My mother told me to listen.

"You'll want to save them all," she said.

I woke coughing, vomiting saltwater that burned my throat. Hot sand stuck to my face and my wet skin and clothes. The sky was blue though I'd been running in the night only moments before, the white sunlight scalding the muscle through my skin. Waves pushed and foamed around my legs. No one was on the shore with me. I couldn't see anyone who might've saved me.

It wasn't a surprise, that I hadn't died.

It seemed the spirits were never done with me.

Praise for

QUEEN OF THE CONQUERED

"A brilliant analysis of power and privilege set against an alternately beautiful and brutal background, you will root for Sigourney even as you question both her actions and motives. Searing and painful, Kacen Callender has managed to create a book that will stick with you long after the last page."

—Justina Ireland, *New York Times* bestselling author of *Dread Nation*

"Callender's heart-wrenching work is a story that refuses easy answers, trope saviors, or all-is-well endings. Lofty as it seems, if you imagine *Hamlet* and Agatha Christie's *And Then There Were None* fused in a narrative that finds its soul from the pain of our cruelest histories, you'll have captured a piece of the powerful fantasy Callender has wrought in *Queen of the Conquered*."

—Evan Winter, author of *The Rage of Dragons*

"Told in gorgeous strokes of color and emotion, rendering even the most disturbing scenes of horror and loss with haunting insight.... It's a fine balancing act, and the book's absorbing setting, captivating lead, and relevant themes of race and class complement each other with alternating delicacy and savagery. At turns philosophical and feral, *Queen of the Conquered* represents the scope and spectacle of the fantasy genre with a vengeance."

—*NPR Books*

"Kacen Callender depicts colonialism, rage, and the terrible price of power with haunting, unflinching eloquence. *Queen of the Conquered* is a heart-stopping masterpiece."

—Tasha Suri, author of *Empire of Sand*

"A fascinating exploration of how power corrupts and drives a person toward self-betrayal."

—*Kirkus* (starred review)

"Dynamic characters and rich, spellbinding action come to life in this epic story. . . . It's a thrilling supernatural adventure."

—*Women's World*

"An ambitious, courageous, and unflinching novel that uncovers the rotten core of our colonial heritage and yet also celebrates the fierce resistance and heroic endurance of the most abused and exploited."

—Kate Elliott, author of *Black Wolves*

"Callender's first adult novel draws race relations, conquest, magic, and politics into an imaginative, layered story that will keep readers twisting until the end."

—*Library Journal* (Pick of the Month)

"An utterly compelling look at slavery, power, and complicity. Uncomfortable, heartrending, and utterly necessary."

—Aliette de Bodard, Nebula Award–winning author

"From the very first paragraph, Callender's adult debut stuns. A complex and furious examination of colonialism, *Queen of the Conquered* is a storm of a novel as epic as Alexandre Dumas's *The Count of Monte Cristo*. I've been looking for this book half my life."

—Tochi Onyebuchi, author of *Beasts Made of Night*

"Callender deftly handles the subjects of rank and racism, cruelty and privilege, while also providing an exciting whodunit in the fashion of Agatha Christie's classic *And Then There Were None* or the more recent *Gideon the Ninth* by Tamsyn Muir."

—*BookPage*

"Set against a lush Caribbean-inspired backdrop, this critical and multilayered story features Sigourney Rose, whose devastating losses compel her to risk her life fighting slavery and injustice and kick some colonizer ass in the process. This is resistance reading at its most entertaining."

—*Ms.*

"Intricate, powerful, and brilliant, with vivid worldbuilding, compellingly flawed characters, and a plot full of exciting action and creepy twists!"

—Melissa Caruso, author of *The Tethered Mage*

"Sinks its teeth in early and forces the reader to confront privilege and revenge through an electrifying voice. With an unforgettable ending, *Queen of the Conquered* is one of the most refreshing fantasies you'll read this year. There is simply nothing else like it."

—Mark Oshiro, author of *Anger Is a Gift*

"Gripping and emotionally compelling; a stunning novel about power, privilege, and survival in a world where you must fight even after everything has been taken from you. If you can only read one book this year, make it *Queen of the Conquered*."

—K. S. Villoso, author of *The Wolf of Oren-Yaro*

KING
OF THE
RISING

BY KACEN CALLENDER

ISLANDS OF BLOOD AND STORM

Queen of the Conquered

King of the Rising

Hurricane Child

This Is Kind of an Epic Love Story

King and the Dragonflies

Felix Ever After

KING
OF THE
RISING

Islands of Blood and Storm: Book Two

KACEN CALLENDER

orbit

orbitbooks.net

Copyright © 2020 by Kheryn Callender
Excerpt from *The Obsidian Tower* copyright © 2020 by Melissa Caruso
Excerpt from *Brother Red* copyright © 2020 by Adrian Selby

Cover design by Lisa Marie Pompilio
Cover images by Arcangel and Shutterstock
Cover copyright © 2020 by Hachette Book Group, Inc.
Map by Charis Loke
Author photograph by Beth Phelan

Orbit
Hachette Book Group
1290 Avenue of the Americas
New York, NY 10104
orbitbooks.net

First Edition: December 2020

Orbit is an imprint of Hachette Book Group.
The Orbit name and logo are trademarks of Little, Brown Book Group Limited.

The Hachette Speakers Bureau provides a wide range of authors for speaking events. To find out more, go to www.hachettespeakersbureau.com or call (866) 376-6591.

Library of Congress Cataloging-in-Publication Data
Names: Callender, Kacen, author.
Title: King of the rising / Kacen Callender.
Description: First Edition. | New York, NY : Orbit, 2020. | Series: Islands of blood and storm ; book 2
Identifiers: LCCN 2020014720 | ISBN 9780316454940 (trade paperback) | ISBN 9780316454964
Subjects: GSAFD: Fantasy fiction.
Classification: LCC PS3603.A44624226 K56 2020 | DDC 813/.6—dc23
LC record available at https://lccn.loc.gov/2020014720

ISBNs: 978-0-316-45494-0 (trade paperback), 978-0-316-45495-7 (ebook)

Printed in the United States of America

LSC-C

Printing 1, 2020

For those who watch over.

to Koninkrijk

Valdemar Helle

Skov Helle

Norup Helle

Hans Lollik Helle

Ludivik Helle

Årud Helle

Rose
Helle

Niklasson Helle

Solberg Helle

Larsen Helle

Jannik Helle

Lund Helle

PROLOGUE

They chased me through the groves. My heart pumped, fear slowing the blood in my legs. Air caught in my throat. Sharp stones cut the undersides of my feet as branches and brush and thorns ripped into my legs and arms and cheeks. Wet dirt sank beneath me, the root of a mangrove tree twisting around my ankle. I fell to the ground hard, rocks digging under the skin of the palms of my hands. I could hear their laughter. I knew that if they caught me, I would die. I'd made the mistake of reminding the boy that we shared blood. This wasn't something he liked to acknowledge. He didn't like what I'd implied. That he and I weren't so different, even if he called himself master, and me slave.

Their footsteps crunched and paused. I hunched in the thorns of brush, air wheezing from my lungs. I could sense the power that filled my father's son. His kraft let him see the abilities of others. He could see my ability—could sense me as I sensed him. He felt me hiding. He walked closer.

"I see him."

I didn't wait for my brother to grab me, to pick me up and tie his rope around my neck. I leapt to my feet. I ran in the only direction I could, through the thorns and weeds and the tangled roots of the mangrove trees. I burst out of the green and into the sloshing water that pulsed onto the rocky shore. I dove into the sea. Salt burned my eyes and the cuts across my skin. I swam as if I meant to swim to the northern empires and to freedom.

I stopped, because my arms and legs were too heavy and weak. I turned to see my brother and his friend standing on the shore, their hair and clothes and skin pale in the white moonlight. They waited for several minutes, and then they left, bored with the game they played. I should have felt relief, but I knew this wouldn't be the last time they chased me through the groves of Hans Lollik Helle. It was impossible to feel relief when I knew I would forever have this body and forever have this skin.

The thought crossed my mind. It's a thought that often does. The question of whether there's a point to living this life. I'm going to die, whether it's by the hands of my brother or by the whip of my father or by the years that always manage to catch up with us, regardless of the color of our skin. Does it matter if I die in a few days or a few years or now, saltwater filling my lungs? The result will be the same. If I were to allow myself to sink beneath the waves, it would be a death that would bring mercy. No more racing through the brush of this island. No more beatings and whippings, layers of scars growing on my back like the rings of bark covering the trees, marking how many years I have survived. And there would be no more nights when I was called from the corner of the wooden floor I slept on, marched through the groves and to the pain that waited, as it always does. Letting myself sink into the sea would bring me peace. It would bring me freedom.

The thought crossed my mind—but so did the urge to live. My desire for death and life was a contradiction. Both desires constantly battled inside of me. In the end, life always won.

I began to swim back for shore, but I didn't notice that the waves of the ocean had already begun to suck me farther away from the island. The tide moved against me as I kicked. Waves became higher, knocking me beneath the surface. Seawater forced its way into my nose and mouth, filling my lungs. I choked with every gasp. Blackness covered my vision.

When I opened my eyes again, I sat on the sand of a shore. It was powdered white without any sign of seashells or footprints or life. The ocean was as still as glass. The sky was red with fire. Islands grew from the sea. Waves rippled as the hills formed, spreading toward the black clouds. My mother was there with me. She stood in the shallows. I could only see her back and the thick scars that wove over her skin, but I knew that it was her. This was often how she came to me, in my nightmares and in my dreams. She would tell me stories. Stories forgotten. Stories buried. My mother told me to listen.

"You'll want to save them all," she said.

I woke coughing, vomiting saltwater that burned my throat. Hot sand stuck to my face and my wet skin and clothes. The sky was blue though I'd been running in the night only moments before, the white sunlight scalding the muscle through my skin. Waves pushed and foamed around my legs. No one was on the shore with me. I couldn't see anyone who might've saved me.

It wasn't a surprise, that I hadn't died.

It seemed the spirits were never done with me.

CHAPTER ONE

Shock vibrates through me and I feel a fear that isn't my own. It's a fear I know well—one that betrays the body whenever death is near. My heart begins to work in my chest. Sweat sticks my shirt to my skin. My limbs feel numb when I stand up. I'd been asleep on a hardwood floor, one I'd known as a boy in the room of an empty slave house where no one will sleep. The others take the empty mansions of the dead kongelig, living like they are masters. I prefer the slaves' quarters only because I'm alone here, with nothing but the shadows and the ghosts. When I look out of the window, I can see the lights—pinpricks of red and orange fire in the night. The flame reminds me of the night of the revolt. The fire that had spread across the island, the screams and pleas for mercy, the metallic taste of blood that mixed with the salt air. The blood sank into the dirt, and for weeks it smelled as though the island of Hans Lollik Helle was rotting.

It's not the night of the uprising, and these aren't people who mean to set the island on fire. I feel their intent. I leave the quarters, shaking as I step down the splintered steps, walking along the dirt that's filled with rocks and weeds that cut into the bottoms of my feet. The nights are always colder in these islands, but in the time following the storm season, the sun becomes hotter during the day, the dirt capturing the heat that lifts into the air.

My legs are weak with sleep, but I force them to run. This fear that fills me doesn't belong to me. She's realized that the men are coming for her. She can sense their anger, their hatred. She can see the images of what they plan: to force her legs open, to cut her until she screams for death, to hang her body from a tree. The men are already halfway up the sloping path of the hill. And at the top is the main manor of Herregård Constantjin.

The manor is white against the black sky, glowing in the light of the full moon. It had once appeared like a castle that the northern empires might have, but it crumbles into ruin now, vines and brush and leaves attempting to swallow the manor and pull the stone into its grave, where its masters lay. It was hard work to put the kongelig with their pale skin into the dirt, but the Fjern of these islands believe they will find paradise if they are burned and buried at sea. We would not give them this.

I reach the top of the hill, past the garden of wildflowers and weeds, and walk into the courtyard. The stones are cracked and charred. The fountain, which had once shined in the center of the parties of the kongelig, collapses into chunks of rock. The men stand in a circle. They carry torches that gnats and moths follow, wings flickering in the light. One man comes from the front doors. He pushes the former Elskerinde Rose down the steps. She falls, skinning her hands and knees. When she looks up, her gaze lands on me.

Sigourney Rose could be mistaken for one of us. Her skin is dark enough to hold hues of purple and blue, and her hair is thick with curls. She has the features of an islander. We are known only as islanders because the name we once had was taken by the Fjern, along with our history and our freedom. Our stolen past is what connects our people, yet Sigourney has never been one of us. The proof has always been in the way she looks at us. With fear. Contempt. Longing. She wishes we would accept her, even as she believes she's our better.

She stands to her feet in the center of the six men, her hair tangled, her dress of white torn and stained. She has been beaten, her bruises and cuts unhealed. Her face shines with sweat and fear in the torchlight, but she raises her chin. She was already prepared to fight for her life. Sigourney's kraft has always been powerful. It might be one of the most powerful abilities in all the islands. She can enter the spirit of another. She can hear their thoughts and feel their emotions. She can take control of their body, if she so desires. Sigourney was prepared to take control of any one of these men with their machetes and have him cut all the others down, but she knew the chances of her surviving the fight were slim. She wouldn't be able to take control of more than one man at a time. Even if she had managed to survive, she couldn't fight her way to freedom from the entire island. She would be executed for killing guards, no matter that they'd attacked her first. I understand the mix of desperation and relief in her eyes when she sees me.

My voice echoes in the courtyard. "What're you doing?"

The group of men whirl around. They're surprised. They weren't expecting to see me here. I recognize them all. I know each of their names. They were once guards that belonged to the Fjern across all the islands—guards who were trained to give their lives for the kongelig. They took the lives of the kongelig instead.

Sigourney doesn't want any of these men to see her fear, and she worries I'll feel her desperation. She takes a deep breath and holds the air in her chest, counting in her head, just as Marieke had once taught her to do when she needed to calm herself.

"Why have you taken Sigourney Rose from her chamber?" I ask. No one responds. Night birds and crickets and frogs make their noise. It's almost hard for the men to hear me over the chorus. "Whose orders are you acting on?"

"Our own," one of the men says. His name is Georg. He's

young—as young as I am, though taller and more solidly built, with the muscles of a man who had been made to work the fields before he was brought into the guard. He hasn't been trained as a guard long, only a year and a few months, but he could still best me in a match if he were to attack—especially when I would be reluctant to fight him. I don't see the point in hurting another islander. We already have too many enemies.

The other five men are guards trained under Malthe. I can see that they're afraid that they will be punished for acting without their commander's consent. All of the men look away from me with a mixture of shame and fear. One man named Frey, older than the rest, curses Georg in his head. It'd been the boy's idea, and Frey had been stupid enough to follow along. Frey thinks he came only because of the guavaberry rum they'd drunk around the fire at camp. He can't admit to himself that even without the rum, he might have come here so that he could help kill Sigourney Rose. Frey had belonged to her cousin Bernhand Lund before the man died, and for the last years he had been the property of the former Elskerinde. Frey wanted to see her die. Now, because he's followed the stupid boy's idea, he could be tied by his wrists to a tree and whipped by Malthe himself. This would be the lucky option, considering the chance that he could be hung by his neck instead. No one fights Malthe's methods. These are the ways taught to us by the Fjern. It's the only way that we know.

Only Georg holds my gaze. It isn't that he's braver than the rest. He has more anger. Rage pulses hot through him. He wants to see Sigourney Rose dead, like she should have died the night of the uprising. No, she is not a Fjern. But she, too, was a kongelig. She had her slaves. She's had us tied to trees and whipped, myself included. She ordered my whipping and didn't have the respect to stay and watch as the whip cut into my back and the scars already woven there, rising from my skin. Elskerinde Rose had ordered my execution. She stood and watched as I stood on a chair, a rope around my neck. She was as evil and merciless as any of the kongelig on this island. Georg doesn't understand why she still lives. He doesn't understand why I stop him from killing her.

Sigourney looks from me to Georg and back to me, watching us like someone might watch a game of cards. She learned from an early age that there's power in pretending to hold control of herself and her emotions. But she sees that whoever wins this match will decide whether she will live or die.

"You don't have the authority to take Sigourney Rose's life."

"Authority? You speak like the Fjern."

"We each have our roles. We each have our commands." I pause, looking from Georg to the other men. They still won't meet my eye. "If we didn't have our orders, the revolution would collapse."

"And who's to say we haven't fallen apart already?" Georg demands. I can feel the frustration in him. The frustration has streaks of anger, but it's tied to a helplessness and a hopelessness. It's been nearly a month since the initial uprising, and we haven't done anything more to force the Fjern and their royal kongelig from our homelands. Georg believes that we stay on this island, waiting for the moment we will be slaughtered by the Fjern. He isn't the only person who worries that this revolution has been lost before it's barely begun. At least in this, Georg will feel like he's doing something of importance. Something that will help the war.

But he's wrong. "Killing Sigourney Rose is a mistake."

"It's a mistake that she's still alive." He looks to his friends for help, but none will come forward. They fear me. This isn't something that makes me glad. "You can't keep her alive with no good reason, when everyone else wants her dead."

"We don't know if we'll need her," I say.

"Why would we ever need her alive?" Georg asks me. He speaks with an exasperated tone. He thinks that I'm lying to him. He thinks I believe him to be a fool. "Do you think the Fjern want her? She isn't a hostage. We can't use her in negotiations."

I hesitate, but only for a moment. "You're right."

Sigourney sucks in a breath. It's slight. Only she can hear it, but I feel the surprise in her. Even if this is the truth, there was no need for me to speak it. I could have said that the Fjern have declared a ransom for her, or that they declared they needed her kraft and were willing to negotiate—any lie I could think of in the moment to make these guards leave without attempting to take her life. But I'm not like Sigourney. I do not lie. When she had me as her slave, working as her personal guard, and as I took my steps in the downfall of Elskerinde Rose and the kongelig, I would always tell her the simple truth. I told her that those closest to her wanted her dead. I've never seen the point in lies.

"She isn't useful collateral, and she's made too many mistakes," I say. "It would be satisfying to kill her and be done with it." Sigourney worries that I've changed my mind. I continue, looking at her with the pity I can't help but feel. "But she's still an islander. We have a chance to rebuild our home. When you envision our homeland, what do you see?" I ask the men. "Do you see a land of blood and violence, fighting for power, an echo of the Fjern? Or do you see a land as it was meant to be?"

I feel the emotions of the men in front of me. Their rage. Their pain. They've all lost so much. Georg's brother didn't survive the night of the uprising. I see his memories as though they're my own. His brother wasn't family by blood but was a man Georg had always looked up to, who had cared for Georg as if the boy was his own. His brother had been made to join the guard years before. It was the reason Georg joined as well. He was trained under the heat of the sun, so searing hot that some men fell under its mercy and died of stroke. Georg was whipped nearly every day for any mistake he made in his training, his back a tangle of scars. And it was all so he could have a chance to be closer to the only family Georg had. His brother stood like an unbending tree in front of the kongelig. Even when he was whipped, hung by his wrists from a tree, it seemed to Georg that the man was unbreakable. The day the whispers had spread of a revolt, Georg's brother had asked for him to stay in the barracks—to stay out of the fight. Let him and the other guards fight for their freedom. Georg was too anxious for his blade to cut flesh and bone. He joined the fight the night of the revolution. His brother learned that he hadn't stayed in the safety of the barracks and left his position to look for Georg. Georg had found his brother dead on the beach, his stomach cut open. Georg punishes himself. He should have stayed in the barracks like his brother asked him to. Georg believes that he should be dead instead. But he's still alive. This is what makes him angriest of all.

I scoop my hands into the anger. It's wet like white clay, molding in my hands and draining between my fingers until I'm only left with the sharp glass of his pain. I push the glass into my palms, wincing as I try to absorb the emotion. I can't take all of it. His pain is inconsolable, with the depths of the sea. But I do take some of the burden from Georg. I can see his face soften as he stands in front of me, his rage quivering as his eyes become wet. Sigourney Rose has always had the kraft to sense another's thoughts and emotions, to control their mind and body—but she never considered how she could use her power with a little bit of empathy.

Georg doesn't realize what I've done. His heart pounds and he tries to force down the swelling grief for his brother.

I continue to speak to him and all the men. "How do you envision our land without the Fjern?" I ask them. "When I picture the islands, there's only peace. We rely on one another without attempting to cut each other down for power or coin. This is what separates us from them. We won't use each other in the way that the kongelig have used us. If we want to be different, we need to begin that change. We won't abandon our own people."

The men hesitate. Georg works his jaw back and forth. The frustration he feels is with himself. He had been determined to see Sigourney Rose dead, but he's beginning to waver. He doesn't understand why he wavers, though I can see the shift in emotion. Sigourney sees it, too. She gazes at me openly. Fear echoes, but she's curious as well. Astonished by the power she's witnessed. She wants to understand how I managed to control Georg as I did. She wants that power for herself.

"Sigourney Rose could help us win this insurrection. We don't know how she could be useful yet. But if we kill her, it'll be too late when we need her in the future."

The hesitance remains, but only because the men, Georg included, are afraid of what I will do once Sigourney is released. I could tell Malthe what happened here tonight. Malthe is not as merciful as I am. Though the kongelig are gone, Malthe has still used the whip on his guards when they don't obey his commands. I've suggested that he not, as has Marieke, but Malthe has told us that we shouldn't concern ourselves with how he leads his men.

"I won't tell anyone what you've done tonight," I promise them, my voice low. "You won't be punished."

Though anger and hatred still rages through him, Georg steps away. Without another word, he begins to march down the hill, returning to the barracks where the guards under Malthe have slept. The other men follow, their torches flickering. Some look over their shoulders at me as they walk. It's strange to them that I would spend so much effort in saving a former member of the kongelig, especially one that had been my mistress—one that had tried to have me killed. It was only because of the weakness of the tree branch and the mercy of the spirits that I still stand here. I understand their confusion. I see how that confusion could take root and grow into mistrust and disdain. I need to be careful. The hatred that the men hold for Sigourney Rose could easily transfer to me.

When the guards leave me and Sigourney alone, we stand in the dark of the courtyard in silence. With the torchlight gone, the only light is from the silver full moon above. Sigourney's legs are weak and shaking. She almost falls in her relief, but she would never willingly show me that vulnerability.

"Thank you," she says. Her voice is hoarse.

There's an echo between us. An echo as she feels that I know her thoughts, and that she knows mine. The longer I have been in Sigourney Rose's company, the more her kraft has melded with my own. It's an uncomfortable feeling. To suddenly enter another—their minds, their emotions—is invasive. The power is strongest with Sigourney. Her thoughts reveal that she believes it's because she is the source of this kraft. She finds it interesting, the way my kraft has evolved. The ability to end another's power and take that power as my own has grown tenfold.

"You've grown stronger," she tells me. It's been weeks since I last saw her.

I don't bother to answer. She senses that I see this is true. Though it was a shadow in comparison to my ability now, my kraft hasn't changed. I could stop the abilities of those around me for a time and borrow a shadow of that power in turn. But it feels like my kraft had only been embers, glowing dimly in the dark—and that Sigourney's power was oil, sparking my kraft into a blazing flame. My power has begun to evolve in ways I'm not sure I understand. It's odd to feel indebted to Sigourney Rose for this. I don't like the feeling of owing her anything.

I gesture, and she walks without struggle. She marches back up the stairs and through the heavy front doors, down the dark hall of mold and dust, air covered with a layer of ash and salt. Paintings were torn from the walls, leaving faded shadows where they'd once hung. Rooms hold overturned pieces of furniture and rotting and tattered curtains. Some rooms leave scorched evidence of little fires behind. Sigourney wasn't put in the dungeons, but in an empty room at the top of a set of collapsing stairs. One wrong step, and the staircase of stone might come crashing down. The room's door is usually barred from the outside, locking her within. Inside of the chamber, part of the wall has fallen, giving a view of the island and the black night. The shadows of bats flit across the sky, and the chorus of birds and frogs and crickets rises to the moon and smear of stars. I can see the shimmer of the black sea in the distance and hear the gentle hush of the waves washing ashore.

Sigourney had once considered jumping from the fallen wall and risking death, but she'd decided against it. She was left here with her cot and ragged sheet. Marieke has taken care to nurse her wounds with aloe and herbs. The woman brings her food— salted goat and fish, mango stew and porridge in the mornings. She brings books to Sigourney so that she can read. She carries a bucket of saltwater to help Sigourney wash when the sun is at its height to help her cool off from the heat since she lives in this room without much shade from the burning light. Islanders see Marieke do this every day, and they see Sigourney living in a room of Herregård Constantjin, and they're angry.

Sigourney wonders why I saved her as she steps into her room. I've saved her several times. I was supposed to have cut her throat the night of the uprising, and the day that I imprisoned her here, Malthe sent me with a blade to complete the job—but each time, I let her live. Sigourney can recognize that I hate her as much as I hate any of the kongelig. Why, then, do I show her mercy? She wonders this without speaking, knowing that I hear her thoughts. I leave and close the door, pressing the bar back into place.

CHAPTER TWO

The meeting room hasn't changed. Mold still leaks from the stone floor, and the wallpaper cracks and peels like dirt under the sun. Seven of us are here. The newcomers, the ones who have joined us in this meeting room—Geir, Olina, Tuve, and Kjerstin—are at the other end of the table, while Marieke sits to the right of Malthe, and I'm on his other side. Malthe is at the head, where the dead king once sat. Agatha's seat remains empty. The girl died almost a month ago, but we haven't had time to properly mourn. Her burial at sea had been a quick ceremony without tears. Her memory deserved better, but there were too many plans and strategies to discuss, too much training to oversee, too much work to be done.

Malthe doesn't look at her chair. He's angry that he allowed her to leave the room that night, costing her life. He's angry with me as well. If I'd cut Sigourney Rose's neck as I was ordered to on the ship as she attempted to escape the islands, then Agatha would still be alive. Instead, I'd brought Sigourney here because she'd asked me to. I brought Sigourney here, questioning the decision to kill her and hoping to show her mercy. Malthe was furious. He demanded that Sigourney Rose be killed, and Agatha volunteered. Agatha had been eager for the chance to prove her power against the Elskerinde for a long time. She'd chased Sigourney from the room, hunting her across the island.

The events of the night are unclear when I see the memories in Sigourney's mind. Too much of it had been muddled by Agatha's kraft, and she couldn't tell what had and hadn't been real. The only fact is that we'd found Agatha's body on the rocks, a deep wound in her side. Malthe guesses that she'd smashed her head as she fell from the cliffs. Agatha had been stubborn, and she'd let her anger control her, but her youth had promise. None of us said this, not out loud, but we hoped that Agatha would be the savior we needed. Her power—her kraft—had been the strongest I'd seen. She was stronger than me. Stronger than any of the kongelig—stronger than even Sigourney Rose. She'd had the potential to save us all, if she had lived.

We've spent hours in the meeting room already, as we do every day with our updates and maps and strategies and plans. Malthe is frustrated. "What are we waiting for? The spirits to come and free us from the Fjern? We must attack Niklasson Helle."

Niklasson Helle is where the kongelig wait with their power. It's where Lothar Niklasson went after he and other kongelig escaped from Hans Lollik—where he orders his Fjern to attack our islands.

Geir, an older man, is thin and gives the appearance of someone who might break if he were to fall, with gaunt cheeks and white hair. He'd spent his years hidden away on Nørup Helle. The man had been a part of the network of whispers, helping to organize the attacks to the north whenever messages came to him from Hans Lollik Helle. He made a habit of singing the songs of islanders in his mind, again and again, so that no one would be able to discern his thoughts. Whether they had kraft or not, it wasn't a risk he was willing to take. Songs fill his mind. The old habit is difficult for him to break.

His voice is low when he speaks. "They outnumber us with

both resources and the number of Fjern guards who will fight for them."

Olina is against this plan as well. "We would lose the battle. We're safer here on Hans Lollik Helle. Would be safer, if we moved our command to the north." Olina is older, perhaps in her thirties or forties, though she isn't sure of her age. She has always been a cautious woman. She doesn't take unnecessary risk.

"We're in a war," Malthe says. "We'll never be safe. Don't delude yourself."

"It would be better to stay here, barricaded against the Fjern, and wait for aid. I've prepared letters making requests." Olina has mastered the tongue of the Fjern and can write in their hand, trained by her master, now dead, so that she could write his letters for him whenever his fingers cramped in his old age. Olina regrets poisoning the old man, a cousin of the Solberg, when she really did have much to thank him for. These are the ways the Fjern have taken our minds. We should be grateful to them that they haven't killed us and that they provide us with food and clothes as they take our freedom. There are some islanders that believe these lies. It worries me that Olina is one of them.

Malthe shakes his head. "You've prepared letters that won't make it past Skov Helle before the Fjern find the scouts and send us back their heads."

Though I agree with him on this, I also realize that we can't attack Niklasson Helle—not yet. We aren't ready. "We need to wait for the right opportunity."

"*This* is the right opportunity," Malthe says. He still can't look at me. He hasn't been able to, since Agatha's death. "They wouldn't expect an attack. We hold the advantage of surprise."

"We have no advantage," I tell him. "Our power is here, on Hans Lollik Helle. We need to communicate with the other islands first."

The islands to the north. Our revolution was meant to spread to all of the islands of Hans Lollik as we took back our home from the Fjern. But our people lost the battles of Larsen and Jannik, and by the time the message to begin the slaughter of the masters had spread to Solberg and Niklasson and Lund Helle, the Fjern had been warned by the fires and smoke in the distance. Scouts and survivors that returned to the royal island reported that the Fjern attacked the islanders before the battles could begin. Guards, whether they had agreed to be a part of the rebellion or not, were gathered and indiscriminately killed. Solberg, Niklasson, and Lund Helle are the strongest of all the islands of Hans Lollik. They've become a safe haven of all the Fjern of these islands, including the few kongelig who managed to escape Hans Lollik Helle.

"When we attack, we need to ensure that all of the islands are ready to attack as one instead of as a disjointed ambush." And with patrols of the Fjern and daily battles between scouts and guards at sea, it's been difficult to pass messages to the islands of the north. The islands we do hold haven't been helpful in this war. Valdemar, Skov, Årud, Nørup, and Ludjivik Helle have not proven useful when it comes to resources or strategic positioning.

The others agree with me. It's better to wait until we can attack as one, instead of sending smaller troops of guards to their deaths. Malthe isn't pleased.

"And what, exactly, is it that you do, Løren?" Malthe asks me. "Why are you allowed into this meeting room, giving your opinions and making decisions?"

I feel frustration rip through me at Malthe's question, and then shame. I don't like to feel emotion. Emotion is a distraction. Even something like anger, rage—the hatred I feel for the Fjern—can cloud my mind. Still, I need these emotions, or I'll become complacent. Some islanders have convinced themselves that a life of slavery is all that they are meant for, happy to live under the foot of their masters. There were some across the islands that fought for the Fjern, willing to betray their own people for the only life they'd ever known. They were too afraid to take their freedom. Disappointment, pity, rage. It's necessary to feel emotion so that I'll have the will to fight.

Every person at this table has a task and a purpose. I have none. I'm only here because my kraft had been helpful once. But it isn't helpful, not anymore. I have no role. When Malthe asks me what it is that I do, the others look at me and wait for my response. What else can I say?

"Nothing," I tell him. "I do nothing."

No one speaks. Malthe clenches his jaw in his silence. The kraft isn't mine, but I can still feel the echoes of Sigourney Rose's power move through me. It's difficult to determine if the disdain I feel in Malthe is his own or if it's one that I've imagined. *You do nothing*, I can feel him think, *and yet you have the respect of all.*

"We've achieved everything that we can for the day," he announces. "Tuve, your messenger will leave before morning light."

The messenger will likely die in an attempt to reach Årud Helle to update the islanders who wait for their commands. Few messengers have reached the other islands alive. It was only in the early days of the rebellion that we were able to contact them and share our updates and plans. It's been nearly two weeks since we last heard from any of the other islands. Tuve acknowledges Malthe's order with a nod, and the older man dismisses us, but Marieke interrupts. "Wait. There's still a point we need to discuss."

Malthe doesn't hide his impatience. He understands which point Marieke means.

"We can't just leave her in this manor," Marieke insists. "What will we do with Elskerinde Rose?"

"You still call her an Elskerinde," Kjerstin notes. Kjerstin is younger, only nineteen years old. Her hair is plaited and falls down her back and shoulders. Her skin is a warm brown that gives a feeling of the sun as it sets, sky red and orange with fire. The same fire is in her brown eyes. Even with a face she keeps blank, trying to hide any emotion and expression from us, I have the sense that she's laughing at everyone around her. She laughs because it's amusing to her that we think we'll win this insurrection against the Fjern, when it's obvious to her that we will all die.

"It's an old habit," Marieke says with an apologetic tone. "I would always call her Sigourney when I spoke to her directly, but in the company of others..." She doesn't finish her sentence. It doesn't matter now. She looks at each of us expectantly.

"We know what you would like to do with *Elskerinde Rose*," Kjerstin says. She doesn't speak with kindness. She doesn't respect Marieke. Kjerstin feels Marieke is an old woman who still has love for her master. A master who should be dead, no matter the color of her skin. "You would like to bathe her and dress her wounds and give her the warm spot on your bed. Even though you're free, you're still a slave."

"Watch yourself," Olina says. "If it weren't for Marieke, the revolt wouldn't have happened at all."

Marieke's arms, wrinkled in their age, are tense. Though I can't see them, her fists must be clenched in her lap. Her gaze meets mine. She hopes that I'll agree with her. I've shown Sigourney Rose mercy before.

"The girl is a distraction," Geir tells us. "So is the other we keep in the dungeons. Patrika Årud." The Elskerinde Årud had attempted to leave Hans Lollik Helle before the night of the uprising, along with many other surviving kongelig. Our ships were waiting for the attacks at sea, and the woman was brought back to the royal island in chains. We thought perhaps that she could be used as leverage, but Geir believes it would have been better to simply kill her. "Lothar Niklasson will have no need for either of them, and the people of this island are angry that they still live. We lose our people's respect with every passing day that the two kongelig still live."

Some on the island underestimate Geir. He seems too distant and distracted, his eyes glazed. But while his eyes suggest his mind is elsewhere, I see the sharpness in him. He notices every detail, every twitch and breath. The man has a mind for strategy. Geir promises us that he has no kraft, but he lies. He's met my eyes as we dissected the maps of Hans Lollik, discussing which way the sea turns and which island of the Fjern would be best to attack first. He looks at me, having already realized that I can sense his kraft because of the power that I hold. His kraft seeps into me, and I see the answers appear before me: Yes, the current would take us directly to Solberg Helle, but this is what the Fjern would anticipate. They would be ready for us, but they wouldn't think that we'd be willing to sacrifice guards—our people—on a battle that we would lose. The best strategy would be to sacrifice our people in a plan to distract the Fjern as we simultaneously send guards directly to Niklasson Helle while their defenses are down, preoccupied with the battle of Solberg Helle. Geir sees this is the best course of action, and I understand this, too, but neither of us say the words, because the Fjern are right. We would not sacrifice our own people in the way that they happily would. Sigourney's kraft, still inside of me, lets me see that for Geir, keeping his kraft a secret is a strategy as well. He keeps this strategy well hidden from me, refusing to think on it while in my presence, the words of old songs filling his mind.

When Geir says that the women should be killed, it isn't only his opinion, but the kraft that tells him the best strategy. "They should both be publicly executed to reinforce the loyalty the people have for their leaders."

Olina disagrees. "The free nations are paying close attention to how we treat our hostages."

Olina has been instrumental. At the table, Marieke, Olina, and I can read and write, though no slave should be able to. Marieke also has her connections to the north. She would travel the empires years ago when Sigourney Rose was only a child, passing messages of plans for the oncoming insurrection. But she does not understand the societies of the northern empires or the Fjern, whereas Olina has had the chance to study and learn their customs, and her own connections are more far-reaching. Olina had penned three letters on our behalf, requesting the surrender of the islands of Hans Lollik. The letters were sent to Lothar Niklasson. The messengers were returned to the shores of Hans Lollik Helle on unmanned boats without their heads. Olina focuses on her letters to the empire of Rescela, a nation that is along the coastline of the northern lands. She requests aid from aristocrats of the free nation, but many scouts never returned. We can only assume that they had been captured and killed by the Fjern at sea. For the scouts that do return, the letters have gone unanswered. Still, Olina has hope for one woman in particular who has seemed moved by our plight, though she hasn't yet promised the aid that we need. Olina wants to leave for Rescela on her own so that she can explain in person the atrocities we have faced, but we can't risk losing her.

"I speak to a dame of the Rescela Empire who is against violence toward the defenseless," Olina says. "I can't write to the ambassadors, saying we have survived the atrocities of the Fjern, only to kill our own prisoners in cold blood. They will call us hypocrites. They will say we cannot govern our own freedom."

"They're eating food," Kjerstin says. "Drinking fresh water. They're using our resources."

"Two more mouths to feed isn't the issue," Marieke answers.

"The issue is the damn guards eating more than their fill, drinking rum into the night—"

"How would the ambassadors learn of their deaths?" Malthe asks. The table quiets.

Olina frowns. "I'm sorry?"

"Do the royals of the free nations know that Sigourney Rose and Patrika Årud are still alive?" he continues. "The Fjern themselves aren't sure who has survived, beyond those who managed to escape. The others were killed in the initial attack. For all anyone outside of this island can tell, both Sigourney Rose and Patrika Årud are already dead."

A silence follows and stretches. Malthe can see that I hope for mercy for Sigourney Rose. I hate the woman, but she's also an islander who has withstood the horrors of the Fjern, just as any of us still alive have. I see the memories that haunt her—her sisters, her brother, her mother. I can't help but sympathize with her. I can't help but want to show her what she's been unable to see: the possibility of these islands, us all living in freedom and peace.

Because my power mirrors the kraft of those around me, I was able to see into Sigourney in the months leading to the rebellion. I rarely liked what I saw, but I could also see the hatred she had for herself. I saw the love she had for the family she'd lost and the respect and admiration she'd held for her mother. I saw the hatred she had for the Fjern and how, on the quietest of days, she would sometimes wish for a life away from these islands. Beneath it all, she'd wanted a life of peace. She has the potential to change and to join her people. And with a kraft like hers, no one can deny that she's powerful. If Sigourney were to join our side, she could be an asset. She could help us win this revolution.

I want to show her mercy. It's for no other reason that he says, "We should execute them. Both of them. There's no need to keep either alive."

Kjerstin is pleased. She openly smiles. Geir gives a single, stilted nod of approval. Only Olina purses her lips. If Tuve has an opinion on the matter, he doesn't share it.

Marieke raises her chin. The woman has had her reasons to hate the Fjern as much as any of us. She has wanted her revenge against the kongelig. She blames them for the deaths of her daughter and the child's father. She wants to see each and every one of them burn. But in her haze of fury and grief, she has a harder time seeing that she has attempted to replace her daughter with Sigourney Rose, and she doesn't realize that she can't love a woman who is her master, no matter if Sigourney claimed Marieke was free. I can feel the roil of emotion inside of Marieke. It's a wonder that she manages to keep her voice steady. "You have no reason to kill Sigourney Rose. If you do, her blood will be on your hands, and the spirits will hold no love for you."

"My hands are already stained red. All of our hands are, whether you held the machete that cut the necks of the kongelig or not. Tomorrow night. They'll both die by beheading."

Malthe would not admit it, but his decision is only because of his anger for me. He's angry because he blames me for Agatha's death, but he's angry, too, that I do nothing, and yet seem to have the love of all the islanders on Hans Lollik Helle. He wants to kill Sigourney Rose—not because he feels her presence matters one way or the other, but because he wants to remind me of my place. He wants me to see that he has the power to declare the death of the woman that I wish to see live.

I don't speak without thinking. With my father and brother, I learned early that to speak without thinking can be fatal. It's a calculated risk that I say what I do. "No."

Marieke looks at me with hope. Kjerstin, frustration. Olina glances between me and Malthe with uncertainty and Geir with a similar hesitation. Tuve looks up from the surface of the table, a quirk of his lips in slight amusement that he quickly hides.

Malthe doesn't ask me to repeat myself. He heard me. Still, I say it again. "No. Sigourney Rose will not die. We need to keep her alive. Patrika Årud—yes, you can do whatever you want with her. But not Sigourney Rose."

There's a moment of quiet before Kjerstin gives a small laugh of disbelief. "I suppose what everyone says is true."

Despite the respect so many have for me, islanders have questioned the closeness I kept with the woman I called master. They've thought that I might have shared Sigourney Rose's bed. If it were true, most would see it for what it would have been: me, a slave, without choice and without pleasure. So many of us have been forced into the beds of our masters. Kjerstin herself understands this well. She realizes that she's cruel, to suggest what she does—that I was a personal guard, looking for power or rewards by pleasing my mistress. I would have rather killed Sigourney Rose myself. There have been enough rumors on my past. There have been enough whispered stories of the ways the kongelig had treated me on this island when I was a child. Even now, the memories tighten my muscles beneath my skin. The insinuation by Kjerstin is a betrayal.

I tell her this. I speak the words plainly, and I can feel the shame in Kjerstin rising. It's a long pause before she apologizes. "I spoke in jest. I see that it wasn't funny."

She lies. She hadn't spoken in jest at all. But there isn't anything I have to say to this. I address the others. "I want to show Sigourney Rose mercy because she is one of us and because she is powerful."

"All the more reason to kill her, before she finds a way to become a threat," Geir says, voice low.

"She was taught only one way to survive these islands. She was taught that she is a master. If she can relearn, she would be invaluable."

"I do think she could learn, if given the proper amount of time," Marieke adds.

"I gave her a choice," I say. "She could have taken her own life to escape us. She knew she would face imprisonment, possible torture, and yet she chose to live."

"Any coward would," Malthe says. "This isn't proof that she's willing to join us."

"She's one of us," I argue. "She's an islander, skin dark as any of ours."

"Don't be so naive," Malthe tells me, his voice rough. "Skin as black as night does not make her one of us. If we judged by the color of skin, then you would be dead with the rest of the Fjern."

He misspoke. He sees it the moment the words leave his mouth. My skin is brown, and my hair and eyes as well, but the blood of the Fjern is still in my veins, and I'm paler than many islanders. Malthe doesn't see this for himself, but perhaps this is what he hates about me most of all. But his words have gone too far, and everyone flinches on my behalf, except for Geir, who can see that the odds have shifted because of Malthe's mistake.

"She will join us in this fight," I say in the silence that follows. "Sigourney will live."

CHAPTER THREE

My head begins to ache as I leave the meeting room. It's a slow pressure that grows behind my eyes. I don't often have headaches. As a boy training in my father's guard, some of the other islanders might sometimes complain of pains shooting up their back after long days of hard work whether the whip had been used on them or not—and even then, most would keep the pain to themselves, their faces twisted into grimaces. Not many complained of headaches or pains that were caught in their muscles or stomachs or chests. It didn't seem worth complaining about when everyone was hurt, when everyone had felt the bite of the whip and the blow of the fist.

The pressure grows and sharpens. I pause, my vision going red. It must be the stress. I haven't had so much responsibility before. I don't have a clear role in comparison to the others, but I'm still in this meeting room, in our created inner circle as leaders, voicing my thoughts and opinions and being constantly reminded that any misstep would mean all of our deaths.

When I close my eyes, the red of my eyelids covers my vision, and with my eyes still closed I begin to see images—but they aren't the halls of this manor. I see a cot, the broken wall with its fallen stone, and the island: the burnt fruit trees and the groves of mahogany trees and the field where Malthe's guards continue to train without his watchful gaze. The sea, as blue as the sky above, shimmers in the heat as its salt comes on the breeze. This sea, so beautiful, is the grave of so many of our people. I often wonder if their spirits walk the ocean floor. As she admires its beauty, Sigourney can't stop the fear that trickles through her. Whenever she sees the ocean, she's reminded of the way she'd fallen from the cliffs, Agatha following her—the force of her body hitting the waves, the saltwater pressing its way through her nose and mouth and throat, filling her lungs as she desperately swam through the water, black in night—she'd been so sure she was going to die—

I open my eyes. The headache had grown so much that I was sure my head had been split open with a machete, but it's gone now. There's a distant relief of pressure tingling over my skull, like it was a limb that'd fallen asleep. After the feeling is gone, I stand where I am, breathing slowly and taking the air into my lungs, reminding myself that I hadn't fallen into the ocean and that I hadn't almost drowned. I'm not confused about what's happened. I already see the answer, and she does, too. I don't understand why, but for that single moment, my kraft had connected me with Sigourney.

It's happened before when I'm standing in front of her, not using my own power to block hers. But I'm not standing in front of Sigourney. She's on the other end of this manor, down several halls and up a broken staircase, inside the chamber that has become her prison. The night before I'd woken and realized, without a doubt, that guards were on the way to kill her.

When Malthe asks to speak with me, his voice echoes in the otherwise empty hall. I'm still reeling, but I can't let him see my weakness. I force myself to stand straight and face him. I pretend that I'd only been lost in thought. Malthe doesn't force a smile in greeting as he approaches me. The tension between us has grown. I don't like games of the mind or of actions spurred by emotion. I thought that Malthe was the same. He has a silence that engulfs him. It was a silence I'd once admired, but I can see how dangerous it actually is.

I'd spent years as a child training under Malthe, cutting his targets down with a precision that impressed him, though he would never admit to it. I'd looked up to him then. He was the only example I'd had of an islander with his dark skin and thick hair who was close enough to be a father. He didn't love me. I didn't think so then, and I know this as a fact now. He didn't love me as he might've loved a son, but he did respect me. He had been suspicious of me when he first learned that I was the son of Engel Jannik, and he assumed that I would think myself better than all the other guards. It wasn't a wrong assumption to make. I did have some years where I considered myself better and stronger than those around me. I was angry that they would look at me with disgust because of the Fjern blood I had in my veins. I would work hard to prove myself greater than all of them. I'd convinced myself that if I could best them in sparring and training, the other guards would begin to see me and accept me as one of them. As the islander that I am. These were the dreams of a child. I've always been held at a distance. I've never been accepted as one of my people.

I'd worked hard enough that as a boy Malthe noted my talent, but he had pushed me away when I came to him, asking him to let me join the uprising. He feared that I'd been sent by my father to root out the rebellion. It was months before I was able to convince him that I hated the Fjern as much as he does, if not more. Malthe didn't love me as a son, but he had loved me as someone who might be able to follow in his footsteps one day— who he could train to continue his legacy. He didn't consider that I might one day surpass him.

We walk the halls of the abandoned manor together. I can feel the echoes of Agatha's loss in every step. Her kraft had made this manor seem like a place of power. She'd fooled all of the kongelig and the islanders who weren't a part of the oncoming rebellion, making Herregård Constantjin look and smell and feel like a castle of the Koninkrijk Empire. Now, the walls rot, the marble floor is cracked, and mold spreads from the ceilings.

"She'd been gifted," Malthe says.

"Too gifted," I add, not because it's something that I think, but because I can feel the words come from Malthe's mind. He doesn't miss the moment, glancing at me. We haven't acknowledged, not any of us, that it seems my kraft has evolved in ways I wasn't expecting. This isn't new. Kraft can grow, just as the person it belongs to grows. I'm not sure what it means yet, that I can still feel the power of Sigourney Rose's kraft inside of me, even when she isn't anywhere near, or that I can sense the strategic thoughts filling Geir's mind so much more vividly than I would have been able to months ago.

"Yes. Too gifted, perhaps," Malthe concedes. "Her gift made her powerful, and she loved power. It made her foolish."

"Do you think it's wrong to feel drawn to power?" I ask Malthe.

He doesn't answer me. "Your own power has grown," he says.

"My kraft, you mean."

"Your kraft, but your power as well. The others look to you for leadership. Guidance. Is that a role you're ready for?"

"You don't think that I am."

"No, I don't," Malthe agrees. "You lead with your heart."

The comment surprises me. I don't consider myself someone ruled by emotion.

"You want to show mercy to everyone around, including our enemies. That isn't how one wins a war. Mercy is the downfall of revolutions."

"I won't show mercy to the Fjern. The real problem is that you believe Sigourney Rose is the enemy, and I'm not convinced that she is."

"But how could she not be the enemy, Løren?" he asks, frustration cracking through.

"You're unable to see because of your own biases."

"My own biases," he echoes.

"You hate her."

"Yes, of course I do. I hate all of the kongelig."

"You hate her especially."

"And don't you?" Malthe asks. He stops and turns to me. A window behind him is shattered, filling the hall with the white heat of the island. "She was a traitor. She left all of us enslaved, and had she been granted the throne, she would've kept the islands as they were, wearing her crown and dresses of white."

"I believe she can change."

"You're a fool," he tells me. "You'll be the end of us."

"How can we claim to be different from Sigourney Rose? How can we claim to be different from the kongelig, or any of the Fjern, if we torture and kill without mercy, just as they've done to us?"

"We aren't claiming to be different," Malthe tells me. "We're only claiming our freedom."

He leaves me there as I stand in the direct light filtering in through the window, my skin prickling with sweat. From where I stand in the silence of the halls, I can hear the evening songs and prayers beginning to rise around the island. The people speak to the ancestors. It was something the Fjern had forbidden us to do. Anyone caught murmuring their prayers to the spirits of our ancestors had their tongue cut from their mouth. Our people had become skilled at practicing our faith in secret, on the bays and in the groves at night where the Fjern could not see or hear us. The songs were taught to most of us as children. I still remember the older woman, whose name I'd never learned, teaching me our prayers of gratitude. She told me this was something that separated us from the Fjern. We prayed to our ancestors to show our thanks, while the Fjern prayed to their gods so that they could beg for more.

I walk out of the manor and into the courtyard where I'd stood so many times, watching the kongelig with their glittering parties of white and where I'd saved Sigourney just the night before. I can see the white manors that had belonged to the kongelig families, scattered across the island as I walk down the sloping path that leads to the groves. Most of the trees were burned down in the battle. The ashes and blackened carcasses of palms and trunks remain. Women sing their prayer songs as they work to clear the debris, their skirts tied into knots around their knees. Some bend over the dirt, replanting seeds. If we don't survive this war, our people believe that after we've lost our bodies, we'll live on in the islands alongside our ancestors. The trees, the sea, the hills of green: This is what we must respect more than our flesh and bone. One woman named Ulrike sees me. She stands, dusting the dirt from her legs, and she comes to me as she always does, taking my hands and gripping them in hers. She squeezes her eyes closed as she murmurs a prayer.

"Please watch over him," she asks. "Please bless him with strength and wisdom to lead our people to freedom."

Ulrike had seen me hung by my neck. She witnessed the branch breaking, and was among one of the first to say that I'd been blessed by the spirits. Ulrike believes that I was sent by our ancestors to save our people. She isn't the only one who thinks so on this island.

"Thank you," I say to her, but she only kisses my palms before she returns to her work. I can feel the women's stares as I walk from the groves to the line of slaves' quarters. Everyone has heard about my kraft. It scares me that so many people know, when it was something I'd desperately hidden for so many years. The women whisper to themselves. *He was blessed by the spirits with kraft. He has the power to take the kraft of the kongelig—take their power, and use it as his own*. They see this as a sign that I am meant to destroy the Fjern and lead our people to freedom.

The quarters are ten shacks along a dirt path, some of which were claimed by the guards as barracks, though no one else will sleep in them. Next to the barracks is the valley's field, where the guards train. Malthe oversees the guards of the island, as well as anyone who had not been a guard but is able to carry a blade. He works his guards harder than when we had been under the rule of the kongelig. I work alongside him to teach formations and techniques for hours beneath the burning sun, to the point where some have fallen unconscious. Malthe risks them dying of heatstroke, but it's a risk he thinks must be taken. The Fjern have already attacked Hans Lollik Helle twice since we took the island, but we have the advantage of the mangroves as a natural fort, and the manor on the hill allows us to see the ships coming. We work hard to keep our lives and our freedom.

The exercises are over for the day. Only a few men linger at the edges of the field, sharpening machetes and crafting arrows. When I check on them, a guard named Steef tells me they're worried they won't have enough materials.

"We're running low especially on flint stones," he says.

"Check with everyone who is clearing the groves," I tell him. "They might be able to find more resources under the remains."

The others nod their agreement, and Steef thanks me. There are plenty of guards who follow Malthe with unwavering loyalty, but it makes me uneasy that I can also sense a particular level of respect for me in some guards, Steef included. I can feel that he wishes I was in command of the guard. I've shown more mercy than Malthe. I've been more patient in teaching and running the drills. I can only hope that these are thoughts Steef and the others will keep to themselves.

In the field, some children play with sticks they pretend are machete blades, chasing each other with high-pitched screams.

One girl named Anke runs at me with a stick clutched in both hands, ready to strike. I step around her and pick her up so that she squeals. Anke has a kraft that she hides. She's able to heal wounds, by putting a hand to an injury and watching the cut heal and disappear. It's still a young ability, but there's potential for it to become strong. Had the kongelig learned of this power, the girl would've been hung from her neck. She's still afraid to tell anyone. I don't see any need to expose her secret.

Helga, the woman who watches over Anke and all the children, frowns from the firepit, where she and others chop cassava and ready a pot of stew. There aren't many children on the island—only seven, all orphans who were brought to the royal island for safety when their parents were killed in the fighting. I carry Anke back to Helga. She scolds the girl, telling her she needs to learn to sit still.

This field is where I'd want to have a village built. We would have our own homes, not quarters where there'd only be enough space for all of us to sleep, cramped on the ground. We would have our own gardens. The groves, once replanted, would be for everyone's use. The Fjern came here and put a price on fruit and fish and water, but these would be provided without any cost once we're free from the kongelig's reign. We don't stop anyone from eating food if they're hungry.

Marieke argues that the food still has to be more carefully rationed. Yes, we're no longer slaves, but this doesn't mean we can eat like our former masters. There are about seventy islanders on Hans Lollik Helle. Nearly fifty are guards under Malthe. The islanders who don't fight came to us in the aftermath of the uprising, and with the Fjern patrolling the seas, very few have been able to leave. There were only enough goats to last the kongelig the storm season, and they've all been slaughtered. We've overfished the bays, which had never been plentiful, and half of the groves were burned down in the battles. The trees that remain aren't growing fruit quickly enough. If we continue this way, we won't last another month.

The prayer songs slow until the only sounds are the birds and crickets. The sun is setting quickly, the sky turning pink and then a deep red. I can hear laughter throughout the groves. I walk without purpose, accepting prayers and blessings and giving what little advice I can offer to those who need it. Maybe Malthe is right. What have I done since the night of the first revolt? I've attended the meetings and given my opinions. I've walked the island, observing those who pick fruit from the trees. I've helped to teach the newer guards how to hold their machetes and fix the position of their feet and their arms for a swifter kill. But is it enough?

Marieke has followed me from the manor, through the groves and to the field. She approaches me without speaking. She wonders if what the others say is true—if I really have taken Sigourney's kraft. If I have, she worries that this would be used as an excuse to execute the former Elskerinde. Sigourney Rose's power contributes to the debate of whether she should be alive or dead, and she wouldn't be needed anymore if I have her kraft as well.

"It isn't as strong," I tell her. She isn't surprised that I've noticed her. Marieke has witnessed too many things in this lifetime to startle easily. "It's a shadow in comparison to hers. She could look at a person and see all of their past, their wants, become that person entirely. I feel and hear only snippets. I can't control their bodies."

"It's still astounding," she says as she walks to join me. "Your kraft inspires people, Løren. I hear them whisper about your power."

I understand what she implies. Whereas Malthe doesn't want me to lead this insurrection, Marieke does.

We walk as the sky darkens, toward the mangroves and the

bay. She seems to realize what I'm thinking, even without a kraft of her own.

"The others look to you for guidance," she tells me. "They feel comfortable with you and trust in your judgment." When I don't speak, she continues. "I see the way everyone looks at you. They have hope. You have the spirit of a leader, Løren."

But being a leader is not a position I want. It's strange to have anyone's confidence when I'd once been the boy on the floor of the slaves' quarters, listening to the others whisper that I couldn't be trusted because I was the slave master's son. I'd been hated. The other islanders saw me and only saw the blood of the Fjern that was in my veins.

It didn't matter that they knew how I'd been treated. I'd learned to try to avoid my brother and my father and especially the Elskerinde Jannik whenever I could, but when any of them were in the mood for torture, I was their entertainment. My father would beat me, sometimes because he was angry and other times because he was bored. He would find ways to use me against Aksel. To humiliate my brother and make him feel lesser than me, a slave. Aksel would then find his ways to punish me for it, chasing me through the groves with a rope so that he could attempt to hang me from my neck. He'd wanted me dead, though he was too afraid to take my life himself.

Elskerinde Jannik was the worse of them. She would call me to the sitting room to wait on her, whether I was in the middle of training or other duties. Her torture was caused by her biting tongue and the quick slap across my mouth if I ever displeased her. And after surviving the masters, I would return to the slaves' quarters, to the burning gazes of my people. The boys my age would give me their angry stares. In our training for the guard, they would do what they could to beat me into the ground. I wouldn't fight back. If I did, they would use it as proof against me, that I hated my own people. There was nothing I could do to show the love I had for us. We had survived the massacre and attacks of the Fjern. We still lived with love and passion as full humans, despite the Fjern's attempts to make us feel that we were nothing but animals. I love that we hold power in our veins. Even without kraft, there is a silent resolve and determination in us all, sustained by our ancestors who still watch over us.

It'd hurt me then. It hurt that the others would see I was treated as they were, but that they would still refuse to claim me as one of their own. It's ironic. In this way, I understand Sigourney Rose. I understand what it feels like to not be accepted.

Marieke and I cross through the mangrove trees that weave through the dirt and turn to the bay. On this side of the island, the wall of mangroves that fan out into the shallows are a natural fort against the sea. The waves are ripples against the white sand. Marieke has a favor to ask of me, but she's hesitant to say the words. Instead, she says, "No one wants to follow the rations. And can I blame them? Now, we feel the freedom of eating like kings, not waiting on scraps from our masters."

"The problem is that we're not free," I tell Marieke. "Free from the work and chains and whips, yes—we're free from that. But until we've won this rebellion, and the Fjern concede and leave these islands, we don't have our freedom."

We'll still have the pain that racks our memories. The scars that carve our backs. The mourning that fills us as we think of those we've lost. The pain is so deep that I can feel it burrow its way through my skin and flesh and bone and into my spirit. I often think of the time I will no longer be a part of this world. It sometimes feels like I've already left this life and that only my spirit remains.

"I wanted to thank you," Marieke says, more quietly. "The others—they don't understand. They don't try to understand. They see her as the enemy, but it was her circumstance. Is it

so wrong to love her? I cared for her like she was my own. I'd
made a promise to her mother, to keep her children safe if any
harm had befallen her. I'd agreed to Sigourney's death, initially,
because I didn't think there was any choice but for her to die.
I agreed to sacrifice her, for the sake of the rebellion. If it was
between her and the lives of thousands...But there are other
ways. I see that now. Elskerinde Rose doesn't have to die."

"There's a chance we won't be able to save her," I say. She
nods. "And there's so much else we have to be concerned about."

"I'd half hoped that Malthe would just agree to let her live as
the list of tasks grew."

"He thinks that the others need to see her die. A symbol of
the uprising." And Malthe has to prove to both himself and me
that he holds the true control.

"Have you been to see her?"

I've seen Sigourney two times. The first, when I'd gone with
a knife with orders to complete the job Malthe had given me.
The second was the night before in the courtyard as the guards
planned to cut her neck. I don't want to tell Marieke about the
men who had tried to kill Sigourney. It would only worry her,
and Marieke has enough to worry about.

"I have," I say without elaborating.

"It's too painful for me to see her that way." This is what
Marieke tells me, but I feel a glimmer of satisfaction in her. She
shouldn't want to see Sigourney Rose in chains, and yet she can't
help but think that this is what the woman deserves after keeping islanders as slaves of her own. Though Marieke tells herself
that she loves Sigourney Rose, she sees that this is a painful lesson that the former kongelig must learn.

"Do you want me to visit her?"

"It would ease my mind," Marieke admits. "I bring her
food, water, fresh clothes—but if I ever stay longer than a few
moments, or if I ever speak to her, I can sense the judgment from

others. If you go, you can speak to her—see that she has everything that she needs. The others—they won't mind if it's you."

She's wrong about this, and I don't think she believes it herself. I realize that the other islanders will judge me just as they've judged her. They already have. But I can see the hope shine in Marieke's eye. I feel guilty. When I go to Sigourney Rose, I'll only be looking for reasons to see her die.

CHAPTER FOUR

Sigourney is silent when I open the door to her room. She sits on the edge of her cot, her back facing me. She pretends that she wasn't expecting me, but she could feel me coming several corridors away and could hear my footsteps echoing on the stairs. She also sees what had happened in the hall as I was leaving the meeting room earlier today. Sigourney is aware that, for one blinding moment, I was connected to her here in this room. I feel the curiosity in her. This is the second time this has happened: that suddenly I could see through her eyes like I had become her, and she could see through my eyes like she'd become me. The fact that we have the same kraft becomes a hall of mirrors, with us reflected in each other infinitely, creating a connection between us like nothing she's ever experienced before.

She doesn't look any better than she did last night. Her hair is still tangled. Her dress is still torn and stained. A faint smell of salt and dirt and sweat emanates from her. This is what humiliates her most of all. She can attempt to control her appearance. She can force her expression into one of serenity. But she can't control something this base. It's a symbol of all the power and freedom she's lost. She doesn't swallow this humiliation well. Sigourney's been humiliated many times in her life. People have found joy in watching her suffer. It makes me ashamed for a moment that I enjoy the same. There have been too many people who've delighted in her pain. The Fjern, the islanders. She has no allies. Is it so wrong that I would feel sympathy for her?

With the sympathy is another emotion. I'm hesitant. Cautious. Sigourney doesn't immediately speak on the kraft that seems to connect us. This is what I want to speak to her about, so she purposefully ignores the topic.

"Did you come to laugh at me?" she asks.

It isn't a question worth answering. She already knows that I haven't. She only hopes for my pity. She wants me to console her.

She tries again. "I thought you'd be too busy to visit me. You have an entire insurgency to run, an island to rule."

She's baiting me, but I still answer. "I'm not ruling Hans Lollik Helle."

"Oh?" She turns to look at me over her shoulder. She's become thinner, her cheekbones hollow. "Who is, then? Is it Malthe? Maybe it's Marieke. Someone must be ruling the island."

"No one is ruling the island." She can see this truth inside of me easily. "We have leaders for the war, but when we've won, the people will rule themselves."

"As you've imagined peaceful islands would exist," she says, turning away from me again. "How long do you think that will last?"

Anger simmers in me. She mocks the rebellion. Mocks her own people. "I've pitied you."

There's a spark of anger in her. She wants to be consoled, but she feels humiliated that I've said this. She thinks I mean to suggest that she's beneath me. "You can keep your pity."

"You're a victim in a way," I tell her. Finally she quiets and listens. "You were never taught about our people—our culture. You were never given the chance to properly learn the prayers of the spirits or the ways of the islands."

She stands up and faces me. "And you're here to teach me?"

"Learning might be the one thing that could save your life."

If I didn't fully have her attention before, I have it now. She narrows her eyes, silently waiting for me to continue.

"The only way you understand how to live in this world is how you've survived the Fjern. They are willing to steal and enslave and kill to fulfill their greed. That's where we differ. We don't need to take advantage of others to live. We rely on one another. Everyone is able to live because no one person prospers over another. There is no throne, there is no crown. There's only our community and our people."

"It's difficult for me to believe that anyone would rely on one another and share willingly without conflict. It's inevitable that someone will want to have more power than all the others."

"It's only difficult for you to believe because you've never witnessed it for yourself." I try to control the exasperation. I invite her to look inside of me, so that she can see examples for herself. She sees the community that's already begun to grow here on the royal island in the midst of the war. She sees what I have in my years on Jannik Helle: I wasn't trusted, but I could still witness the ways our people would come together and help one another, whisper their prayers in the night and at dawn.

"And you believe I'm capable of joining such a world," she says, voice soft. There's a peace inside of her. She thinks of the life she'd wanted for herself, away from the Fjern.

"I know that you are."

She meets my gaze again. Her expression hardens in defense, but she doesn't look away. "Do you think I could be forgiven?" she asks. When I don't respond, she says, "Would you be able to forgive me?"

I'm not sure of the answer to that. I tell her the truth. She takes a deep breath. The wall between us is still down. She sees how I used her kraft to work through the emotions of the guards. Georg's pain was in my hands. "You aren't so different from me," she says. "You also manipulated someone to do your bidding. You controlled that guard's emotions."

"I empathized with him," I tell her.

"Empathy," she says. "Something you're worried that I'm incapable of feeling."

I don't answer her. She's already seen the other reason I've come, and she says that I should tell Marieke that the food and water isn't enough, but she assumes she won't be given more.

"How long will you keep me here?" she asks.

"Until the others agree that you can leave."

"Until I've learned to be a true islander, you mean." She's already seen the discussions we've had. She realizes that there's a high possibility that she won't leave this island alive. "And do you think that I should be able to leave this prison?"

"There have been worse prisons."

"It's still a prison," she says with a hard voice. "I want to leave. Let me out. I can't be any threat on an island where I'm surrounded by enemies."

"Malthe disagrees."

"What does he think I'll do? There isn't any way that I can take control of dozens of islanders. Someone would kill me before I got far." She walks to the wall, but her back faces the hole that has caved in. She eyes me, curious. She's always been curious about me.

"You know this well yourself," she says. "I'm not surprised. My own kraft changed and evolved as I grew older and as I became more powerful. I wonder if this is the end of your kraft's changes, or if there's still more to come. Is it only with me, this kraft? No," she says, feeling the answer of Geir. "You've experienced this with another on the island. But you might be only reading his mind. What of other abilities? Can you take those powers also? It might be a question worth finding the answer to."

She falls into silence, letting the idea settle. There's only one other person on this island that I know of, besides Geir and the young Anke, that has kraft. Patrika Årud is still locked away in the dungeons. Sigourney must have a motivation to send me to the woman. Sigourney doesn't have the ability that I do, to use a mental block between us and hide her true intentions. I can see that she hopes I will go to Patrika Årud. She hopes that the woman will anger me, and that I'll have her killed. Patrika Årud and Sigourney Rose are the only remaining kongelig on this island. If Patrika was to be executed, then Sigourney believes her importance as a hostage would rise.

"Do you really think you have any value to the Fjern?" I ask her.

"I suppose there's really no way to know until that question is tested."

"It's a gamble," I say. "One that could end in your death."

"The chances that I won't make it out of this alive are already quite high," she says with a small smile. It's one that might have been considered enigmatic by the Fjern, once upon a time—the sign that she was raised to be a part of the kongelig. The smile is a mask that she uses to hide the fear. I can feel it inside of her, twisting through her body. It clouds her mind. She's desperate. She doesn't want to die.

She turns her back on me once more. "If you aren't here to kill me, and you aren't here to release me, then there isn't a point for you to stay, is there?" Before I leave, she tells me, "I'm not sure I can be the person you want me to be, but I can try."

I leave the manor with its white walls that crumble to stone and then to sand. Dusk falls and fruit bats are shadows against the purple sky. I remember the sky as it was in my dreams and in my nightmares: the fire that had been set in the clouds. I'm not sure if this is a fire that was set before the Fjern arrived on these islands, or after they came. A fire set by the hands of my own people, so that we could rise again.

I'm angry with myself when I stop outside of the doors in the broken courtyard. Even when she can't control me, Sigourney Rose finds a way to manipulate me. I turn around. I walk down the halls, caped in shadow. Down the stairs and into the leaking dungeons. I'm surprised none of the islanders have formed their mobs to pull Patrika Årud from her cage and hang her by her neck. It's possible that they're glad that she suffers alone in her prison. It's possible they simply could not find a key.

She does suffer, that much is clear. There is little light here. My eyes take a while to adjust to the shadow. I stumble, hand on the slick wall that sweats in the heat. When my eyes do adjust, I see the three empty cells and her, in the corner of the very last one. She sits, knees pulled to her chest. Her hair is matted and frayed. She is bruised. A mob did not come here to kill her, but someone has visited and given their own punishment.

When I stop in front of her cell, Patrika looks at me with dread. She doesn't try to hide it. She is broken and she's realized she won't leave this island alive. The anxiety in her eyes, the tightening grip of her arms and hands, the hitch in her breath—I see it all, but it doesn't bring me the pleasure I'd hoped it would. I see her, and I can only feel the quickening of my own heart and the fear racing through my blood.

It's a fear that once made me ashamed. I'd wished I could be braver when I was summoned to her. In the stories my grandmother would whisper to me at night, the heroes were the ones who faced their fears with bravery, no matter the circumstances. Even if they knew they were to die, they stood with their heads high and their backs straight. There was once an angry spirit who'd walked from the bottom of the ocean floor and onto the sand of the bay. The spirit, enraged that his life had been taken from him, demanded the life of a girl child every time he came—until, finally, there were no more girls for the islanders to sacrifice, and a woman volunteered her life instead. She went to the bay, where she knew the spirit would drag her into the sea so that she could drown in its depths. And when she went to the sand, she rolled her shoulders back and stared at the sea with fearlessness. The spirit was used to the cries and screams. He asked, "Why don't you fear me?" She said, "What do I have to fear? The worst you will do is kill me." The spirit took her, and she drowned in the sea, but while he had her body, that was all he was able to take.

I wish I could say I was like the woman from this story. I try to force the courage, the bravery, the strength. This is what's expected. This is what my mother wants from me whenever she visits me in my dreams. But I'm a coward. There was a time, once, when I told myself that I was fearless. My life wasn't my own. What did I have to fear? I would test the line between life and death time and again. I would risk the waters of the sea and would spit at a Fjernman's feet. I would hang from the trees, waiting for death to finally take me. I told myself that I didn't care if I died, because at least then I would truly be free. But I was always afraid then. I'm even more afraid now. There's a chance we could win this war against the Fjern. There's a chance I could know what true freedom would mean, the kongelig dead at my feet. The closer I am to owning my body, the more I want to live. The desire to live vibrates through me, rumbling with the quiet intensity of darkened clouds.

There isn't anything Patrika Årud can do to me. I'm not the child I once was. I can stop her kraft. She can't hurt me anymore. But the memories flood through me still. Memories of standing alone in her room as she examined me. I'd only been a child, but she hadn't been ashamed of her interests. She treated me as all the Fjern treat my people. I was a game to her, and each night my father sent me to Patrika, she had a goal of discovering how to inflict the most pain on a body. Maybe some of it was experimentation or practice for her kraft. But I also remember the pleasure in her eyes and the twist of her smile. She enjoyed the way I cried and pleaded and screamed.

Patrika watches me from her cell. She thinks I've finally come for revenge. She's never acknowledged what she did to me so many years ago. She eventually stopped her game as I grew older. Maybe she was tired of me. Maybe she wasn't interested in my body as I became a man. If Patrika ever met my eye on the island of Hans Lollik Helle, when I was brought here with my brother as his personal guard for the storm season, she would only pretend not to remember me. I'd wondered then if she really could not tell that I was the boy she'd tortured for so many nights, but with Sigourney's kraft lingering inside of me, I can see how clearly Patrika always knew who I was. She would often look at me and remember with a flint of pleasure the times I'd been brought to her rooms. As an adult, I wasn't worth the acknowledgment, and she had nothing to fear—not my anger or my retribution.

She fears me. She's so afraid that she doesn't speak. She's worried that the wrong words will anger me. She's worried that I'll kill her no matter what she says.

I could ask her questions. I could ask her why she tortured me. I could ask her if she realizes how she has affected me. The way I flinch away from touch. The way I've never wanted to share another's bed because I can only remember the way she'd pulled me into hers. How some nights, pain will rack through my body and I'll jerk awake with the taste of blood in my mouth. I could ask her many questions, but the words won't leave my throat, and I realize I don't want to hear her voice.

I step closer to her cell. She tries to press herself back against the wall, like she hopes she can disappear through it. "Please—" she begins.

I close my eyes as I reach for her kraft. I can feel the power in her veins like a thread I only have to pull for it to unravel. I tug. She wouldn't be able to use her kraft on me if she tried. This isn't why I came. I let the thread unravel inside of me. I can feel her kraft like a snake, cold and unsettling beneath my skin. It coils and tightens. I open my eyes again, and I let the power ricochet from me.

I reach for Elskerinde Årud, imagining needles piercing her skin. Her eyes widen with surprise and realization, and she releases a breath—then a scream as the needles spear through her flesh and her bones. Her screams echo through the dungeons and fill my ears. I want the noise to stop. I can't stand the sound of pain, even if it's from the lips of the woman who caused me so much of my own. I try to imagine withdrawing the needles, slowly, and she bends over, grasping at her skin as she sobs. There's confusion in her, at the very back of her mind—how did I manage to use her kraft?—but the pain has taken over all sense. Patrika Årud has never felt a pain like that before. She'd wondered sometimes what the pain of her kraft might feel like, and as a child in morbid curiosity had tried to turn the kraft against herself, but it'd never worked. Now, she knows.

I turn to leave.

"Wait," she gasps. I pause. She curses herself, afraid that I might use the power against her again, but she has to ask. "How did you—my kraft," she says, an unformed sentence that I still understand.

I don't owe her any answers. She's my prisoner, and if anyone is to be interrogated, it's her. I had only one question when I came here, and it's been answered. I move again, toward the light at the top of the stairs.

"Did you steal my kraft?" Patrika Årud asks behind me. "How did you take it?"

Her words follow me as I walk. She asked her question like I had stolen her power. She still has it. Her abilities are still in her blood. But she thinks I've stolen what isn't rightfully mine in the way the Fjern believe we have stolen our own freedom.

I walk down the hill and toward the bay. The rocks offer me calmness. Their solid form was here before I was born and will be here after I die. This is a place I can untangle my thoughts and return to a state where I'm not ruled by my rage or hatred or fear. I walk across the sand, and I see that someone is there. A shadow, an outline. They work with a boat. Their kraft is powerful. This is what I immediately feel. Their kraft allows them to hide their ability, as they have hidden it for some time. Because they think they're alone, there's no reason to put in such an effort. It's only when they see me that their kraft spikes.

I walk down the hill and toward the bay where I often like to stand with my thoughts. The rocks offer me calmness. Their solid form has been here before I was born and they will be here after I die. It's only as I walk closer that something tugs on my mind. There's something I've forgotten. I can feel the edges of the memory slipping away like the details of a dream I try to grasp after waking, until the realization that there's something I must remember begins to fade.

CHAPTER FIVE

It's almost dark. There's no moon in the purple sky, and the other islands of Hans Lollik are faded in the dimming light. I can see their outlines on the horizon. I wonder what their names were before the Fjern arrived. I wonder what we had named ourselves. The people who had been here before the Fjern, before their land and sea and flesh were taken—what would they have wanted? Would they have wanted us to save our home? Or would they prefer for us to burn the Fjern, even if it meant burning these islands with them?

We could start again. This is what I think my mother wants me to see. Burn the islands to ash, bury the bodies of the pale-skinned Fjern beneath the dirt, and start again.

There's singing and dancing. The old house that had once belonged to Lothar Niklasson has been filled with islanders. Lothar had a house deep in the brush with many rooms and comfortable beds, softer than the straw and hardwood and dirt floors we've been so accustomed to sleeping on. There's a celebration at the manor almost every night. The food and drink is a waste, and Malthe is angry we celebrate a war that hasn't been won, but I smile. The laughter I hear, the drunken voices that tell stories of memories not marred by the whip or the machete or the rope—I think this is a sound that would fill the air of all the islands if we'd always had our freedom. It's a sound that I hope I'll hear often. There isn't anything wrong with wanting to experience joy, especially when faced with the fact that in this war we will likely die.

I don't join them. The sky turns to black with no light as I walk farther away from the flickering torches, the music and shouts, and into the scratching brush of weeds and branches and thorns. I use my memory and strain my eyes in the dim light to follow the path toward the slaves' quarters where I spend my nights alone. I love my people, but it's difficult for me to forget how I was treated as the master's son. I was angry that they refused to see that I was one of them. I was enraged that they would sit idly by, watching as my father whipped me. We could have all easily overpowered him. We could have overpowered the Fjern a thousand times and taken our freedom. But this was a child's anger. There was still so much that I didn't understand. I can't blame any of them for having looked away. I can't blame any of them for distrusting me, either. I am an islander, but I'm also a Jannik. I'm not sure I trust myself.

I hear a whisper. *It's him.*

I pause and turn, expecting to see someone on the dirt path behind me. The brush rustles in the cooling night breeze, then stills as the trade wind dies.

A whisper, again—but I realize it's not a whisper I'd hear out loud. It's too close for that, not in my ear but in my head. *Now.*

I spin and catch the hand that holds the blade. It's inches from my neck, wrist quivering—a Fjern dressed in black, blending into the island's shadows, holds the machete. He presses, the tip piercing my skin, but Malthe has trained me against this maneuver a thousand times. I fall back so that he stumbles over me, and I throw him to the ground. I roll onto his back and twist the knife from his hand, grab a handful of his hair, and slice open his throat. Blood spurts then gurgles and pools. The twitching body, struggling against death, stills beneath me. I swallow and breathe hard while I grip the machete.

Sense comes back to me. I should've questioned the man. It's too late. He's dead. But there have to be more. There wouldn't be only one Fjern sent to this island, just to kill me. I jump to my feet and race through the brush, roots and leaves tangling around my feet. I burst out onto another path and run to the house where the fires glow. I can see the brown faces, shining with sweat and laughter.

"An attack!" I yell. Faces swivel to me, freezing with surprise. Georg is the closest. He stands, eyes wide as he takes in the blood that covers my hands and the machete I hold. "The Fjern—one tried to ambush me. There have to be more—"

The explosion is a bright flash, a blast that punctures my ears and leaves a roaring silence. There's a ringing in its wake. White dust and debris sails through the air, and fire catches on the plants around us. There are bodies, too many bodies, on the ground—I realize that I'm on the ground as well, though I'm already mindlessly crawling back to my feet, machete in my hand, swinging at the first of the Fjern that comes running from the brush with a scream. I cut him down, then the next. Georg takes the machete of a dead man and fights beside me. I can hear shouts echoing across the island. How did the Fjern sneak onto Hans Lollik Helle without our noticing? Where were the guards watching the seas?

I cut a Fjernman's throat just as Georg kills the last of them. He doubles over, breathing hard. There are only four others still alive, reeling with shock. My throat stings in the burning ash of the ruins of Niklasson's manor. There's a hole in the side, people crushed beneath rubble. I run to them, trying to heave rocks and stones, but they're all dead. I recognize Ulrike, red staining her dress. Her gaze is empty.

"We have to get to Malthe," I shout, voice hoarse.

Though he fought well, I can see the uncertainty in Georg. He's still young, and he hasn't seen very much bloodshed. The night of the uprising was the first time he'd killed another person. His voice shakes when he speaks. "He'll be in the barracks."

The barracks are on the other side of the hill that holds the main manor. Malthe will want us to come to him immediately, to take our orders and fight for our commander. He'll have the best sense of positioning, will be able to lead us against the Fjern. If he's still alive, Geir will likely make every effort to find Malthe as well, to lend a strategic eye to the battlefield of Hans Lollik Helle.

But I can see the truth reflected in Georg's eyes. There's no time. From the sound of the screams echoing over the hill and the fields, the Fjern have come in waves from all sides. They came without their battleships altogether this time, sending in what seems to be an overwhelming number of men under the cover of night.

"What will we do?" Georg asks me.

All resentment he'd felt for me has disappeared. In its place is desperation. He watches me, waiting for orders and for me to reassure him with my confidence and commands that he will live. I see the same expectation reflected in the faces of the survivors around me. There are five of us, all guards. The survivors hold their machetes, taken from the dead Fjern at our feet. I've never led anyone in battle before, but I'll have to try if we want any chance to survive.

"We need to make it to the barracks," I say. "To join with Malthe and the others." The smell of smoke gushes through the air, clogging my throat and burning my eyes. "They've likely set fire to the rest of the groves," I tell them. "The only way to the barracks will be south, to the mangroves, up the bay and around."

"To the beach?" one of the guards, named Ivar, repeats. "If

this is a battle to take Hans Lollik Helle, it will be flooded with Fjern."

"It's either to the bay or through the fire," I tell him. Ivar doesn't respond with his preference.

We move together as one, through the brush—too tight for formation, we could easily be flanked and slaughtered, but speed is more important than technique and precision. Branches and leaves crack beneath our feet. We could awaken the entire island with our noise. We sound like a dying beast crashing through the groves. I hear a whisper, feel a presence at my neck—I whirl around and shout at Georg to stop. He's spun with his machete in his hand, ready to cut down the shadow at his side, but it isn't Fjern. Helga clutches Anke. There are more women following them, six in all. They'd escaped from the Larsen manor, where they'd begun to spend their nights. A quick scan of Helga's thoughts shows me that they'd managed to surprise three Fjern who wandered from the path. The women killed the men and took their blades.

"Is everyone all right?" I ask them.

"We'll be fine when we've got the Fjern off our island."

I nod. Everyone's ready to move forward—ready to fight. Anke shines with determination. She has the fearlessness of the heroine from the tales, facing the spirit of the sea—or the courage of a child, who doesn't yet understand the permanence of death.

We move forward as one. The trees become thinner, and the clearing of the beach is ahead of us. There are Fjern as we expected—but I'm surprised to see them fighting islanders. Scouts, I realize, the spies and messengers—Tuve's people, caught by surprise and still battling for their lives. There are only four left, countless others dead on the sand, perhaps herded to this bay to be massacred. The Fjern who remain seem to be playing games, a group already beginning to search the dead, others laughing while some lazily stab at the remaining guards who swivel and spin and block, slashing with their machetes—

I put a finger to my lips. The others nod. We move as quietly as we can from the trees and onto the beach. I move faster, until I'm running. The closest Fjern turns to me with wide eyes before I slice his head from his neck. It falls to the sand, and I spin and stick my machete through muscle of the Fjern that has turned to stab me—the machete is lodged in bone, and I can't pull it out, so I take his blade instead, slicing his neck when he still fights and spinning to the Fjern who swings at Georg—

The scouts, reinvigorated by our arrival, fight harder. One of the kitchen maids takes a knife to her shoulder with a scream, but she only pulls it out and slides it into the Fjernman's stomach. I see Anke in the corner of my eye—she'd wandered into the battle, frozen with terror, and a Fjernman runs at her, seeing not a child but an easy target, but they're both too far away for anyone to stop him—

I don't think. Remnants of kraft still inside of me surge forward, and the man drops to his knees with a piercing scream. I imagine fire licking at his skin, searching through his body, and he contorts in pain. Ivar chops a machete into the back of the man's skull, and he falls to the sand. Anke's chest rises and falls like a mouse caught in a trap.

The man Ivar killed was the last of the Fjern. We all stand in shock for a moment, staring at one another as if we want to be sure we're actually still alive. We are. We were outnumbered by about ten, and we managed to kill all of the Fjern without losing any of our own. Confusion over the man Ivar killed, and why he'd dropped to his knees in excruciating pain, is eclipsed by the amazement that we managed to survive.

"Is everyone all right?" I ask, breathless. I realize that this isn't something a commander would ask his guards. I can't imagine Malthe asking it of any of us, anyway. But I decide in the moment that I don't care. I see the blood, the wounds, the wheezing breaths—but when I ask my question, everyone stands straight, fire in their eyes. Anke returns to my side. They all nod as one.

"Good," I say. "Let's keep going."

CHAPTER SIX

We move up the beach and along the mangroves, cutting down any Fjern we see, before we move up the path back into the trees and around the burning fields toward the barracks. We find survivors along the way. Islanders hiding in the brush and behind the ruins of old manors, guards who had been left for dead are helped to their feet. By the time we reach the barracks, there are dozens of us, easily overpowering any Fjern in our path. Georg, Ivar, and other guards help keep the untrained islanders in formation. I can see the assurance growing in the others, the possibility that we will survive this battle swelling inside of them. But I can only feel dread deepening with every step. Where are Malthe and his guards? There should be a raging battle as they fight for control of Hans Lollik Helle, but as we come closer to the barracks, I only hear silence.

Georg is stiff beside me. He's also noticed the quiet. We come to the edge of the groves. The field where Malthe leads his drills has become a grave. The dead are piled on top of the dead, blood soaking the ground and heavy in the air. Small fires burn the dry grass and the remains of most of the barracks and slaves' quarters, disintegrating them into embers and soot that stings my eyes. Fjern—my eyes scan about twenty, maybe thirty—stand in rows, wearing their uniforms of black. They face a line of islanders.

Malthe's guards are prisoners, hands on top of their heads and weapons gone. There'd been at least forty guards, but over half that number are dead on the field. Malthe is at the very end of the line, face swollen and blood staining his shirt, though it's difficult to see if the blood belongs to him or a dead Fjern. Someone gasps behind me, but another hushes them quickly. I can feel all of the others waiting for me to give my command. From where we hide in the trees, I can see who I think might be the commander of the Fjern. He speaks to another with an expression of boredom. He's deciding what to do with the prisoners. He gestures at them, and his guard nods.

"To your knees," the Fjern guard orders.

Our people don't move. The guard marches to Malthe and kicks him behind his knees, forcing him to the ground. Other guards do the same to the remaining islanders. I can see what will happen. The Fjern don't need to question Malthe and the rest. They'll simply slit their throats before hunting the island for any survivors.

My voice echoes in the quiet. "Now!"

We run forward as one with a scream that rips through the air and into the sky, machetes drawn, feet pounding the dirt. The closest Fjern, still in formation, haven't drawn their weapons when they're cut down. The prisoners see their opportunity for life and grab the Fjern who were seconds away from cutting their necks and struggle to take their weapons. The commander of the Fjern stands among the chaos, surprise switching to irritation. He locks eyes with me and draws his blade. Battles clash around me, but I see the challenge in his gaze. I walk to him, gripping my machete, handle slick with blood and sweat.

"Løren Jannik," he says. "I was warned about you."

Words meant to crack my concentration, but I take the bait. "What were you told?"

"That if I have the chance, I should take my time and kill you slowly."

He takes a step forward, ready to charge, but a blade sticks through his neck and red spurts out. His eyes widen in surprise, and Malthe pulls his machete back so that the man falls at his feet. Malthe gives me one long, grim look that's impossible for me to read, even with Sigourney's kraft. He nods, and we turn away from one another, blades slashing. My arms shake and my chest is tight, but my body continues like it doesn't belong to me. The spirits take control, moving me from one neck to one stomach to one chest, until all I know is the smell of blood and intestines, the blur of pained and surprised expressions, the shouts and grunts—a whisper in my mind, a last thought and prayer. The final thoughts of dying men are incoherent. Thoughts on the scent of salt and grass, whether the gods will accept him.

My machete is stuck in the chest of a Fjern guard. I yank it out again, blood spilling on my arm. I turn, expecting another, but there's no one. Fjern are at my feet, some in piles. I turn again, and I see islanders watching me. Malthe had told me once that I fight like a dancer. Rhythmically, methodically, losing myself to the movement. I feel like a dancer with an audience might. The surviving islanders stare at me as I pant, nearly stumbling in exhaustion, covered in red. Alongside the awe, there's also fear. *Inhuman.* This is the thought I can feel rise from the others. I fought like a monster from the stories we're told as children. Like a man possessed by a spirit set on revenge.

Malthe's heavy expression has not changed. The Fjern are dead, but we lost most of our own people as well, and many are injured. Helga presses a hand to Anke's side, where blood spills between her fingers. Others of us are on the ground, groaning and pleading for help. Malthe begins to snap his orders.

"First garrison," he shouts, voice echoing over the battlefield. There are responses of survivors, both those who had been here on the field and those who had followed me along the bay. I count seven. I'll need to know how many guards remain. "Search the island for any remaining Fjern. Kill them."

The guards move without hesitation. Malthe calls on the second garrison, six survivors in all, to find any injured islander and to bring them here to this field. He believes we'll be safest in numbers until we have a better sense of the condition of the island, and how many of us remain. The third garrison was almost wiped out, but its four guards will stay here and keep the rest of us safe, in case there's another battle to be had.

There are only seventeen guards on this island. Seventeen, out of what had been fifty. The Fjern, if they were smart, would have sent in this first wave to kill us, and then a second to make sure that the first had completed their task. But the Fjern have always underestimated us. They probably thought they'd sent more than enough men to slaughter every single one of us on this island. Technically, they had. It's luck that we're still alive. Marieke would say that it was the spirits that watch over us.

Georg is with the third garrison. Twelve of the nonfighting islanders are still alive. The surviving three orphans are grouped together with the adults who sit in a daze. Cloth has been ripped into strips, and Helga helps to wash Anke's wound. There's a deep cut in her side. It's the sort of cut that can turn yellow and then green. Anke will not survive a cut to the stomach like this. Anke, still determined to be brave, doesn't cry. She's been used to hiding her kraft all of this time, so she's surprised when I approach her and ask if it's true that she can heal another person's wounds.

Helga is as old as Marieke, but her hands are steady as she cleans Anke's cut. She'd been on Niklasson Helle working under Herre Lothar Niklasson before she was brought here for the storm season. She's worked closely with Marieke both in the kitchens and in the network of whispers. When I ask my question, she looks at Anke with surprise. Helga thought she knew of everyone who had kraft, and she especially wouldn't have expected this of the girl that's been running underfoot for nearly a month, laughing as she hid from Helga and anyone else who called her name. Helga pretends that the girl annoys her to no end, but she enjoys Anke. She enjoys the reminder of why she must continue to fight.

Anke looks at me with frightened eyes. I tell her not to worry. "You won't be in trouble for the power you have."

It hurts her to speak, but she wants me to think that she's brave, so she does her best to hide this. "There was a girl who was whipped by the master. My mother said she was my sister, so I had to help her. I put my hands on her back and asked the cuts to heal. It worked."

"Have you ever tried to heal yourself?"

She shakes her head. I help guide her hands to the wound. She flinches. I can feel the pain in her, like iron from a fire searing into her flesh. But as Anke concentrates on the wound, asking it to go away, the pain eases. The blood stops seeping. Helga looks from the bandage and back to me before she begins to unravel it. The wound is still there, but it isn't nearly as deep. Saltwater to clean it, a fresh bandage, and rest is all Anke needs.

I remember Sigourney's suggestion that I can take any kraft I want. I remember untangling Patrika Ärud's kraft in my veins. I close my eyes and breathe, imagining that I'm holding Anke's kraft in my hand. The power is warm and still has an innocence. I'll be able to help heal anyone on the field, but if we want to save as many people as we can, it won't be enough.

"I have to ask your help," I say to Anke. "I know that you're hurting, and I know that you're tired, but I need you to be strong." Anke is eager to prove herself. She nods her agreement with determination.

Helga helps Anke move from one person to the next. I go to a woman, lying on her side and crying, her stomach cut open. She would have died without question, but I hold my hand to her and feel the warmth spread from my chest, down my arm and to my palm. The kraft takes a lot of energy. Black haze covers the corners of my eyes, but when my vision clears, the wound is much more shallow. We spend hours of the night like this. Torches are lit as we hurry to the sides of those pleading for help. People run back and forth from the bay with buckets of saltwater to clean the wounds. Anke is exhausted, but she continues to work. She cries when a man beneath her hands stops breathing and can't be saved.

I stand from a woman I've helped Helga bandage. The woman fell unconscious, the blood leaking from her thigh turning black. I survey the field as I walk and see that all of the survivors have someone tending to them.

Georg releases a heavy breath as he positions himself at my side.

"The commander should thank you," he says to me. "If it hadn't been for you, this island would've been lost."

"That isn't true."

"Yes, it is," he says plainly. "Without your warning, I wouldn't be alive. Without your guidance, we wouldn't have made it here in time to save the commander and the others. We would've had our necks cut."

"It was thanks to all of us," I tell Georg. "I didn't save this island. Everyone who held a machete did."

Georg eyes me warily. His voice lowers. "The way you fought—it was like you were possessed. I've never seen a man fight like that before."

"I'm grateful to the spirits for their guidance in the battles."

"As am I," Georg says. "But there are some who think that your connection to the spirits is beyond their guidance. There are too many old superstitions connected to kraft."

Though our ancestors always believed that kraft was a blessing from the spirits and something to be honored, generations of seeing our people slaughtered because of kraft has twisted our traditions. Many consider kraft to be something that brings ill luck and bad fortune. This is what Georg refers to.

"I'm telling you this so that you can be careful," he says. "There are some who respect you, and there are some who do not." Georg eyes me for a moment before he adds, "I respect you. Malthe is our commander, but you have my loyalty. I think you'll find I'm not the only one."

I'm not sure what to say to this, and thankfully, I don't have to find any words. Malthe comes to us. I'm afraid he might have overheard Georg, but if he did, he doesn't indicate this. "A moment, Løren."

We walk to the edge of the field and stand together in the shadows of the groves. We watch as people begin to clear the land of the dead, murmuring their prayers and asking for the dead, our ancestors, to forgive us and watch over us. It'll be work that will last days, especially as we try to give our islanders the respect they deserve in death at sea and bury the Fjern beneath the dirt. If we aren't careful, the dead could poison what little water supply we have, if the fresh waters from the streams haven't been poisoned already. The most devastating blow is losing the last of the fruit trees. The Fjern were quick to set fire to the rest of our food supply.

I remember with a flinch. "Where is Marieke?" I ask Malthe. "Tuve, Geir, all the others?"

"Tuve is dead," Malthe says. "He was supposed to be patrolling the bay with his scouts."

I curse. "And Marieke?"

"I don't know about Marieke. If we're lucky, she was hiding in one of the manors that wasn't set afire."

I think of the explosion at the Niklasson manor, the oil and fire that must have been set up in advance. There are pieces of this ambush that don't make sense. Pieces that I'm sure Geir will have opinions on, if he's still alive. "We need to find the others and reconvene."

"I see you're becoming more comfortable making your orders," Malthe says.

I hesitate. I recognize the silky steadiness in his voice. I've waded into dangerous territory. Malthe has always had a certain control over me. He's been my commander since I was a boy, beating me into submission whenever I misspoke and punishing me for any failures. My fear of Malthe isn't an easy habit to break. "I didn't make any orders," I tell him, but he doesn't respond. I try again. "If I did, I didn't mean to."

Malthe still doesn't speak as his eyes rove over the work that's begun. The high of the victory is dropping. As the backbreaking work begins, so does the grief. Some sit, dazed. Others have begun to cry, a woman wailing over the body of a friend, another woman who had worked the fields at her side since they'd both been children. How many were lost on the island tonight? More were killed in this battle than in any of the battles of Hans Lollik Helle before, more than the night of the first revolt. Georg was right about one thing: This is the closest we came to losing the island and the revolution. I glance at Malthe. I see in the set of his jaw, the coldness of his gaze, that he realizes this as well as I do. He usually hides himself so well, but I feel embarrassment at the root of anger. He's ashamed that he didn't see this attack coming and that he had been caught unprepared. He's humiliated that he was caught on his knees, and that he needed me to rescue him.

He turns his anger toward me. "You're a guard, Løren. A guard, under my command. You should have been in the barracks where you belong," Malthe says, "instead of wandering the island as you always do."

I'm not sure what the purpose of this statement is or why it would matter if I'd been in the barracks or not. "If I'd been in the barracks, there's a high chance that I would be dead."

"Dead, having followed orders, is better than living as a traitor."

"A traitor?" I repeat. Anger bites through me, but I temper it. Malthe doesn't say anything else to this, and neither do I. I ask Malthe for permission to leave the encampment and help in the search for survivors. We need the clear thoughtfulness of Marieke, the steady mind of Geir, the voice of Olina's reason and Kjerstin's biting nature to come together after such a loss. We need to strategize how we will survive the coming months.

"No," Malthe tells me. "Stay here and help with the dead."

He begins to walk away from me.

"We need to find the others."

"You heard your orders, Løren."

To disobey Malthe would mean a whipping, at the very least—though with the anger raging beneath his still and calm expressionless mask, he might just try to execute me for refusing to do as I'm told. But I know what's important. I can't stay here at the whim of Malthe's games of power. I don't bother to try to convince him of the need. I leave, and while he doesn't speak, I can feel his gaze following me.

CHAPTER SEVEN

There's only one place I can think to look for the others first. I climb the hill to Herregård Constantjin and move through the courtyard, seemingly untouched by the bloodshed. I'm tense, machete drawn in case a last surviving Fjern bursts through the bushes, but no one does. I climb the stairs and walk through the shadowed halls, to the room where I have been meeting with the others for the last month. No one is here. I pause, disappointment thrumming through me, before I'm struck with a thought. I backtrack through the halls before moving up the stairs of the tower where Sigourney is imprisoned.

The door is already unbarred. I creak open the door and step to the side just in time to dodge the knife that slashes at my face. Sigourney must have known it would be me—must have felt my presence—but she tried to use the moment as an excuse to attack me anyway. She meets my eye with the slightest smile, acknowledging the truth, while Marieke gasps behind her.

Are you sure killing me is a good idea? I ask her, then send her a simple reminder. *You don't have many people on your side.*

Her smile falters.

"Spirits above," Marieke says, letting out a breath and hurrying over to me. She takes my arm and holds it up to inspect a cut I hadn't noticed, blood dripping from my elbow. "I thought you'd be dead."

"Thank you for the confidence."

"It's not meant as an insult," Marieke tells me, ripping cloth from the bottom of her skirt and dabbing at my cut. Only now does it sting. "The battle, the fighting, the number of Fjern we could see from this tower—we assumed the island had been lost, and it was only a matter of time before we were found and killed, too." Marieke has always been straightforward when it comes to death. She's seen it enough times that its presence doesn't affect her. And the revolt, everything she had worked for—she's always had the patience and the faith that, if we fail, there will be others who will try again.

As Marieke cleans and bandages my wound, I ignore Sigourney's careful gaze. I have my kraft working as a wall against her thoughts, a cliff that she's unable to climb. She's waiting for a moment, a crack, a breach—I can always feel her waiting for a chance to see into me, to learn my secrets and my thoughts and to take control of me in a way that no Fjern or kongelig were able to before. This is what I hate about her most of all.

"I'm sorry," she suddenly says, taking me and Marieke by surprise. "I shouldn't have tried to attack you. It's an old habit, to protect myself from you."

It's difficult to tell if she's speaking honestly with my block between us, but her gaze is unflinching. "Thank you," I say.

Marieke is confused, glancing between us. "Where are the others?" I ask her.

"I left Olina hiding in the dungeons of the Solberg manor. Kjerstin went to find and warn Malthe of the ambush. I'm not sure about Geir or Tuve."

"Tuve is dead."

Marieke isn't surprised, though she shakes her head all the same. "I suppose we couldn't all have survived Hans Lollik Helle."

"Tuve and the scouts should have had some warning, but

for them to have been ambushed—" It's difficult to finish the thought. Sigourney won't look away from me. "There were also explosives at the Niklasson manor. Almost a dozen were killed in that attack alone. Someone would've had to set that up, realizing that it was a popular gathering place for the guards."

Marieke's eyes cut to mine. "What are you suggesting?"

"It's obvious enough," Sigourney answers for me. "He believes there's a traitor on the island."

I don't acknowledge that Sigourney has spoken, but I watch Marieke for her response. Marieke looks between the two of us. She almost seems annoyed by the suggestion. "A traitor, on Hans Lollik Helle?"

"There have been traitors before," I tell her.

"Idiots who wouldn't know what to do with freedom," Marieke says. "Fighting for their masters because they're so brainwashed they can't see their own humanity."

"Yes," I say. "Why couldn't one of them be here on this island, pretending to be a friend, while secretly passing on information to the Fjern and acting on their behalf?"

"There would be too many possibilities to interrogate each and every one of us."

"I suppose a particular kraft could help with that," Sigourney says. She hears how desperate she sounds, trying to find a place where she would be needed to save her from her own execution.

"It's a kraft I hold as well," I remind her.

"You want me to change," she says. "This is an opportunity to show that I'm different—that I do care about our people. Let me help."

Marieke interrupts us. "You both seem so sure that this is even a possibility," she says, then speaks over me when I try to insist. "It's something that we'll keep in mind and discuss with the others, but it's hardly the priority in this very moment. Right now, we need to find the others. Make sure that they're alive, and then meet with Malthe. There's too much to be done to stand here speaking of a traitor who may or may not exist."

She's right, of course. It's why I've always valued Marieke's word. It seems that Marieke is always right.

"It might be safer if you stay here," I tell her. "I'll look for the others and then circle back around to you."

She nods her assent.

Olina is where Marieke promised she would be, hiding in the dungeons of the Solberg manor. She's too afraid to leave even when I promise her that the battle is won. She hasn't seen so much death. There was a man, once, that had displeased her master when she was a child. He had been hung by his wrists and starved. The man had seen Olina pass one day and had begged her for water with a rasping voice. She told him that she would not. He had disobeyed their master, so that punishment was what he deserved. She grips my arm as we move through the brush.

"I told the girl to stay," she says, meaning Kjerstin. Her voice is high-pitched, her words streaming quickly. "Stay—Malthe will learn of the battle soon enough, but she insisted. Gods, what if she was killed on the way to the barracks?"

We make it through the brush, finding only a few dead. Bodies already bloated in the heat. We make it to the battlefield and the barracks, where firepits have been lit. The sky lightens with the promise of a rising sun, and the prayer songs begin, rising across the island. They swell, the sound of sorrow heavier than I've ever heard the songs on this island, until the voices fade away. Islanders are still hard at work. I remember the same expressions of exhaustion, the backs bent as we worked the fields. I'm not the right person to speak to Malthe. He oversees the work from his position at the edge of the battlefield. He sees me, but he doesn't say a word as I put a reassuring hand on Olina's and convince her to let go of her grip.

"Maybe a word to Malthe," I suggest to her, "to give everyone a moment to rest. It doesn't help if we kill ourselves with exhaustion."

She nods, panic still in her eyes. "Where are you going?" she whispers, though I don't know why she speaks softly.

"To find Kjerstin."

If Kjerstin had made it to the barracks, she would be with Malthe, giving him her many opinions. Olina doesn't argue as I slip away, back into the groves. There's still a chance that there are Fjern hidden on the island, but I decide to take a risk and call out Kjerstin's name. I find the bodies of islanders and Fjern alike. I see one young girl lying on her stomach. With the twist of my gut I kneel to her side to turn her over, but it isn't Kjerstin. I march to the fields where the fires are dying, turning to smoldering embers in an early morning drizzle, pink light shining on the horizon. I walk the same path I did the night before with the guards that followed me, to the mangroves and the beach where we'd won our first battle—and I see her.

She sits with her back against a rock, machete in her hand, a dead Fjern at her feet. Red soaks a wound in her side. Her eyes are half closed, but she still breathes when I run to her side. I grasp her shoulder.

"Kjerstin," I tell her. She struggles to keep her gaze focused. "Keep your eyes on me. Don't close your eyes."

She smiles. "Do you really think looking at your face will keep me alive?"

She hasn't lost her humor at least. I rip her dress open and involuntarily wince at the wound. It's deep, and the black-red blood has pooled and congealed. I put a hand on her abdomen and focus the energy of Anke's kraft. Warmth spreads, and Kjerstin clenches her jaw against the pain. I see movement as the organs begin to mend, but it stops short. Her skin is still torn open. I'm weak after healing so many on the battlefield, and

Anke's kraft is still too young to fully heal. There's still too high of a chance that Kjerstin could die from this.

I could carry her to the battlefield, but I'm not sure if she would survive the trip. I yank off my shirt, but it's covered with dirt and blood. While I might not understand much about the sciences of the body, I know enough about infection. I hurry to the edge of the sand where the sea pushes and pulls onto the bay. I dunk the shirt into the saltwater, wringing it out as I run back to Kjerstin's side.

"This is going to sting."

"Not much more than getting a machete in the stomach, I bet."

I press the shirt against her side and she cries, but she doesn't push me away. "Hold it there," I tell her. I rip the ends of the bottom of her dress and dip this into the water also, then try to use the cloth to clean her wound. Her head lolls at one point, and I think that she's gone unconscious, but by the time I begin to wrap the strips of cloth around her stomach, she tells me that I'm better at bandaging wounds than she thought I'd be.

"Malthe trained us for as many aspects of battle as he could."

"He's a good commander, then," she says, but there's something sarcastic about her tone that makes me glance up at her. She smirks. "Isn't that what we're supposed to think, anyway?"

"Your words could brand you a traitor."

"A traitor, or someone who is worried about my chance of survival on an island run by a man too in love with his own power," she says. Her voice is weak, but the words come out in a constant, strong stream. "The hypocrisy of it all makes my head spin sometimes. How much he hates the kongelig and the Fjern, but loves giving his commands."

"You shouldn't be speaking."

"Why?" she says. "Will my silence keep me alive longer, too?"

I sit back, checking the work of the bandage. It'll keep her from losing blood, at least, but she'll need the steady hand of a seamstress back at the camp, as well as the tea of herbs I'm not sure we have to fight off the infection. How many wounded are like this at the camp? Though we managed to win the battle, we lost so many, and we could still lose more.

"Don't look so concerned for me," Kjerstin says, her voice a whisper. "I never expected to live very long anyway. We are in the middle of a war, after all."

I frown at her. "The point is to survive the revolution. Win, and finally live a life of freedom."

She laughs at me, though regrets it as she winces. "The people who fight the revolution will never get to enjoy the freedom, Løren," she says. "We're not going to live through this. You know that."

"If we're not going to live through this, then what's the point in fighting?"

"That's the thing," she says. "There is no point. No point to living, either. So I might as well give my life, trying to do something right."

Light is dimming from Kjerstin's eyes. She closes them, lashes fluttering against her cheeks, but she still breathes, her chest heaving with the effort to live. I pick her up and carry her, as gently as I can, while the sun rises and paints the sky.

The wounded are taken into one of the barracks still standing. What little supplies we have left are gathered for aid. I circle back for Marieke, as I promised her I would. When I arrive, Sigourney asks that I let her out of the room.

"I could be of help," she says. "I can't prove that I'm willing to change if I'm locked away."

Marieke is hopeful that I'll release her also, but I can't—not yet. There's too much to worry about on the island still. We have to care for the wounded and find supplies and resources, figure out our next steps. It's enough without having to think about whether Sigourney is somehow using her kraft to harm others, or if another mob has decided to hang her from a tree. She's disappointed when I promise her that I'll return to release her in a few days' time, when I'll be able to keep a closer watch on her, but she doesn't argue with me.

By the time Marieke and I return to the battlefield, Geir has appeared at Malthe's side like he'd been there all along. When asked where he was, he simply says, "I was hiding."

Marieke, Olina, and Malthe are frustrated by his lack of explanation, but Geir only watches me. He expects me to use my kraft—his own power lets him see that this is the only plausible action I could take—and I do. I sink into him to see the truth: He'd been in the secluded Nørup manor, as it was his preference to be far away from the revelry and social politics and emotions of humans that he just could not understand. He was studying the stars when he suddenly realized he'd missed the obvious. The Fjern would never stand to have their islands taken by the people they consider savages, yet they hadn't attacked in weeks. Why not? The answer came to him:

The Fjern must have learned somehow that we had certain preparations in place. We depended on the mangroves as a natural barrier, and scouts surveyed the sea from the hilltop and the bay, ready to warn of any oncoming ships. It was a realization that couldn't have come without the help of someone on this island. Yes, Geir saw what I've also begun to suspect. There must be a traitor. And if there's a traitor, then they must have told the Fjern how lax we'd become, expecting victory from battle on the sea. The only obvious result would be an ambush by foot, sneaking onto the bays and managing to take Tuve and his guards by surprise. The only night for such an ambush would be when there was no moon and the sky was a cloak of darkness. It was then that he began to hear the screams.

Geir knew that the manors, where so many islanders had

taken residence, would be attacked. Geir had studied the island of Hans Lollik Helle enough to know of an alcove hidden away from the main bay. He went there, and when he saw a boat abandoned by the Fjern in the sand, he pushed the boat out onto sea. It was the safest place to hide on an island that was being attacked. He simply waited for the battle to be over.

Malthe eyes Geir with suspicion. He thinks it's strange that the man knew of the attacks but did nothing to prevent them himself. "You could have warned us, Geir."

"It was too late," he says. "By the time I realized that we were ambushed, I could see that the only possibility of me surviving was to escape myself. My death wouldn't have helped this rebellion."

He's right about that, at least. We do need Geir and his kraft if we want to have any chance at winning this war. At one point, only Geir would have inspired any sort of suspicion from me. I don't get the sense that Geir is lying. I don't think he's responsible for Tuve's death, and I don't think he's the traitor on this island. But I still question why he keeps his kraft a secret from the others. If it's for a strong reason, it wouldn't do any good to expose his secret at this moment. I'll have to ask Geir to speak alone with me later.

"We've lost Tuve," Marieke says, matter-of-factly. There isn't any time for emotion. "We'll need a new spymaster. Someone to lead the scouts."

"Might I suggest Kjerstin," Geir says without pause.

"Are you sure that's wise?" Olina asks. She doesn't appreciate Kjerstin's brash personality.

"She's young," he acknowledges, "but she has the mind for it." I can feel the thought that follows: *Perhaps more than Tuve did.*

"We'll have to see if she recovers," Malthe says. He hasn't looked at me since I returned to the camp with Kjerstin in my arms, but I've seen that expression many times before. I feel his mind planning my punishment.

"Morale is low," Marieke says, gazing out at the encampment. The bodies have been cleared for the most part, the worst of the wounded moved into the barracks, but we don't have many supplies. The last of the fruit groves were destroyed. The sun is rising higher. The sky turns a pale blue, and within a few hours it'll be at its height. We'll be hungry. Tired. We were comfortable, at least, fighting off the Fjern before—but they've forced us into the position where we have to make a move.

"Everyone needs to keep their heads down and continue working," Malthe says. "That's the only way we will survive this."

"You forget that not everyone here is a guard under your command," Marieke says with more bite than usual. She's been frustrated with Malthe all along, as I've seen at the meetings—for commands she disagrees with, and especially for his plotting against Sigourney.

Olina agrees. "We can't simply *keep our heads down*. We're hungry, and there's no more food." She's always deferred to authority. She'd always followed her master's orders without complaint, or any desire to fight. It's interesting to see someone like her be such an instrumental part of the uprising. But with the near loss of the war, she chooses to voice her anger. "What do you propose we do? That's what everyone wants to know."

"I have given my orders," Malthe says.

Marieke continues. "They don't want commands to continue training. They don't want a commander at all."

I understand what Marieke is implying, and I wish she would stop. But she looks directly at me.

"I've heard from several that they would like to see Løren as our leader," she says.

There's silence following her words. Malthe still refuses to look at me, but I see a flicker of an image of me hanging from my neck. "Who has said they'd like to see Løren as our leader?"

"It doesn't matter who."

"It does if you're spreading lies."

"She isn't lying," Geir says. "It makes sense that the people would want this. Løren is young, charismatic, offers hope with his kraft—and from what I've heard, he was the savior of the rebellion last night."

"I haven't heard anyone voice their desire for Løren Jannik to lead us."

"Then let me voice it now," Geir says. Surprise sparks through me. Geir's words are powerful, though he won't meet Malthe's eye and his shoulders hunch, his back bent in his older age. Malthe could pick him up and break him in two. Geir is very aware of this. Yet he still speaks the words. "I would like to see Løren as our leader."

"I would, too," Marieke says without hesitation. She has no trouble meeting his gaze as she speaks the words.

Olina nods. "I would as well." She's still angry, but she can sense the danger in voicing this particular opinion. Even as she tries to meet Malthe's eye, she blinks again and again. But she feels safe voicing her opinion when the others have also.

Malthe stands tall. Fury pulses through him. He hides it well, except for the twitch of his nose, the downturned corners of his mouth. "The guards would not follow him."

Marieke has had enough of Malthe. She turns on her heel and shouts to the field. "My people," she yells, voice unwavering. Heads look up and turn to her. I nearly reach out to put a hand on her shoulder, to stop her from continuing. She speaks without the full consent of the group. I wouldn't want to move forward as the leader without Malthe's agreement, too. But she only ignores me. "We have survived a night of hell, thanks be to the spirits, and it was due to the courage and leadership of one man. Shout his name."

There's no hesitation. My name is yelled, again and again.

I close my eyes. I can feel the vibrations of power, strength, admiration—and Malthe's rage. I can feel how he wants to strike me down with his blade.

"My people," Marieke yells again. "It's clear, more than ever, that we need a true leader. Someone who will shine a light on a path, littered with the bodies of the Fjern, and guide us to freedom. Tell me," she says, "who you want your leader to be."

I watch the crowd of our people, invigorated by Marieke's words. Some stand as they clap and stamp their feet, and one beat rumbles through the ground, one pulse as they shout my name again and again. And suddenly, I realize that this moment isn't about me, or Malthe, or any one of us here on this island. This moment is about all of us and the revolution for our freedom.

Malthe disagrees. The name shouted from everyone's lips isn't the name he wanted to hear. A spasm cracks his expression of calm, and finally he looks at me with a gaze that lets me see just how much he would like to cut my neck himself.

"What say you, Løren?" A sliver of him hopes and expects that I will decline. I might have, once. But I cannot. I accept the cheers that rise across the island.

CHAPTER EIGHT

I'm expected to leave the slaves' quarters. The people wouldn't want a leader who sleeps alone in the dust of where we'd been oppressed, no matter my reasons. Marieke suggests I take residence in the manor of Herregård Constantjin instead.

"I'm not ready."

I whisper this to Marieke as we walk from the fields and up the hill to the manor.

"You are ready," she says, "and if you aren't, then you must make yourself ready. We need you, Løren. You're the only one of us that can hold the people together as you have. If Malthe takes control, we won't last much longer." We've all seen that he hasn't made the right choices in leading our people. He would send us to our deaths to attack Niklasson Helle, would train each and every islander into the ground under the hot sun. He continues to use the whip, holding on to the old ways of keeping power. Marieke is right. If Malthe were to take control, there's little chance that we would win this war.

We continue, Marieke taking my arm, out of breath as we walk up the slope of the hill. We stop to survey the island beneath us and the dying embers of its smoking groves. It isn't lost on me that the closer we come to the manor, the harder it is for Marieke to take her eyes away from the tower that holds

Sigourney Rose. It isn't lost on me, either, that with me holding more power than Malthe, Sigourney's chance of survival has heightened.

Marieke gives me one of the chambers least touched by the battles. It's where a guest of the king would have stayed. She and I agree that sleeping in the room of the king himself would be tempting the spirits too much, and that the dead Konge Valdemar could somehow find his revenge.

The room itself was once beautiful, but now the wallpaper yellows and dirt is spread across the marble floor, weeds growing from cracks between the tile and walls. The sheer gauzy curtains were the sort most of the Fjern had in their chambers and their sitting rooms. They're tattered, and the breeze blows through its holes. A wardrobe holds one lone spider and forgotten pants and shirts that Marieke says may fit me when she holds them up. The balcony doors, glass shattered, open to a view of the mangroves and the sea. The bed is too comfortable when I sit on its edge, the white sheets too soft. I think to myself that I might end up on the ground at night anyway, preferring the hardness against my back. I've only ever slept on a wooden floor at night, and I prefer the reminder of where I'd come from and who I am. If I allow myself to sink into a soft mattress at night, I might become comfortable and complacent with my position. I might forget that I'm at war, only to open my eyes to find my neck already cut.

Marieke has decided that we all need a few hours of sleep. It wouldn't do any good if we went from battle and into the meeting room to make key decisions on the next steps. We plan to reconvene when the sun is on the western end of the island, beginning its descent. I lie in the bed, but I don't sleep. The sunlight is too bright and my mind is too restless. I spend the afternoon staring at the cracks in the ceiling. I close my eyes and I think of my memories of this island. I'd attempted to escape from Hans Lollik Helle many times. The island was farther north than Jannik Helle, so I would wait for the storm season, when my father would bring me here as one of the Jannik personal slaves. I'd nearly drowned once. I decided to attempt swimming to freedom. It was impossible. I knew that as I dove into the black water at night. But the moment I decided to swim to freedom was also the moment I decided that I would rather be dead than return to Hans Lollik Helle alive. That's what I told myself, but when my arms and legs weakened and I began to swallow water, salt burning my eyes and nose and tongue, I was afraid to lose my life.

I woke on the shore of Hans Lollik Helle. I coughed water, thinking of the images that'd flashed through my mind as I sank beneath the waves. My mother, her back to me always. The islands that burned with fire. I asked the spirits why they hadn't let me drown. None answered me. I wonder if this was why: this moment, this rebellion. The spirits were never done with me. But when I have fulfilled my purpose, death will collect its debt.

By the time the sun is about to set, I can hear the prayer songs rising across the island. I'm the first in the meeting room. I almost take the seat I regularly do, but I realize I'll be expected to sit at the head of the table where Malthe has been sitting. The chair is heavier than the others. Its rough wood splinters beneath my fingers when I pull it out, scraping it on the stone floor. I sit. I've already begun to worry that I've made a mistake in taking the position as leader. I try to remind myself that this role has nothing to do with me, and everything to do with the revolt. The people need a symbol of a leader that they can unite under. They need someone who can give them hope—someone they respect rather than fear. If I am the person they need to play this role, then I will.

Olina, Marieke, Geir, and Malthe each come into the room and take their seats. Malthe sits to my right without speaking. He seems calmer than he was hours before, but I can still feel an undercurrent of rage inside of him. Kjerstin is still unable to leave her bed, though a healer said that her condition seems promising.

The discussion we hold this evening is more tense than ever before. This isn't surprising. The battle slapped us awake. We had been hesitating, waiting for the right moment to strike. We haven't been aggressive enough. We'd become complacent—too confident in our strategy in fighting the Fjern at sea, eating and drinking like we aren't at war, waiting to be attacked instead of making a move against the Fjern first. We were just happy that we still lived against all odds. Since the battle, the stakes are higher. There isn't much food left. There are stews of fruit that will quickly spoil and dried strips of meat from the carcasses of goats that had been slaughtered and roasted in the first nights of the celebrations. However, Marieke estimates that, rationed to only one meal every day for each person on this island, we would last two weeks at most.

Geir can see that we only have two options, but I can sense him waiting for me to speak the strategy instead. "Our hand is being forced," I say to the room. "We have to make a decision. First, we could have the island evacuated. Everyone could escape to the north, and we could allow the Fjern to take hold of the royal island."

"That isn't an option at all," Malthe says. "We can't abandon the island."

But Marieke disagrees. "There isn't much that's left for us here. Our supplies and food have dwindled. There isn't any point in staying here if we can leave."

The loss of the latest battle still shudders through us all, shattering our morale. Maybe it's best to leave the island behind and start fresh elsewhere with a new base and more supplies and more guards to rely on.

"Still," I say, "while surrendering the royal island of Hans Lollik Helle doesn't mean surrendering the revolution, it does mean a retreat and giving up a vital piece of the board." Papers are spread across the table, including a map of the islands. The most central island to all the islands of Hans Lollik is an important position in this game. Giving it to the Fjern could allow them to continue pressing forward and pushing us back, taking all of the islands of the north until we have nowhere else to run.

"We should start again," Marieke says, "in a place with more access to resources."

"This was the first option," I say, "but I think I agree with Malthe." My words surprise everyone at the table. "We should stand our ground. We can't give up such a vital position."

"And our second option?" Malthe asks.

"The second option would be to send anyone who is not a fighting guard to another island for food and safety. Not everyone needs to be here."

"Those who are injured and those who do not train to be a part of Malthe's guard could leave the island for Årud and Nørup Helle," Olina says thoughtfully. "Perhaps even farther north."

The northern empires have always felt more like an abstract concept to me and to all of the islanders who have never left Hans Lollik. I've only ever seen flashes of the empires to the north from Sigourney Rose's memories. I don't think we could send ships so far, but any of the other islands will have more capacity to hold people who do not fight battles in our war. People leaving Hans Lollik Helle would also lengthen the time fighting guards can survive on this island with our rationed portions. The main danger is whether the Fjern are in the waters surrounding us, waiting for an opportunity to strike. Their ships have scouted the sea for the past two weeks. They've relentlessly intercepted our messengers and killed them so that we can't reach the guards of the northern islands with our orders. If the islanders were to escape to the northern islands without the guards to protect them, they would likely be killed. We're not sure if the north has been attacked. The Fjern could have been working to surround us here on Hans Lollik Helle without us realizing we've already lost all of the other islands.

"And what about the people?" I ask Marieke. "Do you know where the majority stands?"

"There's a desire to attack the Fjern directly, rather than concerning ourselves with surrender and retreat. They're angry. They want vengeance."

"We're not exactly in a position to attack," Olina says.

"We can't just stay on this island and wait for the kongelig to make their next move," Marieke says.

Geir agrees that we're taking too much time. "The Fjern could be planning another attack on Hans Lollik Helle as we speak."

"We should send a message to each of the northern islands," Olina says. "We don't need to wait for Kjerstin's recovery to move forward."

Marieke looks to me. "Løren?" She wants me to say what we will do. I'm uncomfortable with making the decision for us all, but this is my new role.

"We'll evacuate anyone who isn't with the guard from the island," I say. Olina nods her agreement. Malthe is silent, both with his voice and his mind. Geir has no response. He can see just as I can that neither option has a high chance of ending well.

We decide that the best option is to evacuate to Valdemar Helle. The seas between Hans Lollik Helle and Årud and Nørup Helle have been under constant attack, and it would be best to avoid the Fjern, especially when we'll be traveling with such a low number

of guards. The scouts report that the seas between us and Valdemar Helle haven't been under the patrol of the Fjern as frequently.
They've also reported that some islanders who survived the battles of the south escaped to Valdemar Helle and created their own
camp. There are only about twenty total, five guards and the rest
islanders. The kongelig hasn't bothered to lead an attack against
the island. Though it's close to Hans Lollik Helle, there is no
source for supplies or food besides the fish in the sea. The soil is
too hard and rocky, and the brush too thick with thorns. There's
no natural fort that the Fjern guards could use that compares to
the mangroves and cliffs of Hans Lollik Helle. Geir believes this
is why the kongelig will leave Valdemar Helle alone: They would
rather focus their attacks on Hans Lollik Helle than waste their
time and energy and supplies on an island for which they have
no use. There is also the fact that us taking their royal island is
the greatest injury to the Fjern. They won't stop until they have
Hans Lollik Helle under their control once more.

There are twelve surviving islanders who aren't guards on
Hans Lollik Helle. I'm not sure if they'll all be able to stay on
Valdemar Helle, but if we can prioritize taking them to safety,
then we can attempt to send messages to the northern islands as
well, asking for their aid in transporting our people away from
the battles. Helga holds Anke's hand as she guides her to the
bay alongside all the islanders who carry their few belongings.
The wind is strong today, whipping sand that lashes across our
skin and into our eyes. The air is filled with tension. Everyone
has heard of the dead scouts. There have been rumors that their
headless bodies were left in boats that were returned to Hans
Lollik Helle on the current. The Fjern could attack us at sea and
slaughter us before we make it to Valdemar Helle.

Anke pulls on my hand. She complains that she wants to stay
and fight with us. It doesn't matter that she's a child. She wants
to kill the Fjern. She wants to punish them. Anke had watched

as a pale-skinned man took her mother away from the slaves' quarters on Niklasson Helle to be sold on the docks. When Anke cried in front of her mistress, she was slapped, and when she bit the hand of the woman, she was whipped for the first time in her life, though she was only eight years old. She's a child, but we islanders are never afforded the chance to be children. We've never experienced the innocence that the children of Fjern have. Anke reminds me of myself when I was young. She has the same anger that I did, for the other islanders who refused to fight back against the Fjern. I hated the fear the others around me held. They would divert their gazes whenever my father and brother tortured me. They would accept their own whippings without complaint. I didn't realize then that some didn't want their freedom; that others couldn't imagine lives that were not in chains. Anke doesn't understand this yet, but she will.

I kneel to her in the burning sand and suggest that Valdemar Helle will need guards to protect them from the Fjern as well. It's only then that she agrees to leave with the other islanders. We take boats out to the clear shallows, sunlight leaving patterns on the seafloor. We row to the single ship that waits. We decide to use only one so that we can keep the other two ships with Hans Lollik Helle in case the Fjern strike again. Boarding the ships to abandon the royal island if attacked by the Fjern isn't an option, but if we can see the Fjern coming, the ships will need to be used in battle on the sea.

The ship we use comfortably holds about ten. With the twelve we're evacuating and the ten guards, plus me and Malthe, there isn't any space to move about. One woman unused to the sea falls ill, head in between her legs. Another man, injured badly from the ambush of the Fjern, lies on his back while a friend clasps his hand, promising he'll live through the voyage, though this isn't a promise he should so easily make.

The journey is a little more than half a day when there are

clear skies and still seas, but the wind becomes stronger, as if we're still in the midst of the storm season. The ocean is rough. Waves swell and make the ship lean dangerously, back and forth without end. With so many of us on board, there's a possibility that the ship could become unbalanced and capsize, sending us into the depths of the sea. Everyone senses the danger. The journey is silent. If anyone speaks, they only whisper. I hear the murmurings of a prayer. I hope that the ancestors are listening. Rain begins to fall, splashing us with its cold water. We shiver and shake in the wind that pushes us across the sea. Helga believes that she's going to die. She always felt she was meant to drown in the sea. She has had nightmares of falling into the ocean and of the spirits of islanders, angry that she still lives, pulling her beneath. She's afraid to die, but she's also resigned. She accepted years ago that hers was not a life she was meant to keep. Helga allows me to take her hands. She doesn't question me when I close my eyes. I imagine reaching into her spirit and grasping her fear. The fear comes to me as a little girl, a child huddled and shivering. I wrap my arms around her to comfort her. Helga, an older woman, looks at me with a steady gaze. She doesn't understand what I've done. There's a trickle of unease, but gratitude also flows through her.

A woman screams. I stand, unbalanced in the rough waves, as I slip across the deck, avoiding the tangle of arms and legs. I hurry to her side to see what she sees, along with the islanders around her who turn to look. There's a beast in the ocean, gray and with skin like sand. It has one beady black eye that looks at us as it rolls beneath the waves. A spout of water sprays from a hole and it lingers beside us. It could push our ship into the water, but it doesn't. Its tail rises from the sea and crashes back to the surface, and within moments it's disappeared into the black depths of the ocean. The rain stops, the wind clears, and the sea stills. Valdemar Helle appears through the haze on the horizon.

Sharp coral reefs make it difficult for the ship to get too close to the shore. Malthe, the guard named Steef, and I all take a smaller boat, the waves bloating beneath us, saltwater spraying as we row. I'd met Steef before on Hans Lollik Helle. He was a guard who'd asked for advice on the crafting of arrows. He's nervous that he doesn't row quickly enough and that Malthe will promise to have him whipped for his slowness.

Steef is older than I am and has been training in the guard for many more years, but he doesn't feel that he was meant to hold a machete. He can never remember the formations, and he doesn't cut with the same precision as others. He'd seen me fight when the Fjern ambushed us. Steef believed what the others had whispered around the campfire: I wasn't a human being. I appear to be a man that has flesh and blood and bone, but many devils and monsters in our legends do.

Steef remembered a legend his mother had told him many years ago, before he was taken away to be sold to a new master on Larsen Helle. There'd been a slave who tried to escape, but he was captured and hung. His body was left to rot in the tree from which he swung, but the following night he pulled the rope from his neck and tried to run again. He was captured once more, but the Fjern were confused, for they'd been certain the man had died. They burned him alive this time, but the next night, he walked out of the ashes. It was only then that the Fjern decided to let him leave with his freedom.

The islanders knew that Engel Jannik had been my father, but what of my mother? No one spoke of her. None of the guards knew of her. The islanders said she might have been a spirit who walked from the shore. She might have pretended to be a slave girl. She allowed Herre Engel Jannik to think he forced her to his bed. She gave birth to me, hoping that I would be the one to take revenge on the Fjern, before she walked back into the sea again.

Steef believes this might be true. There's no other explanation for the way I hold a machete and dance through the bodies of the Fjern. Some of the guards envy my ability, but Steef doesn't envy me. He doesn't envy any guard who has a talent for killing. Steef wasn't meant to be a guard. He's too gentle for the task. He hates the way the machete vibrates in his grip as it tears through skin and muscle and knocks against bone. He hates the sound of anguished cries and the smell of blood. But this is what he was ordered to do, so he has no choice but to fight. Steef has a large body, so many assume that he is talented on the battlefield. He fears disappointing us. What will Steef do once he isn't forced to hold a machete anymore? He fears not having an answer to this question most of all.

Malthe doesn't speak as Steef and I row. His mind has returned to his natural silence. For a moment I can feel how infuriating I must have been for Sigourney Rose when she attempted to read my mind but could not, seeing that I had thoughts and emotions but unable to access them. Malthe must be enraged. I wish I could sense what he thinks so that I could have a chance of calming him. But he hides his feelings as we make it to the rocky bay.

The closer we come, the easier it is to see the two figures who wait. Both are islanders, one with a machete strapped to her waist. There are women who've picked up machetes to join the fight under Malthe's command, so this doesn't surprise me. What does surprise me are the grim expressions and the biting anger in the woman who steps forward to greet us.

The woman is short for a guard. Her skin is raised with scars. Her name is Erla. She has kraft that she'd managed to keep hidden from the Fjern for nearly twenty years, since she'd discovered her ability at ten years old. Her kraft is powerful. She's able to weaken anyone of her choosing. She looks at her victim and imagines sucking the energy from their veins and the strength from their muscles. It's a useful kraft. This was partly why she'd been asked to join the whispers on Solberg Helle and became a key contact. Her memories of the night of the first battles are a dark shadow that sink into me and cloud my mind. The memories explain the dimness in Erla's eyes and the fresh scar that lashes across her cheek. She'd been a personal slave of Jytte Solberg. Erla had come to the royal island for the storm season for many years, and she expected to be on the island the night of the uprising as well. She was prepared to kill her mistress with her own hands when the time came. But without any explanation, Elskerinde Solberg had ordered Erla to stay behind. Erla felt helpless on Solberg Helle, waiting to hear word of the attacks and whether we had finally won our freedom.

The manor was quiet that night, but Erla had been awake, watching the horizon for any sign of the fires and the smoke from Larsen and Jannik and Hans Lollik Helle that meant the attacks on Solberg Helle were to begin as well. Another woman, now dead, had whispered as they stood awake in the fields that they should attack without waiting for the signal, but Erla understood the importance in waiting. The islanders had to rise as one. If any island was too early in its attacks, we all risked the Fjern overpowering the islands one by one and winning the war.

But hours had passed, and the fires had not begun in the distance like they were supposed to. Hans Lollik Helle was difficult to see, more difficult than Erla had expected—it was bad luck that clouds hung low in the distance—and the clear outlines of Larsen and Jannik Helle didn't burn. The night passed and the sun began to pale the sky. Erla and the others worked in the kitchens as they were expected to, preparing breakfast for the Fjern of the manor, cousins and guests of Jytte Solberg who tended to stay throughout the year. Erla was tense. She made silent eye contact with the islanders around her as she chopped the cassava root and spiced the goat meat. When a Fjern messenger finally arrived, he was out of breath and red in the heat. He yelled for Herre Antoon Solberg, a cousin of Jytte Solberg's and an older man who had a habit of taking residence in the manor whenever Jytte was away for the storm season.

The messenger stood outside in the sun and held the reins of his horse as he yelled to Antoon Solberg and all the rest of the Fjern who had gathered in the manor's entryway. He yelled like he wanted the islanders to hear him. He spoke of the slaves that had revolted on Larsen and Jannik Helle. They'd attacked their masters while the Fjern slept. They acted as cowards, killing innocent children. They attempted to take control of the islands, but the slaves had been subdued before the night passed. The messenger declared that hundreds of islanders had been executed. Blood soaked the streets and bodies filled the sea. He also announced that the royal island had been stolen by the savages. They only knew that Herre Lothar Niklasson still lived, but it seemed most of the kongelig had been killed, even those who had tried to leave the island only days before. There was still no word on the islands to the north, but it was clear that all of the slaves of Hans Lollik had meant to kill their masters in a bid for their freedom.

Antoon Solberg wasted no time. The islanders of Jytte Solberg's manor were all ordered to the fields. It didn't matter the age, and it didn't matter whether they'd been a part of the insurgency. Erla could sense what was to come. A Fjern holding a machete had come to the kitchens to order them all into the fields as well. She used her kraft on him, sucking his energy until he fell to his knees. She ran to the slaves' quarters before any of the other Fjern could stop her. She burst into the rooms and warned everyone not to go—to try to escape right there and then, immediately. She begged them all to leave Solberg Helle with her, but not many believed the danger.

The islanders who followed their orders didn't think that

their masters would kill them all. The ones who had nothing to do with the rebellion believed that their masters would let them live. After all, though the Fjern didn't see the islanders as human beings, they were still worth enough coin that they wouldn't be cut down. Erla knew that they underestimated the Fjern. The Fjern loved their coin, yes—but hadn't they seen how the Fjern loved their power more? They loved the whip, loved their blades, loved how islanders screamed and pleaded for mercy they knew the Fjern wouldn't give. Especially if the Fjern had convinced themselves that the torture they inflicted was justified, they would relish in the islanders' attempts to convince the Fjern of their humanity. Erla had realized the Fjern would never see her as a human being. She could see that she would be killed if she went to the fields.

In the end, five women agreed to run with her, three with their young children. Dozens of others did as the Fjern had ordered. Erla was grateful she had run so that when the screams began, she wouldn't have to see the killings. The Fjern hadn't yet begun to patrol the sea, so she managed to steal a boat and lead those who'd escaped here to Valdemar Helle. They hid in the brush without food or shelter. It was under Erla's guidance that a suitable camp was built and enough fish was caught to last them days.

At that time there was still confusion over which islands had been taken back by our people and which still remained under the control of the Fjern. She decided to brave the seas herself to investigate first Jannik and then Larsen Helle. The islands had been destroyed. The docks and villages were burned, and trees held the bodies of islanders swinging in the breeze. She crept through the fields and destroyed villages, finding women who hid, shivering with fear. Erla had once been a girl shivering with fear, too. Antoon Solberg had a habit of ordering her to come to his rooms at night when she was young. She would try to hide sometimes, in the kitchens or in the fields, praying to the spirits that she would not be found, though she always was. Erla helped each of the women escape and come to Valdemar Helle. Where Hans Lollik Helle and our leadership has been lacking, Erla has stepped in to fill the spaces. I'm grateful to her, but Erla wouldn't accept our gratitude. She doesn't want to be a hero. She wants us to do our jobs and to free our people.

Erla recognizes Malthe first as the commander of the guards and gives a bow of respect, a ritual taught to us by the Fjern. She nods to me as well, but when Steef tells her that I've been named the leader of the revolution, she glances at me with surprise and eyes me with some disbelief. She sees me as a child, not a man who is prepared to lead. Maybe she's right.

"Fine," she says. "Come to the camp. There's a lot to discuss."

CHAPTER NINE

Erla leads us through the brush and to a clearing that islanders had cut from the thick tangle of thorns. The grass is still sharp, cutting my shins as I walk, and gnats stick to the sweat on my skin. Wasps linger on the sweet sap that leaks from thick leaves. There's a rustling in the grass, the movement of an animal I can't see, and birds call to one another high above in the mahogany trees that tower over us. The air smells like wet dirt and sweat and salt and piss, like the islanders haven't been relieving themselves far enough away from camp. Sheets of different colors, already bleached yellow and brown beneath the sun and rain and salt-air breeze, are tied from the branches of trees and pulled taut to the dirt, held in place by stones. The sheets form a circle around the ashes of a fireplace where the sharp needlelike bones of fish are scattered in the weeds.

Though there are some guards that had escaped here from Solberg Helle and some who were rescued from Jannik and Larsen Helle, the majority are islanders who haven't been trained. Most are women who bounce their children on their knees. Some talk to each other in hoarse voices, speaking of how they will find their food today. Many don't speak at all. I don't see the same joy that I've seen on Hans Lollik Helle at night, islanders laughing as they drink guavaberry rum and dance and sing over meals usually reserved for the king. There's silent resolution in some of the islanders I see here, but others act like they've accepted their fate to join the spirits. Even the children seem to think they won't live much longer. They're thin, listless. One child's head turns to look at me with hollow eyes. She and her mother were rescued from Jannik Helle. Her mother had hidden with her by the bay. It'd only been luck that Erla had seen them and led them to her boat on the shore. The child is barely five, and yet she's seen more than any child should. She's seen men cut open and fires set to skin, heard the earsplitting screams that still haunt her while she sleeps.

Erla doesn't bother to introduce us to the people who sit and watch because they wouldn't care. They're all too hungry, too thirsty, too tired to deal with a newcomer and his guards, striding around their camp with self-importance when he's forgotten the people he's supposed to care for. That's what Erla believes. It's what I can see is true. We on Hans Lollik Helle have forgotten survivors of the rebellion. We've been too concerned with the war and our battle plans and scouts and spies to think about the people who are supposed to be the reason we fight. We didn't make it a priority to reach the other islands. The scouts have only been sent to Årud and Nørup Helle to request assistance, and as far as we know, our messages were never received. It's been two weeks of silence from the royal island. How many other islands are like this? Are the people on Årud and Nørup and Ludjivik Helle huddled around dead campfires without any food or water, wondering how much longer they will live?

I sit with Malthe and Steef facing Erla and her helper Lieve, who had been one of the guards and survivors of Jannik Helle. Erla asks us to tell her why we've come, and we do.

She shakes her head. "No. We can't accept any more people into this camp."

Malthe doesn't take well to insubordination. "It isn't a request."

"Do you see the camp?" Erla demands. She gestures at the islanders who sit, watching us with blank eyes. I can feel the vibrations of resentment that Sigourney would have felt had she been here. I think of how she'd always felt this hatred. Everywhere she turned, she could feel our disgust for her, the woman who had betrayed her own people in search of power. I wonder if this is what she'd experienced, along with the shame that bubbles inside of me.

Erla doesn't hide her anger. "We can't fight. We can barely stand on our own feet. If the Fjern were ever to attack us, we would be dead. And you want to give us more people to protect so that they can eat what little food we have left? No," she says again. "You need to take your people elsewhere."

"This is *our* people, not just islanders of Hans Lollik Helle," Malthe responds. And though he's right, I also understand Erla's meaning. We've treated her and other islanders as if they aren't our people, so how can we expect her to treat islanders from Hans Lollik Helle like they are hers? Already I can feel the cracks splitting through the revolt and spreading like a spider's web. We're supposed to be building a world different from the one of the kongelig. Instead, we're falling into the same patterns.

"I'm sorry," I say. Malthe looks at me with anger, Erla with surprise. "You're right. We haven't done what we could for you and everyone here on Valdemar Helle."

Erla wasn't expecting this response. For a moment she's silenced, but she collects herself quickly. "An apology isn't enough. What will do you?"

"What do you need?"

"Supplies. Proper protection and shelter. Pass us resources of the freed islands."

Malthe interrupts. "You can't make demands."

"We're not sure about the state of the northern islands," I tell Erla.

"How can you not know?" she asks me.

I admit the truth. "We fell out of contact with them. Any messenger sent has been killed. We've been too preoccupied on Hans Lollik Helle."

"Too preoccupied to care for your own people?"

She's right. We should've made a stronger attempt at contact sooner—not just when we decided we were ready to attack the Fjern and we needed the help of the other islands. "It's difficult to learn what the state of the northern islands might be, but if we could have you moved from Valdemar Helle to any of the others—"

"To what could be a worse state?" Erla says. "You haven't been in contact. How do you know the islands haven't been taken by the Fjern?"

The Fjern wouldn't have been able to pass Hans Lollik Helle with a fleet of ships to attack and take islands without our knowledge. Something like that would be too difficult to miss. But what if they had sent smaller ships along the current? They could have killed our messengers and taken positions to strike the other islands, stopping anyone from warning us of their slow attack. Geir has suggested the possibility before.

"You want to stay on your royal island, making your decisions about the revolt without thinking about your people," Erla says. "I suppose not much has changed from the time of the kongelig. Maybe you'll find your necks cut soon, too."

"Watch yourself," Steef says. He hates confrontation, and his voice shakes when he speaks. But he's also had many years of training. His hand twitches automatically for his blade. This doesn't escape Erla's or Lieve's notice. Lieve puts her hand on her own machete's handle.

Malthe watches Lieve with narrowed eyes. He considers these the actions of treason. The women have moved against him, the commander of the guard, and me, the leader of the islanders.

This is punishable by death. I see how Erla and Lieve sense the danger.

"I suggest you remove your hand from your blade," Malthe tells Lieve.

"Will you be executing any subject who proves disloyal as well?" Erla asks. "These truly are the islands we so know and love."

The others sitting around the camp watch us carefully. None have the strength to object or to fight, but I feel the anger they have for the people who threaten Erla and Lieve, the only two who have helped them and supported them and given the islanders any sort of hope. Anger has fueled many rebellions before.

If Malthe sees, he doesn't care. He answers Erla's question. "Yes," he says. "We do execute anyone who is disloyal. We can't hold space for traitors."

"Am I traitor because I've asked for aid?"

Malthe stands and his voice rises with him. "You're a traitor because you have no respect for your commander."

"You're right," Erla says. "I don't. If that makes me a traitor, then so be it."

Malthe steps forward, ready to hit Erla across her face, but her kraft flares. She takes energy from Malthe and he gasps, shaking on his feet before he falls to one knee. He struggles to stand, to remain conscious against the black that trickles into his vision. Erla stands over him. I can see how easy it would be for her to continue to take his energy until there's nothing left but a body on the ground.

Malthe looks at me from where he kneels. I understand what he expects. He waits for me to call for the execution of Erla. Erla has claimed to be a traitor. She attacked Malthe using her kraft. She can't be allowed to live. Even here with people who do not fight, with mothers and their children, Malthe wants me to make an example out of Erla so that the people will remember our power. So that they won't be as quick to question our authority again.

Sigourney Rose would have had Erla killed. Sigourney would've had her excuses and reasons. She would've felt that her shame was repentance enough. She would've looked to Malthe and given the order, and Erla would be dead.

My gaze lands on Steef's hand. He understands and lowers it from his blade. Malthe's coldness shifts to me, but I ignore him as I face Erla. "I don't see you as a traitor," I tell her. "I see you as a savior. We've failed you. I'm sorry for that. Let us stay here for the night, along with the others from Hans Lollik Helle. We'll have discussions on next steps to help you and everyone here on Valdemar Helle."

Erla remains skeptical. She doesn't trust Malthe, and now that she's finally escaped the chains of the Fjern, she won't willingly submit herself to a man like him. She wants to kill him before he can kill her. I feel her rage and her anguish. Her emotions are tangible the more they fill me. I hold her fury and pain in my hands. The rage becomes my own. The rage at the feeling of helplessness and hopelessness that covers her like a layer of skin. It's a feeling I recognize. We only want to live. This is all that we ask. And because the Fjern have such hatred for us, even this we aren't given. There's so much that Erla has seen. Every strike and every whip and every scream. The Fjern would rather see us dead than live with our freedom. She stares at the sky, wondering if it would be easier to walk into the sea.

The more Erla's emotion floods through me, the less it fills her. And the less emotion storms through Erla, the more clearly she can see. Yes, she could allow us to stay the night. Though Malthe isn't trustworthy, she can sense how I mean to help them.

"Fine," she says. "You can stay, but only for the night."

There's hesitation when the islanders arrive from the ships. We're all the same people, and we should greet one another as we would our family, but those of Valdemar Helle are worried that the last of their supplies will be taken by us. They already struggle enough to survive. Helga sits with Anke as the girl looks at the islanders around us with curiosity. The silence is taut. I'm worried one person will say one wrong thing to splinter the forced peace. I watch Malthe especially from across the clearing, afraid that he'll decide to carry out executions on anyone he finds traitorous despite my orders.

I sit separately with Erla at the edge of the clearing. "I don't think the islanders of Hans Lollik Helle should stay here," I tell Erla. "I don't think anyone should be here on Valdemar Helle. It was the safest option when escaping Solberg Helle. This was the closest island. But there're no fruit trees, and the bays don't have as much fish. You have no protection, if the Fjern were to attack."

"They haven't attacked."

"That doesn't mean they won't. You should leave with us."

Erla is skeptical. "And go where?"

"We'll travel first back to Hans Lollik Helle to regroup, then to Nørup Helle, Årud and Skov and Ludjivik. We'll see if there's a place suitable for you—for everyone. A place with enough food, supplies, and shelter to wait out the rest of the war."

She has to admit that they have been struggling. Fishing the bay hasn't been easy, and some have gone days without eating, always opting to feed the little ones instead. Erla has wondered about the other islands. She'd considered gathering everyone and attempting to flee north, but she knew that it was too dangerous to leave the island on their own, and especially with so few who could fight the Fjern if they were caught.

"And what will you do with me once we've arrived in our new home?" she asks. "Will I be executed? I've been branded a traitor by your commander, and I have kraft as well."

"I don't think you're a traitor for speaking the truth," I say. "And we would never execute one of our own for having kraft.

Those were the ways of the Fjern and the kongelig. We need your power. If we can find a way to teach people about their kraft, to help them harness their abilities..."

"Don't you worry?" she asks me. "People with power could desire more. They could betray you. Overthrow you."

I agree. "But maybe this role isn't mine to keep."

We end the discussion as the sky becomes dark. Steef and the others lie on the dirt ground that's sharp with stones. Only six fish had been caught. I declined a meal along with most of the adults, making sure the children were given their food first. I leave the camp to walk through the thorny brush and to the shore to be alone with my thoughts. I cross the black sand and stand in the shallows, saltwater foaming around my ankles as waves pulse onto shore and back to sea. I close my eyes and think about my dreams. I remember how my mother would stand with me. Her back of scars, her rough voice. I wonder if this is what she would want of me. Am I doing everything as she expected I would? Am I pleasing her and the other spirits of these islands? But when I ask my question, I'm only met with the hush of waves.

When I open my eyes again, I see the ship in the distance. Ours is still anchored beyond the coral reefs, the boat that had carried islanders back and forth is on the sand farther down the shore. But the ship I see in the distance comes behind our own. It moves fast, sail pulled tight in the wind.

Everyone at the camp is already on their feet and panicked by the time I arrive. Lieve had seen the ship from her post and had run to give the warning. Malthe tries to shout his orders, demanding that Erla and Lieve hand out the machetes to anyone who can fight, but Erla argues.

"Even if there'd been proper training, we're exhausted. Hungry, tired. We can't fight."

"It's our only chance of making it from this island alive."

Lieve shakes her head. "There has to be another way."

"We can't retreat. They're positioned behind our ship."

"What of yours?" I ask Erla. "You must've come here on boats."

"There are five hidden on the other end of the bay," she says. "Not enough to carry everyone at sea, and if the Fjern catch us and attack us on the ocean, we won't survive."

Geir's kraft works itself inside of me, numerous possibilities sifting through my mind. "There're other options for retreat," I tell her.

The plan is simple—foolhardy, but with the shine in everyone's eye, I can see how we hope it might work. The Fjern will come to shore and to this camp from the south. Most of the islanders will retreat to the north of the island to where Erla's boats are hidden, while I, Malthe, Steef, Erla, and Lieve will stay behind to stall for time before escaping. Those on their boats will circle the bay while the Fjern are distracted. They'll pass to the south to return to our ship, and take the Fjern ship as well. The five of us who stayed behind as bait will run to the shore and take our passenger boat and rejoin the others at sea. If we don't manage to escape the Fjern and this island in time, as Steef notes, we'll be dead.

The islanders leave for the north, Anke looking over her shoulder at me before she disappears through the wall of leaves and thorns. Erla and Lieve brandish their machetes. Malthe and I wait in the shadows with Steef silently, the only sound the breeze rummaging through the leaves of trees, and our unsteady breathing, my heartbeat pulsing in my ears. We hear the voices of the Fjern as they march. There aren't many of them. They come through the brush as they speak about the message they'd received. They'd learned that islanders had fled here to Valdemar Helle and were hiding in the groves. The sight of our ship confirmed this. They've realized that we're on the island. One Fjern guard asks his friend if he's sure that the leader of the insurgency will be here as well.

I meet Malthe's gaze. The Fjernman responds with doubt. It's likely that this was a false report. He's angry that they must scour this dead rock. Islanders are here, but so what? They will be killed within seconds. The guard wants to be held in higher esteem than being sent to execute a few escaped slaves.

Steef is confused beside me. How would any of the Fjern have realized that we'd come from Hans Lollik Helle? Their scouts would've had to be watching us closely. If they had seen us come to Valdemar Helle, they would've known for a fact that I am here, along with Malthe. They would have sent fleets to attack if it was their desire to find me and capture me or kill me. Instead, they sent guards on a possibility. The guards are here on hearsay. This is the sort of information that would be passed on by a spy. Malthe has already come to this conclusion and has moved on, deciding to focus on the more immediate problem. They've finally crashed through the brush and into the clearing. There are ten of them. They all freeze, staring at the sheets and the deserted campfire. They pull out their machetes.

"Search the area," the commander orders. The others nod and start toward us in the brush. Erla chooses the man farthest from us. She closes her eyes for a brief moment, and in that second the man falls with a groan. The other guards turn to look at him with alarm. Their backs are to us when we emerge.

Malthe wraps his machete around a guard to cut open his throat. Steef tries to attack the guard closest to him as well, but he moves too slowly and the man spins around and dodges the blade in time. The eight standing outdo us in more than just number. These are Fjern who have been trained for battle. They immediately fall into a formation to flank us, and the clashing of blades begins. Steef has always been too large and slow and clumsy. His machete slips from his hand as the Fjern cuts Steef's arm from his shoulder, then slices open his chest and stabs through his ribs. He falls, still breathing, but he won't live. Erla tries to use her kraft again, but the power pulls her energy as well. She weakens as she aims her kraft at the nearest Fjern, but he only stumbles as he rushes forward, his machete sliding into her belly. She gasps and Lieve screams, running at the man with her machete too high to block—he pulls the machete from Erla and cuts Lieve's throat so deeply her head hangs from her neck. Steef's breathing stops behind us. Still Malthe and I fight.

I can't find an opening. I'm breathing hard, blood shining on my machete and sliding to my hands, already wet with sweat. I try to use Erla's kraft on the guard I fight, but another comes at me from my other side and I must spin to meet his blade. My shoulder is slashed open just as I manage to dodge the man behind me. Malthe swings his sword, forcing the Fjern to back away from him. We stand side by side as the Fjern circle us, waiting for the moment we drop our guard. Malthe sees that we will die if we allow it. He refuses to allow it.

Løren. Are you listening to me?

I look at him with a quick nod and must pay with the slash of a Fjern. I block him and push him away with my blade.

We need to run. We can't die here.

He wants us to run for the southern shore. The others must be on their boats. We could make it to the shore and to the passenger boat. This is what he thinks. Without any warning, he charges forward, rushing at the nearest Fjern and cutting the man down. He escapes into the brush. I run after him, trying not to feel like the coward I am. My ancestors—my people— would expect me to stay and fight and avenge Steef and Erla and

Lieve. But even if I am nothing but a spirit sent for vengeance, I wouldn't survive seven armed Fjern coming at me at once. I'm not ready to die. Not yet.

Malthe and I race to the southern end of the island. The Fjern guards crash behind us through the brush and thorns. We burst from the green and into a clearing of the black sand of the bay, their yells chasing us toward the shore. I pray to the spirits that the others have already safely made it to the ships. A Fjern guard runs faster than the others until he's nearly overtaken me. He cuts his blade at me and I'm forced to spin and block him. The moment has given three more of the Fjern a chance to catch up and surround me. I look behind me to Malthe. He's stopped as well on the beach, staring at me. For a moment his gaze holds an emotion I can't understand. And then he turns away. He keeps running for the bay, pulling at the boat that was left by the islanders. I almost shout his name, but any pleas for help will go unanswered. It'll be easy for Malthe to tell the others that I was cut down—that he couldn't save me.

I slash at each of the Fjern when they come at me. I look at the Fjern to my right and imagine his skin being ripped from his flesh. He screams and falls to the ground, clutching at himself. The Fjern to my left stops in shock, and I use the chance to pull the energy from him. I yank it so forcefully that I can feel his life leave his body and he falls to the ground, dead. The last looks at me and thinks of the stories of monsters he'd heard as a child. I fit the description of the tales he'd heard about a man with skin as dark as mine. I don't need kraft to cut open his neck. The Fjern we'd left behind are running to me, but I turn and race across the black sand. Malthe is already out at sea on the boat, boarding the ship of the Fjern where the other islanders wait. He means to leave me here, but I jump into the waves and swim for the ship that waits beyond the reefs.

A rope is thrown to me and I'm pulled up. I fall to the deck of the ship, soaked through with saltwater and coughing, my heart still pounding. Malthe already stands on the deck. He won't meet my eye. Not out of shame for what he'd done, but with disappointment that he hadn't succeeded. He realizes that he should have killed me himself if he'd wanted me dead.

CHAPTER TEN

When we arrive on Hans Lollik Helle, there's relief among the islanders that they've survived. But there's confusion on land. The guards watch us drag our boats onto the sand of the bay. We were supposed to evacuate those who couldn't fight. Instead, we returned with our own islanders and more from Valdemar Helle.

The return journey was longer than it should have been, wind pushing against our sails. The coming night is quieter than in the past on the royal island. The songs are replaced with Marieke's prayer, her words echoing across the sand and sea. Everyone on the island gathers on the bay to listen to her speak in remembrance of Steef, Erla, and Lieve. We weren't able to retrieve their bodies to give them the proper burial they deserve, so she asks for their forgiveness. She asks for their wisdom and guidance in winning our freedom against the Fjern. Her prayer ends, and we carry flickering torches back to the field and barracks.

I need to speak to the other members of the circle immediately— to give an update and decide next steps, to discuss the fact that there might be a traitor on the island and maybe in the room itself. But Marieke and Olina are busy with the new islanders, and Malthe disappears from the field altogether. I notice that there's a smaller group of guards that leave with him. Geir is also nowhere to be found, and I assume that Kjerstin is still resting.

I decide to wait, standing with my arms crossed as I lean against the wall of the barracks.

The quiet continues as the sky grows darker. No one is used to having strangers on the island, and the guards watch the newcomers warily from their own firepit, only a few paces away from the fire the new islanders sit around. Marieke and Helga help to pass bowls of stew to the young ones and the people of Valdemar Helle. They'll eat first, as a sign of welcome. The silence is broken by whispers. There's tension as people discuss when the Fjern will next attack. The anticipation of the attack is more maddening than the war itself. A voice carries, from a guard named Arend. He's a large man, built with muscle. He stands at the second firepit, his back to the islanders of Valdemar Helle.

"The Fjern will come any moment, and we're playing host to strangers. We can't give away our food," he says, his complaint heard across the field. The guard named Frey tries to tell him to be quiet, but he's ignored. "What is it that we're doing in this revolution of ours?" he asks. Though he wasn't speaking to anyone but the guards beside him, I can see everyone who has heard him agrees. There are some nods from the islanders who sit together near the barracks, while others walking past stop to listen. The islanders of Valdemar Helle stare at the bowls of stew, not meeting anyone's eye.

Arend continues. "We're not doing anything to win this fight against the Fjern. We're only waiting on this island. We might as well send them a written invitation to come and slaughter us all."

Though no one speaks their agreement, I can feel the thoughts of assent. Marieke meets my eye from across the fire, but I only shake my head at her. I'm glad that Malthe isn't here. He would begin to shout, to demand silence and respect. This wouldn't help.

I'm not surprised when I feel Georg at my side.

"The other guards want to know what happened on Valdemar Helle," he says, watching Arend as well. "They want to know what happened to Steef."

Guilt thrums through me. "He fought bravely, but we were outnumbered. I couldn't save him. I'm sorry. I should've done more."

"I have a lot of respect for you," he murmurs. "There aren't many who would take the helm of the rebellion and willingly admit to their own mistakes. They're more preoccupied with how others view them."

He's speaking about Malthe. I don't want to speak ill of the commander, so I don't say anything at all.

"But," Georg says, his voice lowering more, "not everyone agrees. They prefer a man who acts more like a ruler, whether he's a good leader or not."

Arend has continued speaking, galvanized by the other islanders who watch and listen. "We have our leaders," he says, "who lock themselves away in a room and make their decisions so that they can give their orders. They expect us to do as we're told without complaint. There isn't much difference between how I'm treated now and how I was treated before the war."

I push away from the barrack walls. I can see the glint of eyes following me, heads turning. I walk up to Arend, who spins to meet me. His brown skin shines in the orange firelight. There's a breath of uncertainty, but he steels himself when I stop in front of him.

"You're right," I tell him. He's surprised. Others are also, watching us. "We've made too many mistakes. You've entrusted us, and we've failed you." I look at the islanders of Valdemar Helle, huddled by the fire. "Not only you, but all of our people in these islands. You don't like that we make our decisions behind closed doors, like the kongelig." Arend frowns, opening his mouth, unsure of what to say. "We could allow anyone who is interested to join us. We could have the meetings here, in the field."

Olina wants to speak against this. Too many voices could lead to too many distractions, too many arguments. But I only look at Arend, waiting for his answer.

He narrows his eyes. "I don't need to listen to you talk for hours every day. Just figure out what we need to do to get out of this war and win against the Fjern. Get us on the path to cut their necks and get them out of our islands."

The silence is heavy. Everyone waits, watching me expectantly. I wish I could say the words he needs to hear. I wish I could promise Arend and all of the islanders that we'll do what's needed to find our freedom. But I can't say the words when there's a chance we might not win. I've never seen the point in lying.

Instead, I nod. "We'll do our best."

I go to the meeting room though night has already fallen and there's little chance that the others will come. I'm surprised when I see Malthe inside of the room. He sits by himself, arms crossed as he watches me enter.

"Where are the others?" he asks.

"Marieke and Olina are still helping the islanders of Valdemar become situated. I'm not sure about Geir and Kjerstin."

Malthe stares at me. He remembers how he'd left me on the island to die. He knows that I saw him look at me surrounded by Fjern—knows I realized he meant to see me killed. He smiles a little, wondering how I'll address this with the group, or if I'll be a coward and won't speak on what'd happened at all. I've already decided that I don't see the point in bringing this up with anyone else. Everyone already sees how Malthe wants to lead, and complaining about his loyalty will do nothing but distract us from the urgency of reaching the northern islands for the safety of our islanders and those from Valdemar Helle. I grieve the losses of Steef and Lieve and Erla. Erla gave her life for the people she so desperately wanted to save. I must honor her memory by focusing on bringing them to safety. And then there's the matter of the spy.

"There's a traitor on the island," I tell him.

He realizes this as well. He suspects everyone, me most of all. He doesn't trust the connection I have with Sigourney Rose, or the fact that I've fought to keep her alive when it's obvious to everyone on this island that she should be dead.

"We'll have to question everyone in the room," I say.

"Yourself included?"

"Yes," I say. "We need to root out the spy immediately, before they spread our plans to the Fjern."

He narrows his eyes. When there's a shadow behind me, I'm surprised that someone's managed to sneak past me.

I stand in the hallway, on my way to the meeting room. I'm not sure why I'm standing alone. My head hums with fuzziness. Through a window of broken glass, I can see that light is already starting to turn the night sky gray. It feels like I've lost hours of my life—like there's something I've forgotten, that I must remember, but even that thought is fading away. I continue to the meeting room. The others sit at the table, turning to look at me as I walk through the doors.

"Where have you been, Løren?" Olina asks me. "We had to begin without you."

I shake my head, uncertain. I must be more exhausted than I'd realized. I apologize and sit at the table, and the interrupted pause is filled as the others discuss the new strain on our resources. We're in a worse position than before, and Olina isn't afraid to let this be known.

Malthe is silent beside me. He doesn't acknowledge the fact

that he abandoned me on Valdemar Helle, and I don't see the point in bringing this up with anyone else in the room. Everyone sees how Malthe wants to lead this rebellion over me, and complaining about his loyalty will do nothing but distract us from the urgency of reaching the northern islands for the safety of our islanders and those from Valdemar Helle. I grieve the losses of Steef and Lieve and Erla. Erla gave her life for the people she so desperately wanted to save. I must honor her memory by focusing on bringing them to safety. I think there's something I must remember about Valdemar Helle—something that was equally important, if not more urgent—but there's only a hole in my mind, filled with a black haziness.

Marieke watches me closely as Olina speaks. She's worried for me, though she doesn't say the words aloud. She's surprised by my appearance. We'd only been gone almost two days, but she thinks it looks like I've aged years. Maybe I've lost some of my naive innocence. I recognize that we're in war, and I've also lost friends before at the hands of the Fjern—but the loss of Erla, Lieve, and Steef feels heavy in my chest. They'd all worked hard for the revolt. They'd sacrificed their lives, but they'll never see freedom for themselves. Maybe I take the losses too heavily. Malthe doesn't seem to care about their deaths. He acts as he always has with his cold and expressionless stare. Maybe there's a reason for this. He rejects emotion so that it won't pull energy from him.

Geir's mind has wandered as the discussion continues. He thinks about the next potential steps. Now that we have more islanders under our watch and protection, we have no choice but to go to the northern islands for help. But according to our recount of the battle, we left Fjern alive on Valdemar Helle. They will go back to their commander Lothar Niklasson and describe what'd happened. Lothar will be able to see that our hand is being forced. We'd gone to Valdemar Helle for aid and did not find it, so we'll search Skov, Årud, Nørup, or Ludjivik Helle. Herre Niklasson will ready the seas with ships. Another battle could take place within days. We'll need to travel with more guards than before for protection.

Kjerstin has returned to the table as well. She finally managed to escape her nurse in the barracks. She walks more slowly and with a limp because of her fresh stitches, but she doesn't want anyone to see that she's in pain.

Olina ignores everyone as she chastises me. It doesn't matter that I'm the leader of our people. I've made a grave error in bringing the survivors of Valdemar Helle back to the royal island.

"What will you do?" she asks me when she's finished her lecture. "We can't keep more people here. We're already low on food and resources."

I agree with Geir's thoughts. "We need to travel to the northern islands." I remember Erla's condemnation. Everyone on Hans Lollik Helle has been too preoccupied with the state of Hans Lollik Helle and the plans of attack. We should have put greater effort into contacting the northern islands from the beginning.

"And if the islands are in the same state of need as Valdemar Helle?" Olina asks. "Will you bring the islanders here as well?"

"If it's necessary, yes."

"What we need is to send an ambassador to the northern empires," Olina says. "If not me, then someone—anyone—to speak with the nobles. I'm close to convincing the Dame Nage Aris to help us—to send us supplies and guards—but she needs to see with her own eyes someone who has survived the violence and pain we have endured."

I understand her urgency, but I can't continue to make plans of war a priority over our people. "I need to go north with the evacuated first. We can reconsider our position then."

Marieke speaks for the first time since I entered the room.

"My concern is that the people are peaceful now, but they won't remain so for much longer," she says. "Though they're glad to see you as their leader, Løren, there's still frustration that we're not doing enough to win this war. And with the additional mouths to feed, more bodies crammed into our shelters... The people will start to demand change."

I feel Malthe's satisfaction. He believes the food on this island will last longer than I will as its leader.

Geir agrees with Marieke. "It helps that we have named Løren our leader. It gives the people hope for change. But if they do not see that change, perhaps within days, they will turn on us quickly. Without unity, they will rebel against us, and we will lose Hans Lollik Helle without the help of the Fjern."

"What do you suggest?" I ask him.

"Give them something that they want, even if it seems inconsequential." He watches me steadily. His answer is clear. Give them Patrika Årud and Sigourney Rose.

"It isn't so inconsequential," I say. "We're not sure how their executions would affect the revolution yet."

"Their public executions would satisfy the anger and need for revenge of most on this island," Geir says, "especially after the latest bloodshed and the loss of Valdemar Helle."

Malthe is pleased. This is something I've fought against, but everyone at the table, with the exception of Marieke, nods in agreement with Geir's words. As the leader, if I disagree with them all, it could make each of them begin to distrust my judgment. Malthe hopes that I'll make this mistake. The others would see the error of their ways and turn to him. And with a cruelty I'd never seen in him before, I realize that Malthe would find a way to punish me. I shouldn't be as surprised as I am at Malthe's change. We've all changed in some way since the war began. Or perhaps it isn't change so much as coming closer to our true characters. Facing both death and the possibility of freedom has revealed parts of our nature that maybe we hadn't seen ourselves.

Malthe has already planned his punishment for me. He would say that I'm dangerous to this uprising. A traitor. He would claim betrayal is in my blood, thanks to my father. To protect his own title and role, he would have me executed. Malthe hates those with power and those who want power for themselves, but he cannot and will not see his hypocrisies.

Marieke seems to be trembling with the effort not to speak on Sigourney's behalf. She looks at me, waiting for me to save the woman she can't help but love as her own daughter, even as Marieke hates her for being her master. If we win and the kongelig are no more, as long as Sigourney lives, I believe she'll always be Marieke's master.

"I want to speak with Sigourney Rose," I say. "Then I'll make my decision."

I leave the meeting room with much on my mind and anxiety rising in my chest, so I almost don't see the shadow of someone standing outside of the meeting room like they'd been listening to our conversation within. I'm no longer in the hall but inside Sigourney Rose's room. I don't remember walking here, and I'm already beginning to forget that I don't remember. Sigourney waits for me. It's dusk. I can hear the echoes of prayer songs rising. There are longer shadows that seem to move in the corner of my eye like the spirits have come to her chamber to claim her. I've only been gone two days, but I feel again that I've changed. I've become older with the deaths of my allies. I can see Sigourney Rose clearly.

Before, I'd wanted to save her because I wanted to show her mercy, and also because I felt for Marieke. I have hope that she can change, and believe her when she says she wants the chance to prove that she loves her people. But I also see how Geir and the others view this situation: If killing Sigourney will appease the islanders and grant us more time before we begin to disinte-grate, then that is the only path we can take.

Sigourney stands with her back to the door. She knows why I'm here. There's no saving Patrika Årud. She has no allies on this island. The Fjern woman will be publicly executed by the end of tomorrow's light. But Sigourney Rose might still have a chance to convince me otherwise. She might have a chance to save her life. This is what she thinks. A coldness that reminds me of Malthe has begun to fill me, but there's a part of me that fights against this. The part of me that hopes she's right.

"Back again?" She smiles, trying to hide her trembling hands. "You seem to love visiting me, Løren."

This isn't a visit between friends. "You already know why I'm here."

"Yes," she admits. She tells me that she's not so sure I want her to die. "If you weren't hesitant, you would've already had me executed."

"I think it's clear that I am hesitant."

"Why?" she asks. She turns to me, and I can see the despera-tion in her eyes. The desire to cling onto any possibility that she might survive Hans Lollik Helle.

"Aren't you able to see the answer for yourself?"

"I can't find a clear reason if you aren't clear yourself," she says. "Whenever I try to see your reasoning, I find confused thoughts combatting one another. You want me dead because I was one of the kongelig, and you hate me for betraying my people and for keeping you as my slave, but you want me to live because you can't help but have hope for me, and because Marieke loves me, and also because you're too soft and merciful. It'll be your downfall."

I stare at her blankly. She enjoys these moments too much, reading others and feeling the power in understanding them more completely than they understand themselves.

"You're right," I tell her. "I am too merciful."

The words suggest that I could give in to Malthe and let him kill her tomorrow alongside Patrika Årud. Sigourney flinches, though she tries to keep herself steady. She's already begun to play this game. She can't back down.

"There's another path," she says. "You've considered it yourself, if only briefly. This kraft of mine—it's yours now, too. It's created a new power between us. It reminds me of the twins, Erik and Alida Nørup, before Malthe cut off Erik's head. When he lived, Erik and Alida could share each other's thoughts. You and I—we do the same. Sometimes I see through your eyes, and you through mine. What would happen if we focused on our power simultaneously? What if we grew it and cultivated it? We're already two of the most powerful to hold kraft. Together—"

"There is no *together*," I say. "We're not allies. You haven't proven yourself to be trustworthy."

"No, you're right. We're not allies—not yet," she says. "And I'm acting in my own self-interest. I'll admit to that. But if my self-interest can help you win the war against the Fjern, then why not use it?"

I hate that I must ask. She keeps the idea on the edge of her mind, a taste of what she suggests building curiosity in me. "What do you propose?"

"Send me to the Fjern."

I almost laugh. I do smile, watching her as she looks back at me without blinking. "Is that a joke?"

"It's not."

"*Send you to the Fjern*—so, what, you can escape? Do you think I'm a fool, Sigourney?"

Her answer is yes, though she doesn't say this out loud. "Send me to the Fjern so that I can act as a spy against them. We can't be sure of how much distance our connection can withstand, but if we test our power—if you send me to Niklasson Helle—there's a chance that I could pass you invaluable knowledge of the kongelig, their battle plans and strategy. Everything you would need to win this war."

I'm shaking my head. "You would only run the first chance you have."

"I doubt the Fjern would simply allow me to run. There are enough of them living that still want me dead."

Sigourney is right. She has enough enemies that it isn't likely she would survive escaping the islands of Hans Lollik. "I would be risking my life to help further your cause," she says. "You've wanted proof—wanted me to show that I am on the side of our people. Let me go to Niklasson Helle. I can pretend that I managed to escape the royal island. I'll tell them that I will help them with any information I can in exchange for my life, while in actuality I'll be passing information to you."

"You'll betray us."

"The way I see things," she says, "I have more of a chance of life with you and my people, than with the Fjern and the dying remnants of their kongelig."

Her face is impassive when she reads my thought: *She may look like us islanders, but the Fjern are truly her people.*

"I may not belong with the islanders," she says. "Not yet. But I certainly don't belong with the Fjern, either. Let me have a chance to prove myself to you."

I don't answer her. There's confusion, hesitation, desperation inside of me. She can feel this, too. It's difficult to figure out which feelings belong to Sigourney and which are my own.

"If I do leave here and betray you, I won't survive long," she tells me. "The Fjern won't consider me useful. I know nothing of your battle plan on this island, because you don't have a plan yet yourself. You've run out of resources and want to send the nonfighting islanders to the north. This is all that I can tell the Fjern, and they've likely already realized this. They'll probably execute me before I have the chance to pass information on to you."

"Then why take the risk?"

"I have a higher chance surviving by helping you, than staying here as your prisoner, to be executed tomorrow alongside Patrika Årud. If I betray you, Løren, and you manage to find me again, I'll bare my neck to you myself."

There's a lot to consider, and I don't have much time before tomorrow's end, when I have to make my decision—and yet I already know which path I'll choose. From the flicker of relief on Sigourney's face, she realizes this as well. My thoughts come quickly—we would have to move fast, there's too much of a chance that we'll be caught, and how will she leave the shore without anyone's notice?—but she keeps up.

"If you help me leave tonight in the darkness, you won't have to contend with Malthe."

"I will in the morning when he's realized you're gone," I say. "And it isn't only Malthe. The others—"

"They'll respect your decision as long as you face them with command. If they see the fear and hesitancy that controls you," Sigourney says with a slow smile, "then they will try to take your power."

She's insufferable. I let her see this thought, but she only continues to smile, knowing that she is safe and that I've given in. I have no intention of having her killed. Not now. Not yet.

"And what of Patrika Årud?" she asks. "If someone were on this island begging for the woman's life, would you save her, too?"

"No," I say simply. I have too many memories of the woman to ever want to spare her, and unlike Sigourney, she is undeniably a Fjern woman—a member of the kongelig who would do everything in her power to destroy this insurrection if she was given her life. Besides, I can agree with Geir and the others: We all need to see someone punished for the bloodshed of the battle and loss of Valdemar Helle and our allies. Patrika Årud will do just fine.

"A shame," Sigourney says. She does not mean it's a shame that I won't spare Patrika's life, but that she won't be here to see the woman die. "Get Marieke. She'll help in my preparations. You'll need to send a loyal guard, someone you can trust, to help me with the boat." Sigourney doesn't like it, but she'll need to be alone in that boat with few supplies. She'll need to make it look like she really had managed to escape from Hans Lollik Helle. In a way, she will have escaped from us—just not in the way the Fjern will assume.

I leave Sigourney in her room. I still decide to bar the door behind me. This should be a sign. I'm about to send her to work on behalf of the revolution, but I still can't trust her. Is this a mistake? I ask the question again and again as I leave the manor, heading to the fields where islanders still camp along with the newcomers from Valdemar Helle. Marieke is bent over a pan, washing strips of cloth of blood so that they can be reused as bandages. I put a hand on her shoulder and whisper that Sigourney needs her. By the widening of Marieke's eyes in the firelight, I see that she understands my meaning. She grips my hands for a brief moment, unable to show too much gratitude with curious and watchful eyes, and she leaves without another word. When enough time has passed, I find Georg. He eats a strip of dried goat by the fire. He's confused when I ask him to prepare a boat and leave it in the alcove of the bay, but he doesn't question my orders. He assumes that the boat is for potential scouts and nods, setting off to do his work.

The others expect me to stay in my new room in Herregård Constantjin, but I would feel better sitting by the firelight tonight, able to watch Malthe and see that he hasn't suspected anything. The field is more crowded with the islanders of Valdemar Helle, the barracks overrun with the injured and ill. People still sit in separated groups. I notice the guard Arend, who had earlier voiced his anger against me and the other members of the circle. He speaks to Malthe. Malthe meets my gaze, and Arend pauses to look over his shoulder at me. I only nod and continue walking. Even if there has been fear of our people rising against us in anger, I'm heartened to see Anke sharing guava stew with a woman and her child from Valdemar Helle. Though there isn't the same joy in the celebrations as before the Fjern ambushed us, there are gentle smiles as conversation fills the air like its own soft music.

There are other guards sitting around a third campfire. They're surprised when I join them. Though the guards are glad to see that I haven't tried to hide away, I can feel their discomfort, too. The guards are the very same who have not always accepted me. They had been cruel to me as we trained under Malthe. Frey remembers how he'd taken pleasure in knocking me to the ground again and again as Malthe roared at me to get to my feet. I was too thin and weak as a boy. Frey towered over me as my father once had. My father had also taken pleasure in beating me into the ground. I remember wondering how it can be that two men who live such opposing lives can have this one pleasure in common.

Frey offers a cup of sugarcane wine. While the water runs low, there are still jugs of rum and wine to last the entire island another month. It seems that the guards have decided to partake in what might well be the last days of our lives. I take the cup from Frey with a nod of thanks. I understand his apology in the gesture. With my nod, the silence around the fire breaks. Ivar smacks a hard hand on my shoulder.

"He's as thin as bones, but this kongelig bastard can cut down a Fjern," Ivar says. Laughter and shouts of agreement follow.

They recount the battle from before I'd left for Valdemar Helle. There'd been fear in their eyes, but as I sit with them, the fear slowly turns to respect. The respect is mutual. The men before me have battled long and hard against the Fjern, not only in this revolution but for years as their guards, pitted against our own people from the different islands and trained under the scorching sun every day. I ask questions, the answers appearing before me. I try to push the kraft away to give the men the privacy they deserve so that they can each choose to answer in their own ways. I ask if they have families, if they lost anyone on the night of the uprising, what they will do once they have their freedom, how they would like to see these islands once we're no longer under the power of the Fjern. The answers vary: drink and lie in bed all day, enjoy the company of a new wife, swim in the sea without punishment, simply exist in these bodies and this skin.

"And you?" Ivar asks me.

I realize I hadn't envisioned a life for myself. I'd imagined the peace of the islands countless times, but I can't imagine myself alive to enjoy the peace and freedom. I say this to nods of understanding. How can I have envisioned a life when all I've ever expected is death? Across the sparks of the flame of the fire, the air wavering in heat, I see Malthe standing by one of the barracks that remain with his arms crossed. He watches me without any expression or thought. The fear that, somehow, he realizes what I've done fades through me.

When the guard Ivar comes the next morning, declaring that Sigourney Rose is not in her prison, Malthe looks at me.

"What have you done, boy?" he asks. "You'll be the death of us all."

CHAPTER ELEVEN

Patrika Årud dies quickly. She doesn't beg. She would never allow her last moments to be spent begging those she considers savages for mercy. But she can't stop herself from crying. She tries to swallow her tears as she's forced to her knees, and when Malthe swings his sword, she lets out a breath, the beginning of a scream that's cut from her throat. Her head hits the ground. Malthe picks up the head by its red hair and holds it for all of the island to view. Its eyes are already beginning to bulge from their sockets and its tongue lolls, blood leaking from the bone of her severed spine. I'd thought there would be cheers and yells of approval, but everyone is silent. There's satisfaction, yes— but everyone understands her death won't save us. Her death won't bring the end of this revolution. This is only justice, and even this wasn't enough payment for the pain Patrika Årud has caused. Malthe hands the head to a guard with the instructions to put it in a boat that will drift on the current to Solberg Helle.

There are some who wonder how Sigourney Rose could have managed to escape. They want to see her death, too. I go to the tower that had been her prison and close my eyes. We're far away, but I can still feel her connection. I don't see from her eyes as clearly as when she had been in front of me, but when I clear my mind, I see images that are hazy and collide in a blur of confusion. Water black as night, shadows of islands in the dim morning light, waves washing and foaming onto shore. The Fjern waiting with their machetes. I know, without a doubt, that Sigourney has made it onto one of the islands ruled by the Fjern and that she's been captured, just as she planned. The fact that I can still feel some sort of connection with her can only mean that she's still alive. I'm not sure how long this will last.

"The people aren't satisfied with the death of Patrika Årud," Geir says. We sit in our meeting room, discussion having already lasted too many hours. "Though it helped, they'll need more. If we don't answer their concerns, their anger will only continue to build and we will fall apart."

"We should have given them Sigourney," Olina tells us.

"What secrets might she have carried with her when she escaped?" Kjerstin says. Her wound has nearly completely healed. The stitches still pull at her skin when she moves too suddenly, but she hides her pain well.

"Escaped—or released," Malthe says, watching me.

Geir's voice crackles when he speaks. "There isn't any point in focusing on the past. We need to decide what action we'll take next."

I nod my agreement. "We can send the nonfighters to the north and to safety, with the message that we need the guards from the north to come to Hans Lollik Helle for our next attack."

Malthe tightens and extends his fingers on the table, staring at his palm. "Or we can attack now, taking the guards to Niklasson Helle."

Malthe had always wanted to attack Niklasson Helle without hesitation, but the problem we faced then still remains. "We don't have enough guards to win a battle on Niklasson Helle," I tell him. "We need the help of the northern islands."

"Why can't we do both?" Kjerstin says. "We can send a message to the north asking for reinforcements while the rest of the guards attack Niklasson Helle."

"And give up Hans Lollik Helle?" Geir asks. Because this is what would inevitably happen. Us leaving the island would not go unnoticed, and the Fjern would take the royal island back into their control.

"Why not?" Kjerstin says again. "This island doesn't offer anything but a central position. If we're able to push forward and win ourselves another island closer to the Fjern, then that should be the priority in winning this war."

I shake my head. "We need an island that will continue to connect us to the north." Especially after losing Valdemar, we need a base to act as a potential point of sanctuary. "We can't simply charge forward."

"Then we should retreat," Olina suggests. "All of us, to the north—and not just to the northern islands, but to the northern empires. To freedom." This is something she has argued for before, but no one has ever agreed with the concept.

"There is no one who would welcome us," Kjerstin says.

"Though they haven't yet offered help in the war, I can't see why our brothers of the northern empires wouldn't welcome us into their home. They, too, managed to escape and find freedom from these islands. They should be generous and understanding."

"But it isn't a guarantee," Geir says. "They could easily see us as an opportunity: turn us over to the Koninkrijk Empire for coin and good favor."

"And besides," I say, "we shouldn't be so willing to give up our home. These are our islands."

"They are," Olina agrees. "But are they worth dying for? We could create a new home in a new land."

"They are worth dying for," I say simply. "So many have already died for these islands. We can't run away. Not after the sacrifices that have been made. We need to fight."

Silence follows my words. In the quiet, I feel a pressure. It grows in my chest, spreading up my neck and to the side of my head, which begins to ache. It feels as it does whenever I struggled to block Sigourney from my mind with my kraft, but I'm losing. All around me, my surroundings begin to change. I still sit in the same room. This I can feel and taste and see, but only vaguely, like the remnants of a dream.

Before me sits Lothar Niklasson. In his eyes, I can see that he wants me dead.

"Løren?"

I've returned to the room, to the faces turned to me in concern. Marieke continues. "Are you all right?"

"Yes. I'm fine."

"You became stiff, suddenly—"

The others still watch me, worry remaining. Malthe's face is carefully blank, but I can feel the suspicion growing in him.

I stand up. "I'm sorry. It's been a long day. I need to rest."

"You can't simply decide to—" Malthe starts, but Marieke interrupts.

"Go to your new chambers. I'll bring you some stew and lemongrass tea."

I hate that this is how I leave the meeting room: like a child, Marieke caring for me. But as I walk, every time that I blink or close my eyes, flashes of imagery change around me. I stumble down the hall and up the stairs to my room. I burst through the door and nearly collapse on the floor, my head burning from the inside out.

Lothar Niklasson sits before me—but not me, no. He sits before Sigourney. Her hands are tied, but she still straightens her back with dignity and poise. He's been asking Sigourney questions. The interrogation has been conducted with the manner of a polite conversation over tea. This is something I could never stand about the kongelig or any of the Fjern: their false pretenses.

They disguise danger and death with ribbons and lace. I prefer to see the sharpness of the dagger and the blunt truth of hatred and disgust than have it hidden away.

Lothar treats Sigourney as if she's his guest, with her hands tied in her lap. The man's skin is sickly pale. His face is lined, white hair atop his head thinner than the beard that grows. He is a smaller man in comparison to Konge Valdemar when the king had been alive, but his size reminds me of a spider that can't be seen but whose single bite poisons and kills. Lothar and Sigourney had already discussed the night of the first revolt. Sigourney explained how she was nearly killed but survived and was taken prisoner with Patrika Årud, who has surely already been executed, as Sigourney was supposed to have been as well.

"I'm surprised you managed to live this long," Lothar tells her. "And you were able to escape just as you were facing execution? Convenient, truly."

I understand the danger in this conversation with Lothar Niklasson. The man holds a kraft with an ability that compels anyone he speaks with to tell the truth. No lie is able to leave their lips. Once the truth begins, sometimes it's impossible to stop. If Lothar asks Sigourney the right question, she could tell him everything that she means to hide. She could reveal that she is not on Niklasson Helle only as a fugitive, but on my behalf.

The Fjern had declared that only those of kongelig descent were allowed to hold the divine gift of the gods by law. Any islander found with kraft was executed if we dared to, as the Fjern would say, steal what was rightfully theirs. I was lucky that my father wasn't willing to kill me when he found that I had kraft in my blood. I was an islander and a slave, but he couldn't kill his own son. Sigourney, though she is also an islander, had also been a member of the kongelig. Because of this, she was allowed to live.

Lothar could easily declare that, with the killings of most of the kongelig and the insurrection, Sigourney is no longer protected by law. He could claim that she is merely an islander with a power that should not be hers. He could kill her with no fear of retribution. Maybe Lothar would not need such an excuse. Maybe wanting to see Sigourney dead would be enough of a reason for him to kill her, whether her death would be considered righteous by law or not.

Sigourney can feel all of these dangers. This is why she decides not to speak as Lothar smiles.

"I've always admired you in a way," he says. "You somehow manage to find yourself in places where you don't belong. No islander should have made it onto the royal island as a wife of the kongelig. No islander should have made it into the meeting room as adviser to Konge Valdemar. No kongelig should have been imprisoned on Hans Lollik Helle and lived as long as you did. And escaping by boat in the dead of night, to find your way onto my island…"

"I'm blessed by the gods," Sigourney says, and she does believe this to be true, or the words wouldn't have left her lips.

Lothar's polite smile tightens. "Yes. I suppose you are."

Sigourney can sense that Lothar has decided he's impatient and doesn't wish to play these games any longer. Before she can think to prepare herself, he asks, "Why are you here on my island?"

"I managed to escape Hans Lollik Helle—"

"I believe that you were a prisoner on Hans Lollik Helle under the rule of that Jannik boy, as you said," Lothar lets her know. "And so you would have technically escaped. This doesn't mean you weren't also released. Did the Jannik bastard send you here to Niklasson Helle?"

"I came here to Niklasson Helle for help."

"Did you come here, in agreement with Løren Jannik, to spy on me and aid in the slaves' insurrection?"

He's trapped her. Her mouth is open, false words unable to leave her tongue, no matter how much she tries to force them out. She fights the sensation of heaving that trembles through her body. Finally, "Yes," she says. "I came here to spy on you and aid in the insurrection."

Lothar watches her and waits for more of the truth to come.

"They're desperate," she says. "Trapped. The latest battle nearly destroyed them, and now they've lost Valdemar Helle as well. They still haven't decided which action they'll take next, but Løren Jannik hopes that I can send him information to help their decision."

"Send him?" Lothar asks, quick to pick up on her choice of words. "How do you plan to pass along this information?"

"Løren Jannik has kraft," she says. Lothar's eyebrows twitch in surprise. My father and brother and the Elskerinde Freja Jannik had known about my ability, but this was something that shamed them. They were embarrassed that the slave boy with Engel Jannik's blood had power. They were embarrassed that they still allowed me to live. Lothar almost doesn't believe Sigourney, even though she wouldn't be able to lie with his kraft. This is how deep the Fjern's reluctance to see our power runs. But he realizes that my power must be true. He considers his memories of me. Had there ever been clues to the fact that I had an ability in my veins? He thinks of the way my father had always taken such pleasure in beating me—of the rumors he'd heard of my brother's attempts to kill me, of the depth of the Elskerinde Jannik's hatred for me. He wouldn't expect any of the three to love me when I'm an islander and was their slave, but he wonders if they would have given me more peace if I didn't have a power that threatened them. He thinks all three are fools. They should've killed me when they had the chance.

"Our kraft links us in a way that has been previously unseen," Sigourney says. "I didn't understand the power's strength. I can hear his thoughts, and because he has the ability to mimic the kraft of those around him, he can hear mine. Even now, he listens to your questioning. He hears what I'm saying. He sees you, as I do, sitting before me."

Lothar watches her without speaking. In the beats that pass, I can see that he's allowing this information to stew. The possibility that I could be listening to this interrogation without being anywhere near is unsettling to him. He's already unused to the idea that any islander could have an ability, and especially one as powerful as this. For two islanders to have a kraft that combines and doubles the strength in power is unnerving.

He leans closer. "If you can hear me, Løren Jannik," he says, "I want you to know that I'm going to enjoy destroying your play at revolution. Your child's game will not last. Your people will be slaughtered. You will be captured. I'll enjoy taking my time killing you. Do you hear me, boy?"

I can't answer, but Sigourney still says that I can hear him. Lothar sits back in his seat with a satisfied smile. "Good. Your link will be severed once you're beheaded," he tells Sigourney.

But Sigourney has never given up so easily. Not if it meant she might have a chance at life. "I didn't have any choice but to come here," she tells Lothar. "It was the only way I could think of surviving Hans Lollik Helle."

"Then you were right in that you would survive the royal island," he says, "but wrong in that you might survive me."

"I can be helpful to you," she says.

Lothar nearly laughs. "Do you mean to betray your slaves already?"

"Yes," she tells him.

"Isn't your friend still listening?"

She tells him that I am, but that she doesn't care. "I can use the connection that we have. I can invade his thoughts, his mind, his plans whenever need be. I can help you stamp out this insurgency."

"You're desperate, Sigourney," Lothar says. "It isn't a pleasant look."

"I want to live."

"Do you really believe I'd need your help? I'm already close to winning the war."

"You don't know that for certain," Sigourney says. Lothar pauses. The ultimate danger in Lothar is that he's a man who is willing to listen and learn. "The islanders have always been stronger than we think. The fact that they are underestimated is their greatest strength. Isn't it true that three times, you have attacked the royal island, expecting to win, and three times they have held Hans Lollik Helle? I heard they had only five fighting guards on Valdemar Helle, and yet the majority of the islanders managed to escape with their lives."

"Yes," Lothar says, and it pains him to admit this. "But we've also weakened them. One more blow, and they will topple."

"You're underestimating them yet again," Sigourney says.

Lothar watches her carefully. "Fine," he says. "Tell me what we need to do to destroy them."

CHAPTER TWELVE

The link between me and Sigourney is cut. I'm trembling on the marble floor. I can hear Marieke and feel her hand on my shoulder as she attempts to guide me to my feet, but my vision is still blurred, a pain behind my eyes piercing through my skull. She's afraid as she speaks to me. Her words sound far away, but her worry washes through me. If I've had a hidden illness or if I was injured in the battle without anyone's knowledge, and I die, then she's certain that the war will be lost.

She helps me to the edge of the bed and I sit, lowering my head. Speaking hurts, but I force air into my lungs. "Sigourney."

"What happened?" she asks.

"She's made it to Niklasson Helle," I tell her, but I'm not sure how much more I should say. It wouldn't come as a surprise to anyone else that Sigourney has already decided to betray us, but Marieke would refuse to accept this as the truth. I'm having a hard time coming to terms with it. A part of me expected this from her, but another part also had hope that she really did mean to prove herself changed. But this is the reality. Faced with the possibility of death, Sigourney chose the only avenue she could foresee that ended with her survival. She offered herself to Lothar, claiming that she could be helpful to him, freely giving him information against us. The only comfort is that she isn't sure of our next plans, since we still haven't made any definite decisions. She'll have to lie to stay useful, and with a man like Lothar and his kraft, I don't know how much longer Sigourney will last.

"Niklasson Helle," Marieke repeats. "Is she safe? No, that's a silly question. Of course she isn't safe. But is she to be killed?"

"They've taken her prisoner but don't mean to kill her. Not yet, at least."

Marieke is relieved. "Are you still connected to her?" she asks me.

"I'm not."

Marieke is amazed by the strength of our connection and that I could see so much, as if Sigourney was only a few feet from me. This kraft originated with Sigourney. Using her kraft is like an echo of her ability, and mine is much weaker. When I try to connect with her, I can only see blurs and a vague sense of my surroundings. Sigourney, however—when she wants to connect with me, her power comes fully realized. Before she left, I don't think Sigourney realized the full extent of what our connection could mean. That even so far away, she could make me see through her eyes as clearly as if I'd been in the very same room. This ignites questions. If she really has betrayed us and she still has her power over me, does that mean she can control my body, too? Would she be able to use her kraft on me if I'm unprepared and unsuspecting, and force me to harm myself or anyone else around me? It's an answer I'm not eager to discover. I was a fool to trust Sigourney. I'm still a fool. A part of me refuses to believe that she would so easily betray her people. She's wanted acceptance and approval from us for so long. She'd been genuine when she said she wanted to prove that she could change. I'd thought that this could be her chance at redemption. I still think that it is her chance. I tell myself that this is only a ploy for Lothar Niklasson. When she has a moment she'll reach out to me to explain her actions.

I try to leave my room to return to the others. There's still much to discuss. But Marieke insists that I rest. "You'll do no good to us dead," she says. She promises that everyone else has already left the room to rest as well, with plans to meet again in the morning.

"Perhaps it will do you good to think about which path we'll take," Marieke says. "We're running out of time. The Fjern will attack again. We need to decide which plan we'll move forward with."

I agree, and she leaves. I dread the meeting tomorrow. Not because of the choice I must make. I already know my decision. I dread it because I'm worried someone will ask me about what happened this evening. If asked, I won't lie. I'll tell them how Sigourney had taken hold of me and how it seems that they were right—she betrayed us the first chance she was given. I would admit that I had helped her escape Hans Lollik Helle. Malthe would probably use this as the proof he needs that I'm not ready to lead. There's a high chance that Olina and Geir would agree. A part of me agrees as well. I don't think I have the competence or the natural leadership that Marieke or any of the others on this island see in me.

But I can't step down, because the only other person who would take control is Malthe. While he is a natural commander, I don't agree with his choices. I don't believe that he would hold to his promise of freedom for our people. He doesn't see the truth in himself, but I can see it clearly in the man he has become: Malthe is much closer to Sigourney Rose than he realizes. He, like her, might think of excuses after the war is won. That there's still a need to rebuild, and that there should be a single class of people separated from the rest to continue working as slaves while everyone else is given a chance to live freely and like kings. Malthe wants to see himself sitting on the throne. I can't allow that.

When I sleep, my mother visits me on the shore. She would visit me at times when I was a child. On nights when I prayed to the ancestors, she would come to me, even if she didn't always speak. I would wake up with flashes of images in my mind. She would stand in the shallows as she does now with her back to me, showing the carvings of her scars. The tide rises. It moves quickly. Seawater floods around my legs and my knees and my waist. My mother tilts her head toward me as the water grows to my chest and my neck and fills my mouth and nose and lungs. "Do you remember?" she asks me.

There's something I've forgotten. A face in the shadows, eyes rising to meet my own. It's like the remnants of a dream at my fingertips, slipping away the more I try to remember. But I must remember. Forgetting will mean the death of our revolution. I feel the truth with this growing inside of me as I sink in the dark of the sea. Bright light shines through my eyelids. It's morning. Yellow sunlight fills the room and the open balcony doors. I feel the heaviness of a dream clouding my mind, the urgency of a message, but it's already begun to escape me.

In the meeting room I don't acknowledge falling ill the night before. I can feel Malthe waiting for an opportunity to speak on this and suggest that I can't handle the stress of my position. Geir's only loyalty is rightfully to the success of this rebellion, and he would likely agree. Olina tends to sway with the tide, and my small moment of weakness could return all power to Malthe. Before he can speak, I announce my decision.

"We discussed the options of leaving Hans Lollik Helle and attacking Niklasson Helle," I say. "I've made my decision. We will not abandon Hans Lollik Helle, and we will not attack Niklasson Helle—not right away." Malthe takes in a breath of frustration, tapping the surface of the table, but I continue.

"I'll be going to the northern islands with anyone not in the guard. I'll evacuate them to safety and establish contact with each of the northern islands to request the help of any fighting guards so that we can prepare to attack Niklasson Helle as one. After winning Niklasson Helle and cutting the head from the body of the Fjern, we will attack Solberg and Jannik and Larsen and Lund until, finally, we will take control of all the islands of Hans Lollik and kill the remaining Fjern."

Geir is hesitant, but any plan would make him hesitant. There is no clear plan that we can form that will end in our absolute victory.

Malthe shakes his head, but he'll voice his dissent at whichever path I choose to take. "We shouldn't waste time traveling to the northern islands."

"They are a part of this rebellion, too," I say. "We'll have the ships prepared. I'll leave today."

"And what of the islands, left without the protection of the guards?" Malthe asks. "If they die in battle, the other islands will be left without defense."

"If they don't help us win this war," Geir says, "then they will die by the hand of the Fjern anyway. Better to risk possible sacrifice now than inevitable slaughter later."

Marieke is glad that I've made a decision. She has worried that my uncertainty may have meant that I wasn't ready for this role after all. She nods her approval. "You'll need to find the lead contacts," she says. Each island had a lead contact in the network of whispers, who, following the night of the first revolt, should have become the leaders of each island as well. The leader of Skov Helle is a man named Lambert; the leader of Nørup Helle, a man named Martijn. The leader of Årud Helle is a woman named Voshell.

Only Kjerstin's words give me pause. "Let me come with you," she says.

"That," Geir says, "would be unwise."

Kjerstin doesn't falter. "Why is that?"

"The mission would be dangerous for an untrained islander like yourself," Geir says.

"I'm the leader of the scouts," she reminds him.

Malthe agrees she should stay. "You'd be in a better position to handle your scouts from here on Hans Lollik Helle."

"You'll only be in the way, child," Olina says.

But Kjerstin is unmoving. "I need to meet with the scouts of the northern islands to pass on the messages my predecessor wasn't able to," she says. "The northern scouts need to be prepared to go south to gather information on the kongelig and the Fjern before we strike."

This isn't a good enough reason for Kjerstin to risk her life and come north. "It'll be easier for me to pass the messages on myself," I say.

"They need to see that they still have a leader who gives them their orders. Not just the leader of the royal island, too distracted to pay them the proper attention they deserve. And not the commander of the guards," Kjerstin adds before Malthe can interrupt. "They'll only feel they're placed below the fighting guards in importance, when in truth they are our most powerful asset. It needs to be me. I was made head of the scouts for a reason, was I not?"

Kjerstin is uninterested in our opinions on the matter. She wouldn't care if I tried to order her to stay. She would simply ignore me and board the ship headed north. And though my first reaction was to think she'd be taking an unnecessary risk by joining me, I can see her point as well. I hadn't thought about what the scouts to the north must be thinking or feeling. There hasn't been any contact in nearly three weeks, their former leader dead. It will help them to see Kjerstin—to see that they have a leader who is invested enough that she has come from the royal island to meet them in person. They will feel more secure and motivated to do their work. I think again of the possibility of our uprising crumbling from within. It'd be easy for anyone to decide that we are not fit as leaders and fight to take control. It isn't my place to decide if we are the right leaders, but I can see that we'll have a better chance of succeeding if we stay on this path instead of breaking apart.

"All right. You'll come with me to the north. We leave before sundown."

CHAPTER THIRTEEN

Malthe stays on Hans Lollik Helle to continue the training of guards, both old and new. People who might not have ordinarily fought volunteer to pick up blades, both for their own defense and for the sake of the revolt. I'm glad that more of us have volunteered to learn to fight. If they hadn't, it's possible that Malthe would have begun to demand that they join the guard anyway. Forcing islanders to do work reminds me too much of the ways of the kongelig.

Marieke is concerned that I leave the royal island while Malthe stays behind. He could begin to search for ways to grip control. He could spread lies about me and my ability as the leader.

"Be quick in your mission," Marieke tells me. "We can't afford to wait much longer."

We take two ships with us from Hans Lollik Helle. It's a risk to take two out of the four ships from the island, but after Valdemar Helle, we don't want to take the chance of losing anyone else. Nearly twenty trained guards in all come with us. Many are posted on the decks of the ships, watching the seas for any sign of the Fjern. They're in these waters, cutting down anyone who attempts to reach Skov and Årud and Nørup Helle. Ludjivik is the farthest in the distance. There's been no contact with them since the start of the rebellion. For all we know, the islanders there are already dead.

"This is something we should have done from the beginning," Kjerstin says.

It's true. There isn't any point in offering excuses. We stand together by the rail of the ship that leads the way, vaulting over the waves in the high wind. Kjerstin leans against the railing. Her wound has healed, with the help of herbs and kraft and a good amount of luck. She has a brown scar. Kjerstin doesn't have many scars. Not as many as most of the islanders around her. She only had seven scars—eight now, including this one in her side. One on her knee, from when she ran and fell as a child. Another when the woman who worked the kitchens lashed the backs of her legs for dropping a bowl of mango stew. A small line runs over the top of her right lip. A tooth tore her skin when she was slapped by a Fjern overseer when she screamed as he forced his way into her. The one on her arm is when a thorn caught her skin as she ran through the mangroves of Hans Lollik Helle one night. She was fourteen and she decided she wanted to escape to the northern empires. She was afraid that she would be caught and hanged by her neck, so she returned to the barracks. The two rising scars on her back are from the whipping that followed when an overseer saw her trying to sneak through the shadows. No slave was supposed to be outside of their quarters at night. Konge Valdemar had never bothered to have Kjerstin whipped for any mistake she made. He, like all of the Fjern, never noticed her or any other islander when they were in the room, holding their trays of sugarcane wine and serving their dinners of roast goat and stewed fish. The overseer asked for permission from the king to have Kjerstin whipped. A part of her had hoped that Valdemar would feel a protectiveness and say that she could be punished another way. He had not brought Kjerstin into his bed, though she assumed that he would do so one day when he decided she was old enough. She assumed he wouldn't want her skin marked. She was surprised when he said yes, impatiently and dismissively. The overseer took pleasure in whipping her before all the other slaves of the manor. The scar on Kjerstin's wrist is from the night she'd tried to take her own life. She was afraid of drowning, so didn't run into the sea as so many choose to do. Kjerstin hadn't pressed the blade into her skin deep enough, and when she was found bleeding over the kitchen floor, she lied and said that her hand had slipped while she chopped the cassava.

Kjerstin looks down at the clear of the sea beneath us. I want to ask her if she isn't afraid. Most would lean away from the rail, scared that they would fall off balance and into the water and be sucked beneath the surface.

"I shouldn't speak ill of the dead," Kjerstin says, "but I always thought Tuve wasn't the best person for this job."

"Why do you say that?"

"He only ever did as he was ordered. He didn't consider alternatives. He didn't think creatively about ways to get scouts around the Fjern and to the northern islands. He would send the messengers to their deaths without hesitation."

"You could have said something."

"Do you think that?" She glances at me over her shoulder. "You don't like to admit this, Løren, but our meetings have been fashioned after the kongelig. And just like the kongelig, the room is organized by hierarchy. You think that everyone should voice their opinions, but in reality, we can't always say what we really think." I frown. These words pierce me, and I want to argue with them—but I'm worried that she might be right.

"Besides," she says, "I didn't want to take time away from the planning by entering a power struggle with Tuve. I'd like the chance to prove that I'll be a strong commander of the scouts. Don't underestimate me and decide that I can't do it before you've given me a proper chance."

She's annoyed that I'd argued with her in the meeting room,

telling her not to come with me to the northern islands. She's annoyed at everyone, but she's upset with me especially. Her annoyance is justified. Because she's nineteen, three years younger than I am, I think she's a child. Her youth is no reason to underestimate her. Agatha had been the most powerful of us all, and Kjerstin has been as helpful in this revolution as anyone else sitting around the table. Besides that, Kjerstin doesn't want me to see her as a child. She holds my gaze for a moment more before she looks to the sea again.

"We'll be to Skov Helle soon," she says. "We should prepare for our arrival."

The shores of Skov Helle are deserted. I tell the islanders to wait on the sand with the guards, and I ask Frey to investigate the island with me and Kjerstin. It'll be easier for three of us to go unnoticed and escape back to the ships if we encounter something we'd rather not. If all the islanders from the ship come onshore, we'll only risk their lives. Frey isn't happy that he must risk his life. He sees how some have become resigned to the fact that they won't survive this war. He isn't one of them. The man has fought too long and hard to die here in these islands. He wants to live. He wants to survive and feel, finally, what freedom is. It's something he'd always dreamed of when he was young. He'd wanted to attempt escaping to the northern empires, but he'd been a slave of Lund Helle under Bernhand Lund and, eventually, Sigourney Rose. Lund Helle was too far away to have any hope of making it to the northern empires without being caught. This is what he tried to tell another boy who had whispered his plans of making it to the north and to freedom. They worked the fields without stopping for hours every day and sometimes into the night. The boy told Frey that one night, when the overseer was not watching, he would use the dark to slip away in the shadows. He would run to the shore and to the boat he had hidden by the bay. He'd leave for the north. The boy had asked Frey to come with him. Though Frey so badly wanted to know the feeling of stepping onto a shore and realizing that he finally owned the body that was his, he knew there was little chance either of them would survive the trip. He asked his friend not to leave. His friend did anyway. The boy was found by a ship of passing Fjern the next morning as he attempted to row past Niklasson Helle. He was brought back to Lund Helle. He cried as a rope was put around his neck. The body still hung from the tree weeks later to remind all of what would happen if they tried to run. Frey wished he'd been brave enough to cut his friend down and give him the burial he deserved. Frey thinks about his friend. He tries to remember the boy's name, but he can't.

I march with Frey and Kjerstin through the groves, pushing our way through the brush that entangles our arms and legs. We try to cut our path with our machetes, but the island seems to be eating us alive. Mosquitoes swarm and gnats fly into my eyes. Flies begin to fill the air, buzzing all around us until they're so thick that they bump against our skin and become a haze. The sound of their wings echo in the grove. I can smell the bodies before I see them. When we emerge in a clearing, the dead lay sprawled. Maggots cover skin and flesh. It's hard to see what color a body's skin had been in death. There are patches of hair. Some are pale, others dark with curls. Some wear the beige shirts and pants of workers, others the black uniforms of guards. These are both islanders and Fjern. Bodies are twisted, limbs across the dirt, stomachs spilling and necks cut. It was a massacre. Frey gags beside me. I almost do also. Kjerstin puts a hand over her nose and mouth. She walks forward, kicking over the body of a Fjernman.

"This was a guard," she says, voice muffled. "Not just a master killed the night of the revolt."

She points out that the bodies haven't decomposed as much as they would have had they been killed a month before. This was a recent killing. She guesses that the Fjern must have attacked the islanders here and that they must have fought back.

"But who won the battle?" Frey asks.

We search the groves, but all around us are the bodies and the flies and the dirt. Any remnants of the villages are only embers and ash. When we return to the shore and row back to our ship, the others wait expectantly, hoping that we will say we've found a new place for them to live. I only say that we need to leave, unwilling and unable to describe what we'd found.

Kjerstin stares at Skov Helle as we sail. It disappears behind us as the sun begins to sink to the west. "After we've found a new island for the others," she says, "we need to return here and give the islanders the burial they deserve."

The night passes almost without incident. A guard sees a ship in the distance and warns us, and I wait on the deck with Kjerstin to see what the Fjern will do. It turns, heading south. This is one of the very ships that might have attacked and killed us if we hadn't come with so many guards. They must see our numbers and decide not to risk a battle.

"Should we follow?" Kjerstin asks, her eyes also on the ship on the horizon.

I hesitate. "No," I say. "Let them leave. We need to keep as many guards with us as possible." There's no point in risking a battle and losing lives.

Though we believe we're safe, Kjerstin and I don't go back to sleep. We sit with cups of guavaberry rum to warm our empty stomachs. Both of us had given up our meals for the night to make sure the nonfighting islanders were fed. The breeze is cool against our faces.

"Do you think the Fjern won the battle and abandoned the

island?" Kjerstin asks me, thinking of the massacre of Skov Helle.

The kongelig have Valdemar Helle. They could have come on their ship to the island—attacked and slaughtered everyone in sight. The islanders could have fought back. But by the number of both Fjern and islanders, we can't be sure who won. More concerning is that there were no survivors on the island. Why would anyone have fought for Skov Helle, just to abandon it after the battle?

"If it was the Fjern, why would they have left the island?" I ask her. "They would've used the opportunity to attack Hans Lollik Helle."

"And if it was us who won the battle?" she says. "Where are the islanders?"

I'm not sure what to expect as we approach Nørup Helle. The sky is a light purple when the island emerges through the haze in the distance. We come closer, and it's easier to see that the fields are green without any sign of fire. The groves still grow, and the hills are flush with life. Nørup Helle is small in comparison to Lund and Solberg and Niklasson Helle, but it's self-sufficient with land that can be lived from without the help of other islands. If they haven't faced any attack, the people shouldn't have had any trouble surviving without aid. I hope that they'll have enough space and resources to welcome the islanders on our ships.

I row on one of the smaller boats with Kjerstin and Frey. The water is thick with seaweed that flows back and forth with every passing wave, silver fish flitting in between the green. The bay is rocky with sharp stones and shells that cut the bottoms of my feet as I drag the boat farther up onto the sand. Frey climbs out to help. Just as she splashes into the shallows, Kjerstin pauses. I follow her gaze and see islanders peering out from the groves that begin where the sand ends. I count five of them, all younger girls who had come to the sea to wash a basketful of dresses and sheets. After Skov Helle, I'm relieved that anyone is alive on this island.

Kjerstin greets them with a pleasant smile. "We visit from Hans Lollik Helle," she says.

The girls come out from behind the trees. Kjerstin asks for Martijn. "He should have become the leader," she says.

One of the girls speaks before the others can. "Martijn is dead."

Kjerstin's disappointment mirrors my own. "What happened?" she asks.

The girls hesitate. "He was killed," one says.

"Zeger is in charge," another adds.

I haven't heard the name Zeger before, and from the confusion on their faces, neither has Frey or Kjerstin. "Can you take us to him?" I ask.

The girls comply, carrying the baskets by leaning them against their waists or holding them atop their heads. They glance back at us again and again as they walk us down the path of dirt mixed with salt and sand, as if they're afraid we will have disappeared. The trees end and there's a field of thin grass with a narrow dirt path worn down from years of footprints. We see the ruins of a village and a steady stream of smoke rising from a firepit with islanders busy at work. Some chop wood, others collect stones, and most work on the rebuilding of the burnt homes. Children laugh and scream as they chase one another. Chickens peck dirt at their feet. There are people who work the fields, many with the scars of training and battle.

The villagers see us and stop their tasks. Children run to us, eyeing us carefully as we walk closer to the village. I pick out who Zeger is before the girls approach him. He looks like he's a generation older than mine with the muscles and scars of a man who had trained in the guard. He gives orders to others as they patch the roof of a house with palms.

One girl hurries to his side and whispers to him, and Zeger turns to face us with surprise. There's a flicker of distrust in him—anger, that we've made it onto his island—but he hides it with a smile. "Visitors from the royal island," he says, repeating what the girl had whispered. "And what are your names?"

Frey introduces me as the leader of the islanders. There are reactions from all who stand around us—surprise, curiosity. Zeger's concern deepens. He realizes who I am. He's heard how the Fjern want my head. He also remembers that I have kraft. But he shows none of this as he nods in acknowledgment. "Then we must welcome you to our island."

He gestures to all who watch and waves them forward. Frey automatically tenses, hand on his machete. But the islanders only rush to examine us and pat our shoulders in greeting. The islanders of Nørup Helle are of all ages. Most of them aren't guards, and from what I can see, the island has no natural defenses. If the Fjern ever attacked, Nørup Helle would fall. But they don't seem to think on this fact. Everyone on the island has been focused on rebuilding. The village here was badly damaged in the fighting, and one woman explains that the other villages had been burned to the ground completely, the manors of the Fjern and the dead kongelig destroyed.

I'm sat down with Kjerstin and Frey at the ashes of a fire, where I'm told everyone sits in a circle at night to share their meal and give their thanks to the spirits. The questions are unending. Frey shifts in impatience. There are more reasons we've come here than just to satisfy the curiosity of these villagers. But I try to be understanding. The islanders have been alone here on Nørup Helle with little contact. They've done well, rebuilding their island without help. And they want to learn what happens in the rest of Hans Lollik. They want to hear if the other islands have suffered the attacks of the Fjern, if all the kongelig are dead, and whether we are close to claiming our lands. To their shock and anger, we tell them that we have lost Valdemar Helle to the Fjern, and that the islanders of Skov Helle were killed. Zeger sits with us. There's growing panic in him, but the words are too tangled in his mind for me to understand his thoughts clearly.

After we've answered as many questions as we can, Zeger stands and asks me and Kjerstin to join him on a tour of the village. Frey stays behind, children hanging from his arms as he's forced to raise each into the air, though he can't help the smile that makes its way onto his face. We walk the path that circles the village, taking in the sight of the damage. Groves have burned and the scattered ruins of houses are visible across the fields and hillsides, like stones strewn across the ground.

"What happened to Martijn?" I ask Zeger.

Zeger pauses before he answers. "He was killed the night of the revolt." There's a flicker in him. He hopes I won't use my kraft to learn the truth.

Kjerstin asks to speak with any scouts who might be on the island, but Zeger says that all messengers had left Nørup Helle to contact Hans Lollik Helle and never returned. "We assumed they were killed by the Fjern at sea."

This isn't surprising news, but I still feel the anger in Kjerstin. How many will be killed by the Fjern before our war is won?

"And the guards of Nørup Helle?" I ask. "How many remain?"

Zeger hesitates. He considers lying to me and saying that most had been killed in the initial attack by the Fjern, but he realizes I would see through this lie, and he doesn't want to seem suspicious to us.

"Enough to protect this island," he says. "Why do you ask?"

I hesitate. It wouldn't do us any good for me to accuse him of hiding a secret—not now. "We're hoping Nørup Helle can offer shelter to those on Hans Lollik Helle who aren't guards."

Zeger frowns. "We don't have much to offer."

He's lying. I see in his thoughts that there's enough space on

this island for everyone on the ships and enough food and supplies to last them several months. If Malthe were here, he would
force his way onto the island. But I can see Zeger would rather
die than allow us to take Nørup Helle from him.

Kjerstin tries to meet my eye, but I step forward.

"If you're able to help us, we might be able to pay you back in
turn."

His greed isn't something he tries to hide from himself as
some do. He considers me. "How so?"

"Help us, and you'll be helping the rebellion. When we win
the war, anything we can give—food, supplies, resources—will
be yours."

Zeger wants more than this. He wants a promise that he
would become an official leader on this island. He wants to be
given the power to rule over others. I can't promise this. Zeger
isn't the sort of person I want to have control. I stay silent, watching him, until he finally wavers.

"I'll see what we can give," he says.

"We also need you to provide any fighters who would be
willing to return to Hans Lollik Helle with us."

Kjerstin adds, "We're planning an attack on Niklasson Helle.
We need as many guards as possible for the battle."

Here, Zeger becomes quiet. He doesn't want to promise the
guards of Nørup Helle to help us to fight the war. But he thinks
to himself that there's no harm in promising something he has
no intention in giving. "Yes," he says, "of course. As many as
you need."

He begins to ask us questions in turn. When will we attack
Niklasson Helle? Do we have a strategy for taking the island? I
speak before Kjerstin can, giving vague responses. "We still have
a lot of decisions to make."

She frowns at me, sensing that something is wrong.

Zeger has realized I've begun to find him suspicious. He doesn't care. This concerns me more than anything else. We need to get away from Zeger—need to get off the island. The path begins to circle back to the village. On the way lie the ruins of a manor that had belonged to the masters. Standing against the wall, a man waits. I think that it's a man I've seen before, always watching and waiting. He uses his kraft, and I've forgotten how to move or breathe. Kjerstin is frozen beside me, but I can hear her internal scream.

"Why are they here?" the man says to Zeger.

"They came without invitation. I'm as surprised as you."

The man comes into view, but his face is shrouded by haze, black dots in the corner of my vision.

"Should we kill him?" Zeger asks.

"No. The masters still want him alive. Get him off Nørup Helle."

The voice is already distant. My eyes are heavy.

I wake beside Kjerstin, though I don't remember sleeping. She sits on the dirt ground of one of the newly built houses. There isn't anything inside of the house except for the blanket I lie on. There's a hole in the wall that acts as a window. The sky outside is black. Hours must have passed. Kjerstin's gaze is confused, like she's just woken from a long sleep as well. Frey sits against a wall, holding onto his machete as he keeps watch.

"Finally awake," he says to me, some judgment in his tone. "You've been asleep almost half the night."

I remember walking with Zeger and Kjerstin—Zeger agreeing to help, and telling us to get some rest before we continued on our journey. He allowed the islanders from the ships to come onto the island. We ate together with the rest of the villagers, out by the firepits. This is what my memory tells me, but it feels far away, like the fragments of a dream.

I can sense Kjerstin feels the same. She's shaking her head. "I barely remember falling asleep," she says.

Frey frowns. "Are you sure you're feeling all right?" he asks.

It's what he'd asked both of us when we returned from the walk with Zeger. Kjerstin had nodded impatiently, blaming the heat of the sun.

I shake my head. "Something isn't right."

Kjerstin agrees, but not for the reason I'm thinking. "We shouldn't have stayed the night. It's a waste of time, when we should be halfway to Årud Helle already." She stands, dusting off the backs of her legs.

I'm already beginning to forget the root of my unease, though I try to hold tight. I look up at Kjerstin. "You're right. We need to leave."

Frey raises a brow. "In the middle of the night? Surely we can wait until dawn."

I don't often care if my orders are challenged, but this moment matters. Something is happening, and if we don't escape, we might not leave Nørup Helle alive. "Now, Frey. Gather the others—we all need to return to the ships."

Kjerstin looks at me with concern. "The others? They're to stay here, on Nørup Helle—"

I can't explain the instinct that this isn't a safe place for them, but leaving them here would mean risking their lives. Kjerstin's and Frey's confusion mix together, but I don't bother to repeat myself. I stand and leave the shack, walking down the path in the dark of night to the other shelters where the islanders of Hans Lollik Helle were guided to sleep. Dread fills me. Anke, Helga, all the others—I begin to see images of them all dead and lining the ground, like we'd found the islanders of Skov Helle.

Someone calls my name. I stop and turn. Zeger stands on the path behind me, holding a torch. "Is everything all right?"

He's tried to hide the guards who watch and wait in the shadows, but I sense them—five of them, all with their machetes in their hands.

There isn't any point in playing into ignorance. "I'm not sure what you've done to me," I tell him, "but if you let us leave peacefully, it won't matter. Blood doesn't need to be spilled."

Kjerstin and Frey have followed. They both slow down in their confusion, noticing the tension in the scene but not yet understanding it. They stand behind Zeger, who holds his torch in the center of us all. His men begin to approach, skin shining in the flickering light.

"Are you afraid to spill blood, Løren?" Zeger asks me. "We're in a war. It's inevitable."

"Let us leave. You won't have to worry about retribution."

"Not even after we have won the islands from the Fjern?" Zeger asks. "Surely then you'd have me killed."

"What's happening?" Kjerstin calls.

I can see how Zeger plans to hold me captive—to offer me to the Fjern for coin. He's been given orders to keep me alive, so he can see how much I am worth to the masters. Zeger thinks he can get away with demanding coin for my capture. Zeger is a fool. He hasn't seen the Fjern's true forces—only the deaths of the masters. He doesn't understand the number of ships and guards that await us on Niklasson and Solberg Helle. He doesn't see how he and everyone here on Nørup Helle will be slaughtered.

"They'll kill you," I tell him.

"They'll try to," he agrees, "but I'm prepared to fight."

He orders his men to kill Kjerstin and Frey—he has no need for either of them. Kjerstin tenses, and Frey grasps his machete. The same guards who had sat with us around the firepits move to kill us. One man follows Zeger without any question. He charges at Frey, but the older guard dodges and swings around, machete chopping into the islander's back.

Zeger yells at the others. "What're you waiting for?"

Another comes forward. I close my eyes and imagine that the hot embers of the firepits scorch his skin. He screams while another runs to Kjerstin, machete raised. She rushes forward, dagger burying into his neck. One guard swings his machete at me, but I duck. He swings again, slicing open my arm, bright pain flashing through me. He doesn't see Frey behind him. The older man grabs a fistful of his hair, yanking his head back, machete ready to cut open his neck.

I throw a hand out. "Stop!"

Frey stops. The guard clenches his arms, swallowing—shaking with the knowledge that he'd been moments from death. The final man stands, eyes wide, looking between me and Zeger. His friend, held by Frey—the other man, on the ground screaming in pain. He sees that this battle is lost. He curses Zeger. He hasn't wanted to follow the man, but he felt he had no choice since Martijn was found dead. Zeger had stepped forward and given orders, and everyone else had fallen into line. I use Sigourney's kraft to reach into him and grasp his fear.

"We won't hurt you," I tell him, and he believes me. He drops his machete. I release the other from his searing pain, and he stays on the ground, unconscious.

Zeger's rage courses through him. He shoves the man away and picks up the fallen machete, but Kjerstin is already standing over him with her dagger. He raises his hands in surrender, eyes fastened to me as he imagines the ways he'd like to find his revenge.

"Did you kill Martijn?" I ask him. He doesn't bother responding. The answer is obvious. The man had survived the revolt. It was easy enough for Zeger to slide a blade in between his ribs and pretend it'd been the work of the Fjern.

Another thought comes to me, one he hadn't meant to admit. "And the people of Skov Helle?" I ask, my voice quiet. "What happened to them?"

Zeger narrows his eyes. He thinks of how the people there had refused to submit. Zeger had gone to them, asking that they combine resources and fall under his rule. But it wasn't only greed that motivated Zeger. He'd been ordered to do this. He worked for the masters still, not because he had any loyalty to the kongelig or the Fjern in the way that some islanders do, but because he thinks we've already lost this war. He's willing to do anything for the Fjern, if it means that he'll still live. He was supposed to take control of the islanders of Skov Helle, without anyone realizing he still answered to his masters. The kongelig would return to these northern islands after they took Hans Lollik Helle, and he would surrender to them.

But the islanders of Skov Helle did not agree. The Fjern weren't pleased. They went to Skov Helle to kill the islanders and take their supplies, and Zeger waited for his opportunity. He saw when Fjern scouts attacked. Zeger and his guards helped the islanders of Skov Helle, betraying the masters—they would not know it was him. He didn't fear their punishment. And when the battle was won, he turned on the islanders of Skov Helle and killed them as well. He took the supplies for himself and returned to Nørup Helle. Greed and desperation are this man's only motivation.

Zeger wasn't expecting my arrival. He thought that I was so valuable he would be able to escape the wrath of the Fjern if he delivered me to them in exchange for coin. He's a fool, truly. They'll kill him and everyone else on the island.

"You might still survive this night," I tell him. "Stand down. Return with us to Hans Lollik Helle. Tell us what you know of the Fjern. You don't need to be executed."

Kjerstin doesn't understand why I would promise such a thing, when I should take Zeger's head myself. But with his mistakes, and though he's a traitor to our people, he's still an islander. He's still one of us. He deserves another chance, to learn from his mistakes. And he could still be useful. He's been taking orders from the masters. He could tell us of their plans.

But Zeger narrows his eyes. "Imprisoned and questioned," he says. "This sounds like another description of the life I'd had before." Zeger may still answer to the masters, but he doesn't consider himself a slave. He has abandoned the islands and betrayed his people for another path toward freedom—one where he believes he will be a pet of the kongelig, fed scraps and kept alive for helping to end this war.

I try to reach into him, to hold on to the pain—the beatings and whippings and constant fear of death, tangled together to create a man desperate to live. I try to feel empathy for him, to ease his burden so that he can see there is still a chance to undo his wrongs—but he pulls back. He leaps for the machete and grasps the handle as Kjerstin swings her dagger. She misses his throat and instead punctures his cheek. Blood begins slow before it flows. He staggers and falls. His life flickers.

One of the men who'd attacked releases a sharp gasp. Frey holds on to him tighter.

"What should we do with the others?" he asks, expecting that I'll say to kill them.

"Let them go."

All are surprised. Frey looks at me, unmoving. I give him a sharp look. "Release them, Frey."

He does as he's told. He lets go of the man, who stumbles forward. He doesn't seem to believe that I plan on letting him and the others live. If Malthe had been here, he would have ordered the executions of each of the guards, including the ones who had not tried to kill us. I ask the men to lead us back to the village and to wake everyone.

They line up and face me. There are dozens. Helga holds Anke, who is still half asleep. I feel responsible for all of their lives. My voice is hoarse when I tell them that Zeger is dead. There are gasps, furious whispers, but I continue. I owe them the truth. "Zeger betrayed all of us. He meant to abandon us for favor with the Fjern. When he tried to attack, he was killed."

But some of the villagers of Nørup Helle shake their heads. One speaks. "You leave your royal island to come here and kill the only man who has cared enough to lead us."

Kjerstin steps forward. "Zeger was behind the murders of the islanders of Skov Helle."

There are murmurs. Another shouts. "Zeger told us the islanders of Skov Helle attacked him first. He acted in defense."

"He was lying," I say, but the murmurings are growing louder. I can hear Marieke's warnings—that insurrection from within will destroy the revolution before we've had a chance to attack the Fjern. "I gave Zeger a choice. I offer the same choice to all of you. You can join us. We plan to attack Niklasson Helle, and we need guards."

There's dissent. "You come here and kill our leader, and ask us to fight for you?"

"What's the other option?" another yells. "Fight, or die?"

It would be what Malthe would suggest. But I shake my head. "No. The other option is to stay here and live your lives as you wish. I will not force anyone to join us. Those are the actions of the Fjern, and we're no longer slaves."

My words are met with silence. Kjerstin is just as shocked beside me. "Løren," she whispers, but I ignore her.

"We leave immediately. If you want to join us, the choice is yours."

CHAPTER FOURTEEN

Kjerstin shakes with anger as we return to shore and to the boat that waits. She's so furious that she can't look at me.

"You can't be our leader and allow people to choose whether they'll follow your orders," she tells me as I begin to row. Frey doesn't meet my eye. He doesn't envy my position facing Kjerstin's anger, or the responsibility of so much that weighs on my shoulders. He has sympathy for me. He sees me as a boy still. I'm too young to have to face so much on my own, and with so much at stake as well. But Frey also agrees with Kjerstin. He's disappointed that I let the guards choose whether they would go or stay. In the end, only six out of nearly twenty have agreed to come. They went ahead of us, helping to row the islanders of the royal island back to the ship. It went unsaid that they would not be welcome here on Nørup Helle, and I didn't want to risk having tension erupt into violence.

"You're too soft," Kjerstin tells me. "You show too much mercy. This is the result: fools thinking that they don't have to obey your orders."

There's some truth to what Kjerstin says and to what Frey thinks, but I also feel confident in my choices. "What good would it have done to force them to join?" I ask. "The guards would've been resentful. They wouldn't have fought the battles with the same determination and concentration as we would need, and their lives would be wasted. That isn't any different from the ways of the Fjern enslaving us. This wouldn't be any different from the Fjern forcing us to die for them."

Kjerstin sucks her teeth. "They are guards under your command. How do you expect to win this war without any fighters?"

"I can only hope that there are guards who'll fight willingly for our freedom." She shakes her head, but I need her to understand. "I couldn't force them, Kjerstin. We wouldn't have been any different from our former masters. I can't lead a rebellion for freedom by enslaving others."

She lets out a breath. Kjerstin sees my point, but she doesn't accept my methods. She believes that sometimes the brutality of Malthe is necessary. That if we don't take our power, it will be taken from us instead. "This isn't a war separate from Nørup Helle. They have to realize this. If we lose the battles, they will be killed or forced back into slavery."

"They could do as we bid, and after the rebellion and when the Fjern are all dead, they'd still hold anger for Hans Lollik Helle." It isn't only Malthe that I have to worry about desiring more power and doing what he can to take it from me and anyone else who stands in his way. There are others like Zeger across the islands who might want to take power for themselves as well. "One insurgency would end, just for another to begin, and the warring would never end until we're all dead."

Årud Helle is close enough to Nørup Helle that it's only half a day of sailing. We don't encounter the Fjern, and I wonder if they have pulled back from their attacks at sea—if they're planning for a larger-scale attack with the help of Sigourney. The sun is rising by the time we've arrived. Kjerstin, Frey, and I leave the ships behind as we did at Nørup Helle, taking a boat to shore.

Its bottom scratches the sand as we pull it from the waves. After our experience with Nørup Helle, we're tense as we walk from the bay and into the dirt of groves. There's movement. I glance behind us, back to the sea and the ships, when Kjerstin grabs my arm. I turn to look at her, then forward. A line of nearly ten guards have emerged. They stand with their machetes, faces cold. One man steps forward and holds a bow and arrow that he aims directly at me.

A woman comes from behind them. Though her back is bent, she moves fast. She walks past the line of guards and stops ten paces from us. The woman, named Voshell, sees me and the boat and the ships in the distance. "Speak your name and purpose."

I glance at Kjerstin. She doesn't care that a guard has an arrow pointed at me. If she must fight back for both her safety and mine, she will. Her hand searches for her dagger, strapped to her leg.

"My name is Løren," I say. "We come from Hans Lollik Helle."

The woman's eyes narrow. She's heard this claim before. She remembers the Fjern ships that have passed the island, each with the promise of attack. Årud Helle doesn't have many guards that survived. They'd barely won the battle. Without much protection, those on the island are afraid of the ships that pass. The woman named Voshell thinks about how, after the battle they'd won, eight islanders had arrived on the shore in a boat of their own. Four men and four women, all of them young and well-suited to fight. They claimed they were from the royal island, and that Hans Lollik Helle had been ambushed by the Fjern. They said they barely escaped with their lives. They said almost everyone had been killed, including me and Malthe and Marieke and all of the leaders.

The strangers were shown to a house of a Fjern master that still stood. They were given cots to sleep in, and Voshell wished them a peaceful rest. The woman hadn't been able to sleep in weeks, so she was still awake when she heard the screams. She drew her blade and left her room to see the strangers who had claimed to be from Hans Lollik Helle. They'd taken knives they'd hidden in their clothes and cut the throats of anyone too unfortunate to be near them as they slept. The battle that ensued was quick. The strangers were young and strong, but they were outnumbered, and the islanders of Årud Helle wanted to live more than the strangers wanted to kill them. Five were cut down, and three remained.

The remaining three were subdued. Voshell demanded to know why the strangers had attacked.

"We were sent by our masters," one said, "to avenge the killings of the kongelig, and to return the islands to their rightful owners."

They were loyal to the Fjern because this was the only life they'd ever known. But these slaves knew they would not win back Årud Helle. They knew that they were being sent to their deaths. This was the extent of the hold the Fjern had on their minds. These islanders had believed the Fjern when they said their only worth in life was to die.

The woman called Voshell doesn't order that the bow and arrow be lowered. She doesn't care that she sees islanders before her. All she sees are the bodies that have been trained to fight and the two ships that wait at sea. We could just as easily be slaves sent by our masters to attack our own people once again.

"We weren't sent by the Fjern," I assure her. "I'm not like the eight who betrayed you before."

Voshell narrows her eyes, realizing that I have kraft. She's seen islanders with kraft before. Their abilities were always hidden from the masters, but the Fjern would eventually learn the truth. Voshell has seen dozens of hangings of any slave accused of having kraft. She remembers how a girl, only ten years old, was found to have kraft when she accidentally repeated the words of a song her mistress had sung in her head. The mistress took pity on the girl and had her drink a tea that would put her to sleep before its poison stopped her heart. This woman looks at me, a living islander with kraft, and she feels both awe and fear. Kraft in an islander has often been seen as ill luck, inviting death wherever we went.

But Voshell has heard of me. She remembers when I joined the network of whispers, training under Malthe. She may not trust us, but she does believe that I am who I say I am.

"And who is Tuve?" she asks, looking at Frey expectantly.

Kjerstin's gaze falls to the dirt. "Tuve is dead," she says. "I'm the new scout leader."

Voshell is unsurprised. She nods with her mouth in a hard pressed line. "I thought something was wrong when we didn't hear from him in the past week."

This is a strange thing for her to say. The ambush by the Fjern was a week ago, and Tuve was killed in the fighting—but before the ambush, messengers sent to the northern islands were killed. We shouldn't have had any contact with Voshell and Årud Helle—at least, this is what Tuve had described. "Tuve has been in contact with you?" I ask.

She gives me a confused look. "Yes. He came to the island each week to give us updates from Hans Lollik Helle, and to be sure his daughter was still safe."

Kjerstin's eyes widen. She hadn't realized Tuve had a daughter. I only knew because of the memories I'd seen in the meeting room. It wasn't something he spoke about freely.

Voshell gestures at us to follow her. The other islanders of Årud Helle don't hide their animosity. They're suspicious of us, and none want us here. We cross the bay and march into the shadows of the groves. The islanders live in the homes of their dead masters as we do on Hans Lollik Helle, but the homes here are in better condition. Fires weren't set across all of the trees and stone, and in the open fields, only houses that have stood many generations crumble under the weight of time.

Even with the manors of the dead Fjern still standing, the islanders on Årud Helle have begun to build new houses outside of the groves and in the fields. Some have stones held together with wet sand and others have walls of wood or palms. The village Voshell takes us to is buzzing with life. Islanders have their roles as they carry buckets of milk taken from the penned goats. Men use their machetes to clear nearby brush. Children laugh as they play their games, chasing each other across the dirt under the watchful gazes of women who pound dust from sheets hanging from the branches of trees. Someone sings a prayer song as they tend to a garden. The soil of Årud Helle has never been fertile, and it's difficult to grow crops here. But the islanders have been determined to make a home for themselves rather than working the dirt for the sake of their masters. They have tended the soil carefully. Roots have spread and stalks have grown and fruits and vegetables have begun to sprout. It would take attentive work, but Årud Helle could become as prosperous an island as any of the others. Each of the islands have always had their own specific uses: agriculture and crop, fishing, herding, or port and sale like on Jannik Helle. Årud Helle never found its way to profit. In the memories I had seen in Patrika, thanks to Sigourney's kraft, I could see that she'd inherited the island, and that it had been a path away from a life of poverty in the northern empires. She only saw this island as a path to the crown. She didn't care for the island as she should have. Our people will. The sight gives a glimpse into what the future of these islands of Hans Lollik might be.

Årud Helle has guards. Before the revolt, there should have been about seventy on the island. It looks like only a quarter of that number remains. But with the massacre of Skov Helle and the events of Nørup, I would be grateful for any number of guards willing to return to the royal island to prepare for the attack on the Fjern.

As we walk, I notice that the villagers stop their tasks to bow their heads to Voshell. It isn't that they fear her, like the islanders who fear men like Zeger and Malthe. They respect her. She is the oldest of all the islanders. She's witnessed much on these islands for so many years. She has seen her brother tied to a tree and whipped for almost an entire day. She watched as they left his body tied to the tree, and after he died, watched the birds begin to pick at his skin. She has seen her mother run from their master and, rather than be caught, swim into the sea and allow herself to drown beneath the surface. She has seen the beginning and end of different revolutions. She watched the smaller revolts as men attacked the Fjern from the fields, and she has seen them cut down and hanged. She had listened to the impassioned speeches of a few claiming that they could take their freedom, only for a slave too afraid of death to tell the master what they had heard, and for anyone who had ever dared to whisper the word of revolution to be tied by their wrists from a tree so that they could die under the heat of the sun and the sting of the salt. Voshell has seen so much. Survived so much. We all understand this is deserving of respect.

"Tell me everything that you know of the war," Voshell says as she leads us through the village. We tell her of the battles of Hans Lollik Helle and our struggles with sending messages to the other islands, though I don't mention I'd included Årud Helle in this. Voshell seems to have already picked up on our confusion and wonders why Tuve wouldn't have told us that he had been here to the island before he died, visiting his daughter.

I see the girl now. She hides behind the wall of one of the nearby houses, glancing around the corner to look at me and Kjerstin and Frey. She's as quiet and watchful as her father was. She's only ten years old, but she has the gaze of someone much older. She wonders where her father is and why he wouldn't have come here to Årud Helle with us if we were also from the royal island. She feels that something is wrong, but she's too afraid to ask. Voshell will have to tell the girl what's happened later tonight. She doesn't look forward to this.

"Have the Fjern attacked Årud Helle?" I ask Voshell.

"No," she says. "They bypass us on their ships far out on the horizon, but they never come to shore." They've been focusing their energy on taking the royal island, then, like we thought. "Our only problem has been with Nørup Helle." This steals our attention. "Martijn was killed, and the man called Zeger took his place as the island's leader. He never attacked us," Voshell clarifies when she sees Kjerstin's alarm, "but he made his threats."

"Zeger is dead," Kjerstin says. "He betrayed us to the Fjern. Tried to capture Løren and hold him for ransom."

Voshell nearly laughs. "He met the end he deserved, then."

We've circled the village and continued on the path. We see the bay in the distance and the islanders that wait on the sand. We've been gone long enough that they must be worried.

"But why did you come here?" Voshell asks me. She asks this with a smile an islander might reserve for another, but the smile is tight with suspicion.

I tell her the truth plainly. "We need help. Hans Lollik Helle has run low on resources, and we need you to take in those from the island who are not fighting guards."

Voshell doesn't hesitate. "Of course," she says. "We've been careful to ration our supplies. They'll have to work for their keep, but we'll take anyone who needs the shelter."

I give her my thanks. "There's something else," I tell her. "We need guards to return with us to Hans Lollik Helle, to prepare for an attack on Niklasson Helle."

This is where Voshell hesitates. She isn't pleased with the request. She wants all of the fighting islanders to stay here so that they can protect the village. If they leave and lose the battle and each of them are killed, what then? Voshell sees me watching her closely and realizes that I must have heard her thoughts, but she doesn't fear this. Årud Helle has survived on its own so far, without the help of the leader of the islanders, without the guards of Hans Lollik Helle. I can't come here with expectations that they will sacrifice themselves for me.

"You've asked us for help because you run low on supplies, yet you take our people to bring back to your island. Why would you do this if you already lack resources to care for them all?"

"We won't need them to stay on the island long," Kjerstin says. "We'll attack Niklasson Helle as soon as we can. We need the guards to fight if we're to have any hope in winning the battle."

Voshell shakes her head. "The guards are the only defense we have against the Fjern. Without them here, we're too much at risk."

Kjerstin decides it would be better to argue on my behalf. "The true danger is in not winning this war," she says. "As long as the Fjern remain in these islands, we'll always face the danger of attack. If you can risk the weeks it might take, then we will have a higher number of guards and a higher chance of winning our freedom. The battle of Niklasson Helle should be the priority."

Voshell laughs. "It's easy for you to say this when you do not live here on Årud Helle. The priority of the islanders under my care is to survive. We will do what we can to live as long as we can. If it means the Fjern will be in these islands longer than we would like, then so be it. But we will not sacrifice ourselves for this battle when it's obvious that you will not win."

Voshell has figured out what Kjerstin and I have been unwilling to outright say: We are losing this war. The Fjern continue to hold the upper hand in every battle and every position. We're cornered with dwindling supplies and resources and numbers. Voshell is right. There's a high chance, too, that we will lose the battle of Niklasson Helle. She doesn't take this fact lightly.

"This is a pivotal moment for you. This is the first time since the night of the revolt that you will have taken the initiative to leave the safety of your royal island to attack the Fjern, rather than waiting for them to come to you. If you lose your battle," she says, "the Fjern will see your weakness more clearly than ever before. Nothing would stop them from continuing their attacks. They will take back the royal island and Årud and Nørup Helle and all the other islands we won in the uprising. They will punish anyone who still lives." Voshell has seen the ways of the Fjern. She understands there's a chance that they would be willing to kill each and every islander if it meant stamping out any threat of the revolution. This is how much they love their power: Even if it meant the destruction of their crops and coin without any islanders to force into working the fields, they'd kill us all.

Voshell continues. "When you lose your battle on Niklasson Helle, we'll need our guards here to protect us against the Fjern if we're to have any chance of surviving and escaping."

"With the guards here, you wouldn't stand a chance against the Fjern."

"We would stand a higher chance than if they were not here," Voshell says.

I see that she understands our reasoning, but Voshell would rather prolong what she sees as the inevitable—give herself and these islanders on Årud Helle a chance to survive, maybe escape to the northern empires before the Fjern arrive. There must be something that we can do to convince her to allow the guards of Årud Helle to come with us to Hans Lollik Helle.

Voshell senses my thoughts. "If I was more certain that this wasn't a battle where I'd be sending my guards to their deaths,

I would consider allowing them to join," she says. "If there's a chance that they can return with their lives, then this is something that I can agree to."

"What would convince you that this is a battle we can win?"

"Zeger is dead. Did you kill all of his guards as well?"

"No. They're all alive," I say, "except for two that died when they attacked us."

"How many of the Nørup guards will come with you?"

I clench my jaw. "Six."

"Six," she repeats with a growing smile. "And the guards of Skov Helle are dead. And what of Ludjivik Helle?" she asks me.

"We haven't contacted them yet."

"There will be twenty guards at most, if anyone still lives," Voshell tells us. "I will require many more guards than that to allow mine to enter this battle."

"How many?"

She tells us one hundred. The request is impossible, but I can see that Voshell is right. We'd come here in desperation, hoping for any number of guards to help us fight Niklasson Helle. But we need more than only twenty if we're to have any chance.

Kjerstin wishes to continue arguing, but I interrupt to thank Voshell. "We'll keep everything you've told us in mind."

Voshell nods her acknowledgment of my respect. "I'll await your return."

CHAPTER FIFTEEN

All of the islanders from Hans Lollik Helle come onto land, and the villagers of Årud Helle welcome the newcomers into their homes. With Voshell's blessing, suspicion shifts to a sense of celebration. The islanders act like they might if the war had already been won. It reminds me of the nights on Hans Lollik Helle before the attack, guards sitting around their fires to drink and laugh. A feast is prepared despite the strict rations Voshell has had on the island. There's seared fish and boiled cassava and fresh coconut water, goat stew and roasted fruits. She claims our arrival is a worthy exception and promises that the newcomers will have to work hard in the fields to make up for it. There's song and dance, and Voshell stands at the fire to tell the children the story of the woman who dared to brave the spirit of the sea. Frey has been captured by the children, and Anke crawls on top of him with all the others, screaming and laughing, already comfortable in what will be her new home.

The celebrations will go on into the night, but I can feel exhaustion creeping through me. Kjerstin isn't as tired, but she decides she'll also retire. We're given one of the last of the Fjern houses still standing with a straw bed still intact. I've enjoyed being here in the village tonight. It gives me hope to see that, with all we've survived, we can still find joy with each other and ourselves.

The inside of the house is barren. The walls hold no decorations and the wooden floors rot into dirt. There's only one cast iron stove that's left ashes on the ceiling, where it looks like a fire might have started before it was put out. This is where a Fjern would have lived—someone who was not one of the kongelig, someone with little wealth but who still believed that they were worth more than me and Kjerstin and any of the other islanders. I feel content, that this Fjern is dead while I am not. I'm content that the Fjern would've been enraged and disgusted to see that I've taken residence in their house. Kjerstin lies down on the straw bed while I sit on the floor with my back against a wall. We sit in silence for a long while. There's a lot that Kjerstin doesn't like to share about herself. There are depths to her and layers that I'm curious about, but I don't want to enter—not without her knowledge, not without her permission. She notices my quiet and guesses my discomfort.

"Were you always able to see into people the way that you can now?" she asks me.

I admit that the kraft only came to me recently through Sigourney Rose. "My ability stops the power of others and takes that power for myself. I've essentially borrowed her kraft." I don't tell Kjerstin that the bond between me and Sigourney has grown stronger, or that we've been connected after Sigourney left the royal island. Sigourney hasn't attempted to reach out to me, not since the moment she told Lothar Niklasson that she would betray me. I'm not sure if she's done what she promised. I'm not sure if she's even still alive. I can't risk attempting to connect with her again.

Kjerstin notes that it seems I'm always connected to that name. "It's like you can't escape her," she says. "And I'm not entirely sure that you want to."

She thinks of the time I had spent as Sigourney Rose's personal guard and slave—thinks about the fact that I have spared

Sigourney's life multiple times, and that I would disappear so that I could visit Sigourney in her prison. Kjerstin's accusation sits between us. This isn't one of her false allegations that I have shared Sigourney Rose's bed, or that I have loyalty to the woman because she was once my master. This is something that feels a little closer to fact—one that I wasn't expecting to examine. Kjerstin worries that she might have been too pointed with her words. She apologizes.

"I've always been too blunt," she says.

"It's a strength. You aren't distracted from the truth."

"Why are you so drawn to her, Løren?" Kjerstin asks me. "Why did you always show her mercy on Hans Lollik Helle?"

It embarrasses and shames me to say the words aloud. But I also sense how Kjerstin resents that I feel all of her secrets and desires, but she knows nothing of mine. It's a risk to tell her the truth. Kjerstin could easily share with Malthe and Geir and Olina that I've admitted to feeling drawn to Sigourney Rose, who is a traitor and enemy of the islands. She could use this to prove that I should not be the leader in this revolution. A part of me wishes she would, but this is a responsibility I must keep. If I'm not the leader, then Malthe will inevitably take control and destroy all of our efforts for freedom by either losing the war, or winning and becoming another king who will enslave his own people.

I've never been able to lie, so I tell Kjerstin the truth. "Our kraft can allow us to see into others. Sigourney's is much more powerful than mine. Her ability lets her understand another person fully, as if she is that person. I have enough power to see another person like I might know a friend. I learn their histories and wants and pains and struggles. Sigourney's kraft—her connection to me, and mine to her—has made it easy to sympathize with her."

There's more that I don't tell Kjerstin, because this feels more difficult to say aloud. It isn't just the kraft connecting us. I can see some of Sigourney in myself. I can see the way that she is trapped between two worlds and has never truly felt accepted by either. It's a feeling that I understand well. I understand the pain of being rejected by my own people. Sigourney has done nothing to earn the respect and love of us. I can't say she doesn't deserve the hatred islanders show her. But it's still a pain I understand when she looks to us and sees that hatred. It's the same pain I felt in the quarters as a boy, hearing the other islanders around me whisper that I can't be trusted because I'm the master's son.

"It's selfishness that makes you want to save Sigourney, then," Kjerstin tells me. "Selfishness, because a part of you thinks that if you can save Sigourney, then you're also saving yourself. If she is accepted, then you will finally be accepted, too. If she is redeemed, then you will find redemption for your own mistakes."

Defensiveness makes me want to argue. But in that moment, I also realize the sudden flourish of emotion is a sign of truth. Kjerstin notices my silence but doesn't say any more on the matter. She closes her eyes as if she means to sleep and asks me instead what the next plan will be. Voshell and Årud Helle will only help us in the war if we have the help of at least one hundred more guards. Ludjivik Helle can't offer this number, and not half of that is on Hans Lollik Helle. I also know we'll have more islanders like Zeger to contend with. I'd been naive in thinking that everyone—all of our people—would unite against the Fjern for the common goal of peace and freedom. But I see that some will always be more attracted to the idea of power. I'd told myself I would always show mercy to my own people—that we're deserving of being saved. I'm beginning to fear that this is a promise I won't always be able to keep.

We say our goodbyes to the villagers of Årud Helle, who line up in the early morning light. Anke doesn't want me to leave her here on the island. She wants to return to Hans Lollik Helle with us, to fight and train as a guard. She's only satisfied when I tell her that she'll be needed soon, but only if she trains here on Årud Helle to become the best guard that she can.

The trip to Ludjivik Helle is a full day and night. Though we're still in the islands of Hans Lollik, the water seems darker with sand and dirt, the sky gray with clouds. The air is colder here, the trade-winds breeze making me shiver as we row from the ship to land. When we arrive to the rocky shore, splashing into the shallows sharp with jagged shells and dead coral, we aren't greeted with any survivors. I worry that we'll soon find another site of massacre. We begin to walk. I'd been to Ludjivik Helle once before with Sigourney Rose. She brought me here under the orders of her king so that she could execute an old and sickly man who had threatened betrayal to the kongelig. He was a Fjern who was disgusted by islanders, so I didn't care that he died. I felt the same pleasure that Sigourney did when she made the man choke, lungs bursting in desperation for air. It interested me that Sigourney spent so much time trying to convince herself that she did only what was necessary, absolving her of what the Fjern would consider sin under the eyes of their gods. She committed a sin. She killed a man. Her reasons didn't matter. She was evil in this. I am, too. I can't pretend to be the hero of a fairy tale when I enjoy and anticipate the deaths of others, even if they are the Fjern.

The trip was faster on the carriage I had taken with Sigourney, but after an hour of walking across rocky and barren fields, we see three houses standing on the path where only twelve islanders live. They watch us approach. There are no weapons or smiles. I see that the islanders here are hungry and tired and that they don't care if they live or die. If we are here to kill them, then so be it. A few watch us with the expectation that we've come to take their lives. They don't plan to fight us. They're surprised when we only raise our hands in greeting. Ludjivik Helle has always felt separated from all the islands of Hans Lollik, but especially now it feels like they aren't a part of the war. They have been forgotten here by both sides, barely managing to survive on their own.

We ask if there are any Fjern left alive on the island, and they say that the Fjern of Ludjivik Helle have been dead for some time. The cousins of the Ludjivik were traitors of the crown. In punishment, Patrika Årud had sent in her forces to slaughter all of the Fjern—everyone, no matter the age and no matter their innocence. There weren't many to begin with, and those here hadn't put up much of a fight. The islanders were supposed to have been taken and sold on the docks of Niklasson Helle, but some managed to hide. There had been more islanders before we arrived, but most left after the revolt—escaped to the northern empires and to what they considered true freedom. The survivors of Ludjivik Helle couldn't say if they'd made it to the northern empires safely.

We ask the islanders to return with us. We can't bring them to the royal island, but Voshell would be more than willing to welcome more islanders onto Årud Helle. I'm surprised when they refuse.

"Why would we go to any other island, when we'll only be met with the same war?" one man asks. Ludjivik Helle, as barren and isolated as it is, has always been his home, and the home of all the other islanders here. They prefer to stay here in the comfort of the only place they've ever known, even if it means they will die. At least they'll die in peace.

We promise that islanders and guards will come back to Ludjivik Helle, but they have long since been disillusioned and don't believe that we will return. We board our ships to sail for Hans Lollik Helle. The breeze is softer than usual and the waves are smooth. The trip will take days. My anxiety builds with each passing moment. What has happened on Hans Lollik Helle while we've been away? Malthe could've taken control as he's wanted, or the Fjern could have attacked without our knowledge. We might be about to return to find the royal island in ruins, everyone dead. Kjerstin doesn't share her thoughts aloud, but as we stand together on the deck, I can sense the same fear growing inside of her. She worries that this trip was only a waste of time and resources. The only goal we've fulfilled is finding safety for the nonfighting islanders, but that safety is temporary. It's only a matter of time before the Fjern attack Årud Helle. Anke, Helga, Voshell, and all the others would be at their mercy. We have to find a way to get the guards that we need, and attack Niklasson Helle with certainty that we will win.

CHAPTER SIXTEEN

Marieke waits on the shore. She joins me and Kjerstin as we walk into the groves and toward Herregård Constantjin. Marieke doesn't look like she's suffered attacks at the hands of the Fjern or Malthe, but it's easy to see that she's tired. This war has taken a toll on her. The woman had once been fueled by need for revenge. She had been more vengeful than me or Malthe or Sigourney Rose. Maybe more vengeful than any of the islanders of Hans Lollik. Her daughter had been killed in the same massacre that claimed the family of Sigourney Rose. She was willing to wait a lifetime to witness the fall of the Fjern if it meant finding her revenge. But Marieke has changed. We all have. She senses the oncoming defeat. She's tired, and she's realized that she will die. Whether she's killed at the end of a blade by the Fjern in a few days' time or she dies in her sleep in any number of years, she will eventually die.

"What's happened while we were away?" I ask her.

"Fjern ships approached, but they didn't attack," Marieke tells us. "We've been on high alert. We thought we would be ambushed, waiting for your return."

She asks what we learned of the other islands, and we give her updates on all that we'd seen on Skov, of the attack of Zeger on Nørup Helle, and explain Voshell's conditions. I want to call a meeting with all in the circle to decide our next steps, but she tells us to rest.

"You've had long travels. It'll do no good if you both fall to exhaustion. I'll pass the message on to the others, and we'll meet tomorrow in the morning."

I want to argue with her. There's little time to make our move against the Fjern, and there's no way to tell when they will next attack. We have to move before they do. But I also feel myself wavering on my feet. I've had little sleep these past few days, sitting on the decks of ships and by dying campfires. Marieke is right. I need to rest. I do as she suggests, walking the path to the manor of Herregård Constantjin that overlooks the island from its hilltop. It's strange to be back after days of travel. Hans Lollik Helle has never been my home. I grew up on Jannik Helle with my brother and father and the Elskerinde, coming here only for the storm seasons. The manor on Jannik Helle didn't inspire any love from me, but I was still familiar with the paths that would lead me through the gardens and to the field and to the quarters where I would sleep at night. I feel out of sorts returning to the royal island. My mind feels muddled. Maybe I'm more exhausted than I've realized.

Though the manor is falling apart, it's still a symbol of luxury. I feel disgusted walking its halls and sinking into my bed when I think of the starving islanders of Ludjivik Helle. I close my eyes and see images of the dead of Skov Helle lined up as one, and I think that I hear a whisper that there's something I've forgotten. There's something I must remember.

I don't think I'll sleep, but one moment the day is bright and the next I wake to shadows. There's a gentle knocking on the door. I assume it's Marieke, returned with food and water. The moment that I tell her to come in, though, I feel a different presence. I realize that it's Kjerstin before she shows her face, glowing brown in the setting sun's golden light.

She's recently washed. She'd slept and when she woke, she walked to the bay to use saltwater and sand to scrub her skin. It was something she would do here on Hans Lollik Helle whenever Konge Valdemar had no need for her. Kjerstin enjoyed the feeling of the sharp grit of sand. It stung, leaving fine lines on her arms and legs. Her hair is still wet, plaits undone so that her thick hair rises around her ears and shoulders.

I sit up in bed, surprised. I can't think of something to say that wouldn't be offensive. Asking her what she's doing here would make Kjerstin feel unwelcome. She closes the door as she walks into the room. She observes the bed's tapestries, the rotting wallpaper, the balcony doors that I've closed from the saltwater air.

"You really are living like a kongelig," she tells me.

"It's not where I'd prefer to be."

"You don't have to defend yourself against me. I don't really care, either way."

I understand her implication: There are others that do. There are islanders who're frustrated that the war hasn't gone as planned. There are guards that remain on the island who are angry that we're losing this war because of our indecision and lack of action. And here I am, their leader, hidden and locked away in my manor. Kjerstin has seen that Malthe is angry about this, too. She went to speak with him to share an update on the state of the scouts to the north. He stays with his guards in the barracks, but from his comments on how I live like a Fjern king, she can see that he wants to be here in the manor as well, though it seemed there was a silent agreement that living in the main house was an honor fit for only the leader of the revolution.

"Maybe I should return to the quarters where I was sleeping before," I tell her.

"No," she says. "If you were to do that, I'm sure you'd lose the respect we've seen you earn from the guards and the other islanders. People would wonder why you treat yourself as the masters treated you. You can't sleep in the barracks, either. You need to show yourself different, of a higher rank, than the guards you command. Sleeping in the fields with the people would make them become too familiar, like you're one of them."

"I am one of them."

"You're not. Malthe is right, in a way. You're our new king until we have won this war and decide how we want to govern ourselves. There's no winning for you, sadly. In a position like yours, you'll never make anyone truly pleased, and you'll always receive ire and anger and hatred, no matter what you do. You'll always be someone's enemy. This room is the option that has the least backlash. Convenient that it also means you get to sleep with your head on a pillow."

She opens the balcony doors so that the room fills with salted air and the sound of waves. She doesn't step outside. The ends of the curtains begin to drift on the breeze.

"You really are good at reading situations," I tell her.

"Perfect to replace Tuve," she says, understanding my meaning.

"Is it a position you want?"

"It's a position I've already accepted."

"But is it one that you want?"

She shrugs, looking over her shoulder at me. "I wouldn't say there's any particular role I crave. I'll do whatever I can to help. What I want is to be relaxing in my bed with a proper meal in my stomach and the taste of guavaberry rum on my tongue. That's all I truly want."

She continues to look at me for only a second more before she turns forward again. She realizes that, with Sigourney's kraft, I'll know that she's lying. She wants more. There's a reason she came here to my room. She's embarrassed by the thought that I might've realized her hopes, but she doesn't say anything about this. I'm surprised. Kjerstin is usually much more forthright, but with this, she can't meet my eye.

"I wanted to thank you for saving me," she says, changing the subject, her back straightened and humor gone. "The night of the ambush, when I took a machete to the side. I realized that I never did."

"You don't have to thank me. Anyone would've helped you."

"Do you really believe that?" she says with a small laugh. "I'm pretty sure most would've left me for dead if it meant risking their own life. You didn't do that. As Marieke described it to me, you left the safety of the other guards to search for me in the dark of night when there could've still been Fjern hiding in the shadows."

"You're vital to this uprising," I tell her.

"Is that the only reason you saved me?" Of course it isn't, she sees that, but she does also have a sarcastic sense of humor. She watches me for a moment longer, forcing herself to hold my gaze, her chest warming. She considers coming to the bed just to see what I will do. I can see images in her mind—flashes of what she's imagined some nights already, how she would touch me, how she would kiss me—

"I'm sorry, Kjerstin," I say. The images abruptly stop. "I'm more tired than I realized."

She wonders if me saying this was purposeful. She wonders if I'm reading her thoughts at this very moment. I consider admitting that, yes, I feel her intentions. I consider explaining that I don't desire her the way she does me. Not because she isn't beautiful, but because I've never desired another person in the way others do. It's strange and uncomfortable to feel this longing of hers. It doesn't sit well inside of me. The thought of touching another person in the way that she imagines only brings me memories of Patrika Årud and other masters of Hans Lollik Helle, their beds and their hands on my skin, the salty taste of their bodies in my mouth, the excruciating pain that split apart my bones and filled my lungs. I consider explaining all of this to Kjerstin, but in that moment she sees how she wants me, but that I don't want her. She's hurt. It's her hurt that inspires her next words.

"Maybe you really do only have eyes for Sigourney Rose," she tells me.

She knows that she's wrong. Both in fact and for saying something like this.

"I have no interest in Sigourney," I say.

"It's what most people assume. That's another thing no one will tell you. Most of the guards left on our royal island believe you shared Sigourney Rose's bed after all. They whisper that's why she was able to escape. You helped her leave Hans Lollik Helle because you are the pet of a kongelig. There's at least one man on this island who would like your followers to turn on you and drag you to the nearest tree to see you hang."

These aren't false words inspired by hurt any longer. They are Kjerstin's cold and formal observations. Facts, given by our newest spymaster.

"I'll just have to make sure that doesn't happen."

She agrees and says good night as she turns to leave.

"Kjerstin," I say. She pauses but doesn't look at me. She's still too embarrassed to meet my gaze. "The night of the battle—the night that Zeger was killed..."

She turns to look at me, surprised by the shift in conversation. I've surprised myself as well. But having spent time with Kjerstin and learning more about her, I've started to trust her. I've come to see her as a friend. There's been a new feeling in me, since the night of Nørup Helle—a feeling that something has happened.

"I keep thinking that I'm missing something, forgetting... The night that the Fjern ambushed us. How did they know where to attack? And Geir..." I pause. I'm not yet sure why Geir has chosen to hide his kraft, and though I trust him, with every passing moment I feel the urgency in finding him and asking him for the truth.

"What're you trying to suggest?" she asks.

"I believe that there's someone on this island. A spy, betraying us for the Fjern."

She doesn't seem as surprised to hear this as I expected her to be. I can feel that she's already considered the possibility herself. Kjerstin has grown to distrust everyone around her over the years. "Do you believe it's one of us?" Someone in the inner circle, she means. "I could keep an eye on the others, if that's what you're ordering me to do."

It wouldn't hurt for her to keep an eye on all the rest. Malthe, Olina, Geir, even Marieke—but, of course, I also have to suspect Kjerstin herself. Any one of them could be a traitor hiding their thoughts from me. My ability is already weaker than Sigourney's, and with her kraft, we managed to deceive her. Would it be so difficult to believe that someone on this island is doing the same to me?

But I'm making assumptions as well. Someone with close knowledge of our decisions could be a traitor—but it could be anyone else on this island. All of the guards are suspects, too.

Kjerstin understands my thoughts. "I'll have my scouts keep an ear out around the island. If it's true that there's a traitor on this island, we'll find them."

CHAPTER SEVENTEEN

I have a restless night. I barely sleep, and when I do, I have fitful dreams. Dreams of a night sky on fire, water rushing and swirling onto a bay of black sand. My mother. She stares forward only, never looking at me, never showing her face. Her back is a maze of scars, crisscrossing and weaving across her skin. "You dare to forget," she tells me. "You forget me. You forget your rage. If you remembered, you wouldn't want to save them."

I wake to someone standing over me. The room is still black with night. I can't see. I try to roll to my feet before I realize that, while I can feel someone is here with me, they have no body. It could be one of the spirits of Hans Lollik Helle. A kongelig, come for their revenge. The pain begins. It reminds me of the sharpness that'd attacked my senses when I was in the meeting room, but the pain fades into a distant ache, as if my body is growing used to the invasion. And this time, Sigourney hasn't created such a strong connection that I feel like a spirit hovering beside her. She's come to me.

Are you paying attention, Løren? she asks me, her thoughts in my mind like they're my own.

I'm still half asleep, unsure if I'm awake or dreaming. But as breaths pass and my eyes adjust to the darkness, I realize what's happening. I'm awake, and Sigourney is here with me.

I am.

I've been trying to reach you for some time. I have a warning for you.

She says this like I hadn't witnessed her betraying us. She hears my thought and I can feel her haughtiness.

Do you really believe I would betray you? I did what I had to do in order to survive Lothar Niklasson.

She would say anything for me to trust her. She could easily be lying, but she wouldn't have been able to lie to him. His kraft wouldn't have allowed it. She had to have been telling the truth when she said she would give him our secrets.

And so I will. I'll give him secrets that are inconsequential, not of any value. It was the only truth I could think of that would allow me to live. But I am still working for you, Løren. I'm still on the side of our people.

I don't believe her. She's frustrated, ready to snap in her anger, but she pushes her emotion away. She thinks that she has no time. She wanted to speak to me for a specific reason. A warning.

A warning, yes. There's someone on the island who has betrayed you. I know no name. They only refer to the traitor as the islander emissary. They say the emissary works closely with you. The emissary has told them that you've moved into Herregård Constantjin. That you sleep there, alone and unguarded.

My heartbeat rises. I sit up in bed slowly, listening carefully. She tells me this, and that the Fjern have also realized that Kjerstin has taken Tuve's place, but they see that she hasn't moved quickly enough. She hasn't taken to her role as scout leader because of her injuries, and before we left for the north to find more guards to help in our battles, she had not ordered her spies' replacements to watch the seas. A fool's error, on her part and my own, but in the confusion of the days before we left—Patrika Årud's execution and my own illness in response to Sigourney's kraft—

Pay attention, Løren. I don't need to hear your excuses. They've sent someone.

I'm already on my feet, moving for the door, when I realize that I'd dismissed the feeling of someone else being in the room too easily. A man is here, a shadow against the dark, a glint of his blade in the dim moonlight. He moves with the breeze, and I grab his hand out of the air. He releases no sound as another hand swipes for me. I can feel the tip of the second blade pierce the skin of my shoulder before I manage to grab the other wrist with my free hand. We fall into a silent struggle, him pushing the blades toward my chest and my neck. I bring up my knee, driving it into his gut. He bends over with a gasp, and I twist away behind him, pulling his hand to his throat. The blade goes through skin and flesh. The man gurgles and gasps, falling to the ground.

"Who brought you here?" I say quickly, desperately, sinking to the ground with him. He won't be able to speak, but his mind could answer for me. "Who has passed the Fjern information on the island?"

But his mind is unclear, hazy with pain, death coming fast. Sticky wetness floods the floor and wets my hands and knees. He's dead.

I curse, standing. I try to feel for Sigourney's presence, but she's gone as well.

She helped me. She didn't have to. She could've let the assassin cut my neck as I slept. I feel a gratitude I can't control. Not only this. She warned me about the emissary. She told me that, whoever it is, works closely with me. It could be Malthe, Geir, Olina, Kjerstin, or Marieke.

Right now, I don't know who to trust.

I find Geir near the barracks at daybreak by the ashy remains of a campfire. The sky is a soft blue with wisps of clouds. The air is filled with the sounds of early-morning birds singing from the treetops. The salty breeze still holds a chill from the night as it blows over the ocean. Geir stands alone, watching the guards train under Malthe with his arms crossed. The guards rise before the sun and work endlessly under Malthe's watch. The guards will likely exhaust themselves to death in days without proper meals and water and shelter to save them from the heat of the sun. Before, Malthe would take no opinion on how to handle his guards—but I have the power to command him to let the guards rest. No amount of training over the next few days will prepare them for the battle of Niklasson Helle any more than they already have. It's an order I'll have to give, but it's a conversation I'm not looking forward to.

Geir isn't surprised that I've come to him, but Geir isn't surprised by much. He reminds me of Voshell, as does Marieke. They're all a generation older than Malthe, several generations older than me and Kjerstin and Sigourney Rose. Geir is one of the elders of the network of whispers. In his memories, I can see that he'd been only a child himself when he heard of the plans for a rebellion. Not one of the quick skirmishes for death in the fields, where the islander never had any real intention of living. A true revolt—one that would force the Fjern from these islands. Those whispers were as much a part of our history and culture as the prayer songs the elders would teach us on the bays. Not everyone was invited to join. It was a task Geir inherited from his own father. It had taken generations, the slow building of murmurings and meetings and plans, all with the goal of spreading the whispers to only those that could be trusted, poisoning the islanders who showed hesitance when told the truth of the insurrection to stop them from going to the masters. Every person, on each island, knew their role when the time would come. They knew which among them would kill the masters in their sleep, who would set the fires to the manors, who would be prepared with the machetes to battle the guards and the Fjern villagers.

They also knew that they would have to wait, across all of the islands, to rise as one. Geir had been frustrated when he was my age. He wondered why they waited. They all had their roles. They all knew the plan. His kraft had developed by then, and he knew that there was no strategic reason to not attack. He could see that, no matter how long they postponed their plans, there would always be a higher chance that we would lose to the Fjern. Still, the islanders waited for the right moment—the sign, some said, which would come from our ancestors. Marieke believed that the sign was Sigourney Rose. We have yet to learn whether she was right.

Geir barely glances at me before he turns his back, walking away from the remains of the campfire and the barrack walls so that he can go farther into the groves and brush that still remain after the fires of the battle. The mahogany trees give patches of shade from the rising sun overhead. Cockroaches, attracted to the mahogany and smoked out from the fires, dash over the fallen and dying leaves and branches that crack beneath our feet.

We stop beside one of the largest trees. Its branches overhead are sturdy and thick, the sort used for hanging. I remember as a boy watching the hanging of other islanders. My father, before he died of storm-season sickness, seemed to hang men out of habit. If enough time passed where he hadn't killed one of the men he owned, the loathing he had would build until, finally, an islander unlucky enough would be chosen. It didn't matter the reason. For not moving quickly enough when given an order, for not looking him in the eye when spoken to, for daring to look him in the eye when spoken to, for allowing themselves to be noticed as they stood against the wall with their heads bowed. My father didn't care about the reason. He'd choose men only. He had other purposes for the women in his home. Once a man was selected, he'd make the hanging an exhibition of the power he had over our lives. He'd have everyone gather in the fields, and he'd make us watch. The men never bothered to fight. I was angry that they didn't. It took me years to realize what they must have already known. There isn't any point in fighting a battle you know that you will not win.

Geir didn't speak as we walked, but he does once we're under the shade of the mahogany trees. He's nervous as he looks at every shadow that moves.

"You want to learn why I keep the secret that I do," he says. His voice is gravelly and dry, more than usual. He sounds like he hasn't had water for days. "You've wanted to learn for some time."

"It didn't ever seem like there was a moment to ask you alone."

This amuses him. He allows the twinge of a smile. "Do you really trust me so much that you were willing to wait?"

"I never got the sense that you were a traitor."

"Is that a fact?"

"It's one of the positive effects of my kraft," I say. "I can sense when someone is lying and when someone isn't."

"We managed to trick Sigourney Rose," he tells me. He doesn't look at me as he speaks. He keeps his eyes out on the fields, where Malthe trains his guards. His barked orders echo to where we stand. "Anyone could trick you as well."

"Should I not trust you?"

"I'm only telling you to be careful," he says.

I ask him why he chooses to hide his kraft. "I have to admit. You choosing to hide your kraft didn't always make you the most trustworthy person in the room."

"I'm surprised you didn't figure the answer out for yourself," Geir says. He doesn't mean this to be insulting.

"Maybe I should have," I admit.

"The reason is strategy," he says.

This both confuses and interests me. "What strategy could there be in hiding your kraft?" The only purpose for strategy I'd considered was for the war—the strategy behind our decisions in attacks.

As the question lingers between us, his answer comes to me. It's a simple reason in Geir's eyes. Malthe has never liked anyone he considers more powerful than himself. The commander of the guards doesn't have kraft. This is something Geir suspects the man has always resented.

"If Malthe realizes that my talent for strategy is actually kraft, his opinion of me will diminish. And for a man like Malthe, to be a person that holds his poor opinion is a dangerous position to be in. I might find myself without a head in the coming days if he were ever to learn the truth."

I'm skeptical. "Do you really think Malthe would have you killed just because you have kraft?"

"I wouldn't like to find out the answer to that. Would you?"

He pauses. He's already realized that I've felt the tension with Malthe—that I've feared that Malthe would have me killed. It's a fear that anyone with sense would have, and Geir considers me a sensible man.

"Malthe would consider me a threat to his path to power, just as he considers you a threat," Geir tells me. "I don't believe Malthe is the one on this island who has betrayed us. I don't think he's smart enough to have deceived all of us as the traitor does, to be perfectly honest with you. But Malthe can't be trusted. He will be the end of this revolution—the end of us, if we're not careful. I suggest that you find a way to have Malthe executed."

I knew that this is what he would suggest moments before the words leave his mouth. But I'm still surprised that he's said them. Shocked that he'd consider this. Malthe isn't the leader of this island, but the declaration still feels like treason.

"It is, strategically, the best course of action," Geir tells me. "Kill him, before he gains too much control and power over the guards."

"But who would continue to train and command them?"

"You would, of course," Geir says. "You're already a better commander than Malthe is. You hold respect, while he relies on fear. Guards following a leader they respect will fight harder. You inspire them."

"This isn't enough reason to kill the man."

Geir took a great risk by suggesting such a thing to me. I could have him executed for betraying a member of the inner circle. It was a risk that he considered for some time. While I traveled to the northern islands with Kjerstin these past few days, Geir weighed the options. He must either be confident that I wouldn't take his life or he must think the issue is urgent enough that he would risk everything. I sense that he leans more toward the urgency of the situation. I remember Malthe leaving me to die on Valdemar Helle after the attacks of the Fjern guards. I think of the hatred that's burned in his eyes for me. With Geir's kraft, I see that he's right: It would make the most strategic sense to have Malthe killed, no matter the question of whether it is right or wrong.

Geir's kraft flickers in me with another thought. I don't meet his eye as I consider the possibility. Geir could be the emissary. It would be a calculated move if he were to convince me to kill Malthe for posing a risk with his hunger for power. Perhaps then he could tell me that Marieke's devotion to Sigourney Rose is a danger we cannot risk before having her hanged. He could claim that Olina means to betray the islands to the northern empires, and he could accuse Kjerstin of having been the emissary all along with her grip on all of the secrets of the scouts. Geir could be working a strategic plan to turn me against my own allies until everyone is dead and only he and I are left. This would make it easier for the masters he still serves to take this island.

Geir can't read my thoughts, but he can sense something has shifted in me. Something that could potentially be dangerous to him. He curses his decision. He should have found a better way to bring his concern forward. He should have waited until Malthe made a grave error before bringing the idea to me. But he didn't want to wait. He worries that with every passing day, Malthe plots to take control of the revolution. "You don't have to make a decision now," he tells me. "Think on it."

He leaves without waiting for me to speak.

CHAPTER EIGHTEEN

Geir is careful not to look my way as the inner circle meets and discusses our plans. We sit at the mahogany table. I describe to them my and Kjerstin's experience on the northern islands and explain that Voshell will not allow us any of the guards of her island until we have at least one hundred to fight the first battle of Niklasson Helle. The discussion quickly disintegrates into an argument of whether we should act without the numbers, or wait until we can attack Niklasson Helle and win with better certainty. We make the same arguments that we have for the past weeks. Frustration builds in me. We need to make a decision, but we're all too afraid that the next move, if it's a mistake, will be fatal for all of us in these islands. We've worked too hard and for too many years for the uprising to come to an end so easily. Marieke watches me expectantly throughout the meeting. She's waiting for me to say what we will do with the finality of a true leader.

I ask for the night to consider and leave the meeting room with the promise that I will give them my answer with morning's light. I decide to take a walk to clear my mind and give myself the space to make what I think will be the best choice. I leave the manor as the sun quickly sets. The sun always moves fast in the days following the storm season, with longer nights and shorter days. I think that my dull headache, a pressure between my brows and behind my eyes, is just from listening to the others argue for hours. The pain is softer than the times Sigourney has tried to reach me, so I don't realize it's her until I hear her whispering my name.

I walk to the bay and to the rocks where I have spent many of my days and nights, wishing that I had the courage to jump beneath the waves and realizing the cowardice in wanting to die instead of fight within the same breath. I'd hated the islanders around me who refused to fight because they were too afraid to die. I hated my own hypocrisy more. The sharp edges of the rocks cut into my feet and the saltwater is warm as it foams onto my skin. I close my eyes.

Sigourney is alone in a room. I'm surprised that it isn't a dungeon or a jail cell. The room is closed, with no balcony and only one window, through which Sigourney can hear the squeaks of fruit bats and chorus of crickets. The night breeze is cool. She sits on the edge of a hard bed, breathing in and out. She wonders if I'm here, and I tell her that I am.

Relief fills her. She doesn't think of me as a friend—she isn't so delusional—but I am still friendlier than the Fjern that surround her. She hates being on Niklasson Helle with no allies in sight. They've given her a bed, but she's still a prisoner. There's a guard standing outside of her room at this moment. The man's name is Kalle. He's an islander who still works for the kongelig. There are islanders who remain slaves on these islands, afraid to join the rebellion. It was only luck that they were spared after the first night. The kongelig had rounds of interrogations, whippings, and executions. The Fjern didn't believe that everyone they killed was a part of the revolt. The Fjern publicly carved and maimed the slaves only to show what would happen to those who tried to defy their power—to show what would happen to me and everyone else on the islands we've managed to take.

Sigourney recognizes that this is what might happen to her as well if she isn't careful.

They've allowed her to live, for now. It was a tense discussion between Lothar Niklasson and the Fjern who follow him, looking for favors through allegiance and loyalty. The Fjern under Lothar Niklasson argued that Sigourney was a danger to them all and that she should be executed, but Lothar had considered her offer. He didn't think the Fjern truly needed her help to defeat us. Still, her kraft could be useful. If Lothar managed to learn how to control Sigourney properly, then she could be suitable to him and his control over the kongelig and these islands. Others argued that she wasn't worth the risk. They wanted Sigourney Rose dead.

The Fjern have re-created the court of Herregård Constantjin. They haven't officially named their new king yet, but Lothar Niklasson gives his commands all the same. Sigourney is allowed to move about the manor and the island as long as her guardsman, Kalle, is always beside her. I had been Sigourney Rose's personal guard, but Sigourney shares that this man is unlike me in many ways. I have the blood of the Fjern, as does Sigourney, but Kalle's blood as an islander seems to never have been tainted. This is rare. So many of us were born from mothers who'd been forced into the beds of the Fjern. Instead of joining the revolution, Kalle remains loyal to his masters. He believes that the insurgency is a child's game conceived by fools. It's because of us that innocent lives have been lost—not only the Fjern, but islanders as well. Islanders who had no knowledge of the rebellion, punished and sacrificed for our mistakes. The only similarity between me and this guardsman Kalle is the hatred we share for Sigourney. She finds this amusing.

She'd left the room where she'd been locked away. She didn't want the Fjern and former kongelig to think that she was afraid, even if she was. She strolled through the courtyard of the main

Niklasson Helle manor, Herregård Sten. From afar, Niklasson Helle seems to be a sharp rock jutting into the sky, but the island itself has valleys and sheer cliffs. Niklasson Helle never relied on agriculture in the way that most of the other islands have. The Niklasson family's military, one of the strongest in the islands, created its own power.

The Fjern who are at Herregård Sten were not families that lived on the island, but the families of other surviving kongelig. The storm season had officially ended, but they seemed to think it was best to stay together on the most fortified island of Hans Lollik. Lothar's manor is on the very edge of a cliff, a square fort with four long strips of rooms with a courtyard and garden in its center. There are no frivolous decorations of lace and marble. Everything is hard gray stone, including the walls and floors, and there are few windows. The entirety of the manor reminds Sigourney of a dungeon. This is also partly why she decided to leave her room to walk through the manor's halls. She couldn't stand to be trapped inside of her dank, dark chambers.

She walked the halls, ignoring Kalle, who followed behind her, until she made it outside and to the courtyard, where she also found a gathering of Fjern enjoying the sunshine. It was clear Lothar had little practice with entertaining guests. There was an islander playing a stringed instrument and a few others holding trays of sugarcane wine. It was a wonder Lothar made any effort to entertain his guests at all when his focus was so obviously on winning the war. But the other Fjern didn't seem to understand that there was a possibility they could lose against us. They drank and laughed, confident that this uprising was only a brief interruption in their lives; that, once the island-ers were killed and their complete power over the islands was restored, they would return to their homes.

When Sigourney stepped into the courtyard with Kalle at her side, there was a pause in conversation. The pale Fjern knew that she was on the island and knew that she was their prisoner, but there was still surprise that slicked the air—anger, that Sigourney would dare to roam the premises as though she had her freedom, like she were still one of the kongelig. There was anger at Lothar, too, for allowing her to do so. Many felt Sigourney should have been killed the moment she set foot on Niklasson Helle. But others were amused. It was an amusement that Sigourney was familiar with. It was the same feeling that greeted her when she first arrived to Hans Lollik Helle at the start of the storm season. Amusement, that she could consider herself to be equal to the Fjern.

Sigourney saw with surprise that her husband, Aksel Jannik, was also in the courtyard. He stood alone near the gardens, stinking of guavaberry rum. A quick read into him showed that, after leaving Hans Lollik Helle, he'd returned to his own home on Jannik Helle. He'd expected to leave for the northern empires after taking care of a few affairs, but the insurrection began. He had been awake, drinking in the night, when he saw the fires of Larsen Helle in the distance. He could hear his guards coming and could hear their whispers as they searched for him. He was drunk, but Aksel knew that he had to hide or he would die. He climbed from a window and ran from his manor, moving through the rocky fields and into town, which was already on fire by the time he arrived, Fjern slaughtered on the docks and blood leaking into the sea. There were still some alive, continuing to fight against the islanders who had picked up their machetes. Aksel forced his way onto a boat filled with Fjern desperately trying to escape. He should have stayed and fought for his island, but he was a coward, so it was no surprise to anyone that he would leave. It was only because reinforcements were sent from Solberg Helle that the Fjern held the island at all.

Aksel saw Sigourney as well when she walked into the courtyard. She could feel his disgust and embarrassment, since everyone knew that he had married the islander, and that she had used her marriage to him to get onto Hans Lollik Helle. Everyone thought Aksel a fool, and he was one—but their judgment today wasn't as harsh as it has been in the past, not when they knew how Aksel mourned Beata Larsen. She'd been the first of the kongelig to die in our plan of killing each kongelig one by one, and he hadn't been right in mind since that night. Aksel left the courtyard, ignoring the stares to see how he might react to see-ing Sigourney, and ignoring her, too, as he passed her by.

There was one woman who was a cousin of the Nørup fam-ily, Gertrude Nørup. Though Erik Nørup had not survived Hans Lollik Helle, and though Alida Nørup had fled the islands for the northern empire of Koninkrijk, there were still members of the family who remained, squabbling among themselves to see who would take the position of heir of the Nørup family. Gertrude was considered plain by the Fjern's standards, with a small mouth and thinning hair. She was only slightly older than Sigourney and about the same age of her friend Jytte Solberg. Elskerinde Solberg and Dame Gertrude Nørup stood together by the rosebushes. The sight of Elskerinde Solberg shocked Sigourney just as much as it shocks me to see the woman alive in Sigourney's memories. I'm sure that Sigourney had been tricked, or misunderstood her own vision, and that the scene is being fil-tered to me incorrectly. Elskerinde Solberg should be dead. The night of the revolt, Agatha had cut her throat.

Sigourney assures me that Jytte Solberg is truly alive. Sigour-ney reached into the woman and saw that Agatha had cut Jytte's neck and left the woman for dead, but she hadn't cut deep enough. Jytte is the sort of person who will fight for life as blood leaks from her throat. She'd stumbled and gasped through the fighting and foray. She made it to the bay, where Fjern were escaping the island. She was brought on board before she lost consciousness. She was brought to Niklasson Helle, where all of the kongelig had fled, to be nursed back to health. There was a chance, over the next passing days, that she wouldn't survive—and for a while, it seemed that she wouldn't. Fever took her and she wavered in and out of consciousness, whispering to people who weren't really there. The neck wound did not kill Jytte, but there was a chance that Lothar Niklasson would. He could have had poison slipped into the tea of herbs that were brewed for Jytte Solberg. He could have decided to claim she'd betrayed the kongelig the night of the uprising and had her dragged out to the courtyard for a public execution. I can't see why he chose to keep Jytte Solberg alive, but it was bad luck for us that he did—bad luck that, days later, her whisperings stopped and she opened her eyes.

Jytte could still speak. The knife had missed her vocal cords. She and Gertrude Nørup had been discussing plans of potentially taking control from Lothar Niklasson. Jytte and Gertrude were two ambitious women, but no one would take either seriously because of their sex. They knew it was safer to be seen in the gardens, drinking their sugarcane wine as if they were frivolous girls who didn't take the war seriously. Lothar knew the rival he had in Jytte, but he was not in the courtyard, and Jytte enjoyed discussing plans to take control right under the noses of the other Fjern who underestimated her. She wore her kongelig dress of white and had a bow tied around her neck to hide the thick purple scar. She hid it because she knew others would recoil from her in disgust. To the Fjern, a woman must be unmarked. They didn't find scars beautiful, and a scar like the one that wrapped around Jytte's neck would remind them too much of the scars that rose along the backs of the brown slaves that surrounded them.

It was only when she was alone in her room that she would untie the bow and stare at the scar in the mirror. That scar gave her a power she was surprised to feel. A rage, an anger, in this simple reminder. Jytte Solberg had always wanted to own these islands. She wanted to be a queen. But, now, she understood Sigourney Rose more than before. She understood this desire for revenge. The end of the insurrection and executions of the slaves was not just a stepping stone to the throne for her. She couldn't wait to kill each and every single one of us.

Jytte couldn't let Lothar Niklasson take the title of the king. She and her friend had already agreed on the simplest plan: allow Lothar to win this war. Remain loyal to him and grant him any number of guards he desires. When the insurgency is at its weakest, and there is no other possible outcome but for the islanders to surrender, Jytte and Gertrude will leave to begin preparations for battle on Solberg Helle. Niklasson will already be weakened from its battles. Solberg will not hesitate to attack immediately, taking power from Lothar. Gertrude will help. The Nørup clan doesn't have nearly as many guards, but they do have resources, and Gertrude has been forthright with her lack of ambition to take the throne. "There is such a thing as too much power," she's said. She only wants to be the head of the Nørup family. This is something Jytte will declare once she's won her crown.

Sigourney approached them both in the gardens. Kalle tried to order her to remain where she was—not to approach the Fjern, she was a prisoner and it wasn't her place—but she ignored him as she walked to Jytte and Gertrude.

"Aren't you worried Lothar will suspect you?" Sigourney asked. She'd decided she would not stand in embarrassment, isolated at the edge of the garden. She faced Jytte Solberg directly to prove that she wasn't scared of the woman. Sigourney remembered well what Jytte hoped to do once she became queen. She wanted to make Sigourney her slave. Jytte would keep Sigourney at her side like a pet. She would use Sigourney's kraft, which Jytte didn't believe any islander should rightfully have. This is what Jytte had threatened during the storm season.

Gertrude was shocked, affronted that an islander would

approach them. Embarrassed, she looked at the gazes of the
Fjern who watched. Jytte's eyes narrowed dangerously. Though
she pretended to be bored with Sigourney, there was a danger
in the islander's words. If Sigourney declared to all what her
kraft had discovered, there was a chance that Lothar Niklasson
would question her and see what Sigourney claimed was true.
He would have Jytte and Gertrude executed. The man has been
waiting for a chance to kill Jytte, knowing that she still vied for
the crown.

"There's nothing to suspect," Jytte said.

Sigourney smiled. She knew she had Jytte in her hands. "I
wonder if Herre Niklasson would believe the same."

"Why are you entertaining this?" Gertrude asked Jytte. "The
slave must have storm-season sickness if she thinks she can speak
to us this way."

"I'm not a slave, Dame Nørup," Sigourney said. "I may be a
prisoner, but I'm still Elskerinde Jannik, and I still have power
over you. You are not a member of the kongelig."

Gertrude, already pink in the heat, turned red with anger. "I
should have you whipped."

Here, Sigourney paused—for though she wasn't a slave, there
wasn't anything that would stop Gertrude from ordering Kalle
to have Sigourney whipped, here and in front of all the Fjern and
kongelig. Sigourney wouldn't be able to so obviously manipulate
those around her without them realizing her actions and having
her killed—not like when she'd been able to slowly, calculatedly
influence the previous Elskerinde Jannik. There would be nothing to stop her from having Sigourney humiliated. She'd never
been whipped before, not as I have, not as all of her people have
been beaten by the Fjern's hand. She hasn't felt the sting of a
lash over her back. She had ordered the whippings of her people before. She'd ordered mine. A part of me, a dark and angry
part, wishes she had been whipped. I wish that she'd learned that

pain and humiliation, to feel like she's reduced to an animal. But there would be no purpose to this. I feel ashamed at the very thought. I can't wish for the freedom of our people and simultaneously hope for one of our own to suffer, no matter who they are and no matter how they've treated me.

Sigourney wasn't whipped, though Gertrude was tempted. Jytte interrupted the conversation before it could escalate.

"Don't worry," she said, eyeing Sigourney. "She'll remember her place soon enough. Elskerinde Jannik," she said, "would you please hand me a glass of sugarcane wine?"

A slave holding a tray of wine stood against the wall of the courtyard, just as far away from Sigourney as he was from Jytte. Everyone watched, and Sigourney knew that this was Jytte's way of subduing her. The woman might as well have had Sigourney beaten. It was equally as effective. Though Sigourney had the power to tell Lothar what she'd discovered, she also knew that if she didn't do as Jytte asked right then and there, she would risk Kalle's whip, stripped and degraded in front of all. This was a different sort of stripping, a different sort of degradation. The Fjern smiled to themselves as she walked across the courtyard, under all of their eyes, and picked up a glass of sugarcane wine. She walked back to Jytte and placed it in her waiting hand.

"Thank you, Elskerinde Jannik," Jytte said to Sigourney, before taking a sip, eyes still fastened to the woman's gaze. She passed Sigourney a thought.

You can tell Lothar what I plan, Jytte told Sigourney, *but know that I am not so desperate to see you become my slave. You wouldn't live to see its outcome.*

CHAPTER NINETEEN

Waves still crash and roil around my feet. They shimmer under the silver of the moonlight. The moon hangs low, a white globe that brightens the sky like the sun itself. It's so bright that I almost question if I'm in another of my dreams or nightmares, and I expect to see my mother standing, her back to me as she waits in the shallows. The waves that wash my feet are less violent than a few months before when I stood here during the storm season, but there's still a risk that the water could swipe my feet from under me and pull me into the sea. My body's natural response is fear. It pumps through me with every beat of my heart. Fear would crawl through me whether I risked my life on these rocks or not. There's always a level of fear inside of me, just like there's always a sheen of sweat that covers my skin in the heat of these islands. But along with the fear, there's a whisper that fills me. Assurance, that the spirits won't let me die. Not this way.

Sigourney had always been too afraid to join me on these rocks. She'd only ever watch from the bay. She stands beside me. It isn't her, not really—she's only a projection of my imagination, created by the bond of our kraft. She's translucent, like a spirit might be, prepared to haunt Hans Lollik Helle.

I thank her for the warning she'd given me of the Fjern assassin. She saved my life.

It wouldn't do me any good to lose my only ally.

How much longer do you think you'll have before the Fjern kill you?
I ask her this, and she laughs in response, not surprised by my
bluntness but amused. I always have been blunt with the truth.
There's no point in attempting to cloak the truth for the sake of
politeness, especially one as obvious as this.

I think they'll kill me the moment they decide I'm no longer useful.
This is true, I can feel this within her. *And I have to remain useful
to you as well, so that you won't let me die on Niklasson Helle.* And she
can feel that this is true within me, too. Though I wouldn't want
to abandon her, if the others on this island feel that Sigourney has
betrayed us, or that she hasn't been helpful enough for us to risk
our lives to rescue her if need be, she'll be left on that island to
the mercy of the Fjern. She's glad that I don't bother to deny this.

Then listen to me now. She has seen from Jytte Solberg the
woman's plans. Sigourney has also seen how Solberg Helle has
become necessary to the Fjern in this war. The island stores arse-
nal and has become the main site for the training of guards. To
attack Niklasson Helle first would mean the loss of the war. But
if we were to attack Solberg Helle, we might have a chance.

*Even better is the fact that attacking Solberg Helle means destroying
Elskerinde Jytte Solberg. She has a true chance of taking Lothar Niklasson by surprise and taking control of the kongelig, becoming their queen.
If we were to get her out of the way, we would only have to worry about
attacking Lothar in the end, rather than having to battle two families.*

I hesitate. Geir's kraft sparks in me, and I can see that it would
be a better plan to allow Jytte to attack Lothar—for them to
weaken each other further, before fighting whoever is left standing. But I can also see Sigourney's point in taking Solberg Helle.
This island holds the most resources, which we desperately need.
It's also a central position, making it easy to attack the other
islands the Fjern still hold: Larsen, Jannik, Lund, Rose, and
Niklasson Helle.

It isn't lost on me that fighting Jytte Solberg would also be the best course of action for Sigourney. She has many enemies on Niklasson Helle, but while Lothar Niklasson can't be bothered to kill her yet, it seems that Jytte's priority is making Sigourney suffer. It would be most helpful to Sigourney for us to attack Solberg Helle, and give Jytte another priority to focus on. Better yet, we might kill Jytte Solberg in the process.

Sigourney is already fading from my vision. *Is it so wrong for me to hope for this?*

We don't have the number of guards necessary to request the help of Årud Helle, but we have to move forward with our attack nonetheless. I'd gambled on taking the time to travel north and asking the help of our fellow islanders. We wasted time, and we only have a few days before we run out of food and supplies. We have no choice but to attack, before we find ourselves in a worse situation. It's a gamble that I lost, and we have to face the consequences of my mistake.

Malthe is still determined that we attack Niklasson Helle first, but I have seen the island through Sigourney. I see the number of guards. The island is fortified against us. We have no chance in winning. Sigourney's reasoning in attacking Solberg Helle first is sound, but if we were to win the battle, she would benefit as well. I can't trust that she only wants us to control Solberg Helle for the sake of the rebellion. Geir's kraft works its way through me. It would be better to attack the smaller islands first, with their weaker defenses. We could take Larsen Helle and then Jannik Helle, collecting the resources and adding to the number of fighting islanders who can join us in the attacks against Solberg and Niklasson Helle.

I hold a wall between myself and Sigourney. I can feel her continuing to try to contact me, the pain in my head piercing my thoughts. But I don't need her to visit me. I don't need her to continue confusing me, manipulating me and swaying me to make decisions that are for her benefit. I still need more information before I can make a final decision. In the meeting room, I ask Kjerstin to send a chosen scout to Larsen Helle and confirm that the island is one within our ability to win. If the Fjern have learned of the possibility that we will attack, either through their emissary who could be in this very room or through Sigourney learning my thoughts, then we'll need to be prepared for a battle we still might not win.

But the morning after the scout leaves, Kjerstin comes to me, grim and out of breath. She asks me to follow her to the shore. Though decayed by salt and heat and bloated by water, I recognize the scout's head. His gaunt face has eyes that sink into his face. The head is removed and given proper burial at sea. After we've paid our respects, Kjerstin whispers her concern to me. The Fjern had been patrolling the seas to the north, but there's a particular current that the scout had taken—a route usually ignored and unseen. Especially at night, no one would have been able to see the scout so easily, unless they were looking for him in advance.

The others had been expecting me to cut my ties with Sigourney, but I can say without hesitation that she knew nothing of this plan. I'd had my wall up between us. She couldn't contact me, even when I felt the pressure in my head as she tried to break through. She wouldn't have seen our plan to send Ivar south to Larsen Helle.

"There isn't any doubt," I say to the others as we sit in the meeting room. "No one but us in this room knew. One of us has betrayed the revolution."

Olina, who had been watching me, allows her gaze to fall to the surface of the table. Geir is unbothered by this declaration. He's confident I have no reason to suspect him. He instead looks at each sitting at the table as well. Kjerstin watches me unblinkingly. *Do you really believe it would be me?* She wants to ask this aloud, but her thought comes to me clearly all the same. *Do you really believe I would betray my islands to the Fjern?*

Marieke and Malthe are just as silent as the rest. Malthe gazes at me openly as well. He expects me to accuse him. Not because he thinks to himself that he actually has betrayed us, but because he thinks this is what he would do if our positions were reversed. Accusing him would give me the opportunity to have him executed—to be rid of him, in the way that I see he wants to be rid of me. It would make the most sense. It's something Geir hopes I will do as well. But I won't simply accuse Malthe. Not because I fear him and not because I see him as a rival. This is the way that the Fjern would rule—killing innocents just because they are rivals. We need to create something better.

Marieke won't look at me. I can't believe, not for a moment, that she would be the one to betray us. She has been one of the longest members of the whispers. She waited for the right moment to present her allies with Sigourney Rose. She's had more patience and cunning than any of us—a lifetime's worth. Why would she destroy all of her hard work for the Fjern?

Yet as I ask myself this question, I can feel Kjerstin's accusing gaze land on Marieke. The woman continues to call Sigourney Rose an Elskerinde. It could be possible that she would've fought all of these years for freedom, without realizing that once she had her freedom, she didn't know who she was with it. She might have decided that she wanted to remain under her mistress, the woman she considers to be her daughter. I also realize that it could be just as possible that Sigourney is somehow controlling Marieke. She did the same to get onto this island. She controlled the late Elskerinde Jannik. She didn't force the woman's hand, necessarily, but she made enough suggestions that the woman allowed Sigourney to marry her son, Aksel, so that Sigourney could arrive on Hans Lollik Helle for the storm season. That had taken years, but Sigourney might have learned a way to perfect her kraft of control without anyone's noticing. Marieke could be acting on her mistress's behalf without her consent.

"And how can we be sure that it isn't you?" Malthe asks.

"Me?" I repeat.

The incredulity isn't received well. Yes, what about me? The expressions on the others consider me carefully. I've been the most merciful one here to Sigourney Rose. Though I led the others to victory, it could easily all be a sham as I work with the Fjern. I'm the son of a kongelig family, the only of us who leads this rebellion. Their blood is in my veins. Could they really trust me, when I look more like the Fjern than anyone else in this room? It's possible that the kongelig could've offered me a place among them, one that I might have secretly desired all this time. A more frightening possibility is that Sigourney could actually be controlling me without my knowledge. I don't really understand enough about this link between us. She could've found a way to exploit our bonded kraft—and me as well.

"I'm not the one who's betrayed us," I say, but that's what anyone would say whether they were the traitor or not. It doesn't help the circle's opinion of me. Kjerstin seems skeptical of the possibility, along with Marieke, but Olina does seem to consider me in a new light. Geir's expression is carefully blank.

"We don't have time for this—not right now," Malthe says. "We'll need to revisit and question each of us in turn. Right now, we need to decide our next move."

My first instinct is to argue. It'd make more sense to discover who the traitor is, before they can get in the way of our future plans. But I realize that Malthe is right. If we spend hours, days trying to root out the spy, then we'll have lost precious time. Without their intervention, we will have lost the war. We can only hope that whoever it is will decide to be careful and not act with everyone watching one another.

"And who will we attack?" Marieke asks me.

"Larsen Helle." It's the closest island, and we won't be prepared to attack Solberg Helle, no matter what Sigourney suggests.

"The Fjern will see this is our only option," Geir warns us. "They'll be prepared."

"We must hope that they'll continue to underestimate us," Kjersin responds. "Larsen Helle comparatively doesn't have a natural defense. I can try to send the spies ahead again to see if their guards have arrived in force."

"They'll just kill the scouts like all the rest. We need to sail and attack immediately," Malthe says. "We need to bring all of the guards."

"Hans Lollik Helle will be defenseless," Marieke protests. "We could lose the island."

Kjerstin speaks. "I agree with Malthe on this. If we have any chance at all, we need to take Larsen Helle and liberate the islanders there so that we can add to our forces." There could also be resources waiting on the island. Resources we desperately need.

"There's someone in this room we cannot trust," I say. "They will use this information against us and the Fjern will attack Hans Lollik Helle. We'll leave half of the guards in defense and take the rest with us."

"If we do take Larsen Helle, we'd have to move quickly into attacking Jannik Helle, or they'll take the island back within the same night."

"We'll be ready," I answer Geir. "We'll take Jannik within the next day and prepare to fight for Solberg Helle. That's the only way we can win this war: if we take each island, one-by-one, until we have driven all the Fjern from these seas."

Malthe is frustrated. He doesn't want to waste time or resources on the smaller islands. He wants to attack Niklasson Helle immediately. But we don't have any other choice.

I give the order. "Begin preparations for Larsen Helle."

CHAPTER TWENTY

Geir and Olina argue that I should not leave Hans Lollik Helle. I'm the leader, and the battle of Larsen Helle is too dangerous. Marieke agrees. She's afraid to lose me, and I can also sense that she doesn't trust that I would survive, especially with Malthe as my only ally. Kjerstin is the only one who doesn't argue for me to stay. She worries, yes. But she also believes that my chances of surviving here on Hans Lollik Helle are as high as surviving Larsen Helle. It's all the same to her, in the end. We'll likely lose and be executed side by side. It doesn't matter when it's time for us to die.

The journey is short. The tide is strong, and while we do encounter Fjern scouts, we easily overtake them on the ships of Hans Lollik Helle. I can see Larsen Helle in the distance. I remember the island from when I was a boy, desperate to escape to the north. The bay has little cover that could be used to hide. There are only a few mangroves in comparison to Hans Lollik Helle and the island has open rocky shores. The flat fields with grass shimmering in the breeze would leave us too out in the open and vulnerable to ambush. If we manage to win the island, we'll need to move on quickly.

The sun is already rising by the time we're near the coast. We hadn't meant to arrive so close to dawn. If it can be helped, it's always better to fight in the bright midday sun rather than the dark of night. The enemy can't see in the shadows, yes, but neither can we, and our people have trained long and hard hours under the hot sun. The Fjern have never been used to this heat. They always seek the shade and turn pink and red and faint. Fighting in the heat is to our advantage.

The Fjern have seen us coming. Pillars are lit in warning, black smoke ballooning into the sky. I can hear the bells from the helm where I stand, Malthe in his position beside me. Hesitance begins to paralyze me. I think that there will be innocent people on Larsen Helle. Different from the kongelig I have cut down before. Fjern who simply came to these islands to make better lives for themselves away from the harshness of their empire— mothers, children. These will be people who have nothing to do with the kongelig, people who perhaps couldn't afford to own slaves themselves. People, trying to live their lives in peace. Countless will be killed in the fighting. If left to the others—if left to Malthe—every single Fjern will be slaughtered.

I can feel the anger of the others. I can hear Malthe's voice. No Fjern is innocent. A revolution isn't won by showing the enemy mercy. And I try to remind myself that, no matter the age—no matter the innocence—each of the Fjern are the enemy. I think them innocent, but these Fjern children will happily accept the power they were given over my people's lives. If given the chance, they will own and sell my people's bodies and decide that we are not worth the same as them. I tell myself this, again and again.

We anchor our ships in the shallows and take smaller boats, pulled from the ship, to row to shore. There's no battle call. The guards were already given their orders. It's a silent march from the gray sand and across the sharp grass and to the nearest fishing village. The village is a collection of wooden houses that lean in the breeze, small gardens that produce weeds, and a dirt path that leads to the empty docks where boats and nets have been abandoned. The village is small. Most of the Fjern ran when they saw us, but not everyone would've been able to escape. There'll have been the elderly, the ill, mothers with too many children to run. Malthe marches through the center of the village as the guards begin their search, and the screams for mercy begin. He'd already decided there would be no survivors. There's no need for prisoners, and anyone we release will simply return to the Fjern with information against us. I try to steel my heart against the cries. I want to close my eyes, but I can feel Malthe watching me, waiting for a sign of weakness—for a sign that I have too much sympathy for the Fjern. That I really might be the traitor of Hans Lollik Helle.

There's a shout, a gasp of surprise—I turn, and a Fjern boy with a machete has leapt from the shadows. He's managed to chop the blade into a guard's leg. The guard shouts with pain, but before the boy can land a fatal blow, another guard is already parrying him away. The child stands in front of a house, breathless and afraid, but determined to hold his ground against the dozens of guards in front of him.

I see the truth: His mother is inside of the house that he wants to protect. The woman is ill. She has been for some time, a storm-season sickness that hasn't left her lungs for the past few years. She's already near the end of her time. The other villagers didn't think or didn't care enough to help her from her bed. The boy's father died when he was only a baby. There has been a man in the village who took pity on the child and began to teach him how to fish like any proper man should. This man tried to convince the boy to run with him when he saw our ships out at sea, but when the boy refused, the man didn't try very much longer. He left the boy and his mother behind. The boy could tell the man believed they wouldn't survive, and the boy sees that the man was right. Yes, he understands that he will likely die, but he will try to take at least one of us with him.

Malthe is amused. The killings until this moment have been as expected: a scream, a plea, a brief struggle before the neck is cut. He can't help but see this boy as entertainment. When I look at the Fjern boy, I see the similarities between him and my brother and his friend Erik Nørup, now dead. His pale skin and hair and eyes, the coloring of boys so often told they own this land and my people—the coloring that I've come to see as one that coincides with cruelty. My brother and Erik Nørup enjoyed the power they were given. They showed me a different sort of torture. At least when I was brought to the beds of Patrika Årud and other kongelig at night, I didn't have to wait for the pain. They saw no point in drawing it out. The torture was immediate. My brother and Erik Nørup, though, took pleasure in seeing me torment myself with fear. They would chase me on Hans Lollik Helle, enjoying the way I tried to hide, to stop myself from breathing too loudly so that they would not catch me.

I see this Fjern boy and I remember my brother, and I can't help but hate the child for it. But I can also see how Malthe enjoys the same breathless fear. The boy is no older than thirteen years. He reminds me of Anke, wanting to prove herself ready for war. My stomach turns.

I expect Malthe to begin playing his game. To goad the boy, to say something that will make his men laugh. But I've forgotten that Malthe has always been the type to play a quieter sort of sport. His gaze lands on me.

"Konge Jannik," he says. "Your blade doesn't have a drop of blood on it."

He refers to me as king sarcastically. I can feel the amusement of some of his guards, the same who have shown frustration with me as their leader. I see how the nights have passed: They have seen the way I've left the royal island with little explanation, traveling the northern islands and leaving the guards behind with their strict rations and their endless work. They've seen the way I sleep in the manor of Herregård Constantjin as if I see myself as one of the kongelig. I have the blood of the kongelig. They wouldn't be surprised if, after winning this war, I did declare myself the true king of the islands of Hans Lollik, just because of the blood I hold in my veins. It hasn't helped that Malthe has spread his whispers and his lies in the days that have passed. He's told them that I don't truly care for the guards that fight for me. I see them only as pawns, ready to die on the battlefield.

Malthe sees how I stiffen when he makes his comment. I haven't even unsheathed my blade. I left the killing of the Fjern to the guards. They've also noted this. I've proven their commander right. I'm willing to watch them do their work and risk their lives, but I've become lazy, and will no longer fight. Malthe can practically feel how my heart stops in my chest.

He allows the smallest of smiles. "I give you this boy to kill," he says. "It isn't fair that we should be the only ones to enjoy this battle."

The guards watch me. The boy still holds on to his machete, but his arm shakes. This isn't a battle. It's a slaughtering. Disgust crawls through me, but some of the disgust is for myself. I knew that the guards were killing boys just like this in the village. I wasn't witnessing it directly, but I still knew. How would me killing this child be any different? I should hate this child. He's only a boy, but he will grow to become another Aksel Jannik, another Erik Nørup, if he isn't one already. I shouldn't want to show him mercy, but I do.

Malthe sees this. It's why his gaze won't leave mine. This is finally his chance, he believes, to prove that my loyalty doesn't lie with the islands as they should. I've been too soft. I've refused to admit it, but it's true. Any leader who should truly want freedom for my people would cut this boy's neck without hesitation. This is what he believes.

Even as I can feel that it's the wrong choice—even as I feel dread beneath my skin—I speak. "No," I tell Malthe.

It's what he expected, but there's still a thrum of surprise. I can feel the growing confusion in the guards as some believe they've misheard me. Others know they heard correctly. Their surprise is turning to anger. But I can't do what Malthe has asked me to.

I shake my head. "He's just a child. There isn't any need to cut him down in cold blood."

The anger grows in the guards who have circled us and are watching. Anger is a dangerous emotion. It clouds the senses and can quickly turn to rage and hatred. I think for a moment that this could be a turning point. Saying that I refuse to kill a Fjern, no matter the boy's age, will not be easily forgotten. I'm supposed to be here to command them in battle and to urge the guards to kill every Fjern they see—to make the Fjern all pay for what they've done to our people. The mercy I've shown this child is not the mercy the Fjern have shown our children.

Malthe's anger is more difficult to hide. He walks to the boy and grabs a fistful of the child's hair before I can stop him. He pauses. He wants me to see. The boy struggles and cries, and Malthe cuts the head from the neck cleanly. The body falls forward, and the face with its open eyes stare at me accusingly. The boy's expression is frozen in fear and pain. It's the same fear and pain I've seen on so many faces with our brown skin. It's an expression I've made since the day I was torn from my mother's stomach and into this world. Malthe drops the head on the body that's already fallen. It rolls toward my feet. I swallow so that I won't heave. I still have rage inside of me. Rage for the past, and rage for knowing that if I were to show this boy mercy, he probably would never have shown mercy to anyone like me. He would have grown to be a man like any of the other Fjern in these islands. He would have delighted in killing me. But I still can't help the illness swarming through my stomach, the heat of the island prickling over my skin, the awareness suddenly of how each of the guards have begun to look at me. I've lost their respect. They're shocked that I am the same man that had led us to victory on Hans Lollik Helle. Here I stand, too weak to cut the neck of a little Fjern boy. Malthe, though satisfied that I've finally shown the truth of my ways, holds disappointment alongside his contempt.

"Check the house inside," he says to one of his guards, and the man follows through with his order, killing the woman inside by slicing her neck.

CHAPTER TWENTY-ONE

The battles across Larsen Helle continue. Each battle is a massacre: villages abandoned by everyone but those who could not leave, each of them cut down and their bodies left in the dirt to rot. As the sun rises higher and the heat becomes stronger, the smell of smoke and blood rises. We march across the fields, and with every step my tension grows. I can still feel the anger of the guards and Malthe. The thoughts don't come to me clearly, but I still hear snippets. Suggestions that maybe the islanders were wrong in calling me their leader. If I continue on this path, everything that Geir and Marieke predicted and warned me of might transpire. My people could turn on me instead. I could be executed—killed, so that Malthe can take control. While I curse myself for not thinking of a better response to the killing of the Fjern boy, there was no other possible response for me to give.

As we walk, the only sound is made by our own footsteps and breaths and the crackling of fires that we leave behind at every village. Larsen Helle was close enough to Hans Lollik Helle that I would've expected more of a defense from the Fjern. I expect their guards to appear at any moment, to ambush us in the open fields—but I can't see where they would hide. Malthe has also noticed that something is wrong. He doesn't say the words aloud, but his gaze is careful, picking up on any little movement.

The grass is to our waists as we walk, cutting the stalks down with machetes that make metallic twangs on contact. The sound is so familiar it almost feels nostalgic of my days training under Malthe.

We march in silence. A guard to my right hesitates. He doesn't understand why. Something feels wrong to him, and dread fills his body—he takes a step back, and pain explodes. A blade has stabbed through his spine. He gasps, and no one has noticed the blade, the blood, no one but me—I spin to shout a warning, but the sound has the opposite effect. The guards nearest him look at me in surprise and confusion. It's only when they see their friend fall that they realize we're under attack.

Grass shimmers, and all at once dozens of guards yell in pain and surprise. I feel the cut that sparked the shouts: the backs of my calves have deep gashes, but I'm lucky. I can tell the attackers had been aiming to cut the backs of my knees so that I wouldn't be able to move at all. There's chaos and confusion as Malthe aims to have us in formation and order. There's silence for one long moment. The ambushers have been moving in and out of the grass, bent so that we can't see them. I try to keep my mind open for any stray thought, the movement of grass that goes against the wind—

I see the Fjernman before Malthe does. I throw my machete as the Fjern stands, blade ready to slice Malthe's throat. The machete spikes through the air and lands in the man's neck. He coughs blood, staggering back. All at once, the Fjern stand. They surround us in a circle, their blades ready. Arrows fly first, hitting anyone closest. I duck and fall into the grass, hearing the whizzing of the arrows above me. There are shouts and screams, but I move through the falling bodies and for the closest Fjern. I use their own technique against them. I wasn't the only one with this instinct. Other islanders appear, machetes shining as we slice and cut the first line of Fjern down, their bows falling to the ground. Malthe takes advantage of the moment to shout his orders. We fight hard. We aren't like the Fjern. We don't become complacent; we don't feel overconfident. There's too much at risk, too much at stake, to feel that we could ever win this war. We fight like we expect to lose, but we're determined to take as many Fjern with us as we can. We fight until none are left standing.

The battle is over. We've won, but Malthe curses. We lost too many in the ambush. It's difficult to count with the high grass, but it looks like only about ten still stand. The guards that remain breathe heavily. Some have cuts over their eyes, blood dripping down their faces. Others, gashes on their shoulders and arms. Most of us have cuts on our legs from the first wave of the attack. It was an ambush meant to slow us down. It'll give the Fjern the advantage in calling for help from the near islands. We don't have much more time to make it to the Larsen manor, where the rest of the guards likely wait for us. It's probably where the villagers have also gone to hide. They might not have been trained to fight before, but they are bodies that could hold a blade.

I'm not the only one who has these concerns. The anxiety rises in all of us at the possibility of losing this island. If we die here, the Fjern will realize there aren't many of us left to hold Hans Lollik Helle. I'm afraid for everyone left on the island. Marieke, Kjerstin, and all the rest wouldn't be able to defend themselves.

"We can't stop here," I say. The guards have their disgust and anger for me, and Malthe can barely look my way without wanting to spit, but still I speak. "We have to fight on. We have to make it to the Larsen manor, and we have to take this island. Too many depend on it."

I speak the words to frustration. How can I say that I want to take the island when I couldn't kill a little Fjern boy? But alongside the frustration is acknowledgment of the truth. I'm right. No matter how tired we are, no matter how much pain we feel, we have to continue.

As we walk, the grass that had been to our waists eventually falls to our knees and to our shins and ankles until there's no more grass at all but the hard, barren rock of soil that will not grow a single weed. I think this is a strange place for the Larsen manor to have been built. On dead land, as if foreshadowing the family's fate. The manor itself is in ruins. I hadn't realized no one from the Larsen family had returned to take up the mantle of the Larsen name. After the family's one heir, Beata Larsen, was orphaned, she'd moved onto the island of Solberg Helle under the patronage of Jytte Solberg's family—and with Beata Larsen's death, it looks like her family line might have been cut short.

There are smaller houses around the manor where the slaves might have once lived. There isn't any sign of them, just as there'd been no sign of any islanders when we first arrived, waiting to be liberated. As we get closer, my heart is tight in my chest. No one is here—none of the villagers who had escaped, no Fjern guards waiting to kill us. It's in moments like this that I wish my kraft was as strong as Sigourney's, so that I could attempt to reach into the shadows and see if anyone is waiting. It's only as we come to the dead gardens that I can smell what I wish I would not have to see. A wall has an open gate, and inside are the bodies of the islanders.

They've been laid down on their backs, some of their eyes closed to look like they're sleeping, though some keep their eyes open—the last accusing gaze they gave their killers. The bodies are still dressed. They weren't mutilated beyond the single cuts to the necks. There isn't any sign of blood. They must have been killed somewhere else, their bodies placed here for us to find. Malthe has hardened us against emotion. Fighting in the guard means seeing death. It means seeing friends and other loved ones lose their lives. We can't allow our emotion to control us in that moment, or we'll be defeated in the fight. But I feel the swell of pain, not only from me but from all the guards. The heartache as each witnesses the line of islanders. Innocents that had nothing to do with this rebellion. It didn't matter the age. Many are children, lying beside their mothers. One guard turns away and heaves. Georg's eyes are blank but wet. When I meet Malthe's gaze, he wants me to hear his thoughts.

The people who did this. Are those really the people you want to save?

He turns away to speak to the guards under his command. "Stay alert." They might have wanted us to find the dead to break our concentration so that we wouldn't be prepared for battle.

But when we search the grounds and force our way into the house, sweeping the halls, we don't find any Fjern waiting with their machetes. It's only when the guards search the slaves' quarters that the missing villagers are found, huddled and hidden. It looks like it'd been the plan of those on Larsen Helle. If we ever attacked, they were to run here to the manor and hide in the quarters until the battle was over. They didn't seem to consider what to do if they were on the losing end.

"Were those truly the only fighting Fjern on this island?" Georg asks me.

He's incredulous. We all are. The Fjern continue to underestimate us, and it's true that their ambush did take us by surprise. But it almost seems as though they had already given up this island of Larsen Helle. This is a thought that makes me more nervous than before. I wish that the members of the circle were here to discuss next steps. Geir's kraft flashes through me, and I could see the possibilities: how the Fjern would want us to come here, would allow us to feel confident in having won our battle, only to wait for the moment to attack us with all of their force.

We're already weakened, tired, and only ten of us remain. We wouldn't survive such an attack.

"We need to send word back to Hans Lollik Helle and request the defensive guards immediately."

Malthe agrees without complaint and a team of three are sent. Having fought our way to Larsen Helle, the path to Hans Lollik Helle should be clear.

"And what of the Fjern?" Georg asks.

There are nearly twenty captured Fjern villagers. I order the guards to tie them with rope, though some silently question why they should, when we'll likely kill them all. The Fjern sit in the garden, beside the line of dead islanders. Some sit with their eyes squeezed shut in terror, others cry, and still others struggle against their ropes as if they believe they can free themselves and fight us all and still manage to survive. Mothers whisper to their children that they'll be all right, knowing that they're telling lies.

The guards aren't cruel. But I can feel the rage and disgust inside of them, twisting through their hearts. They want revenge. Not only for the islanders that lie dead at their feet, but for the years of pain they've had to suffer. I can feel that desire for revenge inside of them, and while the guards aren't cruel people, I can also feel that they're capable of cruel things. They want to torture the Fjern.

Malthe can feel this bloodlust in them. It's easy for anyone to see in the eyes of the guards who wait for their command. He's thinking of giving them this prize. Do with the Fjern whatever you would like. He's moments from letting the words leave his lips.

"Cut their necks and leave them here in the garden," I say.

The guards are hesitant and disappointed at my words. But there's also gladness that it doesn't seem their leader has lost all of his will to fight and does not show mercy to the Fjern. Only Malthe isn't pleased. He watches me. In his gaze, he sees the truth. It sickens me to order so many deaths, but this was also a mercy. The alternative was something I wouldn't have been able to stand. My command isn't something that he can rebel against, however, not without him receiving the same ire that I had before. I've given my order. He has to follow it.

There are screams from the villagers when they hear their fates, and some try to fight back, but the guards line up, and on Malthe's command, the screams are silenced. The bodies and blood fill the empty garden. There's satisfaction from the others as they wipe their blades clean, but I look at the tangle of bodies before me. This isn't what I saw when I envisioned the islands, free of the Fjern. I'm not sure if this is what freedom means.

We would normally spend a full day and night digging holes for the bodies, but we have no time and no energy to spend. Preparations for the attack on Jannik Helle need to begin immediately. The fear that we won Larsen Helle too easily, and that this must somehow be a trap, hasn't left me. We burn the bodies instead. The smell of charred meat and bone fills the air and sickens me. I want to retreat to the ocean. Standing on the shore, in the shallows, and staring at the sea has always been the only way I can clear my mind. But I can't now. Into the night, Malthe and I sit over a table with maps marking the current of the seas. If we're able to receive the defensive guards of Hans Lollik Helle by tomorrow's end, then we'll have forty guards total. There isn't any way to see how many Fjern wait for us on Jannik Helle. And, even if we survive the battle, there will be hundreds more fortified on Solberg and Niklasson Helle. We will not win.

Malthe and I sit in what might've once been the master's main chambers of the Larsen family manor. It's one of the few rooms that seemed to have survived a fire from long ago. The relics of the past remain. There's a bed with torn sheets. Paintings stained yellow by heat and age remain on the walls. Everything of value has already been taken from the wardrobes and the shelves. Embers die in the fireplace, warming the room. Though these islands fall to the harshness of the sun during the day, the nights have always been cool with the breeze that blows in over the sea. There's a crackling fire, but especially in the days after the storm season, the night gets cold enough that I shiver by the window. Malthe leans back in his seat, a table of maps spread between us, our cups empty of the guavaberry rum that'd been found in the manor's cellars. There's no food, but the rum fills our stomachs and warms our skin.

"We'll be lucky if we live through the attack on Jannik Helle," Malthe acknowledges.

"The spirits are always with us," I tell him. "Our lives are in their hands." I must be tired. I sound like Marieke.

Malthe smirks, sharing the thought. "I would feel safer keeping my life in the hands of the living who still fight." He's also tired, though he doesn't want me to see this. He's self-conscious about how much more tired he becomes in these later years. There were days when he was young, once. He would be able to fight under the hot sun for hours without faltering. Now, he can feel the exhaustion in his bones. It's a constant reminder of how death will always come, no matter whether he will die on a battlefield or in a chair one night after closing his eyes for a short rest.

"We've known each other for so many years," Malthe says. He also realizes how he sounds as he speaks. An old man, surrendering to death, reminiscing on the years of youth when he didn't have to consider that his life could so easily come to an end. "I've known you since you were a boy. A child, younger than the one I killed for you today."

It was a topic I'd been trying to avoid. I still try to avoid it. "I pretended you were my father, once."

Malthe doesn't answer this, and I can't feel any emotion come from him in response.

"Anyone would've been better than my father, I suppose."

"I was nothing like a father to you," Malthe says. His voice has become rougher, harsher, a tone that reminds me of long days of training and sweat and blood. "I always expected the most from you. I knew that you were strong. I could see that you were talented with the blade. This made the others hate you."

"They hated me because I was the master's son."

"That, too," Malthe concedes, "but they also hated you for your power. Not because you have the blood of the Fjern in you, but despite that. It almost seems the more those boys hated you, the better you became in training. It was almost amusing to watch. I expected a lot from you. I pushed you."

"I'm grateful for that."

"And I have to continue to push you," Malthe says. "This revolution—our people, our islands—deserve more than what you're giving us, Løren."

These are words that are meant to hurt. They're meant to make me hesitate, to question myself. For a moment, those words succeed. "You're right," I tell him.

He watches me steadily. Malthe's mind is filled with silence. It's difficult to get a sense of what he thinks of me at this moment. It's difficult to feel if he hates me enough that he might want to cut my neck while I sleep tonight.

"Let me take control," Malthe says. When I don't respond, he keeps speaking. "You aren't ready for this. You aren't prepared. You're still that boy training in the fields in so many ways. You still look to others for help and approval."

"I don't think it's a weakness to look to others for help," I say. "I look to others for wisdom and advice. I don't want to be the king, relying on only my own thoughts and opinions—"

"That," Malthe says, interrupting me. He points and nods. "That is exactly why you aren't ready to command. You *are* king. You should depend on only yourself. The others will only lead you astray." I shake my head, but he continues. "Hasn't someone already led you astray?"

His meaning is clear. We're still not sure who in the circle might be acting as a spy—if anyone truly is, then it's possible that I've already taken false information and bad advice from someone who wants to see us fail. But I also know what I see when I imagine these islands. I don't see one king ruling over us all, with all the power to take away freedom as he sees fit.

"I think that's something we'll have to continue to disagree on."

Malthe doesn't answer this. We'll disagree, yes—but this disagreement will likely end with one of us dead.

Malthe stays in the main chambers for the night. I take one of the smaller rooms several halls away, but I can't sleep. I stay awake with my thoughts and the spirits. On Hans Lollik Helle, there would be the echoes of laughter late into the night as guards drank rum and ate the last of our rations around a fire. The silence on this island is eerie. A reminder of the lines of the dead that wait for us below and how easily any of our bodies could soon be lying dead in the night as well.

When the pain begins behind my eyes and spreads, it takes Sigourney long enough to appear that I think it really might just be a headache, created from a day of stress and misery. But when she appears in the corner of my eye, standing by the window like she can really see from it, I feel a tinge of relief. I shouldn't be relieved. I shouldn't trust her—should not see her as an ally. But with Malthe and the guardsmen who've begun to see me as the enemy, this is my first reaction. I have to remind myself that Sigourney could still be the enemy, the spy that has somehow managed to trick me for the Fjern. Though Marieke hopes and trusts that Sigourney can and has already started to change, there's no evidence of this. None of this internal back and forth passes Sigourney's notice. She's almost smug. She enjoys how unsure I am about her. How I hate her but show her empathy in the same breath. Her appearance solidifies. She might as well be in the room.

"You're still alive," she says. "I wasn't sure you'd survive Larsen Helle. I tried to warn you about the ambush, but you pushed me out."

"I wasn't sure if I could trust you."

"But you trust me now? What's changed?"

I don't trust her now, she understands that. But she can also sense how little choice I have. Sigourney's advice has been helpful in the past, and I feel lost, unsure of which direction to turn.

She can see into me without the block between us. She realizes this isn't the only reason I've let her in. She can see how the death of the boy truly shook my core. Sigourney sees the disgust and hatred, from the guards around me. She understands this hatred well—understands the pain in wanting to be accepted by your own people. Sigourney brings me comfort, in a way. The fact shames me. Maybe Malthe is right. Maybe I have betrayed the islands.

"Betrayed them," Sigourney echoes, "by listening to someone who is risking her life to help the revolution?"

She makes it clear that she didn't come for a simple pleasure call. Something's happened. She's shaken by it. She wants to share what's happened. She needs me to see.

CHAPTER TWENTY-TWO

It would've been easy for Sigourney to hide away in her chambers. It's what she wanted to do, when she was honest with herself. She didn't want to admit the fear that tortured her every time she left to confront the Fjern. It didn't help that she had to pretend to be brave and could not allow a crack in her calm veneer. She was constantly watched by her guardsman, Kalle, which created more pressure in her to never allow him to see her weakness. He was already suspicious of her, and it'd become common knowledge that Sigourney had originally arrived on the island as a spy. Lothar Niklasson felt no need to keep this a secret from his subjects. Sigourney felt this was his own form of punishment: publicly branding her a traitor so that no one would trust her, no matter how much she professed she would work for the kongelig and the Fjern in exchange for her life. Kalle followed her everywhere she went, including her chambers at night while she slept. It seemed the islander rarely slept himself. He took his duty of watching her seriously. If she wasn't careful, he'd be able to easily guess that she could still be working for me and the islands of Hans Lollik Helle as well.

Kalle followed her from her chambers one morning days ago. She'd been invited to join a morning breakfast with the remaining kongelig and their guests. She was surprised to see the invitation at first, and Sigourney couldn't help but have a spark of hope that she was finally to be seen and accepted by the very people she hated, the same people she wished to see burn for killing her family and stealing her islands. Even with her hatred of them, she still wanted them to acknowledge that she was their equal—in some cases, their better.

She was ashamed and embarrassed for this moment of excitement, and after that moment passed, she could see the invitation for what it clearly was: an opportunity for the kongelig to continue humiliating her. The invitation was sent from Gertrude Nørup, whose friend Jytte Solberg would likely be in attendance as well. Sigourney wanted nothing more than to decline. She could only imagine the ways the Fjern would discover to torture her and punish her for being an islander. But she knew that she had to accept. If she didn't, they would delight in the power they knew they held over her—in the fact that she was so afraid of them that she would not leave her chambers.

This was also an opportunity to stand among the Fjern and learn secrets that could be helpful to us, to heighten my chances of winning this war. This is what she thinks, so that I will feel this was the one and true reason she agreed to go, but I can still feel her own ambition. She also saw this as an opportunity to further herself. If the insurgency were to fail, and Sigourney somehow managed to survive, she would still need a plan. She couldn't trust any of the Fjern, but maybe there would be a potential ally at this gathering—or maybe she would learn a secret, not necessarily for the sake of the insurrection, but for the sake of pitting the kongelig against one another. She has a mind for the politics of the Fjern, but it's a mind that I can't admire. I've never understood or appreciated the backhanded ways of the Fjern: the secrets, the plans to destroy one another while sharing smiles and sugarcane wine. I wonder about my ancestors, the first who must have encountered the Fjern. Did the pale-skinned northerners share with them smiles and promises of alliance and friendship? My people, used to speaking in plain words and truths, would've fallen for the lies and tricks so easily. Perhaps it's a lesson I should learn from them.

Sigourney changed into a simple white dress. Kalle still would not leave her room. He'd been ordered by Lothar Niklasson to stay at her side, and that's what he intended to do. He followed her out of the chambers and down the hall and across the courtyard, to the other end of the Herregård Sten, to a wide-open sitting room and parlor where kongelig congregated.

Gertrude Nørup was the ever-pleasant host. It was not her home, but it was a gathering she hosted on behalf of Lothar Niklasson, in celebration of his achievements. She wore a pretty dress of white that did little for her plain features as she greeted the Fjern who entered, chattering as they sipped wine. Gertrude had tried her best in the decorations of the parlor, flowers of white lining the walls and colorful rugs on the hard stone floor. All of Herregård Sten was covered in unforgiving stone that leaked as though they were beneath grounds in dungeons, and there were few windows to allow sunlight and breeze. The effect was a baking heat that simmered no matter where anyone was in the manor. There was little relief. The windows of the parlor were wide open, begging for a breeze that would not come, and the Fjern stood and whipped paper fans back and forth over their pink and sweating skin.

Jytte Solberg stood against the wall, watching the event. She still had a ribbon of lace tied around the scar that wrapped around her neck. Jytte's gaze would not leave Sigourney once she entered the room. Sigourney noticed this, and she noticed Aksel, too. It seemed he would never pass up an opportunity for a drink. The other Fjern avoided him as he sat on one of the sofas. The Fjern considered Aksel Jannik to be an embarrassment to the kongelig. The Jannik name had never held much respect among the other noble families, but with the death of his beloved Beata Larsen, Aksel had sunken to levels of depravity. He called over an islander holding a tray of wine and downed another glass. Sigourney could sense that he'd seen her and knew that she was here, but he was determined to ignore her. Herre Niklasson himself was there, though he was already thinking of how he could escape. The man had always abhorred social functions like this, where the only purpose was to display wealth and alliances. He believed this gathering silly. He had a war to win. But he could not leave a party being hosted in his own honor, in his own home.

He saw Sigourney enter along with all the other Fjern. She could sense how he felt an odd sense of relief. She would provide distraction and entertainment from the overwhelming boredom that had begun to settle—and perhaps an opportunity to learn more about the revolution. Sigourney could feel his gaze on her as she entered the room, and she dreaded him approaching her.

Before Lothar could make his way to her, however, Jytte was already by her side. She offered Sigourney a glass of wine. Sigourney took the glass out of politeness, but she would never be so foolish as to take a sip of anything handed to her by Elskerinde Solberg. Jytte noticed this with some pleasure.

"It isn't poisoned." When Sigourney didn't respond, she added, "Can't you see the truth in my mind for yourself?"

"I've been tricked before," Sigourney said. She hated to admit this. It displayed her weakness: that her kraft isn't as powerful as she would like everyone to believe, including herself.

"Yes, that's what you claim," Jytte said. Sigourney had told all that she'd been tricked by the islanders, by me and Marieke and Malthe—that she hadn't had any idea that the insurrection was brewing right in front of her. Though embarrassing to admit, and though it made her seem like a fool, it was the single truth that allowed her to live in this den of Fjern, so it was a truth she clung to.

Sigourney didn't want to be anywhere near Jytte. Though she would never admit it willingly, she was afraid of the woman— terrified of her kraft. Jytte had the power to control fear. She'd used her ability on Sigourney once before already, and the rising and overwhelming panic had been uncontrollable. Sigourney was sure that if Jytte ever chose to use her power again, especially with Sigourney already in such a state of anxiety, she might choose to take her own life just to escape the fear.

"You probably won't believe me when I say this," Jytte said, "but I admire you, Elskerinde Jannik."

"I do believe you," Sigourney said. The fact was easy for her to feel.

"Not many would so willingly place themselves into their enemy's hands."

"Is that what you are?" Sigourney asked. "The enemy?"

"There's no reason to pretend otherwise. We could form an alliance of some sort, and you would still be my enemy."

Sigourney could see another truth then as well: Jytte had made a habit of having dangerous conversations in the open, where anyone could overhear them. She enjoyed the thrill of having these conversations surrounded by others. It made her feel like the master in a room of fools. It was also less likely that anyone would assume that they were discussing potential trea- son. It would be so much more suspicious if Jytte Solberg sought out Sigourney in the shadows of the gardens at night. If any- one witnessed their secret meeting, Lothar Niklasson would be warned, and the two women would be questioned and executed once the truth was forced from them.

"Why would we ever have any sort of alliance?" Sigourney asked her.

The next thought was sent to Sigourney's mind. Even Jytte would not risk saying the words aloud. *It would be better for you if Lothar Niklasson was dead.*

"It would be better for me if all of you were," Sigourney said with a smile. "Not only Herre Niklasson."

"Yes, well, that isn't going to happen so easily. If you have to choose, he is the one who hopes to see you executed the most of all of us. Though he's agreed to keep you here for the sake of potentially offering information against the islanders, he sees you as too much of a risk to let you live much longer."

"And you don't?" Sigourney asked. This was a far cry from the Jytte Solberg she'd known on Hans Lollik Helle. The woman had claimed to all that Sigourney had been a snake. When it became clear to everyone that Sigourney had managed to trick her way onto the island for the storm season, Jytte seemed to believe this was a crime worthy of execution as punishment. Now Jytte wanted Sigourney as an ally against Lothar Niklasson?

"I would rather see you alive at the end of all of this, Elskerinde Jannik," Jytte said. "That kraft of yours—it'd be a shame to see it go to waste."

Jytte still seemed to be considering ways to have the kraft to read minds and control bodies on her side. Jytte swallowed the last of her wine and handed the empty glass to a slave standing against the wall.

"Consider the possibility," Jytte said. "That's all I ask."

She left Sigourney to brave the gathering alone, whispering something to Gertrude Nørup on her way out of the heavy mahogany doors. Sigourney could feel Lothar Niklasson's gaze on her. He was curious. He wondered why Sigourney and Jytte would have such a seemingly friendly conversation when he remembered how much Jytte Solberg had detested Sigourney. Sigourney could already sense how the man planned to ask her his questions and force the truth from her. Speaking with Lothar was always a risk, so she turned away from him before he could call to her. She walked to the one person everyone else avoided and sat beside Aksel. He barely looked at her. He could hardly see her anyway, with the amount of wine and rum that swam through his blood.

"I wish you would leave me alone," Aksel told her. It was the first they were speaking together on this island—the first they spoke together since Aksel had left Hans Lollik Helle. He was lucky to have gone before the night of the revolt. I doubt he would've survived the fight.

"How can I leave you alone?" Sigourney said. "Everyone would think it odd that I would avoid my husband."

"Let them think it odd," he said. "As far as I'm concerned, we're no longer married."

"Since when?"

"Since you helped in the destruction of Hans Lollik Helle with your other little islander rebels."

"I wasn't a part of the revolt. I was taken just as much by surprise."

"Excuse me if I find that difficult to believe." He took another sip of his wine. "No matter. You'll be executed soon enough. I'll be free of you then."

"But not until I actually am executed."

"You take pleasure in torturing me."

"Yes, of course I do."

"Was this the revenge you'd always planned?" He meant this as a joke, but it wasn't one Sigourney found humor in.

"No," she answered him plainly. "The revenge I'd planned was cutting your neck in your sleep so that I could take the throne."

Aksel laughed, spilling wine on himself. "Death at your hand would be a mercy at this point. I'm trapped on this island because of a rebellion doomed to fail. I should've left for the north while I still had the chance."

Sigourney has some shame for the next moments that pass.

She wishes there was a way to hide these memories from me, but there isn't any way for her to block only bits and pieces of her thoughts. She hated Aksel just as she hated any of the Fjern, but she also remembered how they had shared a bed in the past. She remembered the pleasure she'd felt, and in that moment, she wondered if it was a pleasure she could find again. She slipped Aksel a thought.

Perhaps it isn't so bad that you're stuck on this island with me.

He understood her meaning immediately. There'd been a time when he felt sick at the thought of sharing a bed with Sigourney. Especially in the days following Beata Larsen's murder, he'd felt disgust with both Sigourney and himself for betraying the woman he loved by marrying another. He felt disgust for wanting a woman who was an islander. No matter how much he thought her beneath him, his body reacted without his permission. Aksel still had this disgust for Sigourney, but he felt the edges of desire as well. It'd been a while since he shared anyone's bed. There had been slave girls, but they'd been unwilling, crying and following his orders without passion. Looking at Sigourney, he felt the harsh truth that his body had needs, as did hers. She stood from the sofa, her invitation silent. He hesitated but followed in step behind her as they left the parlor and went into the halls and toward her room. Both noticed the glances as they left the room, but the body has a way of controlling thought and logic. Neither cared in that moment.

"Must he follow us?" Aksel asked, referring to Kalle, always following closely enough to watch, even if it was from across the room.

"Unfortunately those were his orders from Herre Niklasson, and I've found him to be a very obedient guard."

"Then I order you to leave," Aksel said.

Kalle didn't argue—he would not have argued with a Fjern and especially a member of the kongelig—but he also did not take his orders from Aksel. "I'm unable to leave Sigourney Rose's side," he said.

As desperate as Aksel was, he couldn't imagine bedding Sigourney with another man standing in the room and watching them.

"You don't have to be directly at my side," Sigourney suggested. Kalle agreed to stand outside of the room while the two completed their business. He listened to the sounds within, and when Aksel left, Kalle walked into the room to return to his post without any acknowledgment that Sigourney still lay in her bed, sheets wrapped around her.

Sigourney had long since tried to push Kalle to the point of response, but his cold silence had endless patience. She could feel his thoughts and emotions, could see how much the man hated her—but this wasn't something he ever intended to hide. He didn't seem to mind at all that she could see everything about him, including his past. The boy had been raised here on Niklasson Helle. His father had been sold away to another island years ago, and his mother had died of a storm-season sickness. Kalle had been raised in the guard and survived the brutality most islanders have faced in these islands. He worked hard, as he was ordered, and he was always obedient to his master Lothar Niklasson. But Sigourney was surprised to see another truth in Kalle. The man was not like the islanders of Hans Lollik who felt love for their masters and feared their own freedom. Kalle hated the kongelig. He hated the Fjern. He knew that he was worthy of freedom. Kalle believed in playing this game of his masters. Become a commander, gain their trust, let them think of him as a friend. Marriage wasn't often considered legitimate for islanders, but he would convince his master Lothar Niklasson that he was worth marriage. He wasn't fool enough to think he could marry a Fjern, but he would find a woman who was similarly respected and trusted by the kongelig. They would begin a family line that could be separated from the slaves—a new and different class of hardworking, respected, and trusted islanders. They would receive their own freedoms. This is what Kalle strove for.

Sigourney noted with interest that Kalle was a father himself, though the girl and her mother had been sold away as well. He never learned where they were sent. He hadn't loved the woman. He hadn't known her at all. The two had been placed in the same bed by Herre Niklasson, who saw them both as fit slaves with the potential to earn him coin, and they were given their orders. Kalle could tell that the woman, this stranger, was pained by the experience, and it was difficult for him to fulfill the deed, knowing that she had no desire.

When they were done, they only saw one another fleetingly around the manor. She worked inside the walls, while he was always outside in the sun. He saw when her belly grew and when she one day appeared with a baby in her arms. He watched as the child grew from afar. Most men like Kalle didn't care for the children they'd fathered. Many of the guards had been forced into the beds of multiple women, and he couldn't blame them in cutting away the feeling of connection. It would be too painful, to have so many children and have each taken away.

But this girl—Kalle couldn't help but be curious about her. He saw when she began to walk and run on her own, saw from afar that they had the same smile. He tried not to have love for the child. He tried to look away whenever he saw her running her errands from the fields and to the house. One day, he followed her as she held a basket of flowers. He stopped her and asked for her name. She didn't recognize him. She didn't reply with love—only the respect she'd been taught to have for all elders. She gave him the name her mother had given her, and he repeated it like a song. He promised her that if she stopped and looked for him whenever she returned from the fields, he would have a gift for her. He would find pieces of sugarcane to give her so that she could chew on the stalks, balls of gooey tamarind rolled in sugar and shells he'd strung together to wear around her neck. She always accepted the gifts with a thank-you, with no realization that he was her father. He knew that she was not his to love, but he couldn't stop the feeling he had for the child. He saw when she and her mother were put onto the back of a carriage, to be taken to the docks of Niklasson Helle and sold away. The girl had held her mother's hand. She hadn't looked back to see Kalle watching her leave.

Years later, he finds himself wondering about her. If she's well, if she's alive, if she has managed to find a piece of joy in these islands. He'll dream of her sometimes. He worries that the girl is dead, and that her spirit has come to visit him.

Kalle did not agree with the revolution. He thought of the innocent islanders who were killed in the fighting. He had rage for me and everyone else on Hans Lollik Helle who plotted against the kongelig—not for the sake of the Fjern, but because of the islanders who have had to take our punishments. Sigourney could see this easily enough.

"Do you believe that the Fjern should be in power, then?" she asked. "Do you believe your only purpose in life should be to serve them?"

"No," he told her. "We were meant to have our freedom. The Fjern stole that from us."

Sigourney was surprised by how boldly he spoke. "You could be punished for such words."

"I assume you won't have me punished for speaking to feelings you share."

Sigourney acknowledged that he was correct. She stood from her bed, sheets wrapped around her, and moved to the dress pooled on the floor. "We do share these feelings. But I'm confused. How can we share these feelings, but you're against the revolution?

Don't you want your freedom?" Sigourney wasn't confused at all. She only wanted to hear him say the words out loud.

"Of course," he said, "but not like this. This insurrection has taken the lives of so many who didn't consent to being a part of it."

"How would you take your freedom, then?"

Kalle wasn't afraid of Sigourney, and she could sense that he admired her, even with his hatred—admired how she had managed to work her way to her position among the kongelig. "The only way I can envision taking my freedom is by playing the games of the Fjern. Play to their rules. Beat them, according to their own law."

"Treacherous words, truly," Sigourney said, but her words were half-hearted. She was intrigued by Kalle. She allowed her sheet to drop and she dressed. Kalle didn't look away in shame or embarrassment. "I tried to play by the games of the Fjern. You can see where that landed me."

"I can see that you lost," Kalle said. "Maybe you weren't the best choice to play this game. Just because you lost, doesn't mean it wasn't the correct route."

Sigourney laughed. "Help me tie my dress."

Kalle did as he was told. She'd considered his words. "Maybe it isn't too late to try again," she said.

They weren't friends. They weren't allies. But the words were enough to create a shift in Sigourney and one that she could feel in Kalle as well. Sigourney could feel the honesty in Kalle. She could feel how he had no love for his masters and how he was disgusted with any islander that loved the Fjern. She could see how, if he were ever given a piece of power, he would have those islanders executed right alongside the masters they loved so much. She trusted that he was not an ally of Lothar Niklasson or Jytte Solberg or any of the kongelig who wanted to see Sigourney dead. But she could also see that Kalle couldn't trust her as easily as she could trust him. He couldn't see the truth that she could; he would just as quickly have her on her knees, machete ready to cut her head from her neck.

Sigourney hadn't been dressed long when she felt the tension filter through the air. The manor was as silent as it always was—there was no music, no laughter streaming through the halls, but she'd been able to sense the Fjern around her all the same. She could sense their boredom, their confidence that they would survive this war and return to their lives. She could also sense when Lothar Niklasson passed by her room at that moment. It was a coincidence. Sigourney wasn't on Lothar's mind, and he'd been so distracted that he didn't realize that the door he passed was hers. She could sense another man with him. She could feel this man's flurry of fear, his discomfort, his certainty that he hadn't pleased his master—

Without a word to Kalle and without any explanation, she opened her door and snuck out of her room. She padded down her hall, her skirts bunched around her legs, the stone cold beneath her feet. She rounded the corner, but Lothar Niklasson and the islander had disappeared. She wasn't certain. She wants me to know that now. There's no proof that the islander with Lothar, whoever he was, was actually the traitor of Hans Lollik Helle.

CHAPTER TWENTY-THREE

If the man in the halls had really been the traitor, I'd have a hard time believing the spy is actually a part of the inner circle. It'd be difficult, almost impossible, for them to have left Hans Lollik Helle and made it to Niklasson Helle without any interference. It'd be impossible that they would have returned to the royal island without anyone's notice that they'd gone.

Sigourney wants me to understand that I'm thinking too narrowly. I've convinced myself that the traitor is, without any doubt, a member of the inner circle. It's just as possible that the spy could have listened to our conversations. He could have asked questions of any unsuspecting member to gain the knowledge he needed to, before coming here to Niklasson Helle. It would be more difficult for us to keep an eye on every single islander on Hans Lollik Helle, impossible to realize if a guard left the barracks one night after training. It would have taken at least a day of travel to arrive on Niklasson Helle. I could ask Malthe if there was a guard under his command that he'd noticed was missing in the past weeks, or one that had claimed illness or injury to avoid training. And if the spy does happen to be one of Malthe's guards, I realize that this could mean the man is here on Larsen Helle at this moment. They could have left Hans Lollik Helle to arrive on Niklasson Helle days ago, traveled here with us to Larsen Helle for the battle. They could be helping the Fjern plan their next attack at this moment.

"This is why I wanted to speak with you," Sigourney says. "The Fjern—Herre Niklasson…They've realized you'll be attacking Jannik Helle."

Yes, this was already clear. They would have to have known, to allow us to take Larsen Helle so easily. "We're prepared to fight."

"You aren't," Sigourney insists. "They've figured out you will be coming to Jannik Helle, and they plan to unleash the fury of the Niklasson and Solberg guards. The Fjern may be hidden away on Niklasson Helle, but Solberg Helle holds the true power. I'm not sure Lothar is aware of how many ships and guards Jytte Solberg has prepared. There will be ships waiting at sea, Fjern on the docks and shores. Nearly five hundred guards in all. How many do you have with you?" she asks, and immediately learns her answer. She almost laughs. "You don't stand a chance, Løren."

She could be lying to me. She sees the thought, and I can feel her impatience. "Why would I lie?"

"You could be doing what you promised Lothar Niklasson you would," I tell her.

"Working for the Fjern, by warning you of an attack you will certainly lose? By saving your life?"

"You could be dissuading me from taking Jannik Helle so that the Fjern won't have to lose another battle and another island."

"Don't be a fool," she says. "Why would I lie about something like this? You know that the Fjern wait for you on Jannik Helle. They can't wait to take your head, Løren. You should see their excitement in finally having you dead. You can see that I'm not lying."

"You've managed to trick others before. You're tricking either me or Lothar Niklasson."

"I'm tricking Lothar Niklasson. I don't want to betray you. I don't want to see you die." She adds, "I have a higher chance of living if I'm on your side."

These are her words, but I can also see what she hopes that I will: Even though I have no love for her, she has begun to see me as a friend. Sigourney has never had a friend before, besides her sisters and her brother, before they were killed. She might claim to care for Marieke, but she never gave the woman true freedom. She had no allies with the Fjern who she served, and she convinced herself that she was better than us islanders, her own people, because of the power she had. I can sense the desperate loneliness in her. She's been alone for so long that the tentative fear of considering me a friend is fragile. She's seen my mercy and sympathy and thinks that I could begin to care for her. She's wrong. I don't care for Sigourney Rose. The thought that she could consider me a friend angers me. How could I care for someone who treats her people the way that she does? If it weren't for the rebellion, she wouldn't have changed at all. She would have continued to live her life of privilege, perhaps winning the crown and keeping her power and her slaves. Maybe the anger I have is mostly for myself. There's a pinch of truth in her hope. It's the same truth that fuels Malthe's anger toward me and his idea that I am a traitor, whether I realize it myself or not.

Sigourney sees all of this. She isn't hurt by the implication that I don't care for her. She already understands this is a fact. Still, she thinks that we can be allies, even if I don't care for her in the way that she tells herself she cares for me.

"I only want to warn you, Løren. Your insurrection will end if you go to Jannik Helle, and you will be captured and executed. There isn't a doubt in my mind."

Her words are genuine, but I still hesitate. I could trust what she says, but this was the plan I'd decided to move forward with. The inner circle, including myself, agreed that we would come here to Larsen Helle before attacking Jannik Helle. What am I to do? Go to Malthe and tell him that I've changed my mind, and I don't want to move forward with our attack? I can't insist that we retreat without any viable reason. Malthe would inevitably ask why, and if I were to mention Sigourney's name, he would claim that I'm a fool and that I've fallen victim to her lies. I have to admit to myself that this is also entirely possible.

"It isn't so easy to retreat."

"It'll have to be, if it means your life and the lives of your guards."

Despite my hesitations, she's right. I don't need to say the words aloud. She's seen that I've agreed. She says that she must go, and in that moment she's disappeared, leaving me with nothing but my uncertainty of what's to be.

CHAPTER TWENTY-FOUR

Malthe sits by the dying embers of a fire. As the sun began to set, we poured saltwater on all of the fires so that their glow wouldn't be seen by the Fjern in the night. If there's to be an ambush, the light would lead them right to us. The effect means that it's difficult to see anyone in the shadows as the sky becomes a darker blue. Guards rest and mumble in low tones. Only Malthe sits up, watching over the men he commands. Malthe is a lonely man, I realize. He has no true friends. No one he can confide in. He only has allies he works with for one common goal, for one purpose. He has no one he loves and no love that loves him. But if this makes Malthe a lonely man, then I'm the same.

He doesn't acknowledge me when I sit beside him. I wait for a moment, trying to think of the best way to ease into the conversation. But there aren't any words that would soften what I'm about to tell him.

"We need to leave," I say.

He misunderstands me. "I thought we agreed to wait until sunrise."

"We need to leave Larsen Helle," I say, "and return to Hans Lollik Helle."

He pauses here, the words sinking in. He isn't sure that

he's heard me clearly, but in the heavy silence he realizes that he has.

"Why?" he asks, suddenly concerned there'd been an attack, an ambush, something that would force us to retreat, though this isn't possible. He would've heard and seen the fighting. "Has something happened?"

"Nothing yet," I say hesitantly. "We're not prepared to fight Jannik Helle. If we continue on, we'll be massacred."

As the words leave my mouth, I can feel how anyone would take them: the words of a coward, someone who can't be sure of his own mind.

"We decided this was the best course of action," Malthe says. He hasn't been impressed with me as a leader, but this shocks him. "All of us on Hans Lollik Helle. We agreed we would take Larsen Helle, and then take Jannik Helle."

"That's what we agreed on," I tell him, voice low. "But I have reason to believe—"

"What reasons?" he interrupts. "Why are you so sure we would be massacred? Have you no faith in your own guards?"

"Of course I do," I say. His voice has risen, and the nearest of the men have heard. "But there isn't anything that can be done when it comes to sheer numbers. There are more of them—too many. They'll overpower us."

"How do you know this? There were hardly any Fjern here on Larsen Helle."

"And don't you think that odd?" I ask him. "They're luring us into a trap."

"The paranoid delusions of a coward."

"The cautious hesitation of a man that doesn't want to see us lose this war. That's what will happen," I say. "We will lose the war if we go to Jannik Helle. We will all be killed and all of the guards protecting Hans Lollik Helle will be gone. The guards to the north—they'll have no idea what's happened. They'll be taken by surprise when the Fjern suddenly appear in their shallows. We must be smart with our next move, Malthe. We can't rush into the next situation."

Malthe has been watching me carefully. He only half hears my words as suspicion in him grows. "You seem certain that the Fjern wait for us on Jannik Helle."

"It's the only possibility."

"So certain that we would lose."

He already realizes the answer to the next question he asks, but he wants to see how I will react—if I'll attempt to lie, or if I will admit to the truth. "Have you been in contact with Sigourney Rose?"

A part of me thinks that I should lie. He will have no proof against me, while the truth is something that could easily become a weapon. I'm alone on this island with him and guards that have begun to waver in their loyalty toward me. I should wait until I'm back in the safety of Hans Lollik Helle with the other members of the inner circle. But I have never been good at lying, and I've never had the desire to do so.

"Yes," I tell him after a moment. "She reached out to me to pass along the warning. The Fjern will attack heavily if we arrive on Jannik Helle."

Malthe nearly spits at my feet. "Sigourney Rose is a liar and a traitor," he says, his voice low. He has no need to shout. The closest of the guards are listening. "And you are as much of a traitor if you continue to listen to her."

"She isn't lying. I can see that she speaks the truth."

"And a fool, for believing her," Malthe says. "Did you not agree that you would cut off contact from her?"

"It's difficult for me to control when she will reach out—"

"Does her kraft not allow her to see you as clearly as you see her?" He's stood to his feet, towering over me, his anger building. "She can learn your secrets. She might have already told the

Fjern that we wait here on Larsen Helle. They could already be preparing to attack."

"They would've already seen we were here. She hasn't told them—"

He hits me. I could feel the rage in him, but I couldn't see the fist coming, because Malthe himself didn't realize he'd hit me until it was done. There was enough force for me to stagger backward. I think that him hitting me will shock him into silence and stillness as much as it's shocked me, but this time I can feel the calculated thought as he follows me, shoving me down to the dirt so that my head collides with stone. He's already made the mistake of laying his hands on me. This is already something that I could use against him. He might as well use the moment—he hadn't planned on it this way, not now—

He wraps his hands around my neck and squeezes. I choke and try to push him off, air caught in my throat. The power in his grip tightens. It feels like he's trying to snap my neck—feels like he might succeed, and the men he commands are hesitating, afraid to go against him, too afraid to help me—

Hands grab at Malthe's shoulders. He's thrown back and I gasp, choking on air. I turn over onto my hands and knees, sucking in the salt-air breeze, my eyes scanning the scene. Georg and Frey have Malthe restrained, their machetes at his neck. Five guards closest to them have their machetes pointed at Georg and Frey. There's silent tension, and for a breath, no one moves. I could give Georg the order. I could have him kill Malthe. The other guards, though—they could kill Georg and Frey in retribution. The guards and their loyalties are split. The fight that I could foresee breaking out will be deadly, bloody—and we'd lose the few guards we have, already too few to win this war.

Malthe sees this truth also. He sees that killing me and starting this battle would mean halving his chances of returning to the royal island alive.

"I'm sorry," he says. "I was drinking, not thinking clearly."

He lies. This is exactly what he meant to do. He only wishes he'd succeeded before he was stopped. I remember Geir's warning. I should have Malthe killed, before he manages to kill me. But killing Malthe would mean losing a commander. He's more talented than I am in controlling his guards, and if I have their commander killed I might lose the loyalty of the men altogether. They could rebel against me whether Malthe is here to give them the order or not.

"It's all right," I say, loudly enough for the guards to hear my voice. "I understand. I was unnecessarily angry as well. It's the stress of the battle."

I wave at Georg to release him, which he does hesitantly. Malthe rubs his arm when he's let go. He watches me like he might be waiting for another opportunity to attempt to take my life, but he won't do it—not here, not yet. He does want me dead, that is clear enough, but to try now would mean risking too much. When he tries again, it will be when he will succeed, and when he'll be able to finally take control as he was meant to do from the very beginning. He doesn't argue when I announce that we're leaving Larsen Helle.

By the time we arrive on Hans Lollik Helle, Kjerstin and her scouts have already seen us on the horizon. She waits on the bay as we leave our ships and row our boats to shore.

I stride out of the shallows and onto the sand, passing her.

She follows closely. "What happened?" she asks.

She notices when I glance over my shoulder at Malthe, who watches me as he leaves his own boat. The guards closest to him seem to be waiting for their orders. I'm not sure what he'll have planned. He could have his guards attack within hours, maybe minutes, to take this island's control.

"We retreated," I tell Kjerstin. She follows me into the groves, Georg and Frey close behind.

"I can see that. Why?"

There's only one thing I can think of to stop Malthe from having an attack ordered on Hans Lollik Helle. "We need to call a meeting. Immediately," I tell Kjerstin. "Get the others prepared."

She's surprised, confused, but she nods her understanding. She pauses and waits for Malthe to pass along the order as I walk farther into the groves. I wait in the meeting room in Herregård Constantjin for the others. I'm alone. I realize the danger in this. If Malthe comes in first, he could easily overpower me and kill me. He could make up any lie once I'm dead. He could tell the others that I'd attacked first. They'd have no choice but to let him take control, exactly as he'd wanted. When footsteps echo, I tense—but the door opens, and Marieke stands before me.

"Are you all right?" she asks. She's heard the gossip that's spread quickly from the guards and to the other islanders. The yellowing bruises around my neck are the only proof she'd needed. "Spirits, I can't believe that he would—"

"Yes, you do," I tell her.

She quiets and nods. Yes, she does. "But to try in front of so many, so brazenly..."

"I just have to be more careful."

"You need to think of other options," she whispers urgently. I understand that she means I should have the man executed for attempting to take my life.

"If I do that, who will lead the guards?" I say. Geir's answer had seemed simple: I would. But I'm not so sure that I have the same confidence in me that he does. I'd had one lucky night on the ambush of Hans Lollik Helle. I don't have the skills to command so many guards to victory.

Before Marieke can respond, Olina steps into the room. She is cold as she takes her seat. She's also heard what happened, and she finds the fight a distraction, an annoyance. She sees me and

Malthe as children in our selfish struggle for power, when we should be focusing on the freedom of our people. Maybe she's right.

She has another reason to be annoyed. "I'm surprised to see you here, Løren," she tells me. "You should be taking control of Jannik Helle."

"I'm sure he has a reason for it," Marieke says in my immediate defense. Olina doesn't bother to answer her. When the door opens again, it's to Geir, who is silent. In the last moment Kjerstin comes as well.

"Where's Malthe?" Olina asks.

"He said he wouldn't be attending," Kjerstin responds. She's uneasy. She's heard the talk as well. It isn't a coincidence that Malthe will have attempted to kill me and not come here to this meeting. I'd hoped he would feel bound by duty, but he could be by the barracks, giving his orders on the attack that's to come.

Geir sees the fear in my eyes. "He will have a hard time gaining the number of guards he'll need to make a proper assault," he says. "He would have been better off waiting until he knew for sure that the loyalty of all the guards is on his side. He's most likely testing the waters, to see how his guards feel about their leader."

"None of this answers the question," Olina says, "of why you are back here on Hans Lollik Helle."

"We weren't ready to attack Jannik Helle."

"We agreed—"

"We weren't ready to attack Jannik Helle," I repeat.

Olina sits with quiet fury. "You'll have to explain to me, then, how you mean to win this war," she says. "You won't attack the islands. You wait to be ambushed. You wait to run out of food and water and supplies. You will not allow me to travel to the northern empires to request the help that we need."

The northern empires. I meet Geir's eye, and I realize he

thinks the same. I'd been needed here on Hans Lollik Helle to lead—but with the threat of Malthe and the undeniable need for more guards, perhaps it would be best for me to leave while still maintaining the respect as the leader of the uprising. Olina had been asking for the chance to go to the northern empires to request assistance in person for some time. We didn't want to risk her life. But if I were to go with her, along with loyal guards, we might have a chance of making it to the north. I would have a chance of convincing allies to return to the islands with me. Allies who would help me to control Malthe and his guards, before we attack the Fjern.

It's the best course of action. I can already feel my pride hurting from the obviousness of me running away from Malthe to escape his blade. But I can also see that I have little choice. If I return with guards, I can subdue Malthe. As is, he can easily kill me and anyone who claims my loyalty. I have to leave for the northern empires with Olina as soon as possible.

"You're right," I tell her. "It's time to take a different step. We need the help of the northern empires."

She sits straighter in her seat, surprised. Kjerstin narrows her eyes.

"You'll go to the northern empires," I tell Olina, "and to be sure you make it there safely and negotiations go smoothly, I'll come with you."

There's an explosion of emotion, though everyone keeps their expressions still and calm.

"You're leaving the islands of Hans Lollik," Kjerstin repeats, "in the middle of the war?" She sees as clearly as anyone else that Malthe has something to do with this decision, but she's still disappointed that I would run away when I'm needed here. "How many days do you think we would last without you?"

"We won't last even if I do stay," I tell her. "Olina is right. The ambassadors of the free people could give us what we need

to win this war: supplies, guards, their support against Koninkrijk and the Fjern."

"And if we're attacked while you're gone?"

"Malthe is still here with his guards."

Marieke shakes her head. She doesn't think this is a good idea.
It'll be more difficult to wrestle the power back from Malthe if
I leave him alone on this island. But I'm sure Malthe would take
that power with me on this island by simply taking my head.
Some would think I'm taking the coward's path, and maybe
they're right. But it's the path that gives me the highest chance of
surviving Malthe and helping the rebellion succeed.

I realize also that I'm still not sure who in the room might
have been behind passing our secrets to the Fjern. If that person
truly is in the room at this moment, then Lothar Niklasson will
realize that I'll be attempting to make it to the northern empire.
He could send his fastest ships to intercept me and Olina and
have us killed.

"You'll have to be quick," Geir says. "If you manage to make
it to the northern empires, you'll only have a week at most, I
estimate, before the Fjern will realize we are at our weakest and
attack again."

Kjerstin agrees, though she doesn't meet my eye. She doesn't
want me to see how worried she is for me. She doesn't want
me to misinterpret her feelings as growing love for me. Kjerstin
doesn't love me. She doesn't believe there's any point in loving
another when our bodies don't belong to anyone else but the
Fjern, and especially when we are at war. What point is there in
loving another when either of us could be killed at any moment?
She reminds herself of this as the worry in her grows. She must
accept the fact that I will likely not make it back to Hans Lollik
Helle alive.

I tell Olina that we'll leave at once. It's as we stride from the
meeting room, Olina speaking quickly of all the next steps we

must consider, that I allow the full pressure to fill me. I've never left these islands. It's ironic. I'd always wanted to escape when I was young. To make it to the north, where I would be free. Now I'm going to the north for the first time in my life. If I make it there alive, it will be with the hope that I could find a way to free everyone in these islands, and not only me.

CHAPTER TWENTY-FIVE

We leave under the cover of night. The trip to the northern empires will take a week if the winds are favorable and if we don't stop at any of the islands, which we don't plan to do. Georg helps to man the vessel, smaller than our warships. This is one that was used by the kongelig for the viewing of the whales and other pleasure rides at sea, but the ship is still one of the fastest. It cuts through the black waters under the dark sky. There are no levels beneath for sleeping. We'll have to live here on the deck together for days.

The salt air stings the corners of my eyes as the ship's sails whip through the air. Water sprays and mists, and Olina shivers under a torn blanket. When I hand her the one I'd had wrapped over my legs, she hesitates.

"We wouldn't want our leader to get a storm-season sickness."

"The storm season is over," I tell her with a brief smile. "I'll be fine."

Olina is older than me, her lungs weaker. I'll need her to help negotiate in the northern empires and free nations. She takes the blanket gratefully. I can feel the curiosity in her glance. Olina has heard many things about me over the past months, before the start of the war when I became the guard of Sigourney Rose. She hadn't trusted me—not because she thought I would betray the revolution, but because she thought I was too young. I am young. I'm about twenty-two, though I can't be sure, since my father hadn't told me the exact year I was born. Olina was worried my youth would cause me to misstep, and that I'd cost the entire plan they'd taken decades to build. Marieke had truly been a force in the network of whispers; a woman who insisted on patience and who finally brought them Sigourney Rose. Sigourney had been the piece they'd needed. But while we think of Marieke as the mother of the revolution and our savior, Olina had always been in the background, working diligently and silently without requiring thanks or praise or attention. There was always work to be done: messages to pass from Hans Lollik Helle, where she had been stationed and where she'd also looked closely after the girl Agatha, after Agatha was brought to the royal island. She hadn't cared for Agatha like the girl was her daughter, but she still grieved when we found her body on the rocks. She didn't grieve Agatha so much as she grieved the end of a power that could have helped us win this war. Olina had worked so hard to raise the child, to cultivate the girl's ability, only for her to be thrown from a cliff.

Youth, she'd decided—it was because of Agatha's youth that she'd chased Sigourney Rose and found herself dead.

"Yet Malthe is not so young, and he acts just as rashly," I tell her. She's surprised, then remembers the power of my kraft. She immediately becomes uncomfortable and defensive. She doesn't like the idea of me seeing her thoughts.

"That's true," she admits, adjusting the blanket around her legs. "Perhaps I'm looking for an excuse to explain why things haven't turned out the way we'd hoped." She hesitates, but I can feel the question in her before she asks it out loud. "Can you truly see everything that I think and feel, just like Sigourney Rose?"

"Not everything," I tell her. "Sigourney could become her

target. She can know them as well as she knows herself. I can only see snippets of their past and know some thoughts."

"What do you see?" Olina asks. "Tell me."

I can see that though she's uncomfortable with this power of mine, she can't help but be intrigued. I can see that she's always been intrigued by kraft and has often wondered why there are some who're born with their abilities but not others. She'd wished she had been born with power. Even understanding that there was a chance the Fjern would've realized her kraft and had her killed, she wanted to see what such a power must feel like. Olina was raised to believe in the gods of the Fjern rather than the spirits of our ancestors. There are some like Marieke who have always praised the spirits, despite the risk of having her tongue cut from her mouth if any of the Fjern were to hear. It's what our people did long before the Fjern ever arrived. When the Fjern came, they brought their gods with them: the seven gods, each of whom control their aspects of this world, each of whom must be worshipped. The Fjern believe the gods granted them their kraft, and that the powers are meant for the divine rule of the kongelig. Any islander who has taken this kraft has stolen their power and is sentenced to die.

Olina can't help but continue to worship the gods of the Fjern. She fears their wrath. There's a part of her, a part that she won't admit to herself, that can't help but believe that I, too, have stolen the power I have. That this kraft was not meant for me or any of the islanders—that it should only be in the hands of the Fjern who rule us. She wishes she could have kraft, but she doesn't think that she would deserve it.

The days are long and hot under the sun with no shade except for the blankets we try to use as tarps. Olina sits cross-legged while Georg and I man the sails.

"I can't imagine a full week of this," Olina says. She wipes the sweat from her face. "We'll need to prepare ourselves once we reach land. The northerners won't be impressed with our appearances. Especially our contact. Dame Nage Aris of the Rescela Empire. She'd be offended if we arrived sweaty and salted."

"Surely she'll understand," I tell her. "We're in a war. Traveling for a week at sea."

"She won't care about the circumstances," she says. "They care about their looks quite a lot, in the north."

The days pass and begin to meld together. We let a net loose in an attempt to catch our food. The fish that gets tangled in the net are cut from the bone, scales cleaned from their meat, strips laid out on the wood under the heat of the sun. The sunlight isn't enough to cook the fish thoroughly, however, and most of the meat is eaten raw. Malthe had always taken care to teach his guards how to survive in the wild without any resources, but Olina doesn't take to the raw fish kindly. She becomes ill on the third day, vomiting and unmoving under the shade of the blankets, the rocking motion of the ship having her whisper her prayers.

Georg is concerned. "We'd focused so much on what we would do if we found Fjern ships at sea," he said. "I didn't consider the chance of one of us falling ill."

I'm not sure if Olina's illness is so serious that it could be fatal, but his nervousness affects me. We try to take care of Olina, passing her most of our water and praying for a rainstorm that can refill our supply. I attempt to use the kraft I'd learned from little Anke, but her ability had always been for wounds—not for a sickness of the lungs and stomach. We pass the islands of the north without stopping, holding our breath as we pass each island, never sure when a Fjern ship will appear in the distance. We sail until each island is a green hill in the haze on the horizon, and until they are gone and there's nothing but the unending blue of sea. I realize suddenly that the pull I feel, connecting me to Sigourney Rose, is gone. The distance has finally become too much for the kraft that binds us. I'm surprised by the hollowness I feel. There's a similar melancholy when I realize I can't see the islands of Hans Lollik anymore, even if these lands had been the site of so much pain. I have never lived a day when I could not see one of the green hills of my home. The farther I am from the islands, the less I feel a connection to my past and the spirits who have always watched over me.

Time becomes a mix of sunlight and cold night breeze, and it's difficult to keep the days apart. There's nothing but blue sea and blue sky and salt air. I start to fear that we've gotten turned around or become lost. There's nothing to guide us, no landmarks on the ocean's plains, except for the stars at night. Olina becomes sicker with every passing day. As Georg says, "Some just weren't made for the sea."

Olina stops speaking. She keeps her eyes closed. There's something she needs to tell me, but speaking has begun to hurt her throat. But what she has to say is necessary for me to know. It's a matter of survival.

"The people of the north have different customs," she says, her voice hoarse and her eyes shut. "Each nation takes a different view on kraft."

She tells me that there are some nations that honor kraft regardless of who holds the power in their blood. Some empires honor this kraft to the point that anyone who holds the power is taken to a temple worshipping one of the seven gods. They're forced to praise the gods in thanks for their abilities, kept away from those without kraft. To Olina, it's a different sort of slavery under a different name.

"It would be best if you kept your ability hidden," Olina tells me. "Dame Nage Aris is a devout worshipper of the gods."

*   *   *

I think I'm about to go mad when a bird flies overhead. Georg is so overjoyed that he nearly cries. Our darker skin was made for the sunlight on these islands, and it's rare for us to burn, but our skin has begun to peel and crack with nothing but the salt air and sun. Though only five or six days have passed, we've all lost weight. Olina looks like a skeleton already. Georg doesn't say it aloud, but he doesn't believe she will survive much longer, once we've made it to shore. I hope that he's wrong. Not only for Olina's sake, but for the sake of this entire war. We need her if we're to be successful in these negotiations with the northern empires. Without the north's help, we've already lost.

CHAPTER TWENTY-SIX

Land appears as the sun begins to set. As if the wind can feel our desperation, it becomes stronger, pushing us through the water and toward land. Awe overcomes me. The horizon is like the ocean, a sweep of land that seems never ending. The largeness of it feels unnatural. This is where the northern empires lie—where Koninkrijk, the land of the Fjern, rests. I can't see the Koninkrijk Empire with my own eyes. From what I've heard, the empire is the farthest north of the seven main nations. If the Fjern had stayed here in their land instead of leaving to conquer ours, so much would be different.

The docks of Rescela are crowded with fishermen and traders. They almost remind me of the docks of Jannik Helle, except that here, there's too much to see and too much sound. My eyes can't take in everything—the sheer number of people pushing against one another in the crowds, and the different sorts of people, too. I'm used to the beige and brown shirts and slacks of the islanders, the white dresses and shirts and pants of the kongelig. Here, the colors swirl and blend—reds, greens, blues, and all with different patterns. Some people wear jewelry, so much that it covers their otherwise bare chests. Others have markings and scars designed in their skin. The color of skin varies as much as their clothes. There are still the pale-skinned people who had originally come from the north, yes—but there are also tones as dark as an islander's, with golden brown shades in between. There's no separation between the people of different colors. They speak to one another as friends might, some laughing together, others bartering at stalls in the marketplace. I stare at everyone I pass, searching for any sign that those with pale skin might turn on their apparent friends at any second, take out a whip and beat them into submission. But nothing like this happens. I have a hard time believing that the islands of Hans Lollik are so close, and yet we have remained enslaved and oppressed and trapped in our own land. So few had been lucky enough to escape and survive both the waters and the Fjern. There's another emotion as well: anger, for the people who live here in their freedom. They have to have seen how we've suffered, but they did nothing but continue to live in their comforts. It's unforgivable.

Georg clasps a hand on my shoulder, reminding me of the urgency in finding help for Olina. She had mentioned the name of a woman who had already promised aid if we ever needed to come to the docks of the Rescela Empire. She is an islander who had escaped Niklasson Helle years before and worked an inn called the Krage. We leave our ship tied to the docks and push through the tangle of stone and wooden buildings in winding streets that are crowded with merchants and beggars and dirty-faced children and horses and chickens and starving dogs, the smell of piss and rum overwhelming my senses. Sigourney's kraft is too much. The thoughts and memories and emotions all mingle into a low hum that grows until it's a roar that fills my head. I have to put up a block to stop the wave after wave of thought and emotion. I can sometimes feel the spike of kraft in the crowd we push through, but I can't see who the kraft belonged to with every person shoving past and disappearing into the masses again.

We try to ask for help. Olina, her arm over Georg's shoulders, is half awake and so weak she can barely drag her feet. We
ask again and again if anyone has heard of the Krage, but the
response is annoyance and in some cases disgust. For the first
time in all my years, I don't think the disgust has anything to do
with the color of our skin. Others with skin as dark as ours and
darker only sneer, eyeing our tattered and sun-bleached clothes
and the way our skin clings to our bones. Others look at Olina
with fear, as if they worry her illness is contagious. Finally it's a
pale, gruff, and impatient man I hadn't bothered turning to that
helps us. I assumed he would ignore us the way so many others had, and I'd unconsciously been avoiding anyone with skin
as pale as the Fjern. But the man overheard me asking another
person with brown skin, and he points the way, instructing us to
follow the path of an empty alley until we come to an inn nested
between two larger buildings, where the image of a crow will
be painted on a sign. He warns us that it'll be easy to miss, and
he's right. We pass by the sign that swings in the breeze and have
to turn back.

Though the inn is hidden away, many of its patrons have easily
found it as well. The inside is loud with music, someone playing
a stringed instrument I've never seen and a man singing a song
that would've insulted the kongelig's delicate ears. Others laugh
as they sit at their tables, joining in with the song or shouting
over the music to hold their own conversations. I expect to open
the door and for faces to turn, for pale-skinned Fjern to stare us
down and demand where our masters were and why we weren't
where we belonged. But we only receive two curious glances
at most. Georg and I help Olina through the aisles of tables and
chairs, to the barkeep who wipes glasses busily. He reminds me
of my father. He's pale—pale skin, pale hair and eyes, and broad
shoulders. My breath automatically hitches in my throat at the

sight of him. But when he sees us approaching, he only nods in greeting before he notices Olina.

"Not sure she could handle another one."

Georg is too nervous to speak to the man directly. It's easy enough to see from the tension in Georg's shoulders and the pinch between his brows that he's also struggling with the number of people who ought to be our enemies.

"We're looking for a woman," I tell the man. "She's a friend of ours. Her name is Roos."

"Roos?" he says. I get the sense that he knows who she is, but that he's surprised to hear us call her our friend. I can see the click of understanding. He takes in the color of our skin, our thinness, and our worn clothes. He realizes that we're islanders of the south, and that we've escaped Hans Lollik. He hides his feelings on this information. I fear that he considers capturing and selling us to the Fjern. I wonder how aware the north is about the rebellion. If they realize we're in the grips of fighting for our freedom and our lives. If the barkeep does understand, he doesn't comment on any of this.

"Roos is on an errand," he says. "She's expected to return tonight."

Georg and I exchange looks. We don't think Olina will live much longer without the care she needs. The barkeep seems to see Olina in a different light. "We have herbs that could help her," he says, nodding his head at Olina. "Roos is always conjuring her herbal teas. People come from across the nation just for her medicine."

The man offers a room for us, and we tell him that we're grateful. Even as he helps us, I can't trust him. I still expect him to turn on us, to pull out a machete and attempt to cut open our stomachs. He opens a door to a small room draped in patterned colors that seem to vibrate. The barkeep leaves for a moment to get the herbs he's promised us, and Georg helps Olina lie down in the bed.

"Do you think he would bring the Fjern here?" Georg asks, not looking away from Olina's gray face.

"He could be Fjern himself."

He glances at me. "There are kongelig who escaped to the north. Alida Nørup. Cousins of the Solberg and Niklasson. He could be sending messages to them. He could say that slaves who've escaped are waiting like fools inside of his inn."

"We'll have to trust that he isn't."

"Trusting him could be fatal."

Georg could be right, but I don't see the point in arguing. The simple fact is that we need to trust in this man to help save Olina. It's the only option we have.

When he returns later, it's with a woman with dark skin, close to Olina's age. She's beautiful. She holds her head with all the regality of the kongelig, a shawl wrapped from her shoulders and across her chest. The only sign that this woman was ever enslaved by the Fjern is a scar that runs from her cheek and curves down her neck.

Roos doesn't waste time with greetings. She's immediately at Olina's side, kneeling beside the bed. She puts a hand against Olina's temple and uses a finger to force open her eyelids. Olina's breathing has harshened. Roos stands.

"Olina won't live," Roos tells us. "Say your goodbyes while you can."

Georg gives a bewildered expression. "Aren't you going to try to help her?" he asks.

"There isn't any point in wasting my herbs on her if the result will still be the same."

Georg opens his mouth to argue and to insist that Roos try to save Olina, but his tone won't help our situation. I put a hand up to quiet him.

"Please," I tell her. "We need her alive. For all of our sakes. For the sake of the islands."

Roos eyes me. "Are you hoping you'll persuade me by mentioning the islands?" Her eyes are dull, but behind her cold gaze I sense she holds memories she tries not to unleash. "Those islands are no longer my home."

"So you don't care about what happens to our lands? About your people still trapped there?"

"Why should I? You're the fools who still haven't managed to escape in all this time."

Anger swells in me, and I can tell that Georg is ready to hit Roos across the face, no matter that she's the only person in this room that can save Olina. I swallow the anger and close my eyes to take a breath.

"Please," I say again. "Olina said that we should ask for you if we ever needed help. She said that we could trust you."

Roos clenches her jaw as she looks from me to Olina.

"A waste of good herbs," she repeats, but she turns to the barkeep with her instructions for hot water and her supply. We watch as she creates a steaming mixture and helps Olina sit up in her bed to force the tea into her mouth. Most of it dribbles from her chin. I thank Roos, but she says she has done nothing worth thanks. She leaves me and Georg in the room with Olina. We watch as her breathing worsens, and Olina is dead within the hour.

Roos cries as a white cloth is placed over Olina's body and she's carried from the room. I'm surprised. The woman had been hardened when asked to save her.

"I knew that she wouldn't survive," she tells me. "There was no point in wasting the herbs. That isn't a sign of my feelings toward her. Olina was my friend."

They had been on the island of Niklasson Helle together, young girls who'd sworn to one another that one day they would escape the islands. It was one storm season that Roos saw an opportunity. There were trading ships from Rescela, and a man who had promised to help Roos leave for the north as long as she shared his bed for the time of the journey. She agreed, and she begged Olina to come—but by then, Olina had already joined the network of whispers. She'd helped plan the revolution, and she knew she'd be needed. She stayed. Roos never forgave Olina for this. She left her friend behind, angry that Olina would be so foolish as to stay in the islands for a war she knew they would not win. At the root of this anger was shame for abandoning her.

And now her friend is dead. Olina had been free for the first time in her life, the moment she arrived on the docks of Rescela—but she didn't realize her freedom before she died. Roos mourns Olina, but she doesn't see the point in these tears, either. Crying won't help me or Georg, and she understands the three of us came to the northern empires for a purpose. For the sake of Olina, Roos has already decided to help us in whatever it is we need.

"I was Olina's messenger," Roos explains. "Any letter she sent would come to me, and I would deliver the letter as needed. I can't read, so I never knew what the letters said, but I do know that Olina sent her messages to one person in particular. She believed that they were the most likely to aid us."

Roos speaks of Dame Nage Aris.

"The Rescela has been sympathetic to the islanders' plight," Roos says. "Olina was courting her. Asking her for resources, guards to aid in the war. From what I understand, Dame Aris has been hesitant. The Koninkrijk Empire and the Rescela Empire aren't enemies, but they aren't allies, either. Dame Aris could gain a lot of enemies from both the Koninkrijk and Rescela Empires alike if she were to help you."

Olina had been working on convincing Dame Nage Aris for months. All of the work she's done is gone with her death. I'll be starting a new attempt and a new relationship by asking for this stranger's help. Dame Aris has no reason to trust me—no reason to agree. The pressure is already building.

We stay only the night. Roos helps to arrange horses to take us from the coast of Rescela into the countryside where Dame Nage Aris lives. The trip would normally take a week while stopping at inns to rest along the path, but Roos understands the urgency and outfits us with the strongest horses, already marking spots on the map where we will stop to swap horses with people she calls friends who owe her favors. The ride out of the Krage and into the city is as overwhelming as the docks. The city is impossibly large, never ending. And even with so much space, it seems like there are more people. I wonder if this is why the Fjern in Koninkrijk decided to conquer other lands—if they simply ran out of space for all the people in these nations—but it doesn't explain why a nation like Rescela would exist as it does, without need of attacking and pillaging and enslaving others.

Eventually the city becomes a smaller town with wider cobblestone roads, and then that eventually ends, taken over by fields without any trees in sight. The grass seems limp and brown. The sun isn't as bright as in the islands. It's dim and pale and reminds me of the moon, with skies that are dull and gray. For all the horrors of the islands, I can see how they are beautiful in comparison to the north.

We ride into the night, Roos warning us of the possibility of bandits. We're lucky to emerge unscathed as it turns into morning. My body is desperate for us to stop. My hands cramp from gripping the reins, and my legs are sore, my back and neck aching. Pain shoots up my spine with every step the horse takes as it gallops, but I remind myself of the stakes: Stopping means taking more time to meet Dame Nage Aris—more time to convince her to help us, more time for her to send the guards and supplies if I'm successful, more time for the aid to arrive. And in that time, we could have already lost the war. Hans Lollik Helle could have already been attacked by the Fjern. Everyone could already be dead. I ride harder. Georg keeps his pace beside me.

After two days of riding, stopping only for water and quick meals of dried meat and to exchange the horses at inns along the way, we come to a path that cuts through the fields and to a single manor in the distance. Roos leads as we race to the house, slowing down as guards wait in the gardens to greet us. The guards are pale-skinned and carry swords at their waists. I tense, expecting them to attack, but they wave and speak in a language I've never heard. I'm surprised when Roos responds in their tongue.

She jumps from her horse, and I swing a leg over and jump to the ground as well. My palms are bleeding. I hold my hands as fists to hide the cuts. Georg looks faint on his feet, and I stand beside him, ready to steady him if needed.

"Dame Nage Aris's friend Olina sent two messengers in her stead," Roos says, switching over to our language. The guards seem curious, glancing at us, but I see no hostility in their gazes.

"Is Dame Aris expecting you?" one guard asks her.

"Unfortunately not, but we must ask to see her at once."

One guard nods to the other, who disappears into the manor. Barely a minute passes before he's returned with an accommodating smile and a gesture for us to enter.

CHAPTER TWENTY-SEVEN

The house is lavishly decorated, more so than any house I've seen, more than the inside of Herregård Constantjin. There are paintings every few feet with golden frames covering floral wall-paper that has details of birds and butterflies. The marble tile shines, our boots clacking as we're guided down one hall and then the next. We're taken into a sitting room of ribbon and lace. I almost don't see the woman sitting on her sofa. Her dress blends in with the extravagance of the room. She has brown skin, close to mine in shade, and a pretty smile that I sense she likes to use to get her way. There's something about this woman that reminds me a little too much of Sigourney Rose.

Dame Nage Aris stands and greets us like we're friends she's known all of her life. I'm taken aback—not only by this, but by the strong sense of kraft. I can immediately feel the ability Dame Aris has over persuasion. She's a woman who is used to having her way with the simplest of requests. Olina hadn't mentioned that Dame Aris had power in her veins. She'd said, in fact, that the woman was devout to her gods and could potentially have me sent to a temple were she to learn that I have a kraft of my own.

Dame Aris doesn't seem to notice my surprise. Olina had also warned us that the woman would be offended by our appearances, but she isn't fazed by the ragged clothes or the dirt and sweat and blood from our long journey.

"I'm so delighted to meet you," she says, her voice high like a child's, though she seems at least a few years older than me. She speaks with a strong accent that makes it difficult to understand her words. "I consider Olina a great friend. She's a brilliant woman. You must be special to be her friends as well."

I try not to be distracted by the woman's kraft. I don't want her to notice how nervous her power makes me. An ability like hers feels particularly dangerous. She could have me do or say anything of her choosing. If I don't manage to use my kraft against her in time, she could control my will completely. I'm not sure I should use my kraft to defend myself. She'd feel my power used against her, and her view of us could shift from friend to foe. We would not only lose any possibility of help from Dame Aris, but potentially be captured and imprisoned.

Dame Aris would expect me to bow in greeting. If Olina were here, she would be annoyed by my lack of northern manners. But I've never seen the point in mimicking the rituals of the Fjern. "Thank you for inviting us into your home."

"Don't be silly. I wouldn't have refused you. Travel is difficult on anyone, and especially for you. You've come from the islands of Hans Lollik, yes?" Her expression darkens when we nod. "The stories Olina has told. Some of them I can't believe."

In the time leading up to the revolt, Olina had come here to visit Dame Aris whenever she had the opportunity to accompany her Fjern master. She would slip away under the cover of night to visit Dame Aris and build a relationship with the woman, hoping that her sympathy could be useful when the revolt began.

"Hard to believe," Dame Aris repeats, "but the more I asked of others from those lands, the more I realized she spoke the truth. Horrible. My heart breaks."

I'm not sure what to say to this. Her heart breaks, and yet she still hesitates to help us. Olina must have been near madness with frustration. "Thank you," I tell Dame Aris.

Her eyes suddenly brighten. "But where is our friend? She didn't stay behind in those horrible islands, did she? I look forward to her visits."

I glance at Roos, who looks to the marble floor.

"Olina passed away," I tell Nage. Her shock is immediate. She gasps, and the tears that fill her eyes are genuine. When she asks what happened, I explain Olina's illness on the trip here and how it overcame her so quickly.

"She was a spectacular woman. A true friend." Dame Aris wipes her eyes, then claps her hands together. It's startling. Georg flinches. Roos meets my eye. She thinks there's something strange about Dame Aris. Something performative. She's right. The woman enjoys having an audience while she stands in the center of our attention. When I read Dame Nage Aris, she does honestly feel pain for her friend, but there's also a flurry of other emotions that are difficult to pin down. She isn't cold or calculating. It seems she operates on whim. This is more concerning.

"Let us celebrate Olina's life," she says. "Join me for dinner and drink. We'll toast to her."

The dining room has a table too large for the space, made of a lighter wood that I'm unfamiliar with. This is the least decorated of all the rooms, with patterned wallpaper and a golden chandelier that hangs over the table. There are others at the table as well. I hesitate, Georg and Roos at my sides, as Dame Aris sweeps into the room with a wide smile.

There are three guests. A woman who is pale and sallow and looks sickly, with thin black hair and a gaze that doesn't linger. It doesn't seem she would be the type of person to be a friend of Dame Nage Aris. The two men sit side by side, both with dark skin unmarked by scars, wearing bold patterned colors and strings of gold around their necks. They greet us with smiles as pleasant as Dame Aris's, but their eyes skim the state of me, Georg, and Roos—our clothes, the dirt and smell.

I speak for both Georg and Roos as well as myself. "We don't want to intrude," I tell Dame Aris.

"I insist," she says, gesturing to three seats. "Join us. The longer you take, the more time it'll be for us to have our food and our wine and celebrate the memory of our lovely Olina."

We sit as far from the others as possible at the ends of the table—not only out of self-consciousness, but because it's difficult to trust any of these strangers in this foreign land. The woman is introduced as Dame Ione Galatea. She speaks with an accent as well, though it's softer than Dame Aris's. Ione is the daughter of a wealthy merchant from the empire of the Aldies, sent here to Dame Aris's home to learn the etiquette of a fine lady of society. She is only recently of age and believes she was sent here by her father so that he could be free from her. The two men are Sirs Clef and Renate Vashel. Clef Vashel is from an old royal family, a distant cousin of the king of the Rescela Empire and a good friend of Dame Aris. The two men have the same family name, so it's easy to assume that they are related by blood. It's an assumption I can see in Georg, though not Roos, who is more accustomed to the culture of the northern empires. Relationships like these aren't unheard of in the islands. I remember two women I'd seen when I was a child one particular storm season, holding hands every morning on the bay of Hans Lollik Helle when they didn't believe anyone was looking. There was a day when I didn't see them on the sand. I later learned that they'd been caught by their mistress. One woman was sold to another island. The other had dove from the cliffs in her grief, her body washing ashore days later. The Koninkrijk Empire has not been accepting of this sort of love. They view this as an abomination.

It interests me that this isn't the same in all the northern lands. It makes me wonder if this sort of love might have been accepted in our islands before the Fjern arrived as well.

Clef Vashel has decided to be polite, though he doesn't approve of the dirt and smell that covers us. "What has brought you to the Rescela Empire?" he asks. "I have never met any islanders of Hans Lollik. Have they—" He hesitates, meeting his husband's gaze, then asks, "I mean to say, have the Fjern surrendered and given you your freedom?"

Georg barks a laugh. I can see this is inappropriate according to Rescela Empire manners. Georg notices as well, but he doesn't care. He thinks this was a foolish question, and he's right. "Do you think the Fjern would ever willingly give up the land and people they've stolen?"

Clef Vashel raises his eyebrows. "No, I suppose not. I didn't mean to offend you with the question, sir."

"Forgive Georg," I say. "We're all tired. We've traveled far to come here."

"And why did you come here?" Renate asks us. "If you're still at war as you say, then you must have risked much to escape the islands."

"I suspect they hope to start where our dear Olina stopped," Dame Aris says, feigning shyness with a polite smile, her gaze on the wine she swirls around in her cup. "That is to say, they hope to request my support in this war."

Clef and Renate meet each other's eyes with interest. Ione Galatea has not moved or said a word or looked up from her empty plate, but I feel her attention focused on us with intense curiosity. She's never seen an islander before. She's heard much of the war of Hans Lollik in recent days as news has traveled of the slaves who managed to kill their masters.

"But enough of that," Dame Aris says, clapping her hands. "Let us eat!"

Food is brought: chunks of meat, I'm not sure what, and vegetables and fruit in spices, red drink that I learn is wine created from a fruit called grapes rather than sugarcane. Georg, Roos, and I eat like we haven't eaten properly in days, because we have not: We rip into the meat, forgetting the manners of polite society. The others watch with some amusement, and more food is brought for us. As she promised, Dame Aris raises a toast to Olina's memory. She sips, watching me closely.

"I'm glad you're enjoying the food," Dame Aris says.

"Thank you for your hospitality."

"Not at all. Any friend of Olina's is mine as well," she says. "You should try the meat pies."

I'm hungry enough to eat anything on the table. But Dame Aris's slight smile and the silkiness of her voice has me reaching for the pie before I've noticed my hands have started moving. She watches me, satisfied, as I obey the order of her kraft. The discomfort of her being able to control me churns through me.

"What do you think of the Rescela Empire, Løren Jannik?"

I hesitate. It feels like we've begun the game of politics, and that any answer could affect her decision to send aid. "It's a beautiful country," I say. This is met with silence, so I realize it isn't enough—that I'm being too careful. "It's large," I add. "The size is overwhelming."

"Well, I suppose anything would be large when you're used to living on such small islands," Dame Aris says.

Anger pinches through me. Her tone is condescending. "They might be small in comparison to your homeland, Dame Aris," I tell her, "but they're still worthy of respect."

"I didn't mean to imply otherwise," she says with an apologetic tone. "I'm only curious about what you think. Interested in learning more about your lands. It must be strange, to see someone like me, who looks like you, with my freedom and my wealth."

She's proud especially of her wealth. I think of those on the streets of the docks of the city, the children starving and begging for food. People with brown skin might have their freedom in the north, but I suspect there's a different sort of oppression—one that isn't as easy to see, because it doesn't have the name of slavery. "It gives me hope for my people, that we can have our freedom one day, too." I say this because it's true, and because it's what Dame Aris wants to hear.

"There are some across the empires who are disgusted by the Koninkrijk Empire," Clef Vashel says, as if this is a consolation. "They argue on your behalf, that the Fjern cannot classify a group of people as lesser, or as slaves. But it can be difficult to force change in politics that aren't your own. The few Fjern in the north who do argue for your freedom are often branded as traitors and forced into exile."

"It truly is barbaric, the way they treat you," Dame Aris says. "The Aldies had a brief history of slavery as well, but they abolished the practice many eras ago."

At the mention of her homeland, Ione Galatea's eyes glance from her place before falling again. Dame Aris notices. She smiles. "What do you think of my friend, Herre Jannik?"

I look at Ione, who stares at her plate. I understand the meaning of Dame Aris. I'm surprised into silence. Dame Aris means to ask me if I find the girl under her study attractive and if I would be interested in bedding her. Because they are her friends, Clef and Renate understand as well. They aren't surprised by the question. They watch me, also expecting an answer. I can't tell if this casual invitation is a particular custom of the Rescela Empire I've simply never encountered, or if this is a particular habit of Dame Aris and her company.

"Dame Ione Galatea is beautiful," I say to be polite, and because I'm not sure how else I could possibly respond.

Dame Aris sighs like she's annoyed. "You don't actually believe that, do you?"

I look at Ione Galatea to see if her feelings are hurt, and they are—but she's also used to this treatment. She sits straighter without speaking.

Dame Aris continues. "I'm trying to teach her how to be more alluring to attract men who would be worthy of marriage. She can't live here at my house for the rest of her years, and she can't continue to be a burden to her father. I've had her practice with my servants."

Georg looks at me, confused. I can't meet his eye. I've never heard anyone speak so openly about matters of the bedroom before. Roos is more used to the ways of the Rescela people, but she also stares at the food that remains on her plate.

"Danon is the man's name," Dame Aris continues. "He's handsome enough. Anyone would be happy to invite him into their bed. But Ione acts as though I torture her."

Dame Aris is obviously amused by this. Clef and Renate seem to think this is amusing as well. They bend their heads together, hands grazing on top of the table without shame. Georg is transfixed. He can't look away. I have to admit, it's difficult to ignore. It's rare to see such open affection.

Dame Aris notices me watching her friends. "And what about you, Løren?" she asks. "Do you have a bedmate?"

"I don't."

Georg hides his judgment, but he thinks for a brief moment that I lie. He believes Sigourney Rose is my bedmate. I want to correct him, but I can't without admitting to him that I've read his thoughts and revealing to everyone in the room that I have kraft. Though none have been as hostile as the Fjern, I'm not sure if this would change if any were to learn the truth of my kraft. Dame Aris could be like Malthe: accommodating until she learns she's no longer the most powerful person in the room.

"I suppose it's difficult to find love in war," Dame Aris says. "But here, you're away from the battles. You could enjoy the simple pleasures. Ione still has much to learn, but if you find her acceptable—"

"No," I say. Others at the table look at me with surprise with the suddenness of my response. "Thank you."

Ione is offended, but she tries not to show it. Dame Aris watches me for one long moment, and I begin to fear that she'll decide to insist and use her kraft to make both me and Ione share a bed. I would have to use my kraft then—force her to stop her power of persuasion and reveal the power of my own.

But Dame Aris only gives a shrug. "Perhaps Danon would be more to your taste."

She means this to be polite and hospitable, but the words only turn my stomach, the food sour on my tongue. Without Danon here in the room, I can't see if he truly does this work by his own desires, or if this is work commanded of him by his mistress and her kraft. Perhaps there's a type of slavery here in the Rescela Empire as well, even if it's by a different name.

"Dame Aris," I say, "we're tired from our travels. I'm sorry to be rude, but would it be all right if we retired for the night?"

"Oh, of course," she says, though I can feel her disappointment. I realize that she saw us as her entertainment for the evening, as three exotic islanders with our strange ways. She stands and calls for the pale-skinned servant named Danon, asking him to take us to our chambers. Danon ignores us as he walks. He sees himself above us. He thinks that we're only slaves, while he's at least paid coin for his troubles.

We're shown to separate rooms. They're all as extravagant as the rest of the house. This is a wealth none of us have ever experienced. Beds like these, baths, and soft clothes laid out for us by servants—this is something a kongelig might expect, but never a slave. I feel guilty accepting any of this when my people are still suffering. There isn't any sense in living like this, pretending that I'm a king in a foreign land. But refusing the comforts wouldn't help anyone in the revolution either, and it might also insult Dame Aris, who takes pride in being a gracious host.

Roos is shown to a room, then Georg. He's so exhausted that he falls into the bed without bothering to wash or change before Danon closes the door. He takes me to the last room in the hall and leaves without another word.

My body aches and begs for the softness of the bed, but I force myself to wash first, sinking into a tub of warm water that stings the cuts that line my skin. The scars on my back from the whip twinge. My muscles scream. But as I sit in the warm water, everything relaxes. I close my eyes. I wonder about the islands— how those on Nørup Helle are faring, if Anke feels at home on Årud Helle with Voshell. I think about the others: Marieke, Kjerstin, Geir, and Malthe. I wonder if Malthe has already over-taken Hans Lollik Helle and if the others are safe. Marieke didn't hide her support for me. I worry that Malthe could punish her for this—find any excuse to have her whipped or killed.

I also wonder how the others will react to the news that Olina is dead. Disappointment, yes, and grief to be sure. They'll be angry with me and Georg, for allowing it to happen in the first place. I wouldn't blame them. I hold that same anger for myself. I should have done more to protect Olina.

I can hear the door opening in the main bedroom. I immedi-ately stand from the bath. My body is tense, expecting an attack. My kraft can sense that it's only Dame Aris, but I feel ready to fight. Surprise is what calms me when she walks from my bed-room and into the bathroom without hesitation. She sees me where I stand, naked. I sink back into the water, embarrassed, but she only crosses her arms and continues to stare. She isn't ashamed to say what she wants and expects from me. Shame flourishes in me, and there's also a curdling of fear. I close my eyes and see the bedroom of Patrika Årud. Even dead she fol-lows me. Dame Aris notices my silence and my discomfort.

"I forget that people not of the Rescela Empire have such peculiar views on bodies," she says. "There's so much shame. Get dressed. There's something I'd like to discuss with you."

She leaves me to dry. A clean shirt and pants were left by Danon, folded on a shelf near the bath. When I emerge, Dame Aris sits on one of a pair of chairs. A table with wine sits between. She'd considered making herself comfortable on the bed as she normally would but thought better of it. I'm grateful for that.

"Olina told me something I found interesting," Dame Aris says once I've sat. "She mentioned that there's kraft in the islanders of Hans Lollik. The Fjern would hunt each of you down rather than rejoicing in your abilities."

She pauses. I understand her true question. Olina must have forgotten how she had once described how the leader of the islanders had kraft. She'd hoped this would entice Dame Aris into helping us, persuade the woman that we were a blessed group deserving of support. Olina never expected that I would have to come here to the northern empires, or she wouldn't have so easily put something onto paper. And Dame Aris watches me, wondering if I am the leader Olina had spoken of and, if so, what sort of power I possess.

"Do you have the blessed ability?" Dame Aris asks.

Dame Aris has kraft as well, but she could still easily have me sent to the temples to worship her gods while keeping her own freedom. Still, I've never been able to lie. "Yes. I do."

"Tell me of your power."

I tell her. She's in awe. Dame Aris has always been intrigued by the kraft of others. She has an ability herself, she admits. "Being able to persuade anyone to do anything of my choosing has been truly useful."

I don't respond to this. The threat between us lingers in the air.

"You must be eager to discuss the state of the islands of Hans Lollik," she tells me. "I wanted to respect Olina's memory and speak with you on the topic. Fighting the Fjern was something she'd worked most passionately for."

I'm still shaken by the memory of Patrika Årud and of feeling like a scared child again, but this is too important an opportunity to miss. "Thank you," I say. "It must be inconvenient, to host us as guests and listen to our requests."

"It's fine," she says. "I did welcome you into my house, after all. I could have simply turned you away if I did not want to be your host. Tell me. What is it that you need?"

"Olina must have told you of our need for resources."

"Yes, she'd mentioned it," Dame Aris says. The way she says this almost suggests to me that Olina's messages hadn't been written with any urgency. I know that they were. This is only more of Dame Aris's games.

"We need guards," I tell her. "Supplies. Weapons, food. Without guards and supplies, the war is already lost. Olina believed that you would be willing to help us. I hope that she was right."

"She was right," Dame Aris says. "I do want to help. Still, this is quite a financial burden, and you must understand that the royals of Rescela won't be too pleased with me poking into the affairs of the Koninkrijk Empire." She pauses. "What will you offer me in turn?"

Her meaning is clear. I understand what she wants and what she expects. She thinks it will be an easy exchange: my body for only a night, for help to win our freedom from the Fjern. It might be an easy choice for others. I can feel the pressure to sacrifice myself, no matter the discomfort and disgust, no matter the rage of having my body used in the way it has been used, again and again. Sacrifice myself, for all my people and all our islands.

Dame Aris believes the choice is so easy she doesn't wait for my response. She puts a hand on my leg. It feels like my skin begins to rot beneath her fingertips. She's surprised when I take her hand and remove it. She's more surprised when I tell her no.

"I'm not interested in exchanging my body for your help."

There's a heavy pause where she processes my words. "Even for the sake of the rebellion?" she asks. "You said you would lose without my assistance."

"We might."

"Then this is a foolish choice," she says. "And selfish. So many depend on you, and all you must do is pleasure me for one night."

She doesn't see the similarities between her actions and those of Patrika Årud's, or any of the other masters on Hans Lollik Helle that took me into their rooms and into their beds. She doesn't understand the disgust that spills from me—the hatred to the point where I consider for a moment wrapping my hands around her neck.

Dame Nage Aris shakes her head, surprised. Her anger is abrupt. She's embarrassed. Enraged, that she's been rejected, and by someone of such a lower class as me. The Rescela Empire might not have slaves, but their society has found its ways to oppress others. I have no wealth, no status. I should be grateful, like Olina was, that Dame Aris is entertaining me. That she'd bother to have empathy for me and my people. Instead, I reject her. Such an insult cannot stand. Thoughts of possible retaliation flurries through her. She could have me captured along with Georg and Roos. She could deliver us to the Koninkrijk Empire so that we will be executed. Delivering the leader of the slave uprising is one way she could gain respect from the Koninkrijk Empire and influence among her peers. And she thinks about her kraft. She considers saying the words that would persuade me to join her in my bed so that she can use me and my body however she wishes. She decides that this is what she will do.

She opens her mouth and I feel myself pulling the words from her tongue. They strangle her, trapped in her throat. I draw her kraft from her blood and she feels herself weakening, eyes widening. The power stirs through me. I could say the words. I could tell her that she will help us. She'll send the guards of her allies and her resources to the islands to help us kill the Fjern and fight for our freedom. But the longer she sits, powerless, the more the need to speak falls inside of me. I can't take control of another person in the way that they would to me. I know the feeling of not holding control. I can't cause that same pain for another.

I release her. She gasps, breathing hard. I worry that her anger will only grow. That she'll call for Danon, or demand that I leave her house. But she only stands and leaves the room without another word.

Several hours pass. I sit and try to think of next steps, worried that she'll attack, but none comes. I call on Georg and Roos early before the sun rises. I don't explain to them what'd happened— only that we need to leave immediately and return to the islands of Hans Lollik. Before we can reach the front doors, I hear a voice behind us.

"I've sent a messenger," Dame Aris tells us without greeting. "A request to several families for the aid and borrowing of their well-trained guards. These are families who have owed me favors for some time, I might add. I expect nearly five hundred guards to be sent to the islands to fight the Fjern on your behalf."

I'm not sure what to say. Georg is overjoyed, but I worry that she lies out of cruelty in punishment for the previous night. But I can see that she's being honest. She steps forward, uncrossing her arms.

"I also have access to supplies. Dried meats and fruits will be sent from the coast by morning's end. They've been ordered to stop at each of the islands under your control before reaching Hans Lollik Helle. Hopefully they won't be overtaken by the Fjern."

"I don't know how to thank you, Dame Aris," I say.

She waves her hand impatiently. "It's only the right thing to do. Perhaps you could leave with the shipment of supplies. They've been ordered to move quickly. You could return to Hans Lollik Helle within days."

We accept her offer. Polite society would expect a longer display of thanks, but Georg and I are desperate to return to the islands, and Roos has already decided she would join us on the journey and help us however she can in Olina's memory. The guards help to retrieve our horses, and the lady takes the opportunity to speak with me alone and apologize for her behavior the night before.

"Too much wine," she says simply.

CHAPTER TWENTY-EIGHT

We return to sea. I'd spent so much of my life trying to escape these islands so that I could feel freedom. I can see now what I couldn't see then: I wouldn't have been free if I had made it to the northern empires. None of the islanders who live in the north are free, either. No matter where we are, we can't be free when the Fjern are still in our islands and when our people are still enslaved and tortured, beaten, killed. That isn't true freedom.

Georg stands beside me on the deck. He's glad to be returning to the islands, even if it's to war and possible death. The north was too overwhelming. He leans against the railings. This ship is much bigger than the one we'd taken with Olina. We have fresh water and food and herbs that Roos says will fight any illness we might have on the trip back. This only makes me think how we failed Olina. She should be standing alongside her friend Roos. She'd devoted her life to our freedom. It seems particularly cruel that she won't be able to see it to the end.

"There's no use in getting stuck in the past," Georg tells me. He has no kraft, but he can sense my melancholy and guess its source. "We can't be distracted by it."

"No," I tell him, "but we can be motivated by it."

I don't eat dinner. The rocking of the waves and the heavy salt in the air takes away my appetite, and besides that, the less I eat means the more food there is for the people in the islands who need it. The multiple ships given to us by Dame Aris, manned by her guards, will stop at each of the islands to give supplies, while more still will travel with me to the royal island for our plans to attack. The ships are faster than even the boat we'd used to travel north, and we move quickly, giving the villagers of Ludjivik Helle its share of supplies before passing to Nørup Helle. The people are still antagonistic after the killing of Zeger, but they're more receptive when they see the food we offer. More guards agree to fight for our cause, and Roos stays behind to overlook the distribution of supplies. She accepts my gratitude. Without Roos's help in the northern empires, we would've been lost and out of options.

The last of the ships and her guards goes to Årud Helle, where I also stop to check on Anke. She's thinner, tired—all of the villagers are—but she tries to put on a show of good spirits for me. Voshell explains that there was another attack that the islanders managed to fight just days ago, but not before the Fjern burned their groves and half of the houses they had rebuilt. I want to say with confidence that everything will be fine, especially with the assistance of Dame Aris, but this isn't something that I can promise.

"If things don't go as planned," I tell Voshell, "the ships will have to return to Dame Aris, if they survive the battles. I'll ask that they allow you to journey north with them."

Voshell is solemn when she agrees. Georg and I board the ship for our final stop to Hans Lollik Helle, staring at the island fading in the distance. So much has happened after leaving Hans Lollik Helle that it's almost easy to forget why I'd left. Malthe attempted to kill me, tried to take control of the island. Just as much has happened on my journey to the empires, I'm sure that much has happened on Hans Lollik Helle. The time away could have given Malthe a moment to breathe and think clearly—to realize that he'd made a mistake. The time away could have also given Malthe the moment he'd needed to take control of the guards, to kill anyone he saw as my ally. Marieke, Kjerstin, Geir—any or all of them could already be dead.

Georg leaves for the bunks belowdecks, but I can't sleep. I stand where I have all day, thinking of how I would stand on the rocks by the bay. The breeze has slowed tonight, and the surface is still, like glass, almost as unmoving as the sea from my dreams and my nightmares.

I feel a familiar pressure returning. We had been too far away for our bonded kraft to connect us, but as the days went on I can feel Sigourney more than I could before. I can feel her calling to me. Pain spikes in my skull. She's desperate. She's afraid. I move from the deck's railing, feeling like I might fall over the edge. My vision has already begun to waver, the pain in my head forcing me to stagger.

The deck changes. I'm in Sigourney's chamber of Herregård Sten. Sigourney hasn't been harmed, but she tells me that she's in danger. She prepares to leave Niklasson Helle, not by choice. She'd already left once, nearly a week before when she couldn't contact me but had a message she needed to share. It was a message that would affect the outcome of this revolution. She wondered why she couldn't reach me, why she couldn't feel me in the same way that she could before. She realizes the answer as she can see me as clearly as I see her. She sees how I'd left the islands for the northern empires and realizes that the distance between us created too far a strain on our bond. But she had not realized this before. She thought I was dead. She was afraid that an assassin had managed to be sent from Niklasson Helle without her knowledge and without her having a chance to warn me. She was genuinely worried—felt she had failed not only me but the revolution. Days passed without any certainty of what had happened to me, or whether the islanders continued to hold Hans Lollik Helle. She'd been trapped on the island with nothing but her spiraling thoughts and fears. She needed me if she was to ultimately survive the Fjern. If we did not win this war, then she would have no one to turn to. She'd be at the mercy of the kongelig.

Several nights ago, there came a moment when she finally couldn't take the fear anymore. She decided she would leave Niklasson Helle and arrive on Hans Lollik Helle herself to find me, Marieke—anyone—and learn what'd happened. Marieke had always taught her to have patience, but without the woman's guiding hand and no one around her but enemies, Sigourney had difficulty remembering this advice. She waited until night, when she knew Kalle would be asleep. The man had eventually relented to allowing her privacy as she slept at night, and stood guard outside of her door instead—but even he could not stand awake through the night. She opened the single window and climbed into the brush, the thick of the gardens, sneaking through the shadows and running for the bay, where boats were in lines on the sand. Coming to Niklasson Helle was easy: She got into a boat, which drifted on the currents until she was captured by the Fjern and brought to Niklasson Helle as a prisoner. She would be going against the tide for a journey that would last days, and it was more likely that her boat would capsize and she would drown. It was lucky, then, that Kalle found her.

"Elskerinde Jannik," he said. She'd been so wrapped up in her thoughts that she hadn't paid enough attention to her surroundings or the possibility that she'd been followed. Kalle had been asleep when she left her room, yes, but he had always been a light sleeper. The window opening made the slightest sound that had him on his feet. He knocked to no response, so went inside and saw that Sigourney had disappeared through the open window. He followed her silently, curious to know what it was she planned to do. Part of Kalle expected to see her sneak toward the slaves' quarters, to join a meeting of slaves and discuss their plans to revolt. But coming here to the bay and the line of boats, the answer was clear.

"Where did you hope to go?" he asked her. He hadn't bothered to take her arms and force her to march back to the manor. He knew that she could overpower him with her kraft. He knew that she could take control of his body at any moment and force him to hurt himself, kill himself, if she insisted on escaping. Sigourney did consider this for a moment, but she knew that attacking Kalle would also take away options for survival. His murder and her disappearance would make it obvious that she had attacked the man assigned to guard her. The Fjern would realize that she'd escaped the island, and she wouldn't be able to return to Niklasson Helle so easily. If the islanders did not accept her, not without her purpose as a spy, she would have nowhere to turn. Yes, keeping Kalle alive meant she had more chances to live.

He walked her back to Herregård Sten and called on the guards, who alerted their masters. Sigourney knew the Fjern wouldn't be happy to be woken at such an hour. Herre Niklasson had grown bored with her, not necessarily wasting the time in looking for an excuse to be rid of her but open to any reason if it were to cross his path. The man was brought forward to the main courtroom of the manor. He hadn't bothered to change out of his sleeping shirt and pants. It was too late in the night to care about appearances. Other kongelig who arrived had dressed quickly for the emergency calling. Jytte Solberg was there. She hadn't bothered to tie a lace ribbon around her neck, and the purple scar wrapped around her throat like a rope. Gertrude Nørup was there as well, smoothing her hair back uncomfortably. Aksel had come as well. He'd been awake anyway, drinking rum alone in his room, and he found her possible execution to be potential entertainment, just as pleasurable as it'd been to share his bed with Sigourney over the past weeks.

Lothar began the questioning without ceremony. "Why were you attempting to leave my island?" he asked her.

And she told him the truth. "I was attempting to contact Løren Jannik. I've lost touch with him, and I'm not sure if he's dead."

Aksel had startled at the mention of my name, though he didn't show the surprise that ripped through him except for the flicker of a glance.

"Why did you feel the need to attempt to leave this island in the dead of night? If you were truly speaking for the side of the Fjern and the kongelig, you could have come to me to express your concern."

"I can't be sure what will happen to me once I'm no longer useful. If Løren Jannik is dead, then so is your need for me."

"Let's be clear," Lothar said. "We don't need you."

She bowed her head to mimic deference. "Yes, of course. I only meant that I was eager to learn the state of Løren and the insurgency, so I planned to leave."

Lothar eyed Sigourney carefully. "Had you still been in close communication with the boy before his disappearance?"

"Yes."

"What was the nature of your conversation? What was the last thing you spoke of?"

Sigourney couldn't fight his kraft. She had to admit that she'd warned me and my guards not to attack Jannik Helle. And she also went on to say that it was a warning she had given, not for the sake of the revolution as she had told me, but for the sake of the Fjern.

"Your mistake is that you continue to underestimate the islanders," Sigourney told Lothar. "You don't believe me. You would have waited on Jannik Helle for them to arrive, thinking that your number of men and weaponry would overpower them and finally end the spread of the insurgency, but your men do not have the passion and fire of the people fighting for their homes and their lives and their freedoms. The slaves would have won the battle, even severely outnumbered, even without your weapons. You have not seen Løren Jannik with a blade. I have. I've seen him cut down dozens of men who stood in his path, and the commander of the guards, Malthe, is also difficult to defeat. The two together are unstoppable. I lied to Løren, warning him that the battle of Jannik Helle would not have been in the favor of the islanders. He believed me and retreated."

She tells me that this was a lie. She wants me to see that she'd managed to trick Lothar, because there was an element of truth in what she told him. It is true that we are an unstoppable force, and that we could have in fact beat the Fjern. But it's impossible to speak a lie to the man—impossible to trick him. It makes me wonder. Makes me think that, after everything, maybe Malthe had been right all along. Sigourney has managed to trick me into believing her, into giving her chance after chance, exploiting my constant hope that she will change.

"If this is true," Jytte Solberg said of Sigourney keeping us away from Jannik Helle, "then why hadn't Elskerinde Jannik told you this before? She does not waste any opportunity to prove that she's on the side of the kongelig and Fjern to save herself from the gallows."

Lothar looked to Sigourney expectantly, waiting for her response.

"And when would I have told you such a thing?" Sigourney asked. "I'm ignored here at court, mocked and isolated and left to my chambers with my guardsman following and watching my every move. It isn't so easy to ask for a meeting with you, Herre Niklasson."

Jytte rolled her eyes. "If Elskerinde Jannik had truly wanted to, she would've found a way."

Lothar agrees that this is a fact. Sigourney could see that the man already thought this meeting had gone on long enough—that he was moments from declaring he'd rather be rid of her and asking Kalle to take her head. She was desperate.

"I can prove myself to you. I can prove that I'm on the side of the kongelig. The islanders can't keep control of these lands. They don't have the ability."

"She's had more than enough chances."

"Allow me a chance to prove myself to you," she said. "I can give you something that you need."

Sigourney could see that Lothar's interest was piqued. He was curious to hear what she would suggest. He wasn't disappointed by the idea that she presented. She'd hesitated, afraid of the words that she knew she had to force from her mouth—afraid to make the offer when she'd have to follow through. "Allow me to lead a battle against the islanders."

Jytte Solberg laughed, and Gertrude followed, as she always did with Jytte. Aksel squinted at Sigourney, unwilling to believe she'd managed to find a way out of this. Disappointed, because he thought that she might have. He looked at Lothar, hoping that the man would realize that she was only trying to save herself, that she didn't care for the kongelig or the Fjern—but Lothar shifted in his seat, eyeing Sigourney.

He'd needed more commanders. The commanders were meant to be members of the kongelig, but no one on his island was willing to potentially sacrifice themselves for this war. They spoke of the necessity to win the islands back for the Koninkrijk

Empire, but it seemed no one was willing to do the work, only speak about it. The other kongelig were cowards, and Lothar Niklasson could not be everywhere at once, commanding each and every single one of the Fjern guards of these lands.

Jytte Solberg was the only member who was willing to command, but he declared he wanted her leadership here at Herregård Sten. The truth was that he didn't trust her with his guards. It would be too easy for her to take the guards to Solberg Helle, to attack his island and take control. She stayed where Lothar could keep an eye on her, and he continued to attempt to persuade the kongelig to risk their lives and lead the attacks. Sigourney Rose couldn't be trusted. A fool would be able to see that. But she did offer something Lothar needed: a kongelig willing to go to battle, no matter how unskilled she may be. And as she said, it would be a fine opportunity for Lothar to see with his own eyes whether Sigourney Rose would truly be willing to betray her own people for the sake of the Fjern.

When Lothar nodded his assent, Jytte stopped laughing.

"You must be joking," she said to him, forgetting any pretense of respect she might've had for the man.

"Why would I be, Elskerinde Solberg?"

"You can't trust Sigourney Rose."

"Jannik," Sigourney tried to interrupt. Aksel shook his head at the mention of his name, but Jytte responded.

"You may be married to that fool," she said without bothering to look at Aksel, "but you are first and foremost a Rose, which we would all do good to remember. You are the daughter of Mirjam Rose. You came to Hans Lollik Helle for revenge." She turned to Lothar. "And now you mean to hand this snake the control of your guards."

Lothar appraised Jytte silently, waiting for her to go on.

"Beyond that," Jytte said, "is the fact that Sigourney Rose has no ability to lead a battle. She's had no experience commanding guardsmen. None would survive an attack with her at the helm. You will be wasting your men."

"She can't be trusted, this is true," Lothar admitted. "But perhaps this is a moment that could prove otherwise. As for your second point, Sigourney will have the experience of guardsmen with leadership on her side. Kalle," he said, "will join the battle as well."

Kalle had stood against the wall at the back of the room, overlooked and ignored as he was used to. He showed no emotion or reaction to this news, though internally Sigourney could see that he wasn't surprised. Before being pulled from his duties to follow Sigourney like a lost dog, he'd been one of the top guardsmen of Niklasson Helle, on the path to becoming a commander on Malthe's level, though an islander never truly had much power, no matter what the Fjern declared. Kalle knew this as well as anyone else, but it was still a position he had yearned for and worked for, ready to play this game of the Fjern and the kongelig. He'd been frustrated in what he saw as a demotion, watching over Sigourney, though she could see that Kalle had been chosen by Lothar because the man was one of the few islanders Herre Niklasson could trust.

"She will have help," Lothar continued, "and besides that, she does have her kraft. Though it pains me to admit as much as it does any of us, Elskerinde Jannik's ability is powerful. It'd be helpful on the battlefield. She should be able to sense the plans of the enemy, help in controlling their movements and attacks."

"I'll admit that she's powerful," Jytte said with a cracked voice, "but she isn't so powerful that her kraft would allow her to win a battle."

And Sigourney could see that this was a risk Lothar was willing to take—not only because it was a test, but because if she didn't manage to survive, then he would also be rid of a problem that'd been plaguing him. He was interested to see if she would go to battle for the kongelig, eager for a commander to take the guardsmen and attack an island of the north—but he would be just as satisfied to hear the news that she had been killed.

Lothar allowed the barest of smiles. "I suppose we'll have to see."

CHAPTER TWENTY-NINE

Sigourney readies herself in her chambers. She doesn't wear her usual dress of white. She wears a shirt and pants as Jytte Solberg sometimes would with riding boots, her thick hair pinned to her head. It'll be easier to travel to Årud and then Nørup Helle, she lets me know.

This is where Lothar Niklasson has ordered her to go. Because I ordered the retreat from Larsen Helle, it'll be easy to bypass the island and sail north to Årud Helle. Anke, Helga, and all the rest of the islanders who had evacuated Hans Lollik Helle will be in danger of the attack. She'll arrive with her ships of guardsmen, courtesy of Jytte Solberg under the orders of Herre Niklasson. These are far more guards than have ever been sent to battle. "It's because I've warned them so many times that we underestimate the insurrection," she says. "Lothar wants to be sure that we don't underestimate this battle, especially with me leading."

I can feel the fear in Sigourney like it's a living creature that's crawled beneath her skin. She's realized the source of this fear as well as I have. Jytte Solberg has been using her kraft on Sigourney for weeks, slowly building that fear until it's become a constant level of panic. It's something that Sigourney can't control. She tries to breathe, to close her eyes and think through the fear, to realize that it isn't her own and that Jytte attempts to control her in order to sabotage her. This doesn't help as Sigourney hoped it would. She wishes she could meet with me—not only through our kraft, our bond, but in person. If we did, then I'd have the ability to block Jytte's power over her, though I'm not so convinced that all of the fear in Sigourney is there by Jytte's hand.

This wish is why Sigourney is pained saying what she feels she must. "You can't come anywhere near Årud Helle," she says. "I was ordered to destroy the island. I was told to kill everyone, it doesn't matter who. They'll all be dead in a few days' time. Lothar expects me to burn the island completely."

The number of guards being sent, when there are so few defending the island—the fact that it's Sigourney, and she must prove her loyalty...I'm disgusted. Not only by Lothar Niklasson and the kongelig, but by Sigourney herself.

"And you mean to actually go through with this?"

She's surprised by my reaction. "Yes, of course. You do see that I don't have any choice, don't you?"

"This is the lie you continue to tell yourself. Yes, you do have a choice not to lead a battle to an island and slaughter your own people."

"If I don't do as Lothar has asked, then he'll deem me an emissary and have me killed."

"Then be killed," I tell her. She's shocked into silence. "If that's the choice you have to make, choose the lives of your people—hundreds of innocents—over your own. Don't lead this battle, Sigourney."

The pause is long. She's angry with me—hurt, that I would say she should be willing to die so easily. To her, it means that I don't care whether she lives or dies. When it comes to this choice, she's right. "If I don't do this," she says, "someone else will. If it means keeping my life, then it might as well be me."

I'm not sure what to do or say to convince her not to move forward. She takes advantage of my silence.

"Besides," she tells me, "you have a choice as well."

I frown, understanding what she means—yet I still have to hear her speak the words herself. I can't believe she would be so bold to say it aloud. "What choice is that?"

Surrender.

She wants me to surrender—to abandon the uprising.

"You won't win, Løren," she says. "I can see that truth in you as easily as you see any truth in me. You won't win. You definitely won't win this battle of Årud Helle. Give up. Surrender, and save the lives of hundreds. You're angry at me for leading a battle to Årud Helle, but what of you? Choosing to revolt has cost the lives of innocents, too."

These could only be the words of someone who truly has no love or consideration for our people. This is someone who thinks of us as the enemy. I can't see Sigourney's view. I can't understand how she could believe, for a moment, that staying shackled is an option for these islands. I can hear Malthe's words—his belief that my trust in Sigourney would be the end of the rebellion and see us killed. And even now, beneath the rage I have for both Sigourney and myself, is the hope that she would see the correct path. The hope that she will redeem herself. I understand that hope can't overtake my sense. I can't rely on only hope to save Årud Helle.

"And so that's it," Sigourney says. "You refuse to surrender. You'll willingly send the people you so claim to love to the slaughter."

"I won't send anyone," I say. "I'll join my people as we fight for our freedom."

She feels sickened. "You'll die, Løren."

"If that's my fate, then I welcome it."

"What is the point of fighting if it's only to sacrifice your life? You won't win freedom for our people if you're dead. You won't live to enjoy freedom yourself."

"There was a time when you were willing to die for a cause you believed in," I say. "Your family. Taking vengeance against the kongelig. You risked your life by coming onto Hans Lollik Helle. If there's a chance that it will help, then yes, I'm willing to die, though it would mean I won't see the results for myself. This war is larger than just me or any one person. It's about all of us—all of the islanders. That's the difference between you and me," I tell Sigourney. "You fight for only yourself."

"I'm not like you," she says. "I don't have the love of anyone. I don't have the love of the islanders or the love of the Fjern. I have no one but myself. Marieke..." She pauses, and for a moment I can feel the pain and fury in the betrayal of the woman Sigourney had thought had loved her, though Sigourney cannot say she'd loved the woman herself. She continues. "Is it so wrong to fight for myself when no one else will? I won't die by the Fjern's hand for a people who have nothing but hatred for me. I will live, despite their hatred of me."

"So you'll risk dying for the Fjern instead?" I ask. She understands her thoughts are unreasonable. "You fight for them."

"They'll kill me if I don't," she says, "and besides that, fighting for the Fjern offers a future that your rebellion doesn't. You want to dismantle the hierarchy of the kongelig. It isn't fair to the centuries of work my family has put into striving harder, working to free ourselves. We fought our own battle for many generations. We played by the rules of the Fjern. Why should I be punished for that? You'll take away the kongelig and place me on the same level of all islanders. It isn't wrong to want comfort and luxury and power. It's only natural, isn't it?"

This is the first Sigourney has outright said she would choose the life of the kongelig. That if it'd been up to her, not much in these islands would be different, except that we would see one of our own on the throne, treating us in the way the Fjern have treated us for so many generations. This would be its own torture, its own pain—for one of our own people to betray us the way it seems Sigourney Rose plans to.

"I'd hoped you would change."

She has nothing to say to this, and I don't want to hear any explanations. The bond between us breaks, and I'm still on the deck of the ship that pushes across the sea.

CHAPTER THIRTY

Georg and I pull the sails, relying on the strong wind that carries us to the royal island. We see a tangle of mangroves in the distance. Georg is stiff beside me. I understand his concern. If Malthe has taken over the island, it'd be easy for any of the guards to shoot their arrows at us before we've made it to the bay.

No one does any such thing. It's too silent, in fact, when we push through the twisting roots that curve in and out of the water. I step out of the boat and into the murky shallows, pulling the boat onto the sand. It's a testament to Kjerstin and how well she's worked her men that I don't notice the scouts who must have seen us coming and who went to their leader to bring her to us. She seems surprised to see me, like she didn't think I'd come back alive.

"What happened?" Kjerstin asks as she comes to stand beside us. "Where's Olina?" Georg's gaze falls to the sand.

"An illness," I tell Kjerstin. "It happened quickly."

"I hope the spirits welcome her." She speaks softly. She's nervous, turning her head to look over her shoulder and at the groves. "I'm surprised you've come back," she says.

"Why?"

"It would've been safer if you hadn't."

I already know what she will say. "Malthe?"

"He's taken your absence as an opportunity."

"We knew that he might," Georg says.

"Marieke is imprisoned," Kjerstin says. "In the same room that once kept Sigourney Rose. I think he means for her imprisonment to be symbolic. He keeps Geir on a tight leash. I think that he's looking for a reason to disband the scouts. He doesn't trust that I have them under my control. He wants to command them as well."

A man so preoccupied with power would.

"I wouldn't suggest that you show yourself," Kjerstin tells me. "If he catches you—it's hard to say what he'll do for sure, but I don't want to find out."

"I have to confront him," I say. "I have to return to Herregård Constantjin. We have a larger problem. Have a guard release Marieke and escort her to the meeting room. Have the others gathered. Tell them that it's urgent."

Kjerstin can feel the significance of the situation. She agrees and leaves me and Georg alone on the bay. We traveled with machetes. Neither of us want to use them, but we have our hands resting on the tops of the handles nonetheless as we march from the beach and into the burnt and charred remains of the groves, to the training field and the barracks. The guards who work there see us coming. They still and whisper to one another when they see me. I'm not sure what lies Malthe may have told them. He could've said anything without my presence. He could've suggested to them that I'd abandoned the revolution, or that I was too weak. That I couldn't be trusted. We begin to climb up the slope of the hill, toward Herregård Constantjin. It's a blessing, I suppose, that no one has attacked us yet.

We go to the meeting room. Georg is more than worried. He's afraid that any of his brethren could burst through the door on Malthe's orders and attack us without hesitation. The possibility is real, but I'm ready to fight if anyone does attempt to take

our lives. We've barely sat when Geir walks inside quickly. He
looks at me, allowing me to see his thoughts plainly: He thinks
that I'm a fool to have returned as I did, without the protection
of multiple guards.

"Is he meant to defend you against Malthe's forces?" Geir
asks, nodding his head at Georg. "You do realize that Malthe
means to have you killed, don't you? You should have arrived
with a battalion at your side. Is this not what you went to the
northern empires for?"

"Yes," I say.

"And? Where are all the guards? Why is there only one ship?"

"The others were better served helping the northern islands
and preparing defenses."

He shakes his head, disappointed. "You're a good leader," he
says. "It's a trait that might find you killed."

"I'm hoping that Malthe will remember the rebellion before
his personal vendetta."

"Don't be so naive."

Before I have a chance to respond, the door opens again
and Kjerstin comes, this time with scouts and Marieke in tow.
Marieke looks thinner, the skin around her eyes purple and
swollen. She's stiff as she limps into the room, then takes a seat
with Kjerstin's help. She can barely look at me.

"Are you all right?" I ask her with a low voice. I curse Malthe,
but I curse myself, too. If I hadn't been such a coward—if I hadn't
left Hans Lollik Helle—none of this would've happened. But, then
again, I also wouldn't have received the aid of Dame Nage Aris.

Marieke gives a sharp nod, but it's clear that she's not. I remember how quickly Olina had deteriorated on the boat, and I ask for
permission before resting my hands on the woman's shoulders. I
try to imagine breathing life into her bruises and the shallow cuts
that line her skin, and I can already sense her sitting straighter,
her heart pumping in her chest. But my ability is only a shadow

of Anke's, and it isn't enough. I ask Kjerstin's scouts to bring her water and to ask for herbs to be brewed at the barracks. I can't lose Marieke. She's been too much the voice of reason in this room.

"Tell me what happened," I say. Marieke's voice is too hoarse to speak. She swallows, still pained. Kjerstin steps forward.

"The night you left, Malthe declared that Marieke's love for the former Elskerinde Jannik made her a traitor. I don't think that he really cared whether this was true or not. He was looking for an excuse to relate to the people, to punish someone and placate them, to make them feel that he was on their side. It was obvious what he was doing, but I couldn't speak against his decision. I knew that he would've declared me a traitor and had me imprisoned, too. It was lucky, I suppose, that he didn't simply have Marieke killed."

I think this is harsh for Kjerstin to say in front of the woman, but Marieke's stagnant face makes it obvious that she's shared the same thought. It's only been a week, thanks to the speed of Dame Aris's ships, but her haggard form is worse than Sigourney's had been after staying in that room for almost a month. I see that Malthe had forbidden anyone from giving Marieke food or water, except for the smallest of portions once a day. Two sips of water and a piece of dried meat. Malthe's excuse was that the supplies were already so low that they couldn't afford to waste their food and water on a prisoner.

The doors open again, and one of Kjerstin's men returns with a jug of fresh water. Marieke accepts the jug with shaking hands, but she's too weak, and it almost slips from her fingers. I step forward and catch the jug, then help to hold it to her lips. She swallows greedily, almost choking. She breathes a thank-you, but she doesn't look me in the eye. She blames me for this mistreatment. I should never have left Hans Lollik Helle.

"He's dangerous," Kjerstin said. "Malthe has taken too much power."

When the doors open again and Malthe steps into the room, it's obvious to all of us that he'd heard Kjerstin's words, though he doesn't react to them. A line of guardsmen follow him, then stand against the wall. No one has ever brought guardsmen into these meetings before. It's a show of power. A promise that he'll order the guards to cut us down if we do not obey his commands. For a moment, I'm afraid he won't bother with pretenses and he'll only order the guards to kill me immediately, but he doesn't acknowledge me. His gaze lands on Marieke.

"What're you doing from your prison?" he asks. "Who released you?"

"I did," Kjerstin says.

Malthe eyes her. He could declare that she, too, has betrayed us and order his guards to imprison both her and Marieke. Instead, he allows the slight carving of a smile as he sits at the head of the table, where he's always felt he belongs. His line of guardsmen stands behind him silently.

"Løren," he says. "Welcome back."

I'm waiting for the blow, for him to say something that will be devastating, something that will spark this battle between us—but he only eyes me, then Georg. "Where is Olina? Did she stay behind in the northern empires?"

When I explain that she's dead, Marieke gasps, genuine pain and mourning spreading through her. They hadn't always been close, and she hadn't always agreed with Olina's thoughts, but Marieke had respected the woman and had considered her a friend. Geir shuts his eyes for one long moment. This is a blow to the uprising, he sees. He understands that we'd needed Olina's ability to act as our ambassador. If we were to win, she would've been needed to help us establish allies with the free nations to ensure the Fjern wouldn't attack us again. Her death is a serious loss.

Malthe doesn't seem to be as shaken by Olina's death. He wonders aloud if I had something to do with her illness.

"Poison, perhaps."

Marieke and Geir don't speak. It would be dangerous for them to do so. But Kjerstin nearly laughs. "Don't be ridiculous. Why would Løren have killed Olina?"

"It's possible that he could want any of us dead," Malthe says, not taking his eyes from me. "Easier for the revolution to lose the war."

"Are you suggesting that Løren works for the kongelig and the Fjern?"

"The week that he's gone, run away from Hans Lollik Helle, is a week where there have been no lost secrets. He could be using his ability to tell Sigourney Rose our plans."

There's a heavy pause. I realize that in the time I've been gone from the island, whether they realize it or not, all the others have been influenced by my absence as well. Even Kjerstin wonders for a moment, briefly, if it's possible I'd tricked them all.

"There isn't any time for this," I say. The urgency in my voice makes the others pause. "There's another matter we must discuss. There's to be an attack on Årud Helle."

"How do you know that?" Kjerstin asks.

I feel the danger in saying the words, but we can't afford to lose more time. "Sigourney told me through our link." Malthe tries to speak, but I continue. "She wanted to warn me that the Fjern are planning a massacre. She wanted me to surrender Årud and Nørup Helle."

"If we were to do that, the kongelig will have won the war," Geir says. "It'd be easy for them to take the royal island if they take Årud and Nørup Helle."

"We won't give up the islands," I tell him. "We have to ready the guards. Recruits from the north have been sent to the islands."

Malthe interrupts. "All of this, for Årud Helle?"

I hesitate. "What do you mean?"

"The island isn't the most important of the others we hold. Let it go. We don't need Årud Helle to win this war. We could focus our defenses on the royal island instead."

"There are people there," I say, "innocent people who look to us for their protection. I won't just abandon the island for it to be destroyed by the Fjern."

"Fighting that battle could cost us the war if we were to lose the men we brought from the north," Malthe says, his voice rising. "The island itself is useless in this war."

"We will fight this battle," I say. "That is my command."

"You left Hans Lollik Helle. To me, that means you have willingly given up your command of this island."

"You're wrong in that assumption," I tell him. "I'm back, Malthe. Either have me killed, or fall in line."

It's a risk. Malthe considers having his guards step forward. It would be easy to kill me, easy to kill any of the others in this room who try to stand in his way. But still, he hesitates. I can see it clearly: He's told the guards that I wasn't to be trusted, that he believed I was a spy and that I escaped so that I wouldn't be captured, but not all of the guards under his rule believe his lies. He doesn't have enough under his influence to win complete control of this island with my death. I've cornered him, but what's most concerning is that he doesn't seem to be worried by any of this. There's something else here. Something that I'm not seeing.

He nods. "We'll prepare for battle at once."

Marieke asks me not to leave Hans Lollik Helle again. Geir tells me that, strategically, it would be best if I did not join the battle of Årud Helle where, even with the help of the north, the chances we will lose this battle are too high for me to risk my life. But I wouldn't feel right, sending guards to what could be their deaths without joining them. That would be the true betrayal. Kjerstin's scouts leave for Årud and Nørup Helle to pass the message of command. If all goes as planned, they will be prepared for battle by the time we've arrived.

I stand in my room in Herregård Constantjin for what could be the last time. I stare at the seas from my balcony. My mother hasn't come to me in days. Malthe accuses me of being the traitor. I wonder if this is what my mother considers me as well. If she's disappointed in my choices and actions. If she's forsaken me, as I've forsaken the uprising. I see him behind me, as I've seen him so many times before, I realize—desperately needing to remember but always forgetting. He tells me that he wishes he could kill me and be done with it, but his master is excited to see the battle of Årud Helle. He leaves me, and as the familiar black haze covers my vision, I still try to remember as I feel the memory slipping away.

I leave my room. A figure waits for me in the hall. I spin, expecting the blade of an assassin, or Malthe himself, but it's only Marieke. She limps forward, her bones weak. It's only been two weeks, but Marieke looks like she's aged several years.

She has a similar thought. "You've changed," she says, her voice still hoarse. "There's a look in your eye. The look of a storm."

Marieke walks with me down the hall. "I was near death," she says, "and I almost joined the spirits. When I closed my eyes and dreamed, I could see everything, feel everything. I could see you. I could see that I was wrong. You were not ready to lead us." She pauses, her eyes roaming my face. "The spirits spoke to me. They warned that we would not win. Not this uprising. In the future, yes. There's always hope for the future."

Marieke doesn't say this to hurt me. Only to relay what she sees as the truth. "Sigourney will be leading the attack against Årud Helle," I tell her.

She closes her eyes and takes a deep breath to fight the wave of emotion that crashes into her. The fear for Sigourney, the anger at herself for continuing to worry about and care for the girl, the rage at Sigourney Rose herself. She has betrayed us time and time again when we have given her the chance to redeem herself. She's taken advantage of our mercy without hesitation. Marieke has anger for me, too. I should have killed Sigourney that night of the revolt. Then we would have moved forward as planned. We wouldn't have attempted to take power from Malthe for the sake of Sigourney's life, and Malthe might not have lost balance of himself, attacking anyone he thinks a threat. Marieke wouldn't have wanted me to be the leader of our people. And the spy, the traitor—I have no proof, but it's possible that it really was Sigourney all along. She could have lied about the image she'd seen of the figure on Niklasson Helle. She could have found a way to trick me, taking me for a fool as she relays all of the information she can to Lothar Niklasson.

"It's too late to admonish ourselves," Marieke says. "There's no point in thinking of what we've done wrong, and what we should have done differently. We have a chance to right ourselves. The battle of Årud Helle."

I understand what she wants me to do without her saying the words aloud. We must win the battle against the Fjern, yes—must protect our people and the island, must keep the kongelig from taking control of the north. But this time, once we've won the battle, I can't show Sigourney Rose mercy. We can't allow her to live. Not any longer. It pains Marieke to admit this. It hurts a part of me, too. Not because I have any love for Sigourney, but because I must admit that I was wrong. I was wrong to continue showing her mercy, wrong to think that she would see the truth and join us as an islander, wrong to hope that she would use her power to free her people. She has done none of that, and must witness the consequences unfold.

Marieke has one last hope for Sigourney. "Don't let Malthe kill her," she says. "He'll draw it out, make her feel pain. Kill her yourself. Make it quick. That's the one last mercy we can show her."

CHAPTER THIRTY-ONE

I stand at the helm of a ship that leads us north to Årud Helle. Four ships are situated behind. Malthe leads two ships and Geir the other two to flank the eastern and western ends of the island. Scouts have already sent word that the ships led by Sigourney Rose—ten ships in all—are approaching from the western end of the island. She will likely not hesitate to begin attacks on the people. Guards have been sent ahead of us, to warn the islanders and evacuate them north to Ludjivik Helle, but I worry there won't be enough time before the battle begins. There is no specific location, no field where we must meet. All of Årud Helle is to be the arena.

"Are you sure we should do this?" Kjerstin asks beside me. "We could focus on evacuating the people."

"We can't lose Årud Helle," I say. "Not to the kongelig. Not to Sigourney Rose."

Kjerstin wonders for a moment if my decision-making has been taken over by emotion, by an anger I have for the woman and a desire for revenge. She wouldn't be wholly wrong. But more than anything else, I feel a need to punish myself. This is my punishment. Doing what I'd hesitated to and righting my wrongs in trusting Sigourney.

"As long as innocent lives won't be sacrificed unnecessarily," she says, thinking of the guards who will be thrown into this battle. Some have already decided that we will lose. Sigourney comes with enough ships and guards to defeat all of the northern islands. We have half of her weapons, half of her supplies, and half of her men. There's potential for this to be a massacre. When word initially came of the number of ships and guards the Fjern had sent, there was an uproar among the guards. They were angry that we would send them to die. But I reminded them of the battle of Hans Lollik Helle—reminded them how, each time we've been outnumbered, we have found a way to win. We don't lose to the Fjern because we have more at stake than them. The battle of Årud Helle, I declared, would be no different.

Boats carrying islanders have begun to leave the bay, passing us on the waves, people looking up at us as they pass. A line of smoke wafts into the air from the beach. The signal that more than half of the islanders have been evacuated. Guards on the island will continue to evacuate and protect those that haven't been reached yet, but we can't wait and give Sigourney the chance to gain ground. The sails unfurl and the wind sweeps us closer to the shallows. Boats are lowered and we row to shore, past the gnarled coral that scratches the bottom of the wood. Men climb over the sides of the boats to pull us the rest of the way, onto the sand. The ships led by Malthe and Geir do the same along the curve of the beach. Our voices echo. There's no point in staying quiet. Sigourney knows that we're here as well.

We march forward. There're few places to hide on this island. A line of coconut groves block perfect vision, but there are still villages in the distance, empty of the islanders who had taken the homes from the Fjern. Kjerstin marches alongside me. She wouldn't listen to the insistence that she stay on the ship for her own safety. She doesn't care that she hasn't been trained as a guard.

"If my scouts are here, then I will be, too."

We reach the first of the villages. Most of Årud Helle relied on fishing, with villages along the bay and the sea with docks. Looking at his maps, Geir told us that this would be one of the few inland villages, which could be used as a good checkpoint and base for our second wave of guards as the first pushes on to meet Sigourney. The village itself is eerie. Though it should be empty only because guards had been sent to evacuate the people here, I smell death. Kjerstin is tense beside me as well. There's a thin line of smoke from a stove with a fire that still burns, and penned chickens peck at the ground, goats chew on dry grass. As I walk forward, I see a hand lying on the ground. The hand is connected to the body of a dead girl, resting on her back, her eyes stuck open in fear. I turn the corner, and bodies of islanders are spread across the dirt. The five guards sent to warn them are dead, their heads placed in a line for display. I'm barely able to shout a warning when the first arrow flies. The arrows thud as they sink into flesh and bone, shouts and screams filling the air. An arrow aimed for my neck scratches my skin. I clasp a hand over the cut and throw myself at Kjerstin, both of us falling hard to the ground as arrows fly around us. We're still in the dirt when shouts rise, and Fjern guards run from the houses of the village, machetes raised. I kick at one that comes for me, and as he stumbles back I snatch an arrow lying in the chest of a dead guard and thrust it into the man's stomach. I spin and cut the chest of a Fjern. All around me is the chaos of battle.

A Fjern is on top of Kjerstin, a knife at her throat. She pushes the man off, and when he falls, a dagger is in his side. She follows, yanking the dagger from his skin and puncturing his throat. She smirks at me before her eyes widen. It's the only warning I need to turn, machete out, to cut my blade halfway through a Fjern's neck. It's lodged in bone and is difficult to yank out. A Fjern yells as he runs at me, blade high above his head. Kjerstin throws herself at him, the machete narrowly missing my shoulder. I abandon my machete to follow, the memory of the night I'd found Kjerstin on the bay with a wound in her side fresh in my mind. By the time I've reached them, the man coughs blood that sprays across Kjerstin's face.

She falls back, breathing heavy. The groans of the dying surround us, the last pleas for mercy as our guards cut the remaining Fjernmen's necks. About twenty of us remain. We lost guards, but not too many to continue—not so many that we have to give up hope yet. Ten guards are to stay behind, as planned, to keep hold of the village in case we lose our battles and Sigourney is able to continue pushing forward. I try not to think of what it would mean for us to have lost our battles—that I and Kjerstin and all the men around us who march forward would be dead. I wonder about Geir and Malthe—hope that, if they've encountered ambushes, they've also survived. We'll depend on them once the battle with Sigourney begins, just as they depend on us. If neither has made it through, then we'll have already lost.

The thin forest of coconut and palm trees offer little shade from the harsh sun. Only sharp shadows sway back and forth across the gray dirt, mixed with the sand of the bay. The trees here are brittle and dying, and the coconuts that have fallen are rotten, untouched by any bird or lizard that might've found the seeds. The entire island might have once belonged to a mangrove forest. Those trees are dead and gone, but I can still see where the tides may rise on nights when the moon is full, polluting the soil with its salt. Through the thin trees, I see movement. I hear hushed voices. There's a whisper behind us, then to the side. I put out a hand to halt Kjerstin and the others. The whispers stop, but I can see the Fjern half hidden behind the trees. They realize we've seen them. They step forward, machetes drawn.

One man, taller and thinner than all the rest, eyes me. "We're in luck," he announces to his men. "I believe we've found Løren Jannik."

I see it clearly, how he believes he will be rewarded favorably for finding me and capturing me, tying me up and bringing me to the Fjern, not to Sigourney Rose—he tries not to think of the insult of an islander commanding him and the other guards when they should be commanded by someone with skin as pale as theirs. But he would take me and gift me to Lothar Niklasson himself. He hopes for a promotion and special treatment. He thinks that if I fight and if he's forced to kill me, he'll simply deliver my head to Herre Niklasson instead.

We're evenly matched. They walk to us, enclosing us in a circle. Kraft stirs inside of me. On my order, we run at each of them with shouts. There's a clang of blade against blade, grunts and yells of pain, the slice of flesh and fresh blood in the air. I lose myself. I could close my eyes, and I would see my body from the eyes of the Fjern who surround us. I can see the way I swing and turn, the way I cut down one Fjern and the next like a vengeful spirit released on this world. I don't stop until each of the men are dead, and I've taken the commander's head.

When the fighting is done, I'm met with silence. Kjerstin stares at me openly. This isn't the first that my people have seen me fight this way. The fear mingles with respect, and in this instant, relief. We're all still alive.

It's when we leave the thin forest of trees that we see Geir and the men he's led to these woods. A quick scan lets me see that Geir hasn't lost a single guard, though he relays a similar ambush that had caught them as they passed a fishing village on the coast. His kraft for strategy made it an easy fight.

"And Malthe?" he asks.

"We haven't seen him."

"He might be in the thick of battle," he says. "What do you want to do? Shall we wait for him, or should we push forward?"

"Isn't it odd, Løren," Kjerstin says, "that we haven't yet seen any sign of Sigourney Rose?"

"It's possible that she waits on her ship while she's sent the guards in to do her work," Geir suggests.

I wish I had thought to question any of the guards we had killed, though there wouldn't have been much opportunity to do so with their blades at our necks. There isn't any way to be certain, but I don't believe Sigourney would have stayed behind.

"She has something to prove to Herre Niklasson. She would want him to hear how she led her guards into victory against us."

"If we do manage to capture her, I hope you'll give me the pleasure of kicking the chair out from under her," Kjerstin says. She means this blithely, but the words feel harsh. I understand now that I can't show Sigourney mercy. She needs to die. But it isn't a laughing matter to me. Kjerstin can see this, but she doesn't care. She thinks I should've killed Sigourney Rose long ago, and she's right.

"We're wasting time," Geir says. "We need to find Malthe and his men and see where Sigourney hides."

We begin to march, nearly sixty of us in all. There isn't any way to hide from anyone who might be watching, so we don't bother to try. We move through the fields of dry and brown grass, dirt beneath our shoes at times like dried clay, peeling under the hot sun, and at other times moist with saltwater that has leaked in from the sea. We come to a saltwater stream. A body floats down the river—an islander, not one of the guards but a villager who had lived here before the battle. As we watch the body pass, Kjerstin whispers a prayer. But another body comes, and more, until the stream is filled with corpses. Geir puts a hand over his nose and mouth. He thinks he might be sick.

"Fjern bastards," Kjerstin says. "All of them." The pain sparks an anger that becomes a fire tearing through her. She's tired. Tired of seeing her people slaughtered like animals, abused like they are not beings deserving of the respect of life. She wants to make the Fjern feel as she does. She wants to see their bodies stretched across all the islands and the sea.

I wish that we could stop to pay our respects, but this can only mean that the villages to the west, where Malthe was meant to send them to the coast, has been taken by Sigourney. I assumed she would split her guards as we did, coming to the center of the island herself with her more powerful forces, but she isn't here, and this is a sign that she has taken all of her guards to skirt around the coast instead. She might have guessed at our strategy and means to kill Malthe and his guards first, cutting down on our number and making it difficult for us to fight back. Kjerstin and Geir see the error we've made as well.

We move west, where the land becomes uneven with rock and stone, paths that slope up hills and then fall sharply. This was planned by Sigourney as well. This is difficult terrain to enter, and she will be waiting here for us. She already has the upper hand. The fear in me steadily grows, but we have to continue.

Kjerstin wonders if we should surrender. We've saved as many of the islanders as we could. We should leave while we still have our lives—regroup, even if it means abandoning Malthe and his men. We have the guards from the northern empires, with more promised on the way. If we lose this fight, we'll be halving our numbers. She wants to say it. She wants to suggest that we retreat. But she suspects that I'm already in her head, reading her thoughts, and from the way I meet her eye, she has her confirmation. She sees that I won't surrender, so she saves her breath for the climb through the rocky path.

CHAPTER THIRTY-TWO

At the top of a hill we climb is a plateau. The wind whips over the field of dry grass. I can see the slope of a valley, leading to the bay, where Malthe's ship is out at sea. But there is no sign of the guards—no sign of Malthe, either. Kjerstin meets my eye with confusion. My heart pumps in my chest. Something isn't right. We came prepared for battle, only to be met by ghosts.

Geir looks about nervously. "We should go," he says. "Return to the east and wait to hear word on where Sigourney Rose is on this island."

I'm about to agree when I hear a clattering. Across the field, climbing up the valley, are Fjern guardsmen. Line after line, they march. Forty, fifty, sixty, seventy of them—and still they come. They overwhelm our numbers. And in front of them all is the woman with dark skin who wears the white of the kongelig. She walks like she's both a prisoner and a queen. The men she commands stop behind her, but she continues forward. I understand what she asks of me. I walk to meet her.

She stops midway, waiting for me to close the distance. I hold my kraft's wall between us carefully. If she manages to slip through the smallest crack, she could take control of my body and have me cut my own neck. She watches me intently.

"You don't have to protect yourself from me," she says. "Take the wall down. I won't attack you. It isn't proper etiquette."

"I'd rather not take my chances."

"You'll exhaust yourself before the battle begins," Sigourney says. She eyes me, and I give myself a moment to take her in as well.

This is the first I'm seeing Sigourney in person in almost a month. She looks different from the version I'd seen through our kraft. She's thinner. She looks older, too. Marieke had seen a storm in my eyes. I'd been disillusioned. I can see the same effect in Sigourney. Though we'd never been children, had never been allowed the childhoods of the Fjern, we still had an innocence and a naïveté of ourselves and what we expected of others. That's different. Sigourney believed that she could someday be loved and accepted by her people as she sat on a throne of our bones. She realizes now how she never will be. She thought she would force the respect of the Fjern—of Lothar Niklasson and Jytte Solberg and Aksel. She knows they will never respect her. The truth creates a dim coldness in her eyes. She'd killed before, ordered executions and whippings while telling herself she simply had no choice. She realizes that she'd wanted to before. There isn't any point in hiding her own cruelty from herself, no point in hiding it from others—especially when they're her enemies. She looks at me, and she sees her enemy.

"You're different, Løren," she tells me. "You've changed."

She can see how I've tried to embrace the same coldness. She can see how I've failed. It's only out of necessity that I think I must kill her.

"I'll give you a chance to surrender," she says. "Allow me to bring you to Lothar Niklasson, and I'll let all of your guards go."

"Where is Malthe and his men?" I ask her.

Sigourney gives me the sliver of a smile. "He didn't leave his ship."

She speaks the truth. Fury beats through me. Malthe didn't attack. He meant to abandon me and Kjerstin and Geir and all the rest of us to this island, knowing we would need him and his forces to have any chance of winning. This was his plan. He doesn't want me to leave this island alive.

"You should know better than to trust someone like Malthe," Sigourney says.

"As I should've known better than to trust you."

She shakes her head. "The option I offered you might have saved your life," she says. "Had you surrendered—"

"You made the suggestion knowing it wasn't an option."

My words upset her. "That," she says, "is precisely why you've already lost this war. You're beholden to this idea you have of yourself, Løren. You think of only being the good person, the one who is not the villain in this story, without realizing that wanting so desperately to do what's right is just as selfish. You don't do what's right for the islands or for your people. You do what's right for yourself. Because you want to feel good about the moral path you take and your actions, whether they're the right choice or not. It's why you will lose this war."

I see a glimmer of my mother, enraged that I have not burned these islands to the ground. Sigourney leaves me there, returning to her guards across the field. I turn as well, marching back to Kjerstin and Geir, who both watch me, waiting for my orders. I don't want to believe that Sigourney is right. She could not use her kraft on me, but maybe this was her way of forcing herself into my head. She has still confused me and made me second-guess myself. I'd thought it was the right choice to go to battle with Sigourney, but her words cloud my mind. She could be right. My choices have only been selfish. I fight Sigourney, not only for the islands but for my pride.

Across the field, Sigourney is readying her men. She walks in front of the line, giving commands. We still have time to surrender. She said she would take only me prisoner and release my guards. They'd be able to escape, and Malthe, though he betrayed us here on Årud Helle, would be able to return to Hans Lollik Helle and lead our troops to victory. The rebellion doesn't need me. I've told myself lies for why I must remain the commander, but I ignored that it was only ever my desire to have a role—to finally belong—that has fueled so many of my actions.

The shame eats through me. I say the words to Kjerstin. "We won't win this battle. We must surrender."

She's shocked into silence. I can feel the disappointment emanating from Geir.

"We've come all this way, Løren," she says. "Fought our way here."

"They have twice as many guards."

"It hasn't stopped us before."

I shake my head. "I can't risk such a loss."

When I face Sigourney's lines of guards, humiliation rages through me. I take one knee, then bend the other—the sign of surrender and defeat. A ripple of emotion stirs behind me. My guards had been ready to fight. Ready to die. There is some relief. Some hope that they will live. But there's an overwhelming wave of anger. I'm a coward to go to my knees to the woman who is a traitor to our islands—disgusting, to willingly lower myself to the Fjern. I should have been willing to fight to the death.

But it's the choice that I've made. I'm not sure if it was the right choice, but if it means the lives of the guards behind me, I'm willing to lose their respect. I wait on my knees, wait for Sigourney to give the call of victory and allow my men to retreat with Kjerstin and Geir. From across the field, I can see the pity in her smile. She raises her hand, and by the time she's brought it down, a rain of arrows falls on us.

An arrow pierces my shoulder. Pain flashes through me, and

the men behind me scream. An arrow has gone through Kjerstin's leg and she's on the dirt beside me. I can't think with the pain that takes over every nerve in my body. I pull out the arrow just as the Fjern descend on us. Sigourney Rose has promised Lothar a massacre. A massacre is what he will receive.

I thrust the arrow like a spear and pick up my machete, cutting down the Fjern that swarm us with my good arm, but I begin to see that this is a battle we will lose. Men behind us yell in death. Geir is lost to the masses of bodies pushing against us, dirt flying through the air, blood slicking the grass. Kjerstin fights beside me, a cut to her side and her arm, her face bloodied and panic in her eyes. She never believed she would make it through this war alive, but this doesn't mean she was prepared to die.

Air is stuck in my throat. I begin to choke. I drop my machete, hands at my neck. It feels like someone is strangling me. In front of me is Sigourney. She appears before me like a spirit. There is chaos surrounding her, battle swirling around her as if she is the cause of it as she remains free of dirt and blood. There's an apology in her eyes. She believes this is the most merciful way for me to die. If I continue to fight the way I do, I will survive the blades of the Fjern. I will be captured and imprisoned and brought to Lothar Niklasson, where I'll be tortured by the kongelig. She thinks she shows me a mercy, taking my life this way. Yet as she can feel her kraft flow through me, her eyes still widen in surprise when she gasps. She puts one hand to her neck as she realizes she can't breathe.

She sends me the simple order. *Release me.*

If I die, you die with me.

She chokes, falling to her knees. She's taken lives with her kraft, but she has never experienced someone using her power against her as I do. Tears sting her eyes.

Release me!

When I feel air rush into my lungs, I nearly fall with relief. Sigourney stands, infuriated, but I grip the handle of my machete. She looks from the blade and to me. Just as I raise the blade to throw it at her chest, she seizes my arm with her power. I can feel her trying to force the machete toward my gut, but I fight against her kraft, straining to keep the wall in place. She's a towering force, and I'm exhausted from the day of battle, distracted from the pain in my shoulder—

There are shouts from the valley. Sigourney releases me in surprise. I throw the blade, but she gasps and takes hold of the body of a Fjern that fights near, forcing him to trip over his own feet and take the blade, slicing into his mouth. He falls dead, and Sigourney looks from me and to the troops that run from shore. Malthe is in the lead. While she'd been distracted with our battle, none of the Fjern realized that Malthe was stealing toward us.

I realize this was Malthe's plan from the beginning. Allow us to take the brunt of the battle, to nearly fall to the Fjern, so that we can cut down the number of guards he would have to fight when he arrived. He would be seen as a hero to the guards—the commander that has saved their lives. Any question of why he hadn't been here as planned would be forgotten once he's killed Sigourney and the Fjern that follow her.

The sight of Malthe revives us. The battle hardens, and Malthe strikes down any Fjern in his way. He focuses on clearing a path straight for Sigourney. She can see this as well. She tries to take control of Malthe, but I hold my wall against her, allowing him to come closer. But Malthe, with his effortless ability with the machete, is still overrun by the guards in his way. There are still too many of them, and any revitalized energy falls to the waves of Fjern that keep coming and coming. The field is filled with corpses. Bodies blanket the ground, and I trip over arms and legs and spilled intestines, slip on the blood that turns the dirt to mud. I see Geir dead on the ground, his chest open to show his flowering ribs. I see no sign of Kjerstin. I can only see the fact, as clear as the blue of the sky above: We will not win this battle. We'll die here on Årud Helle.

I was wrong to bring us here, but there's still a chance we could make it from the island. "Retreat," I yell hoarsely. "Retreat!"

There are some islanders who hear me and continue to fight. They will not retreat. They will not run from the Fjern. They prefer to die here. There are others who hear me and run—others who have already begun to run, down the rocky terrain and toward the thin trees of the coconut groves. The pain in my shoulder is sharp, and my leg was also cut without my realizing, pink muscle gushing blood. I should die here. I think that there isn't a purpose to me, not when I've ruined the course of the uprising. I should die here on the battlefield with my guards.

But my body still moves, my legs running through the pain. After all of this time, I'm still afraid to die. I fall down the hill, rolling into rocks that dig into my sides. I stagger to my feet, limping, arrows shooting past. Other islanders running with me are hit in their backs. They fall, and still I run. I run to the trees and burst out of them, toward the village. The islanders who stayed behind to guard the path are dead on the ground, cut down by the Fjern who must have found them before coming to the battlefield. I reach the gray dirt and the beginnings of the bay.

I hear a heavy breath and see that Malthe runs behind me. I pause, but realize at the last moment that I shouldn't have. He swings his machete at me. I fall to avoid it. I scramble backward, and he raises his machete and hits dirt and stone. He's exhausted, but he realizes this will be his last opportunity to kill me.

I stay on the ground, breathing heavy. He looks down at me.

"Spirits, boy," he says. "You should've just done what I commanded from the beginning."

"You're right."

He's surprised by my admission. There are shouts and screams from the battlefield. More islanders run past, headed for the bay. We watch them go before Malthe's gaze lands on me again.

"Kill me and you won't have as much of a chance to make it from Årud Helle alive," I tell him.

He sees that this is true. "And once we return to Hans Lollik Helle?" he says. "You'll tell everyone of what I've done."

I'm not sure what I'll do yet. I tell him this, and he accepts the plain truth. He extends a hand and helps me to my feet. I almost expect him to take the chance to slide the blade into my side, but he doesn't take the chance, not with islanders who still run past us to the bay and to the ships that wait.

We run to the sand. I see Kjerstin, blood smeared across her face and drenching her shirt. I'm not sure if the blood is hers or another's. She looks at me with dull eyes, then back at the ships on the sea that burn. The Fjern set fires to each.

"We'll die here," she says with a hollow voice.

There are six of us who have made it from the battlefield. Six, out of the sixty who had come. Sigourney and the Fjern haven't followed us yet, but if we wait any longer there won't be much more time. The sand is still lined with the boats we'd taken from the ships. I begin to push one onto the shallows.

"Do you really believe we'll all make it to Hans Lollik Helle on that?" Kjerstin demands.

"Probably not," I admit, "but we have to try."

She hesitates, but in the distance I can see the Fjern walking toward us. There's no need to run. They've won, and once they find us and any of the other islanders hiding on Årud Helle, they'll take their time killing us.

"Hurry," I tell them, and Kjerstin climbs into one boat with me, while Malthe takes another and also pushes it out onto the waters. We row out from the bay. The Fjern set themselves up on the sand, bows and arrows at the ready. They shoot. We try to duck and dodge, but on the other boat, one arrow pierces a guard in the cheek. They take their time reloading their arrows—this is a game to them as we try to paddle as fast as we can against the tide, past the coral reefs. Another set of arrows fly. They thud into the boat. Kjerstin gasps in pain. An arrow has landed in her back. Blood leaks from her mouth. I curse. I want to hold a hand to her wound, but if I stop rowing, the Fjern will only continue to shoot us all down.

Once we're far out enough, the Fjern on the sand are small, and their arrows can't reach us. We don't have much time. Eventually they'll realize that I was one of the islanders on these boats and that I've escaped. They'll send their ships after us so that Sigourney can take me prisoner. Still, I let go of the paddle, leaving the one other guard to move us along on the current behind Malthe's boat. The arrow shaft is stuck in Kjerstin. I'm afraid it's pierced her lungs. I'm afraid to pull. She could bleed out. I rip cloth and dunk it into saltwater, hold it at her back. Kjerstin feels a pain she's never experienced. She can barely look at me. She shakes her head, tears leaking from her eyes. She wants it to stop. She wants it to end. I try to use the kraft to heal her flesh, but the wound is too deep. She should already be dead.

Blood is on her lips. "I shouldn't have survived that battle," she says, her voice hoarse. The pain squeezes my insides. I realize what she means. I understand what she asks of me.

"You'll be all right," I tell her. "We'll come to Hans Lollik Helle—"

"I'll be dead by then," she says. She knows that she won't make it through the night. It'll take hours to return to the royal island. And if she did live—what then? There were no herbs that would repair her lungs, her back, her spine. She can feel how broken she is inside. She can feel that no healer will be able to save her. She will only lie in pain for hours, days, in a torture that will not end—only for her to die then.

"I shouldn't have survived," she tells me again. She hopes this will be solace for me. She was never meant to survive this. But it's no solace. She'd given me hope. The pain is physical, shards in my chest. It makes me bend against my will, cracking through me as emotion grows. Mourning Kjerstin now would do no good. She would only be impatient with me. She braves a steadying breath and puts her hand on mine. I clench the blade and cut her throat as quickly as I can. Her eyes glaze as she gasps, gurgling for breath. I hold her close as her body shudders against mine. I continue to hold her after she stills. Her blood soaks me. The guard has stopped rowing, and the boat holding Malthe rides up and down on the waves as they watch us.

"She'll weigh the boat," the guard says. He doesn't mean to be harsh, only to speak the truth. Kjerstin deserves a proper ceremony and ritual burying her at sea. I close my eyes and ask for her forgiveness, then murmur a prayer once I've pulled the arrow from her back and lowered her into the sea. She floats, her eyes half-open as she stares at the sky. I watch as the water washes over her and she begins to sink into the depths.

CHAPTER THIRTY-THREE

After taking Årud Helle, the Fjern waste little time in spreading their reach. We receive reports of the stream of ships that have arrived from Solberg and Niklasson Helle, taking Nørup. It happens within a day, and the scouts who managed to survive bring messages of carnage. The islanders fought valiantly, but once it became clear that the islands would be lost to the Fjern, the guards of the northern empires retreated. The islanders that survived the massacres came to Hans Lollik Helle. The barracks are overwhelmed, no space for them all to rest, the food supply gone.

We're surrounded. It's only a matter of time before the Fjern attack. When they do, we'll be lost.

Marieke waits in the meeting room when I arrive. It isn't a surprise when Malthe comes with guards who follow. Malthe has already told all of the battle of Årud Helle. It was a battle he has argued against from the beginning, but in my poor leadership, I insisted. While there, I was a coward and surrendered to the Fjern and Sigourney Rose, trusting them to show us mercy. They did not. They killed nearly everyone, and we barely managed to escape with our lives. Malthe has declared, to the agreement of nearly all on this island, that I should be imprisoned and punished for what has inevitably become the cause of the end of our uprising.

I don't fight. Georg holds my hands behind my back without tying them. He takes me from the meeting room, down the hall and to the dungeons. Though he doesn't say the words, I can feel the apology in him. He respects me, but he agrees that Malthe is right. He agrees that the people of this island will need me to be punished for the mistakes I've made, for leading us into ruin. He thinks that I'll probably have to die.

I don't try to convince him otherwise. He takes me into the manor of Herregård Constantjin and down into the dark of the dungeons where Patrika Årud had once awaited her own fate. Georg locks me in my cell, unable to look me in the eye. He's ashamed of betraying the loyalty he once had for me.

"I can't blame you for doing what you think is right," I tell him. But this doesn't ease his mind. He locks my cell and leaves me in the shadows.

This time, when he comes to me, I feel the ache spread through my skull until it becomes a piercing sting. I'd assumed the pain was connected to the bond I shared with Sigourney Rose. While our kraft did cause a pressure, the sharp pain was not caused by her. It was caused by the man who watched me from the shadows always. I remember now. I'd seen him in the halls of Herregård Constantjin. He'd smiled and used his kraft to take my memory, the way he had when I first saw him and realized he had a kraft that he hid from everyone else. He'd also used his kraft to take and change memories of the guards and Malthe himself the night we were ambushed by the Fjern. Tuve has pretended to be dead for weeks. He traveled between the islands with ease, coming to the royal island to gain his knowledge and bring it back to his master, Lothar Niklasson. To the kongelig, islanders are not meant to have kraft. They are executed for the power that the Fjern believe is their divine right. Yet Lothar Niklasson has kept his secrets from the other Fjern. He learned of Tuve's ability and knew that it could have its uses. Tuve has sensed that his master might have him killed one day, but he's chosen not to focus on that thought.

Tuve suggested to his master that he could kill us. It would've been easy to take my memory and make me forget I'd seen him standing in the shadows. Easy to stick his blade into my gut and be done with it. He'd been tempted to do it many times, but his master had asked him to wait. The time would come. But for now, it wouldn't do for Tuve to kill the leader of the revolution. I would become a martyr and in my death my followers would be impassioned. I'd be replaced, and there'd be too high of a chance that Tuve would be seen and captured. Lothar Niklasson would lose his tie to valuable information. No, Tuve was not to kill me—not yet. He lets me know that he'll enjoy the moment when the time does come.

Tuve has hated me and everyone else who has played a part in this rebellion. He's hated how we betrayed our masters. Tuve believed the Fjern when they said he was not a man who could rule himself. He believed them when they said he would need their orders and need obedience to serve the gods that they served as well. Tuve believed that he had no purpose in life but to devote himself to the ones who claimed him. And there is his daughter. He left the girl on Årud Helle. He understood that she was not his. She, too, was owned by her master. But he didn't want her to lose her life, and he thinks that we risked her life and his own by starting this war. He hates me and all the islanders of the revolution. He hates that we sacrifice the lives of innocents.

Gods, how he wants to kill me. But this isn't why he's here. He has information. It'll be valuable to tell his master that the leader of the insurrection has been imprisoned in a coup. The islanders are not united. We're vulnerable. He'll travel to Niklasson Helle at once. Within three days' time, ships will arrive on our shores, ready to attack.

He leaves, allowing my memory to fade. I try desperately to grasp it. I have to remember this. I can't forget, as I've forgotten all the times before.

I try to remember, but I can't remember what I've forgotten, and I'm not sure if I've forgotten something at all. There's a distant feeling of waking from a dream and I'm lost in thought, unable to remember what'd sparked my distraction in the first place. There's fear, concern, the echoes of urgency that I remember. But of course I'm stricken by anxiety. I'm in a dungeon's cell, waiting for the moment Malthe decides I need to die.

When Marieke comes, I immediately see she isn't supposed to be here. She's come against Malthe's orders. I tell her that she unnecessarily risks her life.

"I risk my life just by staying on this island," she says. "Malthe has lost control of himself. He's realized that we will lose this war and seems determined to live his fantasy as king of these islands before that happens."

I tell her that I'm sorry. "I failed you. I failed all of our people."

She agrees. "I'm also at fault. I put too much trust in you, when I could sense you were not ready to lead us to freedom."

"Is it true, what Malthe said?" I ask her. "Is it because I show too much mercy?"

"I can't answer that question for you," she says, but I sense that she believes it's so. She believes she's guilty of this as well. The mercy wasn't for Sigourney Rose or Malthe or anyone else in these islands. I showed mercy only for myself. So that I could play the role of hero in this story, without taking the actions we needed to win this war. I should have killed Sigourney. I should have executed Malthe. I should have taken these islands back, no matter the cost or sacrifice. Even if it meant burning the land to the ground and rising again from the ashes.

"The war is lost," Marieke tells me. "We failed. But we can

try again," she says. "Not you or me. We will be dead. But as long as there are islanders alive, there's a chance that our people will eventually succeed. I can only hope that I'll be among the spirits able to watch them win their freedom." She says that she'll attempt to leave Hans Lollik Helle. She knows she won't likely make it far before Malthe or the Fjern find her and capture her and kill her, but she would like to try to make it to the northern empires anyway. If she makes it, she'll stay there until the end of her years, doing what she can to rebuild the network of whispers again. It would take another twenty, thirty, forty years before they could try to put their plan into motion once more. She wouldn't be alive then. She's far too old. She feels shame for the thought that flashes through her mind. Sigourney Rose might still be alive. She might have changed into the woman Marieke always hoped she would be.

"I'll pray for you," she tells me. This is her goodbye. She leaves, and I know I won't see Marieke again.

My mother has anger for me. This is why she no longer comes. She's enraged that I have failed her and the uprising. I had been born for this, chosen and guided and saved time and again by the spirits for the moment that I would free the islands and our people. But there's only so much the spirits can do. My actions and my choices are my own.

I'm woken by shouts. I hadn't meant to fall asleep, and I curse myself as I jump to my feet and hold on to the bars of the cell, listening closely. The shouts are too far away and muffled for me to hear clearly, and I can't use my kraft to see into the minds of the men who yell as Sigourney might've been able to. I can hear the panic. The shouts fade. There's pressure in the back of my head. Something I'd forgotten, and I need to remember. I try to listen to the yells to make sense of them, but there's nothing.

It's still black as night when a door opens and footsteps come down into the dungeons. Georg is lucky to still be alive. The wound in his side is deeper than he is willing to admit to anyone. It's already become infected, and without the medicine he likely won't live long. The moment I see him I ask him to let me put my hand on his wound, and he agrees. He hadn't come here for my help. He'd come on Malthe's orders. There'd been an attack on the island last night. The Fjern should have won, but somehow they were pushed from the shores once again. Still, the losses were heavy. We've lost over half of our guards. We won't survive the next attack when it inevitably comes. This is a fact that everyone on the island has finally accepted. Winning the battle last night only gave them all enough time to decide whether they would try to run or if they would die here.

They'd almost forgotten me. I could have died here in these dungeons without Malthe. They'd realized finally that my accusers had been wrong. I was in the dungeons at the time of the attack, and the Fjern had realized which shores to come to, had understood that the islanders had abandoned the battlefield and barracks to hide in one of the manors deeper in the island's groves. I could not have been the emissary that passed on this information if I was locked in my dungeon. I hadn't known. Malthe still claims that I somehow discovered the truth using my kraft. That I was able to contact Sigourney Rose. I see that this is really why Georg comes to me. The others have realized the truth, but he's still here on his orders. Malthe has asked Georg to retrieve me and bring me to the shore so that my head can be cut from my neck before all the islanders. Though I'm not the emissary, I am still the failed leader. Malthe claims that I deserve punishment fitting this failure, and there are enough islanders on Hans Lollik Helle who agree.

Georg doesn't agree. He doesn't want to see me killed. He's afraid to say this. Afraid to admit it to me and himself. But it is the truth. He has anger for me, yes. I've failed him and all the islanders. I've been too soft and held on to loyalty for Sigourney Rose. But I also fought with passion. I showed mercy to my own people out of love and respect. These islands needed a man like Malthe to win the war, but needed someone like me to rule over our peace and freedom.

I don't try to convince Georg to free me. It wouldn't be fair to him, asking him to risk his life for my own. He takes me from the dungeons and into the bright light of day. I'd assumed it was night because of the darkness of my cell. The sun's white light burns my eyes. I clench them shut as Georg guides me forward. I can see through his eyes: the death that still fills the air. The bodies spread across the ground. They haven't bothered to give the bodies a proper burial. Not when there won't be anyone alive to give a proper burial to their own bodies once they're gone.

Everyone who still lives has been gathered on the shore. Most are wounded, bloodied bandages wrapped around thighs and stomachs and chests. Marieke is not here. I see that she was found the night before, trying to leave on a boat. Malthe had ordered her captured for questioning, claiming that she could have been the emissary instead. Rather than allow herself to be captured by Malthe, she ran. She waded into the water and kept walking as if she meant to walk the ocean floor until she found the spirits she always prayed to. She never came to the surface.

I mourn Marieke, though I know I'll soon join her. Georg leads me onto the white sand that burns the bottoms of my feet. We stop at the front, my back facing the waves that wash ashore. Malthe stands with his machete. So many of his guards are cut and injured, but he doesn't have a mark on him. He stands in silence for a long moment like he waits for me to speak—to beg for my life, maybe, or to claim that I'm not the emissary and I don't deserve to die. To put a curse on his soul for taking my life. He's disappointed when I don't do any of this, but he isn't surprised. He'd respected me, once. Still does respect me in some ways. I've made poor choices, yes. But I'll hold my head high until it's cut from my neck.

"Is there anything you wish to say?" he asks me. He thinks I'll take this opportunity to apologize to him and everyone before me. I'm surprised when I do.

"I'd only ever wanted what was best for the islands," I say. "I only ever did what I thought was right for our people. I didn't lead us to victory. I didn't win the war for our freedom." I can feel the anger in some. These words are empty. There isn't any point to apologizing when I can't right my wrongs. For others, though, there's grief. I had fought for all of us here.

Malthe gestures to the sand. He would've pushed anyone else to their knees, but he gives me the dignity of kneeling myself. I face the guards. Some are ready to see me die, but others hesitate. Georg shakes his head. This is wrong. He says this aloud.

"He doesn't deserve death," Georg yells.

Malthe is surprised by the interruption. That moment's breath gives others time to voice their agreement. Some yell at Malthe not to kill me, but others shout their responses, claiming that I need to be punished. Malthe and I remain frozen. Malthe looks at me, and I can see how he realizes this is his only chance. He raises the machete. I should stay where I am. I should let him swing and let the blade bite into me. But my body moves. I roll out of the way just as the machete slices through the air where my head had been a moment before. There's an explosion of movement. Georg runs forward to help me. Seeing him inspires others to run to our side. The other guards who fight for Malthe are outnumbered. The battle is quick. Machetes to stomachs, necks cut open. Their bodies fall as one before Malthe has the chance to move. Some who had chosen Malthe's side raise their hands in surrender. They don't feel so strongly for their commander that they're willing to die now. Malthe looks at me, unsteady. He sees he's lost.

I don't want to kill him. But I must. I've realized my wrongs. I've learned that I can't show mercy. I've only realized this too late. Killing Malthe won't save the revolution, but it could give more time to those who want to escape the island—more of a chance to some who might survive. I won't leave Hans Lollik Helle. I already know that I'll die here.

Malthe asks me to consider allowing him to keep his life. I'm surprised. I never thought him to be the type to beg. "Killing me won't save any of us from the Fjern," he says.

The others wait on the shore. I already mourn Malthe. I grieve the man I thought he once was, the man I'd looked up to and who had taught me so much of how to survive this world.

He sees the hardened determination in my eyes, and his pleading expression turns to rage. "You've killed us all."

When I swing, he throws up a hand to shield himself. It's cut from the wrist before the machete slices his neck. His head falls and his body crumples to the sand. Malthe's blood spreads, soaking into the grains. The silence that follows is only interrupted by the hush of the waves. Like it means to remind us that the sea and the land will live on, long after we are gone.

CHAPTER THIRTY-FOUR

So few remain. There are only seven of us. I would have ordered the last of the food brought so that we could enjoy a final meal, but the rations were finished days before. Some have hope. The ones who don't want to admit to themselves that we will be dead whenever the Fjern decide to arrive think that there's a chance the northern empires will return to save us, or that the kongelig might see the error of their ways and give us the freedom we deserve. These are the thoughts of desperate men who don't want to die. I don't want to die, either. But I put us all on this course the night of the revolt—the night that I didn't take Sigourney Rose's life.

I think of everyone we've lost, the people who are dead because of me. I remember them all. And I think that there's something else I should remember. It's a nagging thought. There's urgency. I must remember. The memory is on the edge of my mind, the tip of my tongue, slipping away...

This will likely be my last night alive. I can't return to the slaves' quarters, where I'd spent so many years alone. I can't return to the room where I'd slept in Herregård Constantjin, pretending to be a member of the kongelig and enjoying my power and privilege as if I was Sigourney Rose. This is what I did, even if I didn't want to admit it to myself. Instead I return to the rocks on the bay beneath the cliffs and stand where it feels like I've stood for all of eternity. I wait for my mother—to feel her presence and her guidance—but she doesn't come.

When I feel his presence, I also feel how he wants to kill me. The machete is in his hand. His master Herre Lothar Niklasson didn't give him the order to take my life, but Tuve wants to please him with my head. If he personally delivers my head to his master, he might be rewarded. I'll forget. He'll make me forget that he's come to me, make me forget I ever sensed him, and he'll cut me open before I've had a chance to realize that he's here.

I stand on the rocks on the bay, where it feels like I've stood for all eternity. I stare at the depths of the sea, my heart pounding with fear, though I'm not sure why it does. I'll die soon. I know that the Fjern are coming. But it feels like there's something else. Something I should remember.

There's a glint in the corner of my eye. I spin and grab the wrist of the hand that holds a machete. I see Tuve's face. He allows a flicker of surprise before he smiles. He doesn't mind a challenge. He'll make me forget again and again, until he's successful in killing me.

I grab hold of his kraft. Tuve startles. He'd known of my ability to take the kraft of others, but he didn't think I would be able to remember why I needed to take his power. He's right. Whenever he revealed himself to me, I was too shocked to act, too caught in remembering that he was still alive and that he was the traitor that I couldn't use my power before he slipped away again, taking my memory with him. But this time, he was too confident I'd forget like all the times before. I slip into his mind and I pull his memories to me. I hold them. I could let them spill into the ocean until he's nothing but a husk, living and breathing but unable to remember the past that brought him here. I'm tempted to. But he should also remember. He should know why he's died, and who has killed him.

I twist his arm until he releases the machete. I take it and slide the blade against his throat. He chokes, red gushing from his neck. He steps back and falls into the ocean. He's sucked beneath the surface. Red floats to the top until that is also washed away by the salt.

My encounter with Tuve was like a dream that had come and gone. I don't feel the need to tell anyone that I survived him or that he'd been the emissary all along. Sigourney agrees. She lets me see that she's come. She and Lothar Niklasson and Kalle and only a handful of guards will soon arrive on Hans Lollik Helle. Lothar Niklasson didn't think it necessary to bring an entire fleet when he knows so few of us survive. He wants to keep his ships on his island, ready for the attack of Jytte Solberg, which he anticipates within days. Our revolution is already a thing of the past for the Fjern.

Will you surrender? She wants me to give up the island without one last battle. *You've already lost. There's no point to the additional bloodshed. You should give up, Løren.*

I will not give up, but it isn't fair to the others on this island not to give them adequate warning. We sit in silence around the fire, everyone trapped in their thoughts and their memories and their regrets. Death is such a common thing, yet no one knows how to react when it's their time to leave this world. Some are angry. Others mourn themselves. Georg feels relief. He's always been afraid of when he would die. At least he has his answer.

"They're coming," I say. Heads swing up and gazes meet my own. "Sigourney Rose and Lothar Niklasson and ten guards. They're coming here to end the uprising."

My news is met with silence. None are surprised. We all knew this is how the rebellion would end. They also understand that I tell them so that they may have a choice. The desperation in some spurs a few to say that they will fight until the end, but there's a calmness in others, a resignation to truth. They could fight and kill these guards now, but more will come, and they will not live. They would rather die on their own terms. So many have walked into the ocean before us, rocks tied to ankles. This is the path for a few men. One hopes that this is where his family waits for him. That the spirits live free in the ocean, ready to greet him. Once it's clear that most of the men will not fight, those who had decided to die with a blade in their hand also understand the truth. They agree to walk into the water as one, tonight, before Sigourney Rose and Lothar Niklasson can come here. At least their bodies will be on the ocean floor, out of the reach of the Fjern, no longer owned by the people who had claimed them. At least they will have this one last victory.

Georg is too afraid to speak the words. He holds his hands together tightly. He's afraid to die, and he's also afraid that I'll reject his request. He thinks it's a selfish ask, but he's always been afraid of the sea. He doesn't want to drown. It would've been easier if there was a poisonous herb that he could drink, but there's nothing left but our bodies and our blades. I put my hand on his, and he looks up at me. He understands that I've seen his thoughts, and that I've agreed to his request.

We walk to the bay with the others. One man says a prayer. For himself, for us, for all the people who have come before us and fought before us and died before us. We tell them good-bye. Each walk into the sea, slowly, rocks weighing down their feet. Georg and I wait on the sand until the last man disappears beneath the waves.

Georg is shaking. He tries to smile, but he can't. I'm not sure I can go through with what he's asked of me after all. I try to tell him this, and he has a flare of hurt and anger.

"It's the least you could do," he says before he can stop himself, and he apologizes, saying he didn't mean the words. But he does. Georg has anger for me, but he also considers me his friend. It's why he trusts me with this. We stand beside each other for some time, looking at the stillness of the sea under the silver moon. It'll be the last thing Georg sees. He thinks this is a good way to die.

"What do you think waits for us?" he asks me.

"I hope it's the spirits who wait to welcome us."

He nods stiffly, already thinking of how he's afraid to leave this world, even if it was one that wasn't meant for him and even if death will mean its own freedom. He closes his eyes. He's ready. I'm quick when I cut his throat. I don't want him to suffer. I help him to the sand and he grips my shirt. He swallows, trying to speak words he doesn't understand, until he becomes still.

Grief floods through me. Grief for Georg, grief for each and every single one of my people, everyone who lives and everyone who doesn't. There's rage, too—anger for those who've taken everything from us. Fury for myself for failing to take our freedom. But though I have failed, I can feel the sliver of hope. Someone will try again. Someone will succeed.

I carry Georg to the water to help lay his body to rest. I stand in the shallows, watching pulsing waves take him away. I should decide how I want to die. I could walk into the waves as well or cut open my own veins. Instead, I stand in the shallows as if I'm waiting. I already know who I'm waiting for.

Pink light shines through the sky when the ship carrying Sigourney Rose and Lothar Niklasson arrives. They anchor out at sea, and a smaller boat carrying her, Lothar, and Kalle brings them to the shallows and to the beach. Kalle helps Sigourney out of the boat and into the water, the ends of her dress wet as she walks onto the sand. Lothar Niklasson follows her. He looks older than the last time I'd seen him. His skin has become thinner, blue veins running along his flesh, turning red in the heat. His hair is white, his eyes pale. If he had not died in the war, he wouldn't have had many more years to live. He sees this as well as anyone else. Yet he had his plans. He meant to give these islands to his heirs, so that the Niklasson name would live on as the rulers of Hans Lollik. He would only be able to enjoy his position for a short time, but he would still be written in history as the first of the Niklasson regents. He won't be able to. He hasn't seen what I do. It should be obvious to the man, that she means to kill him and take all of his power, but she has managed to convince him that she truly meant to serve him and all the kongelig. That her only ambition was to keep her life.

She waited until this moment: when she, Lothar, and the slave he'd thought loyal were away from all of his guards. Lothar looks at me with disdain. I've caused him so much trouble these last few months, and he still only sees me as a boy. The bastard son of Jannik, who had his kraft and should have been killed many years before. He curses Engel for allowing me to live. But it doesn't matter. He will have Kalle kill me and send my body into the sea.

This is what he believes. Sigourney looks at me with the slightest smile. She knows I've seen the truth. She feels no urgency. Lothar Niklasson won't survive this island. She walks to my side and looks down at me as I sit in the sand. She finds it rude that I don't rise to greet her.

"Where are the rest of your friends, Løren?"

I tell her that they're dead. Lothar doesn't believe me, but Sigourney sees that it's the truth. She sees that I have been sitting here, waiting for either her or the courage to end my life, which-ever came first.

"I'm disappointed that you'd consider taking that route instead of facing me."

Lothar is impatient with Sigourney's games. He speaks to his guard. "Kill him and be done with it."

Kalle doesn't move. Sigourney keeps her gaze on me.

Lothar is confused—for a brief moment, he thinks Kalle has not heard him. It's only a moment later that he senses the true danger. He isn't sure he can believe this. He'd questioned Sigourney thoroughly, asked her if she would give him her loyalty, asked if she would try to take his life in pursuit of power—and besides that, he couldn't take Sigourney Rose as a serious threat. If she kills him, the kongelig will not willingly follow her. He believes she has no purpose in taking his life. He underestimates her. He looks at Kalle, who speaks no words as he drives his machete into his master's stomach. Lothar gasps, blood on his lips. Kalle pushes him away so that he falls to the sand, groaning. Sigourney means to let him die in pain.

She doesn't spare him a glance. She can feel his pain, his rage at her betrayal, his surprise and desperation and hopelessness. She feels it all and relishes in it. And she can feel me as well. She feels my numbness and my acceptance of death. She asks me to join her in Herregård Constantjin. She tells me she will wait there for her allies to arrive. She wants my acceptance and forgiveness for what she sees as her only choice. There's much she wants to explain to me, before she sees me die.

I've weakened in the past two days. I haven't had any food or water. Sigourney orders Kalle to help me to my feet and down the path. She surveys the island as she walks ahead of us. There's much to be done to return Hans Lollik Helle to its previous beauty. She laments that Marieke will not be a part of this. She's already seen in me that everyone is dead, including the woman that had raised her. Sigourney has already mourned Marieke. She's already assumed the woman had died with each battle that passed. She's mourned Marieke, and she will mourn again in the privacy of her rooms at night. But she can't allow the woman's death to distract her. Not when she's so close to everything she's worked for. Everything she's ever wanted.

Kalle is silent as he grips my arm over his shoulders and drags me toward the manor on the hill. He has such a deep hatred for me that he wants to go against Sigourney Rose's orders and kill me. He's impatient to see me punished. Not for failing the islands, but for leading the insurrection. He thinks that this is what destroyed these lands. Too many people have died unnecessarily. Kalle would rather play by the rules of the Fjern. He would rather play their game, even if it was built to keep him at a disadvantage. The Fjern would not be able to deny him his freedom if he did all that they asked. This is what he believes. He doesn't see the value in burning the islands to the ground and starting again. It's unfair to people like him, who have worked for their freedom all their lives.

I'm taken to the manor, past the broken fountain where I'd saved Sigourney from Georg and the other guards who'd meant to kill her that night.

"I'm grateful that you did save me," she says, not looking at me as she sweeps into the front doors of the manor, Kalle bringing me in after her. "You could have let me die. You did not."

I should have let her die. This answer is clear now, if it comes to her life or mine.

"Perhaps," she acknowledges. "But would killing me have really saved your revolution?" She thinks this is only a lie I tell myself. That I put the blame on her because I don't want to see the truth: This uprising, though it took a lifetime of planning, was doomed from the beginning. She does not think an uprising like ours would have ever won against the Fjern.

She thinks that hers is the only way any islander would have been successful in taking back our power. "You think that you were meant for this moment. That the spirits saved you time and again and guided you so that you could lead our people to freedom. I think the same of myself."

We sit in the meeting room. She takes the head of the table, where I once sat, and where Malthe sat before me, and where the regent of the Fjern sat before him as well. Kalle roughly drops me into a seat farther down the table and takes a position standing behind Sigourney. I feel dazed and faint. The lack of food, the overwhelming kraft—Sigourney's thoughts, her emotions, and memories assault me. She sits calmly as she waits for me to catch my breath. I wish that she wouldn't. I agree with Kalle. It would be better if they simply killed me.

"There are things I need you to see."

"You only want to make yourself feel better about my death and your betrayal of the islands."

She doesn't answer this. In her mind she has convinced herself that I speak illogically, angry that I've been bested. I'm glad that Marieke isn't here to see this. Sigourney had the opportunity, time and again, to become the woman these islands needed. She saw that the path she chose was wrong, and still she took it, deciding instead to tell herself that her selfishness would benefit her people.

"Is it really so wrong to want the power of the crown?" she asks me. "I want to be regent. I've worked for that position. I deserve that position."

I don't want to argue with her. I want Kalle to kill me and be done with it, if that's what he's to do. But she still wants me to see.

CHAPTER THIRTY-FIVE

The battles of Årud and Nørup had been good for Sigourney. Though the Fjern still viewed her as less than human, they did also begin to see her with the positivity that one might feel for a prized pet. She could have used the opportunity to help further the revolution for the islanders. Instead, she attacked her own people and won the Fjern the two islands they needed to finally tip the balance of the war in the favor of the kongelig.

When she returned to Niklasson Helle, it was to a welcome she never before experienced among the Fjern. She knew it was not an admiration she should value. It was the same sort of love one might have for a goat they'd grown particularly fond of, or a horse that had finally been tamed. Yet she couldn't help but be glad that the Fjern had begun to recognize her worth. It was something she had worked for her entire life, something she didn't think she'd ever witness.

The recognition angered my brother. Aksel Jannik had stayed on Niklasson Helle with the other surviving kongelig reluctantly. It was the only place he could remain and stay safe from the battles that'd overtaken the islands and the sea, but he hated being trapped among the other smug Fjern. Before the war, he had only continued his responsibilities as a son of the kongelig because this is what his dying mother would have wanted of

him. He had no desire to be on the same island as Jytte Solberg
and Gertrude Nørup and Lothar Niklasson. Least of all was the
desire to be anywhere near the woman he'd married. His hatred
for her and himself only grew every time he saw her in the
courtyards and sat with her for dinner with the other kongelig
and shared the same bed with her, as he was prone to do when
he'd had enough sugarcane wine. The news that she had won
the islands Årud and Nørup Helle, and the Fjern's congratula-
tions toward her, enraged him. He'd followed Sigourney to her
chambers. His only intention was to remind her that she was still
an islander and should have been a slave of the kongelig. Instead,
he heard as Sigourney spoke to Kalle about her plans. Kalle had
become someone Sigourney trusted. He was the only islander
she knew that, like her, agreed they ought to play by the rules
of the Fjern, but was also determined to win this game against
them.

Aksel heard as she told Kalle that winning the battles of Årud
and Nørup Helle would only be her first step. She would use her
newfound admiration to enter into an agreement with Jytte Solberg and Gertrude Nørup. They'd both wanted her assistance
against Lothar Niklasson, and now that the timing was right,
Sigourney would finally agree. Both families had already lent
their guards to Sigourney's rule. She had already commanded
them in the battles of Årud and Nørup. She would continue
her control once Jytte Solberg was dead. Sigourney would convince the cousins of the kongelig and the woman's friend Gertrude Nørup to have Jytte Solberg executed for conspiring in the
death of Lothar Niklasson. Lothar Niklasson had died on Hans
Lollik Helle. Both she and Kalle would claim it was the actions
of a guard sent by Jytte Solberg, and though Gertrude would
likely sense the truth, the woman would not continue as an ally
with the Solberg when all the rest of the kongelig wanted her
dead as well.

Gertrude Nørup would be easier to manipulate and control than Jytte Solberg. The woman was a fool—as naive as Erik Nørup had once been. Sigourney would use Gertrude Nørup as a puppet for as much time as she needed to, standing at the woman's side, rising in control with her until she would be able to take the role of regent. Sigourney is confident that Kalle's support will be necessary. He can help to convince other islander guards of Niklasson and Solberg Helle to come under Sigourney's rule. They would create a new class of islanders, who would hold all the power as the Fjern once did. It wouldn't do to simply eradicate slavery altogether. There needed to be a system of power in place for all of their protection. Without that system, the islands would only be attacked by the Koninkrijk Empire or any of the other free nations again.

Everything had gone as planned so far. The only question that lingered was what would become of me and all the others who had been a part of the revolution. It was a question that overtook her thoughts for days, weeks. She left Niklasson Helle with Kalle. She went to Lund Helle, where she had spent so many of her years as the leader of the land she'd inherited from her cousin, before she returned to Rose Helle. It was the place of her birth, where she had lived with her family before they were killed by the Fjern. She returned to the ruins of the manor where so many had been slaughtered. She went to her mother, as I sometimes try to go to mine as I stand on the rocks. She wasn't sure what she hoped to find. She wanted her mother's approval. She wanted her mother's pride. She wanted her mother's guidance. She didn't know if she would be able to kill everyone. But she knew that she would have to.

She didn't quite expect that I would be the only survivor of Hans Lollik Helle. This makes her decision more difficult. She had come here with a steeled heart. She had already decided we would have to die to prevent us from rising up against her. But only I remain. It wouldn't hurt to keep me alive, would it? She could keep me at her side. I would be a trophy of sorts—proof of everything she has survived to bring her to this place. She has won. It's a fact she finds remarkable, one that she hopes that I will celebrate with her. Like the Fjern who recognized her worth, this is what she wants of me as well. She sees I will not give it. This disappoints her.

"You don't really believe I would be happy that you've betrayed us," I say.

Sigourney has at least finally admitted to herself that she's betrayed her people and these islands. She admits that she wanted to win against the Fjern, not out of love for her people, but out of love for herself. She wanted the power of the regent. This is what she will have.

"Yet our people will also benefit, in the long run," she says.

"How long?" I ask her. "Years from now? After your death, and deaths of your children?"

She isn't surprised that I've seen the truth: She carries a child. She's realized this for weeks already, after she felt herself becoming ill by the scent of salt. She can feel the being growing inside of her, and she thinks that she will raise the child to be the true regent of these islands. She doesn't think about the fact that the father is Aksel Jannik, and that she has had him killed.

"We could have ruled these islands together," she says. But these are the daydreams of a child. There isn't any way that we could have worked together to create a world that we both envisioned.

I'm placed in the room Sigourney had once occupied, locked in and facing the ruins of the island. The revolution is over. It's a quiet end to the war. And after our deaths, the island goes on. All of the islands will go on as they are, no matter who claims them. I remember Marieke's words. As long as there are islanders in our homeland, there's hope. Even if I don't witness the freedom of these lands myself, it will come.

It's only days until the Fjern ships anchor at sea. The slaves they bring with them begin the cleanup of the island. They erase evidence that there'd ever been a war. They erase evidence that anyone of the uprising had ever existed. The Fjern return to the houses that had not been burnt down. The new heads of each of the kongelig families return to the manor of Herregård Constantjin and to the meeting room to discuss the actions they'll take to find their sense of normalcy once more. To the Fjern, this was nothing but an inconvenient interruption in their way of life. Our bid for freedom was always doomed to fail.

There are few who protest the execution of Jytte Solberg. Gertrude Nørup doesn't want to risk the ire of the kongelig around her. She doesn't want to be killed right alongside the woman who had been her ally. Jytte is hanged, her body thrown to the sea. Gertrude Nørup behaves as Sigourney predicted she would. She is overwhelmed by the confidence given to her by the Fjern and leans heavily on Sigourney. Sigourney quickly becomes Gertrude's right hand, following her into the meeting room. Sigourney plays the role that Konge Valdemar had once expected for her mother: to sit in the room of the Fjern and give insight into the ways of her people. To betray their potential movements, to say what should become of them. She plays her role well, without complaints. The Fjern are all new to their positions in the meeting room. None of the previous kongelig remain. None recognize the ways she grips to the command, the ways she positions the Fjern against one another, the ways she raises herself to the place of leading each of them. She understands that she won't win their admiration to the point that they'll willingly give her the role of regent. But she does think she'll force them to.

She tells them any secret she'd learned from her connection with me. She has ships return to Ludjivik Helle to kill the survivors. She enters agreements with the northern empires: coin and crop in exchange for any slave of Hans Lollik who had escaped to their freedom. She means to rebuild these islands. Only some islanders of her choosing will escape the fate of slavery.

There's a fate that I can't escape. She's already decided that she can't allow me to live, even if it is only by her side as her treasured slave. I am a symbol of revolution. As long as I live, islanders around us will always see the possibility of another uprising. They need to see my death as much as the Fjern of this island crave to see my head.

Gertrude Nørup asks why I still live. It's the simple catalyst that Sigourney needs. She has me taken from my room and brought to the beach. Kalle holds the machete. He's glad to be the one to kill me. He wants vengeance for those who had not been in the war—for anyone who hadn't had any choice in joining the revolution. The Fjern line up to watch my death. Sigourney Rose stands in the center. She won't watch. She'll look away when my head is cut from my body. But she still needs to stand and oversee my execution.

The sand is hot beneath my feet, then as sharp as shards of glass beneath my knees when Kalle pushes down on my shoulder. I face the sea. I've always faced the stillness of the ocean waves, the cycle of water pulsing as it flows and foams and retreats. Sigourney lists my crimes behind me, and with her kraft I can feel the satisfaction of the Fjern. I should not be alive. I should have died a thousand times, and now they're able to witness what they view as justice. I let them and Sigourney fade. I can see my mother, standing on the shore. She turns and looks at me. Kalle raises the blade.

There is nothingness. There is peace. There is rage. There are the spirits of those who linger as I do. There's the salt of the ocean and the islands growing from the waves and the blue of the sky, always enduring.

ACKNOWLEDGMENTS

Thank you to everyone who has helped to bring this book into the world:

Beth Phelan, for everything that you do, and the entire Gallt & Zacker family.

Sarah Guan for ushering in Sigourney's story, and Nivia Evans for bringing Løren's story home.

The amazing team of Orbit: Paola Crespo, Laura Fitzgerald, Ellen Wright, Alex Lencicki, Andy Ball, Bryn A. McDonald, Lisa Marie Pompilio, Lauren Panepinto, Stephanie Hess, and everyone who has touched the series in some way. Thank you all so much.

And, most importantly, thank you to the readers who have shown their love and support.

extras

orbit

meet the author

Photo Credit: Beth Phelan

KACEN CALLENDER was born two days after a hurricane and was first brought home to a house without its roof. After spending their first eighteen years on St. Thomas of the US Virgin Islands, Kacen studied Japanese, fine arts, and creative writing at Sarah Lawrence College and received their MFA from the New School. Kacen is an award-winning author of books for children and teens. *Queen of the Conquered* is their first novel for adults.

Find out more about Kacen Callender and other Orbit authors by registering for the free monthly newsletter at orbitbooks.net.

if you enjoyed

KING OF THE RISING

look out for

THE OBSIDIAN TOWER

Rooks and Ruin: Book One

by

Melissa Caruso

Deep within Gloamingard Castle lies a black tower. Sealed by magic, it guards a dangerous secret that has been contained for thousands of years.

As Warden, Ryxander knows the warning passed down through generations: nothing must unseal the Door. But one impetuous decision will leave her with blood on her hands—and unleash a threat that could doom the world to fall to darkness.

ONE

There are two kinds of magic.

There is the kind that lifts you up and fills you with wonder, saving you when all is lost or opening doors to new worlds of possibility. And there is the kind that wrecks you, that shatters you, bitter in your mouth and jagged in your hand, breaking everything you touch.

Mine was the second kind.

My father's magic could revive blighted fields, turning them lush and green again, and coax apples from barren boughs in the dead of winter. Grass withered beneath my footsteps. My cousins kept the flocks in their villages healthy and strong, and turned the wolves away to hunt elsewhere; I couldn't enter the stables of my own castle without bringing mortal danger to the horses.

I should have been like the others. Ours was a line of royal vivomancers; life magic flowed in our veins, ancient as the rain that washed down from the hills and nurtured the green valleys of Morgrain. My grandmother was the immortal Witch Lord of Morgrain, the Lady of Owls herself, whose magic coursed so deep through her domain that she could feel the step of every rabbit and the fall of every leaf. And I was Exalted Ryxander, a royal atheling, inheritor of an echo of my grandmother's profound connection to the land and her magical power. Except that I was also Ryx, the family embarrassment, with magic so twisted it was unusably dangerous.

The rest of my family had their place in the cycle, weavers of a great pattern. I'd been born to snarl things up—or more like it, to break the loom and set the tapestry on fire, given my luck.

So I'd made my own place.

At the moment, that place was on the castle roof. One gloved hand clamped on to the delicate bone-carved railing of a nearby balcony for balance, to keep my boots from skidding on the sharply angled shale; the other held the wind-whipped tendrils of dark hair that had escaped my braid back from my face.

"This is a disaster," I muttered.

"I don't see any reason it needs to be, Exalted Warden." Odan, the castle steward—a compact and muscular old man with an extravagant mustache—stood with unruffled dignity on the balcony beside me. I'd clambered over its railing to make room for him, since I couldn't safely share a space that small. "We still have time to prepare guest quarters and make room in the stables."

"That's not the problem. No so-called diplomat arrives a full day early without warning unless they're up to trouble." I glared down at the puffs of dust rising from the northern trade road. Distance obscured the details, but I made out at least thirty riders accompanying the Alevaran envoy's carriage. "And that's too large an escort. They said they were bringing a dozen."

Odan's bristly gray brows descended the broad dome of his forehead. "It's true that I wouldn't expect an ambassador to take so much trouble to be rude."

"They wouldn't. Not if they were planning to negotiate in good faith." And that was what made this a far more serious issue than the mere inconvenience of an early guest. "The Shrike Lord of Alevar is playing games."

Odan blew a breath through his mustache. "Reckless of him, given the fleet of imperial warships sitting off his coast."

"Rather." I hunkered down close to the slate to get under the chill edge that had come into the wind in the past few days, heralding the end of summer. "I worked hard to set up these talks between Alevar and the Serene Empire. What in the Nine Hells is he trying to accomplish?"

The line of riders drew closer along the gray strip of road that wound between bright green farms and swaths of dark forest, approaching the grassy sun-mottled hill that lifted Gloamingard Castle toward a banner-blue sky. The sun winked off the silver-tipped antlers of six proud stags drawing the carriage, a clear announcement that the coach's occupant could bend wildlife to their will—displaying magic in the same way a dignitary of the Serene Empire of Raverra to the south might display wealth, as a sign of status and power.

Another gleam caught my eye, however: the metallic flash of sabers and muskets.

"Pox," I swore. "Those are all soldiers."

Odan scowled down at them. "I'm no diplomat like you, Warden, but it does seem odd to bring an armed platoon to sign a peace treaty."

I almost retorted that I wasn't a diplomat, either. But it was as good a word as any for the role I'd carved out for myself.

Diplomacy wasn't part of a Warden's job. Wardens were mages; it was their duty to use their magic to nurture and sustain life in the area they protected. But my broken magic couldn't nurture. It only destroyed. When my grandmother followed family tradition and named me the Warden of Gloamingard Castle—her own seat of power—on my sixteenth birthday, it had seemed like a cruel joke.

I'd found other ways. If I couldn't increase the bounty of the crops or the health of the flocks with life magic, I could use my Raverran mother's connections to the Serene Empire to enrich our domain with favorable trade agreements. If I couldn't protect Morgrain by rousing the land against bandits or invaders, I could cultivate good relations with Raverra, securing my domain a powerful ally. I'd spent the past five years building that relationship, despite muttering from traditionalists in the family about being too friendly with a nation we'd warred with countless times in centuries past.

I'd done such a good job, in fact, that the Serene Empire had agreed to accept our mediation of an incident with Alevar that threatened to escalate into war.

"I can't let them sabotage these negotiations before they've even started." It wasn't simply a matter of pride; Morgrain lay directly between Alevar and the Serene Empire. If the Shrike Lord wanted to attack the Empire, he'd have to go through us.

The disapproving gaze Odan dropped downhill at the Alevarans could have frozen a lake. "How should we greet them, Warden?"

My gloved fingers dug against the unyielding slate beneath me. "Form an honor guard from some of our nastiest-looking battle chimeras to welcome them. If they're going to make a show of force, we have to answer it." That was Vaskandran politics, all display and spectacle—a stark contrast to the subtle, hidden machinations of Raverrans.

Odan nodded. "Very good, Warden. Anything else?"

The Raverran envoy would arrive tomorrow with a double handful of clerks and advisers, prepared to sit down at a table and speak in a genteel fashion about peace, to find my castle already overrun with a bristling military presence of Alevaran soldiers. That would create a terrible first impression—especially since Alevar and Morgrain were both domains of the great nation of Vaskandar, the Empire's historical enemy. I bit my lip a moment, thinking.

"Quarter no more than a dozen of their escort in the castle," I said at last. "Put the rest in outbuildings or in the town. If the envoy raises a fuss, tell them it's because they arrived so early and increased their party size without warning."

A smile twitched the corners of Odan's mustache. "I like it. And what will you do, Exalted Warden?"

I rose, dusting roof grit from my fine embroidered vestcoat, and tugged my thin leather gloves into place. "I'll prepare to meet this envoy. I want to see if they're deliberately making trouble, or if they're just bad at their job."

Gloamingard was really several castles caught in the act of devouring each other. *Build the castle high and strong*, the Gloaming Lore said, and each successive ruler had taken that as license to impose their own architectural fancies upon the place. The Black Tower reared up stark and ominous at the center, more ancient than the country of Vaskandar itself; an old stone keep surrounded it, buried in fantastical additions woven of living trees and vines. The stark curving ribs of the Bone Palace clawed at the sky on one side, and the perpetual scent of woodsmoke bathed the sharp-peaked roofs of the Great Lodge on the other; my grandmother's predecessor had attempted to build a comfortable wood-paneled manor house smack in the front and center. Each new Witch Lord had run roughshod over the building plans of those who came before them, and the whole place was a glorious mess of hidden doors and dead-end staircases and windows opening onto blank walls.

This made the castle a confusing maze for visitors, but for me, it was perfect. I could navigate through the odd, leftover spaces and closed-off areas, keeping away from the main halls with their deadly risk of bumping into a sprinting page or distracted servant. I haunted my own castle like a ghost.

As I headed toward the Birch Gate to meet the Alevaran envoy, I opened a door in the back of a storage cabinet beneath a little-used stairway, hurried through a dim and dusty space between walls, and came out in a forgotten gallery under a latticework of artistically woven tree roots and stained glass. At the far end, a string of grinning animal faces adorned an arch of twisted wood; an unrolling scroll carved beneath them warned me to *Give No Cunning Voices Heed*. It was a bit of the Gloaming Lore, the old family wisdom passed down through the centuries in verse. Generations of mages had scribed pieces of it into every odd corner of Gloamingard.

I climbed through a window into the dusty old stone keep, which was half fallen to ruin. My grandmother had sealed the main door with thick thorny vines when she became the Witch Lord a hundred and forty years ago; sunbeams fell through holes in the roof onto damp, mossy walls. It still made for a good alternate route across the castle. I hurried down a dim, dust-choked hallway, taking advantage of the lack of people to move a little faster than I normally dared.

Yet I couldn't help slowing almost to a stop when I came to the Door.

It loomed all the way to the ceiling of its deep-set alcove, a flat shining rectangle of polished obsidian. Carved deep into its surface in smooth, precise lines was a circular seal, complex with runes and geometric patterns.

The air around it hung thick with power. The pressure of it made my pulse sound in my ears, a surging dull roar. A thrill of dread trickled down my spine, never mind that I'd passed it countless times.

It was the monster of my childhood stories, the haunt of my nightmares, the ominous crux of all the Gloaming Lore. Carved through the castle again and again, above windows and under crests, set into floors and wound about pillars, the same words appeared over and over. It was the chorus of the rhyme we learned in the cradle, recited at our adulthood ceremonies, and whispered on our deathbeds: *Nothing must unseal the Door.*

No one knew what lay in the Black Tower, but this was its sole entrance. And every time I walked past it, despite the unsettling aura of power that hung about it like a long bass note too low to hear, despite the warnings drilled into me since birth and scribed all over Gloamingard, curiosity prickled awake in my mind.

I wanted to open it—anyone would. But I wasn't stupid. I kept going, a shiver skimming across my shoulders.

I climbed through another window and came out in the Hall of Chimes, a long corridor hung with swaying strands of white-bleached bones that clattered hollowly in a breeze channeled through cleverly placed windows. The Mantis Lord—my grandmother's grandmother's grandfather—had built the Bone Palace, and he'd apparently had rather morbid taste.

This wasn't some forgotten space entombed by newer construction; I might encounter other people here. I dropped my pace to a brisk walk and kept to the right. On the opposite side of the hall, a slim tendril of leafy vine ran along the floor, dotted irregularly with tiny pale purple flowers. It was a reminder to everyone besides me who lived or worked in the castle to stay to that side, the safe side—life to life. I strained my atheling's sense to its limit, aware of every spider nestled in a dusty corner, ready to slow down the second I detected anyone approaching. Bones clacked overhead as I strode through the hall; I wanted to get to the Birch Gate in time to make certain everything was in place to both welcome and warn the envoy.

I rounded a corner too fast and found myself staring into a pair of widening brown eyes. A dark-haired young woman hurried toward me with a tray of meat buns, nearly in arm's reach, on the wrong side of the corridor.

My side. Death's side.

Too close to stop before I ran into her.

if you enjoyed
KING OF THE RISING

look out for

BROTHER RED

by

Adrian Selby

Driwna Marghoster, a soldier for the powerful merchant guild known as the Post, is defending her trade caravan from a vicious bandit attack when she discovers a dead body hidden in one of her wagons.

Born of the elusive Oskoro people, the body is a rare and priceless find, the center of a tragic tale and the key to a larger mystery.

But as Driwna investigates who the body was meant for, she finds herself on a trail of deceit and corruption . . . a trail that will lead her to an evil more powerful than she can possibly imagine.

Chapter 1

The Magist

She's been more brave, more resistant to the torture than any of the humans.

"I'll say his name again. Lorom Haluim."

Behind her stands one of her own people, an Ososi, a giant of their kind. Some of the slaves here hail him as a brother, proclaiming that they have been changed from ordinary humans to immortal Ososi soldiers. Full of pride they show me their glistening brains and the artless ruin they've become under the knives of these drudhas who removed the tops of their skulls and experimented with flowers and roots, poisons and herbs in that quivering, warm clay.

She watches me as all the elderly Ososi have in the time since I have served the Accord, as I take their hands, transmit this shivering dust and let what I taste evolve their pain. They look at me with all the contempt a mortal lifetime confers. "It is just power" speak their eyes. Between her cries of pain she hums a handful of cracked notes, a childhood song, I think, for it is a song I heard also the Oskoro children put into harmonies, the Ososi's distant kin that once lived far across the Sar sea in the Citadels. She sings one note in a minor key here, and I marvel at the depth of the change it makes to the lullaby, a note that remakes the song as though she's sending it backwards to the girl she once was.

Then I catch a word – the dust has unlocked something in her, the name of a river, and hearing it sends a rare shiver of happiness through me. In her delirium, mumbling, chasing a memory that must have followed her song she has given me a clue to where the *rest of her tribe may live. I look up at the giant Ososi behind her, known to all in these lands as Scar. Many years ago he had been capped, the top of his skull removed to leave the braegnloc ready to receive the Flower of Fates. It would have made him the tribe's chief. The work done on his skull had only just been completed when the elders of his tribe learned he was not worthy of the honour of leading them. He carved the skin from their faces, cut their own skulls to pieces and stitched both to cover his head again. He is my finest hunter. He knows of the river this old woman's pain has revealed. I'll join his crew and we will find the children belonging to her tribe. I will hope too for that wisp of disorientation, that lurch in the belly if it's close, the power of another magist, of Lorom Haluim, the one I have been tasked to find, to lead the Accord to.*

"Thank you." She frowns, not realising I'm speaking to Scar, ordering her execution. His hands go to her head and chin, a smooth, fast twist breaking her neck.

Scar drags her body past me and out of the tent. We've had some quiet while the drudhas have been spooning out the droop to the prisoners, stupefying them for a while. Many are in persistent agony as a result of our work, the price of progress on any frontier.

A cold wind enters the tent as Scar leaves. This camp is high in the Sathanti Peaks, away from the scrutiny of all but the wretched tribes that live in these heights. The drudhas make good progress for they are working with living slaves that I have provided them. The soldiers they will soon learn to make from these slaves will be more than a match for any army this world could muster. The Lord Yeismic Marghoster has been as generous in the provision of slaves as his word. It took very little to fix the deformities of his younger daughter and his gratitude has been predictably ample. I recall he wept and kissed my feet as she ran about us for the first time in her life. Who alive, after all, has met a magist such as I?

365

Their myths make us out to be gods, understandable given their limitations. His wife, more sensibly, screamed, a horrified suspicion on her. For some time she thought it must have been a trick, some potion that would wear off. I wish I could feel as these people do, their mortality generates such heat.

As I ate and nodded where required at a feast to celebrate the miracle of her straightened bones, Marghoster shared his fears for the prospects of his oldest daughter, a potential marriage to the heir to the throne of Farlsgrad, young Prince Moryc Hildmir. As I told him how little the Hildmirs would soon matter I felt his wife next to me grow more disturbed by my proximity, shifting in her seat, sweating. Yeismic would not have approved of some of her thoughts. She suffered the memories that come unbidden while in proximity to a magist for two whole courses of our dinner before excusing herself, tears streaming from her eyes. We agreed that the joy of seeing a crippled child cured could be overwhelming to a woman's more sensitive disposition.

Scar returns, giving a short grunt as he forces his huge frame through the flap of the tent. He stands once more, silent, eyes following me as I wipe the Ososi woman's piss off the only chair here.

"I don't like this place. I wish I could return home." I don't expect a reply but I need, sometimes, to say it out loud. I unstopper the wine flask and pour a cup. Taste is the second most interesting thing about taking the form of a human.

"I hope we'll find those escaped Oskoro with that old woman's tribe." Scar remains silent, watches me drink. I see a subtle shift in his eyes, a tenth of a smirk, a mote of annoyance. We had tried to capture or kill the Oskoro that lived across the sea in Citadel Hillfast. Bigger than the Ososi, an older race, all of their kind are as dangerous as Scar, and their chief, the Master of Flowers, far

moreso. With Scar's crew we butchered all the Oskoro we could find, for they could not withstand me. They cried out for Lorom Haluim, even his master, Sillindar, one that I dared not hope would appear. Sillindar is one of the Accord's own kind, their great enemy and the reason for my search for Haluim, who has made his home on this world. I quelled as many Oskoro as I could, my dust taking their strength so they could be tied up. But a handful of them saw their chance, aided by the Master of Flowers, drawing in and killing two of our mercenaries, wounding even Scar. The Master, a drudha and five others fled. Worse was still to come, for as we threw lime bombs into the houses that remained, one of the women came out holding a great prize in her arm, a baby girl, her skull newly cut, the skin sewn back and a seed in her skull – clearly marking her as their future leader, the next Master of Flowers. Her mother saw us, saw me and raised a knife. I raised my arms up, a supplicating gesture, waving to instruct my men to stay back. In the sudden stillness, all of us focused on the child, I felt it, like a gossamer skin on every particle of air and tree, flower and body. Sillindar. Sillindar was here not many years past, within the life span of the woman before us. Then she brought the knife down. The baby didn't make a sound. I threw forward my arms, the dust of creation from my hands, a moment too late. The air spun savagely, my thought made material, a force to tear the knife from her fingers. But she'd stabbed herself in the gut, the force I'd applied pulling the knife up through her stomach instead of into the air. She fell to her knees gasping, letting her baby fall to the ground. Scar rushed forwards to it, kicking her back. He took the baby up in an arm while the other reached for a pouch, a salve that hissed hot on the tiny body. He hummed and shushed her as he did so. I ran to them, smoothing my dust over the hole in her chest but she was already dead. Reversing death is beyond me. I attempted it nevertheless. I always do.

*   *   *

The wind scuffs and kicks at the tent flap. I stand and take a fur from the desk nearby. Scar remains still. He's elsewhere, eyes vacant.

"You'll leave tomorrow. Tell your soldiers. I will return to Farlsgrad's capital, Autumn's Gate. The High Red, Yblas, has returned from the Old Kingdoms. I must be at his administrator's side."

Follow us:

f **/orbitbooksUS**

𝕏 **/orbitbooks**

▶ **/orbitbooks**

Join our mailing list
to receive alerts on our
latest releases and deals.

orbitbooks.net

Enter our monthly
giveaway for the chance
to win some epic prizes.

orbitloot.com